ONEY

My Escape from Slavery

Diana Rubino and Piper Huguley

First published by Endeavour Media Ltd in 2017.

Table of Contents

Dedication

Very special thanks go to my friend Piper Huguley, who helped me capture Oney's true voice. The day I asked her to help me was the day her mother passed away, which I didn't yet know about. She wrote me later that day:

"I see your request as heaven-sent, for I think I told you about how my mother told me about Oney. I know that she would want me to work on anything, do anything, to forward that story."

So I dedicate this book to Lilia Huguley, who wanted this story told.

Diana Rubino

Acknowledgments

I am extremely grateful to Mary V. Thompson, Mount Vernon's historian, whom every author mentions when writing a book about the Washingtons. Thank you, Mary, for going over the entire manuscript for historical accuracy. The Fred W. Smith National Library for the Study of George Washington is an amazing place to do research.

Many thanks to my longtime friend Shermener James for permission to use her first name for the woman who took Oney in when she escaped to Portsmouth. Unlike the other people in Portsmouth and Greenland who helped her, this woman's name was lost to history.

-    Diana Rubino

THE SASSY LADIES SERIES
ONEY – My Escape from Slavery

"Indeed I think I am more like a state prisoner than anything else, there is certain bounds set for me which I must not depart from – and as I can not doe as I like I am obstinate and stay at home a great deal." – **Martha Washington in a letter from New York, during Washington's first term as president.**

"May you long enjoy that liberty which is so dear to you, and to which your name will ever be so dear." – **Reply from the House of Representatives to George Washington when he announced his retirement.**

"Whilst they were packing up to go to Virginia, I was packing to go, I didn't know where; for I knew that if I went back to Virginia, I should never get my liberty. I had friends among the colored people of Philadelphia, had my things carried there beforehand, and left Washington's house while they were eating dinner." – **Ona Judge Staines, on her escape, from an interview on May 22, 1845.**

FOREWORD

by Ona Judge Staines

Dear Grandchildrens,

Lady Washington made me her 'personal servant' but that don't mean she made me free. Oh, Lawd, no. I was still her property—them folks never said 'slave'. It just meant she let me come work in the big house. When she told me I'd make a nice wedding gift to her granddaughter Eliza, I thought she meant I'd sew her a negligee or a quilt for a wedding gift. But, no, she meant I'd *be* the gift.

I swore whatever wedding gifts she gave to Miz Eliza, one of them would not be I.

Hence, on May 21, 1796, as the Washingtons ate dinner, I walked straight past them and out the front door. When I shut it, I left them—and my forced bondage— behind me.

They knew I went to Portsmouth, New Hampshire and tried to get me captured a few times, but gave up. I am free now and choose to remain so.

When I heard Lady Washington died, I wrote this story for you to learn from, marvel over and enjoy. There is much about the Washingtons you'll never learn in school. You'll be surprised what went on behind them closed doors at Mount Vernon and the president's house. As the president's wife, Lady Washington always said she felt like a prisoner. She had no idea …

Ona Judge Staines, Greenland, New Hampshire, Jan'y 1, 1847

CHAPTER ONE

Mount Vernon, Virginia, Feb'y, 1793

"Eight more days and we will have a new president, Oney." Lady Washington's tone wavered with a mixture of hope and dread as she X'd over another number on the calendar. Virginia's richest lady and the president's wife, she oughta be happy ... but Lawd, how sad. Her dead husband Mr. Custis left her a plantation, a mansion, and property: slaves. Then she married into Mount Vernon's five farms and the big house. At her fancy receptions in the capital, guests ogled her silk gowns and mahogany furniture, gushin' all over her: "Being the president's wife surely agrees with you, Lady Washington!"

Not true. As her 'personal servant' I knew she put on an act for all them folk.

One warm morn last spring, I hunched over stitching a collar to a bodice for her granddarter Miz Nelly.

"Oney, come here."

Lady Washington stood at the doorway, grasping her wire specs, knuckles whiter'n her face. The way she trembled I knew I couldn't be in trouble.

I dropped the needle mid-stitch and went to obey her summons.

"Come with me," she murmured kindly so I wasn't a'scared. I followed her up the secret stairs to her private chamber. "Sit," she commanded, pointing to the hard stool. She collapsed in her cushioned chair and drew a ragged breath. "I feel like a state prisoner here ..." Sigh ... "I am not allowed to speak my mind on any subject however trite ..." Sigh ... "My life has become so painfully dull." She poured out her wretched heart. "My husband and I never share any intimate moments anymore," I sat upright, struck dumb with disbelieving. How can this rich well-fed lady, married to the president of the United States, be so miserable? But her tears was my answer. She didn't want to be where—and who—she was.

If I'd'a had the sass, I'd'a asked, "Care to switch places?" But every night, lying on my corn shuck mattress on the big house's top floor, I whispered the truth: "She don't have it so good after all."

****

Now this frigid morn as she sat reading in the firelit parlour, I stood polishing the pewter goblets with a flannel oil-dipped rag. Me being her ladies' maid, polishing wasn't my regular job, but housemaids Charlotte and Caroline crouched on hands and knees scrubbing floors. I enjoyed making things sparkle. So she let me.

My feet hurt but I couldn't sit in her presence 'til she invited me to.

The door groaned open and General Washington stomped in. An icy blast of snow and horse smells followed him. "Patsy, we must talk …" He used her pet name to butter her up. *Uh-oh*, I thought. *She ain't gon' like this*. I followed him with my eyes but not my head.

She sprung to her feet. The knitting slid off her lap and the needles hit the floor with a click-clack. "No, George, you didn't."

"I told you I wouldn't accept a second term unless it was unanimous. It was—again." Indulgence colored his voice. I saw Lady Washington's blood start to boil, but my heart filled with pride. A streak of joy shot through me.

"Before I finished writing my farewell address, they begged me." He sho didn't sound sorry.

Now buffing the goblets with powdered chalk, I watched her pace as her slippers scuffed on the rug. She picked up her snuff tin, dipped a pinch and sniffed it in.

"George, you gave me your solemn oath you'd retire." Her voice didn't rise, but her tone spoke her fury. "Another presidency will kill you. Can't you see what it's done to you already?" She gestured up and down, from his unwigged white head to his mud-spattered boots. Her pale cheeks flushed in crimson blotches.

"Beg pardon?" He stooped, knees bent, hand cupped to his good ear, and tilted his head. He'd near gone deaf, blaming "uproarious Congressmen squawking all day." His lips twitched as his tongue rolled round his last tooth.

She grasped his sleeve. "It … will … kill … you." If he didn't hear, he read her lips. "For the love of God, why you?" Her voice quivered. It always did afore the tears came.

"You know why." He unstooped and fixed his sleeve. "This is my providence."

Oh, honey, do I know providence, I wisht I could'a said as I buffed the goblets with a soft piece of leather.

She swept her specs off and rubbed her eyes. "The world won't end if you don't serve a second term."

"No, but our nation might." Then he wheezed a cough. He didn't smoke no more seegars but coughed a lot.

She held her tea cup to his lips, and he sipped. "George, you did promise you'd quit after two years. It's been four. This will be the second broken promise."

I watched through the eyes of an outsider, though I lived in this house. I understood why both of them wanted such different things. They were so very different kinds of people.

He wrapt his arms round her waist, his chin resting on her head. "I'm as distraught and averse as you are, Patsy. After long and painful conflict in my own breast, I allowed my name to be presented for a second term of my servitude. But 'tis not my decision." His voice cracked. "'Tis the people's." He patted her back, as I seen him pat horses' rumps. "We wanted freedom and this is the price we must pay."

"George, they'll give you time to ponder this, surely." She clasped both hands round his arm and made to drag him to the settee.

He shook his head. "There is no time." He stood firm, feet planted. "Election day is over. I cannot be an ingrate, take their confidence and throw it back in their faces. Although I relinquish my personal enjoyments …" His voice trailed off as he gazed out the window at his vast holdings.

"You forget one thing." She cut him off loud enough so he, even half deaf, stepped back. She looked way up at him, fingers balled into fists. "'Tis not unanimous. *I* don't want it."

He narrowed those icy eyes onto her. "Patsy, you're being selfish."

Her mouth fell open. I cringed, knowing she'd blow up at that. If her fan was handy she'd'a snapped it open and fluttered it—or bopped it on his head. "I'm being selfish? I am only thinking of you."

"Huh. So you say," came his haughty retort. The president, also step-grandfather of four, talked like this to childruns, too.

She let out an anguished growl. Lawd, I done my share of growlin' in frustration. I wiped away a tear of my own. I knew how bad she wanted to stay at Mount Vernon with the general all to herself, finally—after four years of public life with no privacy and long stretches of time not seeing their family. All the wealth in Virginia didn't matter to her now. Embarrassed to witness this private scene, I backed up, trying to blend in with the wallpaper.

"Then you do not know me at all." In a rustle of petticoats and overskirts, she striddled up to me. That being my cue, I put down the silver and held out my arm. "Come, Oney." She clutched my elbow and led me from the parlour. Not allowed to address the general 'til he addressed me first, I couldn't wish him good day. But I caught the thin smile that curved his lips. He took no mind what Lady Washington thought of all this. They did what *he* wanted, not her.

The general put on a modest show, but beneath burnt a desire for fame and glory. How could one man lead armies, win a war against a deadly enemy, and now rule this nation, beloved by every living soul? It stumped me. Us folk even loved him, revered him, more as a papa than a ruler. From the moment I first seen him, astride his stallion in his fitted coat with gleaming gold buttons and shiny boots, I knew he'd be the greatest man in the world someday. All that 'providence' and 'paying the price' was fibs and Lady Washington knew it.

I nodded understanding, but didn't make eye contact. It was disrespectful looking straight at white folk, but as her pet, I could look her in the eye most times.

"A second term is more than I can bear, Oney." This from the woman who lost her first husband and how many childruns?

I stood aside for her, then followed her up the secret stairway. We felt our way up the slippery banister I'd helped Charlotte wax to a sheen with rag in one hand, candle in the other. The Washingtons used those stairs cause they were private, and with swarms of guests always dropping by uninvited and wandering the house, they needed something private.

In her bedroom, she settled in her chair and slid her specs on. I stood 'til she bade me sit on my wooden stool. With no back it forced me to sit up straight. I folded my hands in my lap and bided my time, waiting for her to speak, wond'rin' when I could sip some water for my dry throat.

"I found the last four years insufferable and dread the next four even more." She twisted the crumpled serviette, pulling it tween her thick fingers. "The general even said he'd cut his first term short when the government was in place. But I forgive him for staying. I forgive him everything."

The other house servants warned me never to speak to the whites unless spoken to first, but Lady Washington let me—sometimes. Now I nodded, mouth shut.

She tugged her lace cap over her silvered hairline, gazing round at the wide canopy bed, the lacy cushions, paintings of her four grandchildrens, then out the window at the Potowmac—part of Mount Vernon, too, I reckon.

She asked, "Can no one else take his place?" This was one of them questions didn't need an answer. But I had one. Since I become her pet I pushed toward my boundary every day. I'd keep pushing 'til she pushed back, cause I wasn't a'scared like the other folk.

"No, Lady Washington," I answered boldly. "The general is the only man the people wants. If I could, I'd'a chose him, too. Seems the people are right. Again."

She blinked in surprise. "I should scold you for that. 'Tis too fine a compliment, but false. He could turn it over to Mr. Adams, but he told me Adams isn't the fittest man to lead the nation. I asked him who was, but he hemmed and hawed, and couldn't utter a single name. What a sorry state of affairs."

She fixed her eyes on her Bible, open on her nightstand. "You don't understand, Oney. 'Tis nasty at best and evil at worst, politicks is." She dragged her fingers down the brittle pages. "These men want him to serve because of what *they* want." She stabbed a finger out the window at *'they'*. "*They* care not for Geo— for my husband, that he's sixty years of age, losing his hearing and his teeth. 'Tis for their own selfish needs."

She met my eyes looking at her. "You needn't bother yourself with such trials, Oney. You live this life of comfort and ease with nary a worry ..." She fluttered her hand round the clean elegant room—clean as a fiddle cause I cleaned it.

I tensed up to keep my face unmoving. I should'a said, *Yea, comfort and ease compared to the field slaves not allowed in here.* I didn't need to. She knew.

Lady Washington accepted her fate, as all Christians. But I wasn't a Christian yet. I got no moral instruction at the big house, so I was still tryin'a find something to believe in.

I believed about free will, from what Lady Washington read me out the Bible. But how could she read me about free will and still say 'God's will' and 'thy will be done'? The general could refuse that next term if he wanted. He wasn't nobody's property. Some men wanted him to be king, but he flat out refused.

What if he died, tho? He had no sons. If he died, somebody gotta take over. I slapped the side of my head for that wicked thought.

She clasped her hands at her neckline. "Why does my husband put these men before me and scold me for being selfish?"

Another question—permission to talk. "Lady Washington …" I leant forward, our toes almost touching, "… the general, he knows you ain't being selfish. He just got no other way to make you look wrong. He may rule the country but you still rule Mount Vernon. And that's more important to you, ain't it?"

That got a shaky smile out of her as she tossed the serviette on the dresser. "Yes, I know how badly he wants it. I can't begrudge him his glory. But he's being used, and he can't see it. You know the biggest reason he's going for a second term?" She looked straight at me, and I dropped my eyes.

I shook my head. "Uh-unh."

"'Tis to reconcile Mr. Hamilton and Mr. Jefferson. They hate each other and have opposite beliefs about how this country should be run. And the general is torn." She bent her fingers and studied her neatly pared nails. "He loves Mr. Hamilton like a son but can't abide all the bickering. Absurd." Her lips pressed into a thin line, and she opened them for a breath. "I loathe Mr. Jefferson, but am fed up with Mr. Hamilton, too, whom I always liked. I'm sicker of their squabbles than my husband. Why cannot they work out their own differences?"

I knew the answer, already hearing all this during our sewing, at their dinners, and when Hercules the cook read me the papers. So I said, "Mayhap the general don't believe no one else can settle it, since he like them both and wanna keep peace. We don't want another war."

I was born before that war and learnt all about it later. So I knew about the political parties—but who knows why they called 'em parties? They'd always be fighting.

Now, here in her private chamber, Lady Washington assured me, patting my knee—the extent of our physical affection: owners and slaves never touched, unless I was bathing her. "We won't see another war, Oney, not in our lifetime, anyway." She stood, so I jumped to my own feet. "Of course you'll come with me to Philadelphia again."

My breath halted. Not 'til this moment did I think of myself in all this. I been too worried about Lady Washington, wondrin' if she'd refuse to live in the president's house this time. But she'd planned it all as we'd clumb them secret stairs. So, besides the dozen house servants, I reckoned they'd bring us same slaves as in the first term—the general's valet and hunting companion Billy Lee, cook Hercules, my brother Austin as the waiter, Paris as postillion, Christopher, Giles, Molly and me. That meant being torn apart from Mamma and half-sister Delphy again.

Lady Washington swept past me and out. "You can return to your work now, Oney."

"Please let me stay here, Lawd," I prayed. Would He answer my prayer?

CHAPTER TWO

"You can start packing my things tomorrow, Oney." Her command was my prayer denied. I had to leave Mount Vernon again.

That eve, after helping Lady Washington on with her bed clothes, I snuck from the big house and wedged a plank in the front door to keep it open. I fled into the frigid night, my thin shawl clutched round my shoulders. Crouching, I ran past the servants' hall and dashed down the oval drive, gravel stabbing my feet. I slipt past the spinnin' room where Mamma worked. Being one of Lady Washington's favorites cause of her knowledge of textiles, Mamma she was the highest-priced of us all. I heard Lady Washington boast to her lady friends, "Betty spins, weaves, sews and dyes like no other here. She and her son Austin are worth sixty pounds—as a pair, of course. I don't separate families."

No, but the general did. More of that later.

Candles flickered in windows where overseers lived in the gardener's house. At length I reached the slave quarters attached to the greenhouse. The doors were in back. The general didn't want visitors seeing slaves lived there. The cabin had no windows, but Mamma didn't mind none—the cracks tween the logs brung light. But during a storm—ho-lee cow! Rain, snow and ice blew in. Wind whistled through them cracks like hoot owls.

I pushed open the door and it swang on creaky hinges. I ducked into the frigid cabin, stamping my numb feet on the dirt floor to feel them again. Mamma sat in her rickety chair by dying embers, huddled in her coarse blanket, knitting a shawl for Lady Washington. Delphy, exhausted after working sunup to sundown, slept on her pallet in the corner.

Mamma voiced her thanks every waking day she didn't live in slave row, the field folks's line of cabins. Ten or more men, women and childruns packed one room like cattle, sleepin' on a plank, with a bundled-up blanket to rest they head. Mamma and Delphy slept on leaves and straw. They tried moss but it brung fleas.

"Mamma, the general is staying president. Lady Washington is taking Austin and I back to Philadelphia." I got it out in one breath.

She stood and her blanket fell round her bare feet. "Oh, Lawd, girl, not again …"

As we hugged I let my own tears fall. "I promise I'll get Hercules to write to you and Delphy." My sister was too young to go, and not quadroon like me. We was git from diff'rent daddies.

"Child, every time you leave here, is like losin' Nancy and Lucy all over again …" Her outpour of emotion tore at my heart. Two of my other sisters died afore we come to Mount Vernon, on the Custis plantation where Mamma birthed them.

"I ain't dead, Mamma, just goin' to the city. But I gotta go back to the house afore they find me gone." With another hug, I wrenched myself away, dashed back to the house and crept up to my bed. In the dark silence I rolled myself up under the clean cover—field slaves had to haul leaves to the barns with their one blanket, but house slaves didn't—and I smelt the sweet sope I washed it in, with my own lye water, lavender and hog fat. *How lucky you are going back to Philadelphia with the Washingtons, girl,* I told myself. Lawd, how lucky I sho' was!

I closed my eyes and recalled back over the years—four, I reckon, that was the president's term—when Lady Washington first told me the general got elected …

****

"Elected fer what?" I knew it was something bad, cause how she trembled and wrang her hands, twisting her lace handkerchief that I'd sewed. Was the general going to jail?

"To be president." To my dumb stare, she explained further. "The leader of our land. He was elected by a group of men called Congress. He won't be king, he'll be president. They weren't sure what to call it, and someone came up with that. I think it was Mr. Adams."

"Oh." I nodded, up and down, up and down. "He'll be a good leader of the land." What else could I say? I knew the men called Congress was looking for a leader, but in my young mind of fifteen years, I didn't know why they chose the general. He led in battles against the Red Coats and won the war for independence—for theirselves, that is—and ran his farms. But what did he know of leading a whole country? No, I dared not ask that. And from the looks of Lady Washington's vacant stare at the wall, she didn't know neither.

She led me upstairs but didn't sit, so I stood behind her as she turned and gazed out the window at the Potowmac. "I didn't want this, Oney. I tried to talk him out of it, but he told me he must serve. He told me we have a government of *laws*, not of people. 'Tis the duty of leaders to follow the will of the people as expressed by the *laws*. The *individual* who holds office is less important than the office itself."

I then knew for true if the leader of this land believes *he's* less important than his office, us slaves are less than naught.

Lady Washington kept talking, like I wasn't there, to convince herself. "Providence it was, he said. Democracy." She turned to me with puffy eyes. "Oney, something has been bothering me, and I need tell you what it is."

Why me and not her grandgirls Miz Betsy or Miz Nelly? Or the smart Mrs. Powel who knew all about politicks? Two reasons. I did what none of them other ladies could—I understood. We were of like mind—neither of us was free. She belonged to the general, he belonged to the nation—and I belonged to her.

But the biggest reason? I would never repeat her secrets to a soul—I knew what disobedient slaves suffered—punishment, in ways of unspeakable horror. They got shipped to the West Indies on a slave ship or sold away, never to see they families again. The general only sent one slave, Tom, to the West Indies, traded him for molasses and such—and said he'd never break up families, but don' believe him. He broke up plenty families. Not since I been born, but afore. Mamma she told me he held a slave raffle. Raffled off men, women and they babies like prizes, along with donkeys, pots and pans. He never done that again since I been born.

And they called *us* savages!

The fear of being raffled haunted me every minute of my life. But he couldn't raffle me, cause he didn't own me.

She did.

Mount Vernon had five farms. Some of us slaves belonged to the general, and some, like me, Mamma, Delphy and Austin, were dower slaves Lady Washington brung from her first marriage. It being a large plantation, they worked as carpenters, joiners, wheelwrights, coopers, butchers, tanners, shoemakers and watermen—aside from the field hands.

"What is it, Lady Washington? Somethin' 'bout me?" I tensed up, my breath caught.

"No, naught about you." She looked past me, gazing at a distant point. "Since my husband started serving the country, I haven't been number one in his life, and at times that is a difficult burden to bear. He will always be number one to me."

Thank you, Lawd ... she wouldn't raffle me ... I closed my eyes, let out a relieved sigh, and my heart thumped slower.

That was the first of her shared secrets with me, her only confidante. It wouldn't end 'til the day I ran. I didn't muchly fear her raffling me after that. But I feared for Mamma and Delphy. They wasn't her pets like me.

I never hugged Lady Washington, it being improper to have physical contact with her. All I could do was assure her. "The general is a good leader of Mount Vernon and all us people." I never said *slaves* either. Would'a been like vomiting the word.

Her homespun skirts crackling, she glided over and sunk into her chair, but I stood standing. She didn't invite me to sit. "You don't understand, Oney," she said. "He must serve for four years. That's what the Constitution says."

I knew the Constitution—some list of laws them men at Congress wrote, after much rowing and bandying. I learnt when Hercules read me the papers, and when I listened in on Miz Nelly's lessons. I learnt a lot from her lessons—even the beginning of letters.

"We'll have to leave here for a long time and go to New York." Lady Washington fingered the locket round her neck, a braid of her dead daughte Patsy's hair inside it. "That's far up north, where it's colder." She shivered, as if thinking of it chilled her.

"Oh, I'm sorry, I'll miss you and the general." I truly would. Lady and General Washington did treat me kind. I had all the eats and frocks I wanted. I'd be terribly lonely without her nearby.

She shook her head. "Oh, no, Oney, you'll come with me. I wouldn't go without you. And the general will want your brother Austin to join us."

But I didn't yet know they'd leave Mamma and Delphy behind. I just knew I'd go to this New York—the capital, they called it—be Lady Washington's 'personal servant' there, and Austin would be the waiter. Something made me tingle like never afore—a thrill of excitement. I never been off the Mount Vernon farm, except to Alexandria with Mamma to sell the chickens we're allowed, and petticoats we sewed. New York sounded far away as the moon. I wondered how many months we'd take to get there.

I stumbled backward when she said it'd only take six days. "Lawd! What, we'll fly?" That got a sad laugh from her.

23

This wound me tight like a clock, journeying so far away, to another part of the world. I wanted to see more places than Mount Vernon. And learn new things, about the planets and stars and faraway lands. Mamma she was mulatto, born in Virginia, but said her Mamma got sold from Africa. Far across the sea. My white Daddy, Andrew Judge, come from Leeds, England. I knew England was where the Red Coats come from, who our army fought and won our land, to escape the king. They got their freedom and wrote a big Declaration of Independence about it. But it didn't cover us folk. One day I asked Mamma about that as we sat on the general's thrown-away chairs, sewing in our one-room shack.

"Where's *our* Declaration of Independence?"

She got up and shaked me 'til I rattled. "Don't you ever ax that again, you hear me what I say? You wanna git the lash?"

The general never lashed any of us—he got overseers to do it, but for a lot worse than asking questions. For running away, mostly. But I never asked again anyways. It got me wondrin', tho.

So I asked Lady Washington, "What will the general do as president?"

She didn't know much and told me neither did the general. "He won't rule as a king. He'll be a ruler, but not for life as a king. Men elected him, from the laws they made, not an accident of birth."

'*Accident of birth.*' Them words never left me, ever. Accident meant it ain't supposed to happen. Were we slaves cause our births was an accident? I didn't ask Lady Washington that.

"How'll we address the general?" I asked, "He won't be just a general no more."

"We don't yet know." Her shoulders slumped, making her breasts sag. "The general leaned toward 'His High Mightiness' as the Elector of Holland is called that. Congress has been debating it, as they do everything else. Mr. Adams wanted 'His Highness the President of the United States of America and Protector of their Liberties'. But I agree with Senator Maclay who said Mr. Adams suffers from a case of nobilmania. They'll likely call him 'Your Presidency'. He doesn't want to be called 'Your Excellency' or 'Your Majesty'. That's against everything they fought the war for."

"And what will you be?" I dared to ask.

She gave an uncaring shrug. "I'm only Mrs. Washington. But no one will address me for anything. I must tag along with him." She kept saying, "Oh, he doesn't want it, all he wants to do is be a farmer again, he did enough during the war—" But she forced herself to believe all that.

I saw how the general never stopped. He ran the farms, explored farther west, on and on, so I knew he wanted this rulership. Oh, he wanted it. I'd seen him that eve, striding down the hallway for dinner. He sho wasn't crying. He grinned at me with a new full set of teeth big as a horse's. But this time they weren't from an animal. He'd bought them teeth from slaves. One morn, I been passing by Sambo Anderson when the French dentist yanked some teeth out his mouth.

I asked her now, "Lady Washington, may I 'scuse myself? I need to finish them sleeves of Miz Nelly's."

"Of course, my dear."

I curtseyed and she waved me on. I didn't need to finish sleeves either. I was faster with my needle than a runaway slave. I just didn't wanna hear no more. All her bellyachin' rustled up a jumble of emotions in me that I couldn't sort out. I pitied her unhappiness, yet my festering resentment silently screamed, "How dare you complain!"

Back in my corner of the little parlour, I licked the thread and pushed it through the needle eye, thinking as I stitched, *They're free of Britain, but we ain't free of them.* I thought about the paradox—a word Mrs. Powel said at tea. I wasn't allowed to address guests direct, so I asked Miz Nelly what it meant.

"'Tis a riddle—when one thing is one way and yet another. Why do you want to know that?" Miz Nelly screwed up her lips in puzzlement that I'd ask such a question.

"It sounded like a funny word," I'd answered. Slaves ain't supposed to want to learn things like new words.

I knew that freedom was a paradox—they fought for freedom for theirselves, but not for us. My Daddy, an indentured servant, went free after four years as the general's tailor—Mamma believed I got my seamstress talent from him—he then left us to go farming. But Mamma, me, Austin and Delphy—not free.

Didn't matter Daddy was white. I was a slave cause my mamma was. If she a slave, you born that way too. I couldn't do nothing to fight it. All I could hope for was them to let us free. Like all of us hoped. Exceptin' the ones crazy enough to run.

I went out to Hercules to give him the Washingtons' orders for dinner. The kitchen was a separate building so won't no smell get in the big house.

He leant against the wall reading the papers, eyes spilling with tears like he was grieving.

"Who died, Herc?" They put deaths in the papers, but it couldn't be no one round here.

"Worse, Oney. Looky here." He held the paper out to me, and of course I couldn't read it, but he jabbed a finger at a mess of print and read out loud, "President Washington signed into law today, The Fugitive Slave Act. It's 'the right of a slaveowner to recover a runaway slave'. That means slaveowners can recapture their slaves from any U.S. State," he read on, "'Tis a crime to assist a slave in escaping." He lowered the paper, closed his eyes and shook his head. "Now it is written into the law. If you escape to another state and get caught, anybody can capture you and take you back here."

God above, President Washington done signed it a few steps from where I slept.

Now, four years later, he was staying president. But Lady Washington never looked sadder or more anxious. Her hands trembled as she wrote or knitted, her temper cut short. She yelled out at us, at her grandgirls and grandson Washy, for the slightest thing. When Miz Nelly hit a wrong key at the pianoforte, she shrieked, "What is wrong with you, chit? Just for that, you sit and play another hour by this clock."

She jabbed a finger at the mantel as Miz Nelly squirmed on the bench, whining, "No, Grandmama. My hands hurt." She would play and cry, cry and play, five hours a day.

These days I feared making Lady Washington mad enough to sell me away or raffle me off, so I worked real hard at my chores. A young'un, I didn't get much duties yet. Sewing took the most time cause I excelled at it. Then I had to take out slops, wash floors and woodwork, change slipcovers, polish silver, wax tables and chairs, make beds, fill oil lamps, and two hard smelly tasks: dipping candles and making sope. The fats and lye smelt putrid, sometimes the sope came out proper and sometimes not.

After those tasks done, I went into Lady Washington's room, curtseyed and stood there 'til she needed me. Then if she needed it, I'd fill the water pitcher, arrange her towels on the washstand, help her out of her dishabille and into day raiment. I never got a full day off, but my being her personal maid was an honor. Real easy duties in the big house. But since I liked to make things sparkle, she let me polish the silver. I did it better than

Charlotte, who was weaker'n me. I gave it extra elbow grease, having extra big elbows.

When I helped bathe and dress and powder her in the morn, I made sure to tell her how pretty her dresses looked on her—the dresses I sewed—and I buffed her boots extra shiny. I woke early and lit the fire in her chamber where she read the Bible, no one allowed to disturb her. I put fresh candles beside the book and plumped the cushion she sat on. Then I got me out 'til she called me again.I had lotsa shinin' of silver to do anyways.

Next day, Sadday, was cleanin'-out day. Lady Washington, wanting to keep us healthy, lined us up and herself gave us a spoonful of spring tonic—and I know cause I helped Hercules mix it—molasses, sulphur, and sassafras tea to purify our blood. I s'pose Lady Washington reckoned us folk had different blood than them, cause I never seen them take it. I know they thought they better cause they gave the same cleanin'-out mix to the hogs with their slop.

The house turmoiled in a muddle 'til the day we fixed to leave for the second president term. Lady Washington barked out orders for packing, and I stood in her chamber near the whole day helping her decide what to bring. "It will be cold, so I'll need the brown cloak, but 'tis getting a bit shabby—" She held it up. "Oney, you take this, for twill keep you warm. As soon as we arrive in Philadelphia, you can make me a new one."

Slaves got the castoffs—worn-out textiles, cracked stoneware, the worst sheep's wool. But when I become her pet, she made sure I had new raiment, right fancy feathers to match what her kin wore, since I lived and worked at the big house. Her old cloak'd be muchly roomy for skinny me, but I put on a smile. "Thank you, Lady Washington," and put it aside—I didn't like it, shabby or not, but I dared not refuse it.

We packed trunk after trunk with her undercoats, blouses, skirts, chemises, aprons, hats, gloves, shoes, then downstairs packed her favorite dishes and the paintings of dead Patsy and Jacky she made me wrap in muslin.

But the general didn't seem to pack a thing. He still rose at four of the morn, went into his study to write letters, and come out at seven for hoe cakes or slap jacks swimming in honey, or mush if his teeth hurt, then out on his rounds 'til three. I noticed a cold silence tween the Washingtons I never sensed afore. They acted polite to each other, but absent was the affection, the brush of his lips over her cheek, her two-fisted squeeze of his arm. He stopped saying "'til three of clock, then, Patsy," as he stood to leave. She wandered the house room to room, lost in her thoughts, muttering to herself. She hardly said naught to me, 'ceptin' to order me what to pack.

Me and Austin went to see Mamma and Delphy 'til late into the night, knowing we wouldn't be together again for a long time.

On a piece of paper I took from Lady Washington's desk I marked an X with a piece of coal and kept it 'neath my bed, marking the morns 'til we had to leave. I knew how to count small numbers, so ten days became seven, then four, and finally—one.

Tomorrow I'd leave Mount Vernon and not look back.

CHAPTER THREE

Eight of us house servants toiled, loading five wagons with boxes and chests, from sunup 'til our bellies growled at 12 chimes. As the mantel clock's little hand reached three, we got to eat some corn and herring. At four, a team of matching coach-horses pulled Lady Washington's cream carriage down the gravel drive. With her went grandchildruns Miz Nelly, Miz Betsy, Miz Patty and Washy. All a few years younger than me, we got along, except for Miz Betsy—she treated me like one of the field slaves. But more of her later.

Me and Austin bade farewell to Mamma and Delphy one last time. Us four embraced in a tearful jumble. "I reckon we'll be back in the summertime when the general puts a halt to his presidencin'," I assured them. I didn't shed no tears but Mamma done cried like one of us was dead. "Don' worry, Mamma, we'll be back, I know how you feel, bein' left behind again." A sob clogged my throat and I swallowed a lump.

Austin broke away and slunked down the drive with a backward gaze and hopped onto the end wagon.

I held back to give Mamma one last hug and kiss, to remember the feel of my head resting on her breast, her smell of corn husks and sweat.

"Oney!" Austin called me from the wagon piled with trunks. Paris up front jerked the horse's reins. "C'mon, girl, we leavin'. Git on!"

I broke away and blew my last kisses to Mamma and Delphy, not knowing when or if I would ever see them again. I ran backward, turned and leapt onto the hard seat at the back of the moving wagon. I twisted my body towards Austin so not to see them waving goodbye, and grasped the splintery wood. That began the slow bumpy journey to Philadelphia behind Lady Washington's carriage and trail of baggage.

The wagon's rocking motion soothed me. I tried to put Mamma and Delphy from my mind and think of the excitement waiting for us—parties, theatre, the circus. Soon as we rolled through Mount Vernon's gates, Austin began singing *All God's Chillun Got Wings* and I sang along:

"I got a robe, you got a robe
All o' God's chillun got a robe

When I get to heab'n I'm goin' to put on my robe
I'm goin' to shout all ovah God's Heab'n
Heab'n, Heab'n, ev'rybody talkin' 'bout heab'n ain't goin' dere."

We munched apples and sang near every song we knew, down the rutted roads, jostlin' and bumpin'.

Tired of singing, I hopped into the wagon, settled tween two trunks and leant my head back, closed my eyes and re-lived fond childhood memories …

Mamma atold me we'd never be free like Daddy cause he was an indentured servant. He worked his way to freedom. But us, we were dower slaves. I so feared the Washingtons'd raffle or sell us, or sell Mamma alone, or sell me alone, and I'd never see her or Delphy or Austin again.

One day, Lady Washington held up her silver coffee pot I'd just polished. I reckon I hadn't mixed enough rottenstone with the oil to give it a shiny enough sheen.

"Come here, Oney." She stood rigid by the sideboard, clutching the pot by the handle.

I held my breath, my heart pounding painfully, waitin' for her to say she selling me. Paralyzed with fear, I began to shake.

"You needs shine the light on it ensure the entire surface is clean." And she got out the cloth and rubbed it her own self. She held it up to the window, sunlight glinting off it, shining like a star. "See?" Now, this lady had some elbow grease.

"Yes, my lady. You ain't gonna sell me?" My voice quivered, my mouth so dry I could taste the polish in the air.

Her eyes opened wide and she laughed. "Of course not. Now back to work with you." She shooed me off.

I skipped away, feeling she gave me a new life that day.

Every night I knelt, pressed my hands together and prayed, "Lawd, please don't make Lady Washington sell or raffle us." I learnt about God from what she told me in the Bible. He made us all. I asked Mamma about that and she said, "But He didn't make us equal like Mr. Jefferson says."

I made up my own mind. Lady Washington once told me: "He helps those who help themselves."

"Did God say that in the Bible?" I asked her.

"Yes. And Benjamin Franklin also said it in Philadelphia."

Tween them two sources, that was the answer to all my questions. I never ax'd another question about God after that.

Cause I was quadroon and good with my needle, Lady Washington brought me to the big house when Mamma said I turned nine or ten, we don't know my real age. Lady Washington chose me as her seamstress cause she liked the way I sewed hers and her grandgirls' raiment. But only part-white slaves were allowed to work at the big house. If I was all black or dark enough to look like an ink-spitter, I'd'a stayed out in the quarters.

Lady Washington herself came to our quarters where me and my Grandmommy sat sewing. She'd never come there afore. When the door opened and Lady Washington stood there, we dropped our work and jumped to our feet. Smiling, she looked down at me, put her palm over my head, close but not touching, and said, "Oney, you're going to live at the mansion house, to be my personal servant and a playmate to my granddaughter Nelly. Be ready in the morn." She didn't ask if I wanted to. At nine or ten, I thought this an adventure and hardly slept that night in excitement of seeing the big house. I never been in it afore but pictured in my mind of what it looked like—fancy furnishings, shiny floors instead of packed dirt, delicate china cups and plates, not chipped and cracked, like ours.

Next morn, Molly, a house slave, come to fetch me. I floated over the gravel and through the big house door—the front door. I ain't never seen a slave enter the big house through the front door. We stepped into an enormous blue-green room, a long table down the center surrounded in carved chairs with cloth seats. The sun streamed through the ceiling-high windows.

"Whoa, looky at all this!" My head tilted back as I gazed way up like reaching into heaven. I smelt wax and lemons. The rich aroma of bacon and coffee lingered from that morn's brekkus. She led me up many steps. I never clumb steps afore. Never had any. I stumbled 'til I figgered out how to climb, left foot, then right foot.

Catching my breath in my room, I looked out the window at the sun glinting on the river. I never had a window neither. I span round, landing on the corn husk bed. I sunk and sunk into what felt like clouds. I never felt anything so soft, having slept on the ground all my life.

Lady Washington met me in the hallway and showed me to her sewing chamber. "Here—you can sew a sampler." She gave me one to copy. "These are letters of the alphabet." Naught else. Not what each letter's name was. I seen letters afore but didn't know their names or how they made words. But knew I would someday.

She took me on shopping trips, to the theatre and to visit her lady friends. She dressed me in the same finery as her grandgirls Miz Nelly and Miz Betsy, though I sewed it all. I even had a dress in pink stiff silk. I had much more raiment than the one petty coat, two shifts, one jacket and pair of stockings a year the field women got. The menfolk got one pair of homespun breeches yearly. She heaped upon me sweets and treats, while the field slaves got their weekly rations of viands barely enough to exist on—a few pounds of pork, usually poor cured salt herrings, and a handful of Indian corn. The general weighed each grain and morsel so nobody got more'n their share. No sweets. I snuck leftover blancmange, macaroons and brandied peaches out to the quarters when I could hide them in my apron.

The lady and the general were a bit stingy with calling slaves by their proper names, too—a handful of slaves got called Old Wench, Old Nanny, Young Fellow—easier'n remembering they real names. Sambo had to settle for being called Sammy.

But I had a white name, Ona being Latin for 'unity' or 'harmony'. Lady Washington didn't seem to mind my white name, cause she never called me nothing else.

I became playmate to Miz Nelly and sat in my corner sewing or knitting when she took her lessons with tutors who came to the house: music tutors, dancing tutors, tutors for letters and numbers and everything else. That's how I learnt geography, arithmetic, science, music and some French.

"You're going to sit in on Nelly's history and speech lessons." Lady Washington pulled me from my dishwashing and led me into the parlour one morn. "It would be apropos for you to know your history and to speak well should any of my guests wish to engage you in dialogue."

Me? *Engage in dialogue*? I hoped it wasn't some new frocks they wanted me to make. "What's dialogue, Lady Washington?"

She rolled her eyes and clucked her tongue. "Talking, back and forth, you know … chit chat! You need to drop some of that native vernacular and learn to speak more like a … well, a proper lady."

"Native vern—I ain't never heard that big word afore, Lady Washington."

"It's the speech that your people use amongst yourselves. 'Tis fine amongst yourselves, but not in front of important folk. And stop saying *ain't*!" she screeched through clenched teeth.

So I learnt my history and talkin' fancy. But it sho' sounded funny coming out my mouth. I didn't dare talk fancy with them other slaves. They'd'a laughed me right out the house.

Hercules read me the papers and learnt me how the nation got free from the British with the war, how the government formed, these men who wrote their Declaration of Independence and Constitution, and how they fought for freedom. Knowing all this made me think about us folk. Why didn't they free us? I didn't dare ask Lady Washington.

But I did ask Him every night in my prayers.

CHAPTER FOUR

Right she was—six days, what it took, of bone-rattlin' travel over rutted roads, slogging through mud. Every house we stopped at, the slave folk sacked out in the barn. When it rained they slept in the wagons, covered with old sacks.

On the second star-flung night, near Baltimore, we rolled up a long gravel drive to a brick mansion. "Here it is, The Rising Sun." Lady Washington pointed to the shingle hanging over the door. "I stayed here a few times in years past, before the general was president. It's a very exclusive inn."

Inside, plush carpets covered the floors, and a crackling fire blazed in the brick hearth. I know this cause I went in. Lady Washington let me sleep in her room with her. This wasn't for my comfort. She wanted me nearby so I could serve her in the middle of the night and get her washed and dressed early.

It thrilled me to be allowed in such grand houses. Nobody minded me coming inside with her. Lady Washington sometimes traveled with her quadroon niece, cause of her half-sister Ann Dandridge. They shared their Daddy but Ann's Mamma was a slave, so Ann was born a slave. She got good treatment and light duties in the big house, but she was still a slave. Glory be, the lady wouldn't free her own sister. That unspoken rule divided them—mistress and slave.

Lady Washington asked The Rising Sun lady if the general had paid enough in advance for her, us, and the horses' feed and lodging. Inns charged more money than I could ever imagine—twenty-five cents a person for lodging, another twenty-five for a meal, fifty for each horse, fifty for each slave. The general always paid in advance, didn't want to look like he got favors from citizens.

Our hostess gave Lady Washington and I a sumptuous bedroom upstairs with canopy bed, red velvet drapes and plush carpets. I slept on a pallet on the floor, but I ain't never seen such luxury outside Lady Washington's own bedroom.

Along the way, folk decorated their houses with flags and wreaths of bright flowers. Bands of musicians blasted their brass music as our train of coach and wagons passed. Folk lined the streets, cheering and waving at the president's lady. I was too far back to see her, but I knew she didn't relish the adoration. She prob'ly shut the curtains and hid.

We reached the edge of Philadelphia on a gloomy afternoon, me shivering under the cloak she gave me. The general stood in his crimson coat, waving his long arms over his head. His coach and four matched greys glowed. Paris the coachman sat atop the front seat in gleaming scarlet livery.

Austin helped Lady Washington down, and she rushed into the general's arms. They hugged for a long time and stole a kiss. I looked away, ashamed I stood watching. She didn't act mad or sad this eve. I reckon she was just happy to see him, and tomorrow her sullen moods would take over again, with the 'sir's and cold politeness. The general, he wouldn't care none. He didn't let his wife's pain bother him. They seemed to live in different worlds.

They broke apart, still clasping hands, then he rounded us all up. "Good to see my people again." He smiled, those big teeth also belonging to his people. "Are any of you hungry?"

We were starving, so I didn't mind answering for all of us, "Aye, masta, we real hungry!"

"I just had my dinner and there's plenty left over." He patted his tummy.

Their coaches led the wagon train over the cobbles to High Street. We halted at the rented president's house of red brick. Flickering candles glowed in the windows, welcoming and cheerful.

Inside the candlelit president's house, standing on waxed floorboards, slippery as glass, I ran my hand over the smooth banister and breathed in the scent of beeswax. Them servants musta been real busy last few days.

Ravenous, we devoured the slops of the general's dinner, out in the kitchen behind the house. What a feast—boilt beets, potatoes, and onions mixed with mackerel, smothered in fried pork scraps and egg sauce. We washed it down with warm ale. And leftover dumplin's for dessert. Oh, a Hercules-cooked meal filled me so snug and secure, after the morsels we scrounged up on the journey.

When Hercules served up that steamin' stew I even licked the wooden spoon. Who needed cognac and Madeira? We got corned with gorging ourselves.

Lady Washington let us follow her through the house as she did her inspection. In the fading daylight, she either nodded her approval or shook her head upon peeking into each room, but to me it was a palace. Gilt furniture and bright-colored floor cloths in every room. As in Mount Vernon's big house, all we'd need do in winter was close each door to keep out the frosty drafts from the entry doors. The parlour's sofa, curtains, chair seats and fire screens matched in red damask with shiny gold trim. Over the marble mantel, a looking glass in a gilded frame reached the ceiling. The walls were painted in pea-green and cream.

"Hmm ... nicely decorated ... American rather than French style." With Lady Washington's nod as her eyes swept the room, it sho' passed her inspection.

Me and Molly shared a divided space over the kitchen with the grandchildruns. The black men took a divided attic room apart from the white men. The white coachman and black stableworkers got housed behind the kitchen, but not together. Black slaves and white servants didn't stay or eat together. The general's secretary, Tobias Lear, and his wife Polly had the third story to themselves. The other slaves lodged in the old smokehouse, or in a wooden building what they called the servants' hall. The white servants lived where they pleased—nobody owned them.

Hercules now read *The Federal Gazette* and *Gazette of the United States* to me every day. When Feb'y 22, the general's birthday came, nobody in the house, most of all the general, 'xpected what his adoring people gave him. Starting at sunup.

As I lit the fire in the parlour hearth, three blasts rocked the house. I ran to the window. Molly jumped like a bee stang her. "Wha's 'at?"

Two, three more booms. "Lawd, the lobsterbacks attackin' us again!" I crouched behind the sofa. Footsteps pounded down the stairs. I peeked over the sofa back to see the general tearing downstairs, face whiter'n his hair.

Lady Washington followed on his heels, pulling her lace cap over her undressed head. When the general pulled the door open, my heart leapt to my throat. If them Red Coats be attacking us, he's the number one target. And there he be walking straight into the line of fire.

"Masta general, no! Them lobsters come back to kill us all!" fell out my mouth, not thinking.

Afore my yells prob'ly reached his ears, churchbells clanged, first from the left, then from the right. They rang out in climbing notes of the scale then back down again like Miz Nelly's piano playing, and the ar'tillery again boomed out, in time with the bells.

"George!" Lady Washington stood next to the general at the doorway, pulling him down so he could hear her through the ringing and booming. "This is for your birthday." She stood on tippy toe to reach his ear. "Surprise!"

Grinning in the glow of the hearth, he raised his eyes and hands to heaven, his ill-fitted teeth gleaming in the firelight. "For corn sake, I near keeled over when I heard that ar'tillery. 'Tis a bit soon after wartime to be hearing that again." He draped his arm round her shoulders. "But a nice gesture nonetheless."

At noon, with the day off, we all went to the town centre for sweet treats. The soldiers again marched down the street, firing another round of booming salutes. The ships docked at the waterfront flew flags in a rainbow of colors, and flags unfurled from every window.

When I got back to the house, a row of shiny carriages, some with gilt eagles and coats of arms, lined up to the corner. Lady Washington grabbed me in the entry hall afore I even went up to my room. Chatter and laughter floated in from the parlour.

"Oney, no less than the entire Pennsylvania Legislature is in there, along with Congressmen and Governor Mifflin himself. These bigwigs raided our liquor cabinet, emptied the wine cellar, and served themselves, passing bottles and—good gracious, 'tis a free-for-all."

"Never fret, Lady Washington, I dunno where the others are, still out dilly-dallyin', but I'll serve 'em from the kitchen leavin's. I don't reckon there's much leavin's, the way Hercules, Sam and Nathan spiffy up after cookin' a meal, though."

She kept glancing over her shoulder at the parlour door. "Just run to the market and pick up some nuts and—oh, whatever you can carry." She pressed several notes into my hand, turned me round and hustled me to the door. "Grab some satchels from the kitchen, and hurry before the market closes. Keep the change."

Keep the change? Durn, it musta been a panick. I tore down to the market and plucked up handfuls of whatever they had left—Harvey apples, shrivelly grapes, carrots, onions, winter bergamots, walnuts, and a pound of loaf sugar I diddled the grocer down to twenty-five cents. Seeing some queer-shaped nutshells, I asked the grocer, "What are these? I ain't never seen these afore."

"They're peanuts," he answered. "Grown in North Carolina."

Peanuts? I ain't never heard of 'em but scooped a few handfuls. I merrily munched a bergamot on the way back to the house, the juice sweeter'n lemon but more bitter'n grapefruit. I spat the skins into the gutter where pecking pigeons fluttered and pigs trotted over, squealing with delight. I couldn't let on I'd been feasting, so I rinsed my mouth at the backyard pump and spat on the ground.

All them hifalutin' bigwigs swarmed round the trays I set on the table like scurvy'd sailors at sea. Lady Washington stood pale and mortified as they chomped on raw carrots. Some of 'em even bit into the onions, weeping they eyes out.

"Oney, what are those?" She pointed to the peanuts as the men crushed the shells and scooped the nuts out.

"The grocer said they's peanuts," I answered with a shrug. In minutes they gobbled every morsel. Some of them actually addressed me, "Good day" they said or "Nice to see you, young lady", and a few even thanked me. Cause I near looked white, mayhap they mistook me for Miz Nelly.

By then Hercules and Nathan come back. Lady Washington near dropped to her knees and begged them to rustle up some proper viands for those hungry mouths, what kept dousin' with wine, now raiding the whiskey.

Hercules took one look at the peanut shells strewn all over the table and squawked like a plucked chicken. "Where you get those?"

"They's peanuts," I announced, proud I'd found new fare he could now serve at the general's hoity-toity fetes.

"Lawd sakes, girl, peanuts ain't for them kinda folk. Farmers grow 'em to feed 'em to livestock."

Struck dumb, I clutched at his sleeve. "Hey, Herc. Please, don' tell, let's hope they so pickled they don' know what they eatin'. Bad enough they eatin' raw onions."

He turned and with a low whistle, began rustlin' up some decent beefstakes and sourcrout with cabbage he took from Mount Vernon.

Some day off. But Lady Washington did promise us two eves off to attend theatre.

At dusk when the general flopped onto the sofa looking ready to keel over, a messenger come in delivering a note. Perching his specs on his nose, the general read aloud to those still sober enough to stand: "You are hereby invited as the guest of honor at a banquet and dancing at the

Ricket's Amphitheater at seven this eve … " He whistled through a gap in his teeth. "Great God in heaven save us!"

It fluttered to the floor. One of the Congressmen snatched it up and stuffed it into his pocket.

Governor Mifflin, who resembled the general—the wavy white hair, piercing blue eyes and jolly guffaw, but without his commanding height and military bearing—clapped the general on the back. "Don't despair, sir. You've seen enough birthdays to know they come but once a year!"

"Well, having imbibed through at least a hundred of them, you should know, Tommy," the general quipped back to the governor. Mr. Mifflin hid his scarlet cheeks behind another belt of whiskey.

We folk threw our own feast in the kitchen when Lady and General Washington departed in their carriage for that banquet, after my helping dress her formal. Sam and Nathan dished out hearty portions of ham hocks, beans, mash potatoes, and Hercules read Shakespeare to us 'til we dozed, bellies full.

Good thing the general's birthday came but once a year.

Good thing for Lady Washington, too. Next morn she shredded the *National Gazette* to tatters and stomped on the ragged bits, kicking the shreds through the parlour. She grabbed a broom and swept it into the street.

"There. That's where it belongs with the rest of the filthy trash." She brushed her palms together as she slammed the door with her foot. She stomped back in just as the general asked me where the morning's paper was.

"I believe 'tis out in the street, massa general." But her rant done drown'd me out. I poured her morning buttermilk but she looked like she needed more of a nip at the sherry.

"George, I will wring Philip Freneau's scrawny neck if it is the last thing I do!"

"What did he say now?" The general's eyes darted back and forth, as if wishing another paper to appear.

"He accused you of kingly and monarchial leanings again. And do you know why? Not because you purchased a crown, a scepter or a throne, or had a few subjects executed without trial. No, the bee in his bonnet is buzzing about your birthday celebration. 'A monarchial farce', he called it, 'of royal pomp' … why is there not a law against libel?" She huffed, breathing through her teeth.

"There is a law, Patsy. But there's also free speech. To someone of his lowbrow standing, if I'd held the party in the privy, he'd have considered it monarchial. 'Tis all relative, my dear. Remember from whence it comes, let it roll off you like water from a duck." He halted and pondered his words. "Or something like that, the young 'uns always say."

Her breathing calmed. She reached for a hoe cake and buttered it for him. "Fine thing for him to say about a party he wasn't even invited to."

The next message delivered for the general wasn't hardly a banquet invitation. The butler busy in the pantry, I opened the door to a courier who ran to and fro Mount Vernon with urgent messages, mostly bad. His tight lips weren't smiling this time either.

"Oh, no, Mr. Bellamy, what sorry tidings do you bring?"

"I'd best deliver it to the general myself, Oney." He pressed the sealed paper tween his flattened hands.

"He ain't—isn't here. You want Lady Washington to take delivery?"

He shuffled foot to foot, then asked me to fetch her. She was helping Molly do some spinnin' but dropped it all when I announced, "Mr. Bellamy brings a message ..."

"I know what it is," she murmured, raised her head bravely and marched down the stairs.

I figgered it out, too. The general's nephew George Augustine had died. The general trudged in that eve, hat and shoulders snow-sprinkled. She pulled him down to her height and gave him the bad news.

I boldly spoke out afore spoken to, cause leaving it unsaid was more disrespectful. "I'm sorry for your loss, masta general. I'll pray for Mr. George."

We never mentioned praying, but I had to this time. He adored his nephew, now dead of consumption. Head down, he muttered his thanks and dragged his large frame up the stairs.

That eve Lady Washington called me into their bedroom to help me with packing. "The general needs return to Mount Vernon to arrange for George Augustine's burial."

I polished his boots and packed some sugar candy I'd bought with my own money for his journey. I shed some tears of pity for George Augustine's poor widow Fanny and her three fatherless young'uns. I wondered if they'd all come to live with us. I figgered it likely.

****

40

Molly's and mine's stuffy room looked and smelled a mess. Scraps of cloth and ribbon, chicken bones and sweat-soaked raiment covered the floor. With no time to tidy up, I shoved trash into the corners every few days.

Lady Washington had me bathing and dressing her hair and body, washing and pressing her raiment, and accompanying her on visits. In preparing for her Friday receptions, the general's Tuesday levees and their Thursday dinners, I had to move furniture, decorate, drape the parlour tables with carpet covers to protect them from dripping wax, set the dining room table, and clean up after. In daylight, I cut patterns and sewed more skirts in the new style, the waistband huggin' the underside of the breasts.

I had so many chores, Lady Washington had to send loads of tailoring back to Charlotte at Mount Vernon. This greatly relieved me, cutting my workdays down to 12 or 13 hours, but I would'a rather sewed than all them other labors.

Lady Washington showed me a fashion newspaper that a rich lady sent her from Paris, with flowing gowns of dimity and muslin. "Ladies are dressing as they did in ancient Greece and Rome now," she said, "but I do not believe my figure can carry it." She passed the paper to me.

As I studied the low-cut bodices, high waists and short sleeves exposing entire arms and elbows, I assured Lady Washington, "I can make you one of these. If'n you dislike it, I'll cut it up to make a half robe."

She liked that idea. To work I went with a bolt of robin's egg blue striped muslin.

"Oh," she sighed, "they would, I fear, think me a good deal in the fashion if they could but see me."

She let me have the leftover material to make myself a frock with.

Since she started goin' gray, she'd never be seen without a cap atop her head. I began preparing at least three caps a day for her to wear—clearstarching—starching then clapping with my hands, quilling—shaping strips of paper and cloth to make fancy designs, and frilling—adding ruffles and lace to each one. But they had to be high, to make her look taller. She even helped me, cause "this doesn't seem like work," she said. Her lady friends admired her caps so muchly, she let me make some for them, and they paid me real generous, specially if they wanted lace edging.

I worked sunup to sundown. The Tuesday levees were an open house for the general to receive bigwigs for chat, tipple and general hobnobbin'. Lady Washington's Friday receptions came faster'n I could count the days.

Mrs. Adams always stood to Lady Washington's right, on a raised platform, as the ladies bobbed and curtseyed to them. The gowns with foil spangles glittered from the floor to the tips of their headdress, their jewels reflecting the light from all directions. Muchly to Lady Washington's dismay, the general forbade any talk of politicks.

The teas were more informal. For serving so nice, ladies always gave me a few shillings, what I sewed into my petticoat. Lady Washington let us take our money on market day and buy ourselves treats. The first time I ever tasted an apple tart was at market. But I made sure not to get too many of those. Lady Washington liked her tarts—and pastries, and cakes—and they all settled on her hips. I had to keep letting her skirts out. She'd laugh it off but I didn't think it funny. I feared fatness'd kill her.

I finally learnt to tell time, only cause the general got too busy to set his watch. Every noon he walked to Clark's standard on Front and High Streets to set his watch. I seen him there once, on my way to market. All the porters swept their hats off 'til he turned and went back. He then bowed to them and doffed his hat, when he wore one.

Lady Washington sat me down with the general's watch on this day as he sat conferrin' with his secretary, Mr. Lear, in his study. "I'm glad you're a fast learner, Oney. You've got exactly fifteen minutes to learn to tell time and go to Clark's to set his watch."

She showed me on the general's gold watch what time it was when the big and little hands pointed to each number round the dial. I tore down to Clark's in a fast trot, darting tween clattering carts, drays and wheelbarrows. A minute afore both hands met up at 12, I proudly set his watch. Buffing it on my new muslin dress, I strutted back to the house and presented it to him.

"Right on time, Oney," he praised me, attaching it to his chain.

I began a curtsey.

"You tell Lady Washington I said you may pick out a trinket next time she calls on Mr. Bringhurst."

Huh? When I heard that name I near tumbled over. Mr. Bringhurst was Lady Washington's jeweler. "Jewels for me, masta general? Oh, my Lawd!" I scrambled to my feet, trippin' over 'em. "I ain't—uh, never had nothin' lookin' like jewelry. Only once Nathan give me a handful'a oyster shells I strang together and made a necklace. My heavens, a real trinket from Bringhurst Jewelers." I clutched at my heart and he let out a pleased little chuckle.

"Strung together." He started correcting me when Lady Washington told him I was taking fancy speech lessons.

At times the general and Lady Washington made me feel I was their child. *Why was I the lucky one?*

****

I strolled the market next day, taking my time, for Lady Washington told me to be extra careful choosing victuals—they invited some bigwigs over and needed top pickin's. I turned to leave a stall of cabbages and bumped into a lady. Stammering an apology, I remembered meeting her at the General's first swearing-in at New York.

"Why, Oney, how nice to see you!" She admired my attire and ogled my pearl necklace. "I'm Eliza … well, I was Betsy when we met at my pa—at President Washington's first inauguration."

"Yea, I remember you." I held up my sack of victuals. "Just fetching some provisions, learning how to haggle prices."

"Good for you! There's an art to haggling, and I'm dead sure a smart lady like you won't leave a shilling on the table." She eyed my necklace again, blowing a low whistle through her teeth. "Mind if I ask who gave you that stunning pendant?"

I glanced down and brushed it lovingly with my fingertips. "Oh, Masta General—er, the president let me pick it out when I went with Lady Washington to Mr. Bringhurst, her jeweler here. It's a reward for learning to tell time."

"Why, it's lovely." She stepped closer to study it. "You have impeccable taste. The Washingtons are certainly generous."

We strolled the market as I looked over some fruits, not finding any fancy enough for the bigwigs. When we reached the end, she turned to me, eyes wide. "Oney, what's say we duck into a café for a bit—I know you need to get back to work, but I've nothing to do, and I'm sure Mrs. Washington won't mind your staying out just a little longer."

I had no hurry, either, so I pointed to the Brickyard Café on the corner. "Lady Washington brings us girls in there sometimes when we're out and about." I led the way, crossing the busy street, ducking carts and carriages. "Course I wouldn't go in alone, they'd never serve me."

"Someday that won't be the case any longer." She turned to face me, her tone intense, as if she truly believed it.

As we sat and sipped lemonade she paid for, she told me she'd been an actress, and I shared my love of theater. "Lady Washington gives us ample time off to attend Shakespeare plays and lets me—but only me—study with a tutor." We talked about our favorites, Romeo and Juliet, Richard the Third … and Shakespeare led to talk about books.

"I can't read just yet. Our cook, Hercules, been teaching me my letters." I didn't hide my grin, though I knew learning letters was naughty. "I don't tell Lady Washington, cause she may not mind, but Masta General might."

Eliza took a long sip of her lemonade and set the glass down. "How do you really feel about the Washingtons, Oney? Are they fair? Do you believe your—situation—is fair? I know they treat you well, but deep down, what do you hope for from them?"

I looked her directly in the eye and leaned forward. "What I hope for," I kept my voice low, "tween us, they know what got them there and me here—an accident of birth. Them words never left me, once Lady Washington said 'em. An accident is something that shouldn't happen. So no accident will change nothing. It needs to be done on purpose."

"Oney, I feel you and I are nearly kin, and I'll tell you why in a minute. But first—are you telling me you want to be free?" She didn't take her eyes off me, didn't even blink.

Without pause I nodded. "Someday, yeah. But it ain't possible unless she frees us. Cause we're—me and Mama and my sister and brother—we're hers, not Masta General's. When she dies, I'll belong to her grandkids. So it ain't never gonna happen." I fought tears but they came anyway.

She took my hand and squeezed it. Tears spilled from her own eyes. "Oney, every human being has a right to his or her own body. This nation fought for and won independence despite overwhelming odds. But unfairly, and disgracefully, our leaders overlooked an enormous group of people. I can't say if the law will change in our lifetimes. But aside from the law, freedom is within your reach—if you really want it."

I shook my head. "Too dangerous. You know what happen to escapees?"

"How well do you really know President and Lady Washington, Oney?" she asked.

"As well as they let me. They're devoted, have their bickerin's but they always make up. Compared to what I hear about other mastas and owners, they give us enough to eat, comfortable sleepin', nice clothes. Specially me. I'm her favorite. I get more'n the rest of 'em." I held up my cherished necklace.

"I'll let you in on a secret, Oney. I don't blab this to everybody." She took a deep breath, ready to spill. "First—I'd never own a slave, and if I inherited any, I'd set them free. But if that weren't possible, as in your case, being my spouse's and not mine, if some of them escaped, I wouldn't punish them. I'd try to find them and bring them back, but I'd grant them their freedom then and there. You know why? Because I respect and admire anyone brave enough to take that risk."

I shrugged. "So, you tellin' me what you'd do. That's you."

She gave me a sisterly smile. "But there's more. I'm not just the Betsy you met in New York. And what I do know of President Washington, we're very much alike. That's because he is my very own father."

"You … you're his daughter?" I blurted, then clapped my hand to my big mouth. "How you know that?"

"My mother told me. Once in Providence … " She sighed with longing. "Someday I'll meet him and I know deep down he'll acknowledge me. But meanwhile … you never let go of that dream of freedom. And if you keep your eyes open, you'll find a way, and folks to help, but only if you're brave enough to carry out your plan. And you won't get dragged back and punished. I'm telling you that as a Washington."

"But she's my owner," I argued. "I don't dare disobey her."

She half-grinned, half-sneered. "But he's her husband and her president. She don't disobey *him*."

Her words struck a chord deep within me. Sure I dreamed of escape many times. I hungered for freedom with a passion that consumed me. But could I really escape and never be found? Could I get folks to help me? Would the Washingtons punish me? Eliza thought she knew the General, but she'd never even met him. She only told me he wouldn't punish me, because *she* wouldn't, and they were kin. That didn't really prove nothing.

There was only one way to find out—but was I brave enough? No one could tell me this. No one but my very self. Someday.

Leaving the café, those thoughts propelling me forward, I didn't just walk, I strutted. Head high, I threw my shoulders back, my posture showing the mettle I never had before meeting Lady Eliza.

She clasped my hand. "Oney, we might not meet again, but I have a strong hunch I'll hear about you. And I can guarantee you'll hear about me. So this isn't quite goodbye."

"I know, Eliza. I know," I told this woman who'd just changed my life. "And thank you." Oh, yes, I'd hear about her again.

****

45

A few changes happened in this second term, some good, some not. Lady Washington's grandchildruns went to schools cross town, so I couldn't sit in on home classes, but Lady Washington still insisted on that speech tutor. She made sure I'd learn fancy talk. Miz Nelly and Washy now had a dancing teacher come to the house. Every time Mr. Robardet come to teach them lessons, we folk had to push all the parlour furniture out the way and roll up the carpets for their 'ballroom'. Of course I wasn't permitted to dance, but I watched as they glided across the floor, their slippers whispering over the waxed boards. I didn't envy them none these dance lessons. After a minute watching them twirling and sliding, I near dropped from boredom. That ain't the way we folk danced. When we danced, we do some funnin'!

I wondered why Mrs. Lewis and her daughter, the cooks, never arrived from Mount Vernon. Next day I heard the general tell Mr. Lear: "The dirty figures of Mrs. Lewis and her daughter will not be a pleasant sight in view of entertaining rooms in our new habitation."

Hercules didn't mind none. He gloried in the cleanliness and nicety of his kitchen, his underlings flew in all directions to carry out his orders. But now short-handed, he begged the general to let his son Richmond come to Philadelphia to serve as a scullion..

****

"The general done it for me," Hercules gushed, tears streaming down his face. "He says not cause of any desirable qualities in Richmond, but out of respect for me, 'cause he's your son and of your desire to have him as an assistant,' the general say to me. Oh, to have my boy beside me again."

"I'm very happy for you and Richmond, Herc." And I was. But seeing father and son embrace, reunited, gave me a mixture of joy and a stab of hurt. If only this could'a been me with Mamma.

Hercules sat us both down in the kitchen to learn letters. I learnt to write my name at Lady Washington's desk when she was out, using newspaper to write on, not daring to use her good writing paper.

****

Lady Washington took two whole days to get herself and the house ready for the inauguration and party afterwards. She had me wash and press a plain blue homespun I sewed her, to wear for her birthday. Instead, she was wearing it to this second swearing-in neither of them planned or wanted.

They kept their attire and everything else about it simple, due to certain folk, specially the press, accusing them of acting like king and queen.

"Wake up!" Molly shook me. I rolled over on my straw pallet—I wasn't allowed to bring the corn husk bed from Mount Vernon—the floor creaked neath me and I opened my eyes in the weak light.

"Git'cha self up, girl, the sun's nearly rose ahead a'you. Lady Washington needs bathin' and dressin'."

I stumbled down the steps and entered her room. She sat, specs perched on her nose, reading her Bible, still wrapt in her brocade half robe I altered from a gown more'n ten years old. Never waste a stitch, 'twas Lady Washington's watchword.

She looked up over her spec rims and gave me a stern look with knitted brow. "Oney, you shouldn't lie in so. 'Twill make you lazy. Now go fetch my bathing water." Her playful voice didn't match her stern look, though. I didn't fear a punishing.

I curtseyed and went out to the pump to fetch her water, then washed up in my room. I made sure to rinse my body at least twice a week, needin' it or not.

Later I caught a glimpse of the general. Fact is, I bumped right into him coming out the parlour, looking for Lady Washington. "Your lady is supervisin' the wash, Masta General." I backed way up to give him room with a quick curtsey—when he become president, he told us all to cease our bowin' and curtseyin' like he king, but we all did anyways.

"You'll make a mighty fine president once again, sir," fell out my mouth. I couldn't help it. Though he kept his dress low-key today, he looked so regal standing upright in a black velvet suit, watch and chain affixed to his waistcoat, silk stockings and diamond knee buckles. A dress sword with a fancy-carved hilt swung at his hip.

His eyes brightened in surprise. He bumbled, lips moving, but naught come out yet. "Why, thank you, Oney. Do not be so timid—you're allowed to speak, specially when it's of such a flattering nature." He gave me one of his rare smiles but didn't show his ill-fitting teeth. He tipped his hat and vanished.

Today I was allowed to ride in the carriage with Lady Washington and her grandchildruns. My brother walked the few blocks. In keeping with wanting to stay plain, only one pair of horses pulled this and the general's carriage, but the Arms of the United States graced the sides of his. This was only the second time I was allowed to ride with Lady Washington— one of the journeys back from New York, I'd took sick, way too sick to perch on the back of a wagon. But didn't I throw up all over her leather seat! She wasn't cross, though. She'd just made the coachman stop and me clean it up.

Now me, Paris the coachman and Austin stood with the carriage as Lady Washington, Miz Nelly and Wash went into Congress Hall. The general was already inside, practicing his speech, I reckoned. Streaks of clouds skimmed the sky on this hazy, mild morn. We weren't allowed inside.

A steady stream of bewigged gents lined up to enter, looking like owls in an ivy bush. Their gold watch-and-chains gleamed at their paunches. A group of men stood on a balcony above it. At his first inauguration in New York, the general took the oath on the Federal Hall balcony, and I got to see the whole thing from the street. But this time it was inside, in keeping with staying simple. I didn't mind missing it. I knew it wouldn't be happy for the general or Lady Washington, and she'd be fighting tears. I was perfectly happy missing that.

I wandered off, peeking into shop windows, seeing gewgaws I fancied buying with my few shillings, but I saved them for sweets. When I had more money, I'd buy that pink bonnet with streaming ribbons I saw in the milliner's window.

When I got back to Congress Hall everybody was gone. Only scraps of paper and the usual trash and dung lay scattered about. A sway-back horse pulled a rumbling cart piled with dirt. I lifted my skirt and ran all the way back to the house.

Lady Washington stood center parlour, ordering Molly and Austin how to set the table and when to bring the refreshments. When she saw me, her relieved smile made *me* sigh in relief.

"Oney!" She splayed her hands. "Where did you run off to? I thought you'd gone and left us."

"I went wandrin' round and the time just run away from me—uh, ran away."

"Unescorted? You know that is not proper!" She grabbed my elbow and led me to the sideboard where the silver was hid. "Go set the table and clean yourself up. We're having a houseful."

"Clean myself up" meant I was allowed to bathe in the old tin tub in the attic with heated water. She made me wash afore important company came, so my body'd be clean and presentable as my speech. I didn't even mind hauling pails from the kitchen fire up three staircases. Soaking in that tub was heaven. On these occasions I also dressed in my finest. We all needed be well-togged. The male servants wore livery: fancy crimson vests with polished brass buttons, long coats with tails, and clean white jerseys. Us girls wore satin gowns I'd sewed. She made us wear something matching or close to matching. Today it was a color she called eggshell, near to white, her favorite color.

Lady Washington loved wearing white and ordered yards of white fabrics. "You look like a Roman matron," more'n one guest fed her the praise she basked in. I didn't spare no praise either, since it was me who sewed all this white raiment that blended with her fair skin, gleaming teeth and frosty hair, powdered or not.

Now I knew how to tell time, I watched that little hand sweep the dial in a frenzy that eve. I knew it was midnight when both hands met at the '12' afore the last guest, Pennsylvania Senator Maclay, finally stumbled out the door. But I'd relished the night muchly as if I'd been invited. Miz Nelly played her pianoforte along with a string quartet. The general danced with five ladies, Lady Washington not being one of 'em—she hated to dance, so she stayed busy chit-chatin' with her guests. She did call me over a few times. "Oney, tell Mrs. Powel and Mrs. Adams how you and your brother Austin relish living here. Do you like it better than Mount Vernon?"

"Mount Vernon is home to me." I spoke from my heart and they listened rapt. "I'd never relish no house—er, any house—more than the big house, and I'm privileged to live and work there." And that was the truth. Course it was better than the filthy, crowded, noisy city streets, the clamor of wheels on the cobbles, hawkers hollin' their putrid vegetables, rotten fish, sheep heads and cattle hoofs, ragamuffins begging for scraps, scrounging pigs, piles of dung from animal and man, and smoke choking us on cold days. The air smelt, people smelt, muck in the streets smelt. I couldn't wait to get back to Mount Vernon's clean air and clean dirt. And of course Mamma and Delphy.

"I must agree with Oney." Lady Washington's voice quivered. "Confidentially, ladies, neither George nor I wanted this second term. He's a devoted soldier, serving his citizens another four years. But that's all it is. His duty. He wouldn't have served if those men hadn't been so persuasive, convincing him the government would fall apart without him. We so wanted to retire under our vine and fig tree."

"Worry not, Martha, the time will fly by, as did the last four years." The plump Mrs. Adams patted her arm, her and Lady Washington looking alike as sisters. "I hope to relish it more than you are, should providence repeat itself with me and John."

Mr. Adams already was Vice-President but I didn't know if that meant aught. Did the Vice-President take over, like with kings? I never learnt how that worked in this free land of ours—rather, theirs.

"If it isn't providence, 'tis the men who rule, Abby. Either way, 'tis not us," Lady Washington said over a sigh, as my brother appeared with a silver tray balanced atop his palm.

"Madeira, ladies?" he offered.

Only Mrs. Adams plucked a glass from the tray and took a generous quaff. "For my rheumatism," she found the need to explain. "The Philadelphia climate brings out the worst in it."

"No, we rule the roost, they rule the country," Mrs. Powel chimed in, her husband once being Philadelphia's mayor, now a senator. "Don't complain, Martha. Everything happens for a reason. I fear our nation's fate with anyone but George at the helm. We'd risk falling back under British rule." She shuddered. "I wouldn't trust the nation to anyone else. Who could possibly do that job?"

Did Mrs. Powel expect an answer? I knew Lady Washington had one.

"That's just what George said, but I thought it was him being haughty. Someone will have to, next time. Mayhap he'll come out of nowhere. As long as it isn't Mr. Jefferson." Her voice took on that throaty rumble as it always did when she spoke that name. She almost spat it out like rancid cream.

The other two ladies voiced sounds of horridness. "If Mr. Jefferson takes George's place, we'll all be speaking French and dressing like hussies."

Mrs. Powel glanced round the room, no doubt for my brother and a drink. Talk of Mr. Jefferson always sent Lady Washington to the sideboard for a tipple of sherry. But this time I saw Lady Washington blanch as if she'd tumbled over a beehive, and she may've well did, cause Mrs. Adams regarded Mr. Jefferson as the pinnacle of wisdom.

"Cannot the man understand we want to progress and not remain on farms? He's got the mind of a caveman." Mrs. Powel went on, and I knew if Mrs. Adams had her way, she'd've stuffed a dozen socks into the lady's gob.

But Mrs. Adams, never one to sit on the sidelines and miss a chance to speak her piece, gave Mrs. Powel a staid New England flayin', taking her down a peg. "Eliza." She turned her stout frame towards the offendor, forefinger aimin' at Mrs. Powel's heart like a pistol, "I admonish you to withhold your judgments on Mr. Jefferson without proper examination of his temperament and intentions. He is one of the choice ones of the earth. Why, when we resided in Auteuil, he would travel all the way from Paris for dinner with us."

Mrs. Powel's pompadour near swept the chandelier when she raised her haughty head. "'Tis a long journey to mooch a free meal. And I am well acquainted with Mr. Jefferson's temperament and intentions—neither are less than disastrous to our nation."

Lady Washington cut in. "Now, ladies, we cannot all hold every man in high regard. I cannot say I'm enamored of Mr. Jefferson. George and I need maintain cordiality to him in order to keep peace among ourselves, and not to cause another war declaration."

Her smiling eyes and lips flashed round the room. "Personally, we're in different worlds, with nary a thing in common. Mr. Jefferson never even invited George to Monticello. Goodness me, even the Hamiltons have invited us to their humble abode. But Mr. Jefferson—he hasn't the time for entertaining. He's too busy running his farm and thinking up ideas to drive George batty and—oh, never mind whatever monkeying round he does in his private time behind closed—and locked—boudoir doors." She batted her lashes with the hint of a smirk, and I knew what that meant—her way of steering the talk to a more titillating pastime—gossip.

Xcept for Mrs. Adams, whose glare near set the room afire, the other ladies tittered. They knew durn well of his monkeying round. But I didn't. As Lady Washington's pet, I was privy to many of her private conversations; she hardly ever dismissed me when she indulged in this ladies talk.

But when I heard the name 'Sally' hiss past Mrs. Adams's lips, I knew. Sally Hemings. It was once a secret, but not no more. She was mulatto, and Mr. Jefferson's concubine, as well as mother to his numerous childruns, and half-sister to his dead wife. I never seen Sally, but heard she was comely. Though he kept her a slave, she had the run of his house. He promised to free their childruns—someday. Her, no. Only the childruns. I wisht to meet her someday. We'd have lots to talk about.

When the string quartet began packin' up they fiddles, that meant the party's over. Guests dawdled round the front door, chatterin' and stretchin' out their "good eve"s, but the general was known to exit his own parties, with Lady Washington at his heels, announcing, "The general retires at nine, and I soon thereafter." They all filed out but Senator Maclay, who bent the general's ear about horse racin'. He finally shooed the senator out.

I followed Lady Washington upstairs. She moaned all the way, "Oh, my aching feet," and when she collapsed unladylike, legs spread, into her wing chair, I slipt her shoes off and massaged her sweaty feet. "Oh, Oney, four more years of this will kill *me*, much less my husband," she groaned, wiggling her clammy toes in my hands. "This is but the first day of another sad four years. If he lasts that long."

"The general ain't goin' nowheres, Lady Washington," I assured her, "nowheres 'til he's finished."

"If only I could find a way to make him retire and someone else take over, I'd ask his successor personally."

And I believed her. When Lady Washington wanted something, she asked for it—and always got it.

CHAPTER FIVE

I didn't believe in curses or that mumbo jumbo, but knew this second president term would be nowhere happy as the first, if you can call the first happy. Truly it wasn't. Within a week, poor General and Lady Washington got hit with message after message of bad news, mostly deaths of loved ones.

Us folk barely recovered from the party mess, but since Katie and Eliza, the house servants, was ill, the rest of us had to pick up their slack. Me and Molly cleaned up the party leavin's, rotated the carpets, dusted and moved back the parlour furniture while Lady Washington sat, too exhausted to knit or even read. She just sprawled on the sofa and had me lay a cool cloth over her eyes.

That's when the general come in holding some papers. "The backstabbers are at it again, Patsy."

He didn't seem to notice she just wanted to rest. But round here, he was masta. Hence, she took the cloth from her eyes and sat up. "Which backstabbers? There are so many."

"The anonymous letter-writers sent me no less than three missives about Jefferson's sneaky bid for the presidency and Madison's perfidy."

"I believe Mr. Jefferson is two-faced," Lady Washington snarled, her voice barely above a growl. "But by its very nature, an anonymous letter carries no weight."

"The humorous thing, if you can call it humorous, is there's naught in here I didn't already know, so the joke's on him—or her." He unfolded the next letter. "If Mr. Jefferson wants to be president, I wish he would come out and ask me. He can have it!" He sucked at his ill-fitting teeth. "The writer of this is naïve. Of course things go on behind my back. This is politicks."

"Show Mr. Jefferson the letter and see what he says," she suggested.

"He'll deny it, of course. He's looked me straight in the eye and lied before. Mayhap sending him back to France would be best, 'twill get him out of my hair, at least. You know the saying, keep your friends close and your enemies closer."

"By sending him to France?" Her brows drew together and she peered at him with her *there you go again, George* look.

"'Tis a figure of speech, Patsy." His voice took on that talking-to-childruns tone again.

"If that's what it would take to get him out of your hair ..."

He shook his head with a thin smile. "He's told me himself that he plans to resign by the end of the year anyway. And Hamilton is now talking of resigning."

Her mouth fell open. "After all this? After begging, cajoling, wheedling, and naught short of threatening you to serve this second term as president, they're leaving the scene of the crime?" She made a fist and punched the sofa cushion.

"'Tis naught to do with me." He adjusted his specs. "They wanted me to stay president, no matter where they are. Mr. Jefferson can ride off into the bloomin' sunset, I care not. I'm more bothered about Hamilton leaving. There's hardly a mind close to the brilliance of his for the Treasury Department. His assistant Wolcott is barely a shadow of him. But—what's to be done? To whom does the world's best surgeon go for surgery?"

"The second best," she answered.

"Right. I'll have to settle for second best. At least I'm staying." He unfolded another piece of paper.

I knew he'd admit it! I huffed out a silent cheer, fists pumped and punching the air. I quick turned my head and kept scrubbing.

"This is even better." The general cleared his throat afore reading: "I do not believe you know that the *National Gazette* was established under the immediate patronage of Mr. Jefferson and Mr. Madison, and that Mr. Freneau, the printer of it, is a clerk in the Secretary of State's office with a salary as interpreter. The object of these men is to make you odious and destroy Mr. Hamilton."

"Mayhap that's why Mr. Jefferson is resigning," Lady Washington said. "But we all know Freneau and his newspaper. No self-respecting trout would want to be wrapped in it."

"And I daresay," the general said, "I've never even seen the *Gazette* adorning a privy—for reading or any other purpose."

I went out to fetch more lye sope to wash wine stains off the rug. When I come back they were discussing freedom, I reckoned. My heart skipped— were they planning to free us? But no—my spirit sank, as I realized the general was referring to his self. "I don't want to end my life with any regrets, Patsy."

She must've been badgering him about taking that second term again.

The general scoffed, "I'd told Jimmy Madison, Hamilton, all of them—I wanted to end my days in ease and tranquility. I also thought stepping down and letting someone else serve would be more congenial with ideas of liberty." He faltered here. "I know of no one else who could fill my shoes with my ..." I'd seen him stop and search for the right word, as not to sound haughty and self-important, "... my devotion."

I wanted to applaud. A word I learnt last week and no better word for it.

"Oh, if only I could vote." Lady Washington rubbed her eyes in a circular motion, as if fighting off a headache.

"What difference would that have made?" he asked.

"I'd have voted you out. Then it wouldn't have been unanimous."

He patted her knee. "Mayhap, someday wives will vote when their husbands run for president."

"Mayhap, someday wives will run for president," she countered.

He let out a loud laugh. "Please, Patsy ... one crisis at a time."

****

Not three days later, where I dusted book shelves and snuck a peek at a book of maps, Lady Washington busted into the parlour, hands fluttering. I snapped the book shut but she was so frantic she didn't even notice.

"Oney, this is sickening." Her hands pressed together, she looked ready to drop to her knees and pray for the world to be saved.

"Lawd, what is?" I stepped up to her and looked for the expected tears, but none came. "Are you sick?" I trembled. Was the general selling us? He hadn't sold a slave in many years, and word got round we were secure where we were. But I didn't fully trust none of 'em. They didn't fully trust us, neither. That was one given—the well-defined boundary.

She shook her head, her face drained of all color, looking even whiter'n usual. "Terrible news. Terrible, terrible news ... from France."

Mr. Jefferson died! was my first thought. But no, that would hardly be terrible news to her. Sides, he wasn't in France no more. "Who died?" I knew it had to be somebody important. Dr. Benjamin Franklin? No, he already dead.

"King Louis. He met his fate with Madame Guillotine."

"Who she?" I asked. "She a friend of Madame du Barry?"

Her eyes grew round. "Heavens, no. The guillotine is a ..." She made a slashing gesture with her finger across her throat, "... a very sharp blade the perfidious French use to sever unruly heads from bodies." She heaved a heavy sigh, her breasts rising and falling. "And poor queen Marie Antoinette was arrested. She'll be next."

"That's horrible, all right." I shivered. I never seen a guillotine but knowing it had a sharp blade and the French invented it, it must be nasty. "Why couldn't the king just go to prison?"

"You don't know those French, Oney." She took her handkerchief and swiped it along her hairline. "They are a malignant spider, nowhere near as civilized as we are. They're not even as civilized as the British." She gave a little "hmmf" after that. "Marie Antoinette was brought up on a slew of charges, most, I daresay, made up. From what I heard of her, and this from Lafayette himself, she isn't the monster they make her out to be. She isn't even French."

My morbid side wanted to know what these made-up charges were. It wasn't my place to ask, but lucky for me she told me anyways, needing to get all this off her chest. I of course always listened, eager to learn.

"The Revolutionary Tribunal accused her of stealing and sending France's treasury money to her home in Austria, declaring her son king, having orgies at the palace, and worst of all ..." She took a deep breath and near-whispered, "... abusing her son." She paced the floor. "Oh, how horrible. The poor, poor woman. I pray for mercy on her soul. 'Tis a matter of time before she loses her head, too." Her hands stayed clasped and she brought her head down to meet them.

"What's an ori-gy?" I always asked for the meanings of new words, more eager than she to show off to her fine ladies at parties.

"That's a—" She fixed her eyes on me and drew her lips into a tight line. "Never mind. 'Tis naught that you need to know about. Naught like that ever goes on in this nation." She gave a haughty toss of her head, led me to the sofa and patted the space next to her. Here in Philadelphia I was allowed to sit on the sofa. Prob'ly cause this wasn't really they house. These days she invited me to sit by waving a hand at a chair or sofa. In this house I was allowed the chairs and sofas, not my assigned footstool.

"Does that mean the French revoltin is over?" I sat after she did.

"Revolution," she corrected me. Lady Washington encouraged Hercules to read me the papers, thankful for someone to talk to about these things, when her ladies weren't around. The general was far too busy. She never asked my view on politicks, she just needed to let her feelings out. But I told her anyways. I didn't much fancy Mr. Jefferson, either, and reminded her every chance I got. This amused her, cause she loathed him. We had our different reasons—mine cause he'd toss his coat and walking stick to the butler when entering the house, ordered Charlotte to shine his horse dung-spattered boots, and demanded I inspect inside his wig for lice as Molly scratched his itchy scalp. Lady Washington misliked him cause he "kissed France's arse" as I overheard her grouse to the general more'n once.

"Nay. There is much unrest in France, and things may never calm down there the way they did here at our war's end. Too many revolting peasants who cannot accept their lot in life."

I hid my spreading smile by covering my mouth and coughing, when I thought of those revolting peasants. Good for them! I cheered for them the whole time when Hercules read me that they stormed the Bastille in their tattered rags and mob caps, and dragged the king and queen from the palace. I'd never dare say that to Lady Washington, though. But I couldn't find one good thing about monarchy and royalty. So I had something in common with most white folk, besides three-fourths my blood.

The king and queen shouldn't have they heads sliced off, but shouldn't'a starved they people either. But Lady Washington never asked me what I thought so I kept quiet.

"I can only pray that the queen will survive this." She brushed some crumbs off the sofa.

"Me, too." I meant it, now that I knew the queen wasn't a frog, as Lady Washington called the French in private.

Just then the general stomped in, so it must'a been dinner time. He nodded my way, which I always found thoughtful, as most white folk considered us part of the wallpaper. He walked up to Lady Washington. "I've no time for dinner today. I just received a message from Mount Vernon that Anthony Whitting is ill and not expected to recover. I need go back and find a new manager."

Lady Washington stood, and so did I. Barely reaching his shoulder, she looked way up at him. "You're not leaving now, are you?"

"No, when Congress adjourns in April. But I must write some letters, and fast. Have dinner sent in to me and Tobias in the study. Good day, Oney." He turned on a heel and marched from the room.

"Oh, the general had grown to depend on Mr. Whitting, Oney. He's been such a reliable manager." Eyes downcast, she shook her head. "Good help is so rare."

I knew how rare good help was, and how muchly the general depended on Mr. Whitting. He took over after the general's nephew George Augustine died in Feb'y. Was it the back-breaking labor and endless drudgery in the scorching heat and bone-numbing cold that sickened and kill-ded those men? Musta been. It kill-ded plenty'a us folk. This life was work, work, work—and die.

Not long after, as I buffed Lady Washington's nails, a courier from Mount Vernon delivered a letter. "Oh, no," we said at the same time. We both knew a courier always delivered bad news—more'not, a sudden death.

I stood back to give her privacy as she opened it. "Dear God, it's from Fanny." Fanny Basset was Lady Washington's favorite niece. After Fanny's mother died, she lived at Mount Vernon 'til she married the general's nephew George Augustine, now dead of consumption.

I never said a word when she got these letters, just waited quietly off to the side. With a shaky voice, she always told me what was in them after the shock wore off, swiping tears away, blowing her nose into her lace hanky.

"Her father passed of aplopexy while riding a horse on the way to Mount Vernon." She sighed over a sob.

I stepped forward again. "I'm sorry, Lady Washington," I said softly. "I know they was close." Mr. Basset was married to Lady Washington's sister, and always visited the big house. I spent many an eve serving them, listening to their banter and hearing about the Basset childruns, specially Fanny, Lady Washington's favorite. "She is as a child to me," I always heard her say. Poor lady, all her own childruns gone, Patsy of seizures, Jacky of camp fever. Jacky even died at the Bassett plantation.

"Good heaven, within weeks of George Augustine's passing." Her voice broke. "Poor Fanny. That poor waif. I must write and invite her and the children to live with us ..." Her voice wobbled over tears. " I cannot even write to her right now ..." She stood and brushed past me out the room. I wisht I could write. I'd write to Miss Fanny. Oh, how I wisht I could write! That day I made it my business to learn. The Washingtons never kept none of us learning to read or write. But they never hardly gave us enough time to learn.

Lady Washington being too grief-stricken to write to her niece, she let the general write for her. She stayed up in her room with the Lawd for longer than the usual hour, 'til the demands of being the president's wife summoned her down.

Fanny refused Lady Washington's offer, staying at her town house in Alexandria. Always following the death of a loved one, I dressed her in black mourning attire and helped her down the stairs to face the world, with her stiff lip and back. She had her moments but never let no one see her in dishabille, in tears, or in grief. Just the general and me.

CHAPTER SIX

This second president term made life in Philadephia more exciting than the first, muchly more'n our daily drudge at Mount Vernon. Here, we attended plays, birth-night balls, fireworks displays, concerts, waxworks exhibits, Gray's amusement garden on the Schuylkill River, and the circus. When the general departed for Mount Vernon in April, Lady Washington sped straight to her desk. As I fed silver thread through my needle for a dancing dress for Miz Nelly, she pulled out her date book and pen. I was about to ask her where to place espangles on the satin skirt when she called me over to her.

"These are my plans for this week. On Monday we'll go see *The School for Scandal*, Tuesday I'll have the ladies over for afternoon tea—I'll see if that string quartet of students is available—and Wednesday we'll visit the dry goods store for fabrics to cover the sofa and chairs. Would you like to sew some dimity curtains for your room, Oney?"

I ain't never had curtains afore, never had a window afore. And dimity—that sounded right wasteful for hangin' on a window. "I'd like naught more, Lady Washington. Where is the school for scandal? I didn't know there was a school to go learn scandal."

She chuckled, the first laugh I'd heard from her in many months—not since the general become president again, anyways. "No, 'tis a play, in a theatre. An exceeding popular one. I've seen it several times, but I don't believe I've ever brought you to see it."

"I'd'a remembered that name, ma'am."

"'Tis about one Lady Sneerwell whose gossip and lies cause utter chaos throughout. 'Tis all about trickery and forgery and gossip and—" She clasped her hands. "Oh, what fun." She closed her eyes with a dreamy smile, as if savoring a sweet blancmange. "But it does have a happy ending. It imitates life, but on a grander scale,'tis what makes it funny."

Life on a grander scale than this? I eyed her finery—the woven rug, cloth covering the walls, velvet draperies, carved mantelpiece from Swizzaland, and artwork painted straight onto the ceiling by an artist on his back. And this wasn't nowhere fancy as Mount Vernon. But I never heard no scandal round here. I heard about Mr. Hamilton and some woman who wasn't his wife, but only when Mr. Monroe mentioned it to the general, who loudly voiced his disgust about it.

So far I went to the theatre with the general and Lady Washington five times. Each time, I looked round. Slaves stood alongside their sitting owners through the whole show. They weren't allowed to sit. The first time Lady Washington took me, I stood behind her chair, but she clutched my arm and pulled me down in the seat next to her. "You may sit and enjoy the play, Oney," she whispered.

This play, at the Southwark Theatre, didn't have no extra seats. So Lady Washington sent Austin to fetch us two chairs, making sure the nabobs in charge knew the order come straight from her. I felt like royalty itself settled in my chair. Afore the curtain rose, the orchestra burst into the Marseillaise, and there I was, standing again with the whole audience on its feet, most of 'em singing *Marchons! Marchons! Qu'un sang impur. Abreuve nos sillons!*

But Lady Washington didn't sing—or stand.

That play was Shakespeare, and I didn't hardly understand the fancy language, but I enjoyed the costumes and told Lady Washington how muchly I relished it afterwards. It sent me to another world. After that she let me go to theatre with Austin and Hercules, and whoever else she gave permission to.

Hercules snuck a Shakespeare book from the Washingtons' library and in the late hours, we sat in the kitchen by the firelight. He read to me what he could make sense of. His voice rose and fell, mimicking the quirky accents of visitors from over the sea. As he read *Henry VIII*, I got so fascinated with the story, I blurted out to Lady Washington the next day that Hercules read me from the book nearly through the night. "I'm sorry. He put the book back, like it never been touched."

Nodding with an amused grin, she corrected my grammar. "Like it had never been touched." She put down her knitting and sat back. "Oh, I do love Shakespeare. What a brilliant writer. *Henry VIII* is not one of my favorite plays, but King Henry himself is notorious for having six wives, and cut the heads off two of them."

"Dip me in ink and call me a nib!" I sat rapt. "We didn't git to that part. Was he French?"

"No, British. But he was just as heartless," she went on. "When he wanted to discard one wife for another, he'd just accuse her of terrible things—witchcraft, incest, a multitude of sins, and then order her head lopped off."

Now, after learning the French beheaded their king and would soon behead their queen, it made me think: "Did other kings kill they wives—er, their wives?" I asked her, my curiosity burning.

"No more wives that I know of, but Richard III is rumored to have murdered his nephews to get the crown for himself," she answered in a serious tone. "I hope that cannot be true. But 'tis ever so easy when one powerful person, or a mob, has power. Power can be very dangerous. That's why we have a republic here. Not even the president has all the power."

But she didn't address the other side of it: how about the mob, meanin' us slaves? What would happen here if all the slaves revolted like they're still doing in Haiti to this day? I heard of slave mobs revolting in Virginia, but they got hanged or burnt at the stake. I reckon they're more organized in Haiti.

****

Lady Washington held her tea party, inviting Mrs. James Monroe, Secretary of War's wife Mrs. Knox, and Dolley Todd, young wife of a Philadelphia lawyer. Lady Washington preferred younger women, her grandgirls, nieces and me. She seemed younger when around us. I seldom seen Lady Washington with women her age, unless the general invited them with they husbands to the formal levees. If she had a choice, it was always younger ladies.

And she let me stay, rather than serve and leave. I didn't talk 'til spoken to, but except the most snobbish ones, these ladies enjoyed engaging me in their conversation. Seems I was a novelty, the light-colored pet smart enough for chat about things besides which ribbons matched which overskirt or how to dissolve grape stains. And I talked fancy—almost.

That day at tea I become Mrs. Knox's favorite pet when I grabbed Washy's toad Cornwallis after he hopped onto her lap. She let out a scream tremendous as herself as I cupped Cornwallis tween my palms and spirited him from the dining room.

On the morn after the general left for Mount Vernon, I scrubbed Lady Washington's back as she knelt in the tin tub. "The ladies I've invited all dress to the bricks, even for one of my teas, but I don't want to appear as I'm putting on airs. Why don't you lay out the gray striped damask gown and the blue lace kerchief, and you wear whatever you like today."

She gave me more and more—not my freedom, but pretty clothing. I even got a new pair of pink satin shoes when she bought Miz Nelly a pair. Cost eight shillings. I needn't even ask; she just saw my shoes were wore out. She enjoyed indulging me, as I relished making her pretty, and it made my days more bearable.

The first guest rapped on the door as the hall clock gonged four times. I opened the door to the portly Mrs. Knox. She greeted me warmly, as if I invited her myself. I returned her warmth with a curtsey, which I customarily reserved for General and Lady Washington, but she ordered me to curtsey to her tea guests. I couldn't speak, yet, 'til spoken to.

"Good day to you, Oney, and you look well nourished." She looked me up and down with approval.

"I am, thank you kindly, ma'am, and welcome to President and Lady Washington's house."

White folk never treated me mean, I had to admit, cause I did my duties fast, without fussin' and grousin' but mostly cause I looked white enough to be Lady Washington's kin. And unless she told them who I was, I could'a been her mulatto half-sister Ann's git. As I learnt at Mamma's knee, this was my saving grace, looking white … enough.

"Child, the good Lawd done blest you wit' white looks, what'll better yo' life far more'n the ink-spitters." Back then, I was too young to understand what being black and white meant. Neither did I know an ink-spitter was a very dark person.

"Lady Washington awaits in the parlour." I took Mrs. Knox's bonnet stained on the inside with brown hair-dye, waved in the parlour's direction and stood back to let her go first. The fashionably togged Mrs. Elizabeth Monroe and Mrs. Dolley Todd arrived together, in almost matching robes of blue velvet trimm'd with some kinda animal fur, they heads ornamented with flowers. Mrs. Todd's head was topped with a towering plume of white feathers. They fussed over me, too, and praised Lady Washington for how good she took care of me.

"The lady sure dresses you fine," Mrs. Monroe commented as she handed me her gloves.

"Thank you, my lady, but I do all the sewin'—er, sewing of the finery myself." I proudly spread my own finely stitched muslin skirt and twirled about.

That made Mrs. Todd ask Lady Washington if she could borrow me, to sew her some frocks. Being a Quaker she had a queer way of speaking certain words, but I figgered out what she was tryin'a say.

"Lady Washington, I would thank thee more than I can express if thy servant Oney could come with me to assist us. My sister hath needed new raiment nigh on the better part of the year now. And ye've seen my mama's worn raiment; thou canst understand why she needs a superior seamstress."

"I may lend her to you, but not for a while yet," she answered as I led them to the sofa. "This second term has been so busy for us, I could use another three Oneys. So you'll have to wait your turn, Dolley."

"Then I thank thee way in advance." Mrs. Todd tsk'd, smiling at me. "Thy services are as hen's teeth, Oney," she said, "and it seems not that Lady Washington will let thee out of her sight." She trilled a laugh as she opened her snuff tin, took a pinch and sniffed.

Why did ladies never dip snuff in front of gents? I wondered. I hid my own laugh as I headed out to the kitchen to fetch the hot water and silver tea strainer.

When I got back to the parlour, the chatter was well underway. I'd'a never guessed how muchly Lady Washington missed the general. The talk hardly got round to him. They fixed their first sights upon Mr. Jefferson and that same favorite object of odorous odium—the French.

Only this time Lady Washington put a cat among the pigeons—Mrs. Monroe was a Frenchophile and a Jefferson doter. That didn't sit well with the other ladies. I began to think Mrs. Washington regretted inviting her to this party. Squabbles tween the ladies could get just as vicious as the gents. But ladies had claws more lethal than a bash on the head with a walkin' stick.

"You wait and see, Mr. Jefferson will be president some day, and soon," Mrs. Monroe sniffed, holding out her tea cup for me to refill. "He has more support in the Congress than you think."

"But right now the trend is away from his ideas," Lady Washington countered. She didn't often voice her views in mixed company, that is, with gents. But oh, did she relish stirrin' up a cauldron among her lady friends, specially when she knew their views laid at opposite ends. Like now. "Yeoman will be a thing of the past when Mr. Hamilton's manufacturing cities begin growing. We cannot be a nation of farmers and expect to progress."

"At least Mr. Jefferson prefers the separation of Church and state," Mrs. Monroe argued back. "I do not believe men should politicize God in speeches or oaths."

Lady Washington sat forward. "Then you believe my husband was wrong in saying 'so help me God' after taking his oath of office and kissing the Bible?"

"Well, I—" Mrs. Monroe's hand shook, and she spilt tea on her satin gown. "It is acceptable in an oath, I suppose, but not integrating it with how the country is run. Our independence was solely earned by the bravery of our soldiers—and our intrepid generals, of course," she added, with a fawning nod and fake smile to Lady Washington.

I sussed a fake smile when I saw one. I wondered if God would be involved in me getting *my* independence. Didn't stop me from askin' him every chance I got.

Now Mrs. Knox chimed in, "Mr. Jefferson only wants to separate Church and state at the federal level, with no power of religion over government. Religion lies tween man and his God, and I do agree with him on that."

"Well, of course," Lady Washington agreed. "That is what the Pilgrims came here to get away from. And our founders made sure that government is kept from intermeddling in churches and vice versa. Mr. Jefferson did inform us that the federal government has no power to prescribe any religious exercise. It must rest with the states. So I cannot say he is a buffoon in every area."

Mrs. Todd asked, "Why is thy Mr. Jefferson so progressive on that issue and so backward on others? He doth say 'all men are created equal' and owns several hundred slaves."

Mrs. Todd was one of them rare wealthy whites who owned no slaves, I reckoned.

But that topic went on like I wasn't there. Nobody paid mind to us when we stood in the room. Part of the wallpaper, was us. They'd never shoo us away when they wanted to talk delicate topics, or even about us. They thought we minded none being made fun of, or we didn't understand what they said. We learnt to stand there and ignore it with a frozen face.

"Slaves aren't citizens, Dolley," Mrs. Knox berated her. "I personally am against the institution." I caught her glancing my way but made sure our eyes didn't meet. "They should be granted citizenship after a certain number of years of work, if their owners permit it."

For once I wanted to hear Lady Washington say just one word on the subject. But she never shared her feelings about slavery. In her most intimate discussions, never uttered a word on it. I heard her complain of slaves. She never dismissed me from the room, not carin' if I heard. One day she groused to her niece, "The blacks are so bad in their nature they have not the least gratitude for the kindness that may be showed to them," as I scrubbed the floor round their feet.

"Where do you expect them all to go if freed?" Mrs. Monroe gave a stern challenge. "Out into the wilderness to fend for themselves? They need us to feed and clothe and shelter them. Think the whole thing through, Lucy."

"People need not own human beings," Mrs. Knox argued back. "They can certainly pay them a living wage."

Oh, if only I could add some o'my lip to this tiff. But I didn't dare. Nobody wanted to know what I thought about slavery. Even if one of them dared ask me, I couldn't say what I really felt. I'd turn and leave, rather than lie. But since the subject sickened me, I turned and left anyways, telling Lady Washington I needed to fetch more tea and crumpets.

But just as I left the room, one of them screamed. I turned to see all four ladies sprung to their feet, dancing round the rug on tippy toes. What in tarnation is going on in there? I crept back in, holding my ears against their screechin'.

Lady Washington grabbed my arm, nearly knocking the teapot from my hand. "Oney, do something! There's one of those horrible things scurrying across the floor." The ladies parted to make way for me, holding up their skirts as if a horse come and plopped a pile on it.

I saw the offender, a cockroach, scurry towards the corner. Teapot in one hand, I brought my free arm down and slammed my fist on that ugly bug, flattening it. I picked it up tween thumb and forefinger, opened the window and hurled it outside.

The collective sighs rang out louder than the gonging clock.

"Oh, thank you, Oney, you saved the day," Lady Washington praised me as Mrs. Knox shuddered. Her jowls swang like pendulums.

"Us folk ain't—er, we folk ain't a'scared'a bugs." I shrugged. "We're used to 'em."

Mrs. Todd gave me some coins for my trouble. "Buy thyself something pretty." She nodded her beplumed head and patted my arm—sleeved, of course. She wouldn't'a touched my bare arm.

I knew I was rude, but oh, I laughed and had to run from that room. But listening to their goings-on was too much fun to head back down the hall. I hid behind the door and eavesdropped, my laughs drowned in the tea towel.

"Oh, how disgusting, she pounded it with her bare hand."

"Did it stain your rug, Lady Washington?"

"Now do you agree with me that we needs those people round the house?"

With that, I went and fetched their tea and the midday tipple. Knowing better, I got one for each of 'em ladies.

CHAPTER SEVEN

On the day of the general's expected return from Mount Vernon, Lady Washington hovered at the window, paced back and forth, tied the curtains back for a clear view, stood on the porch and peered into the street, heaving impatient huffs. When his coach clattered to the curb at four of the clock, she flew out to meet him.

When they come in, I backed out the room to give them some privacy. Wasting no time, he strode to his study where Mr. Lear sat busy at his bookkeeping, and shut the door. Me being bold, I knocked, opened the door a needle length and peeked in. "Masta, I welcome you home and would ask if you care for some tea."

He looked round as if not knowing where my voice come from. "Uh …" He saw me peeking in the narrow door crack. "Right, that would be fine indeed, dear."

I skipped down the hall. He called me 'dear'! Course he wasn't thinking. His mind surely remained at Mount Vernon where I knew he wisht the rest of him was.

"I have some deathly serious work to do," he told Lady Washington that eve. They sat before the fire while I sewed eyelet holes into a cambric frock for Miz Nelly. She let me keep the extra material to make an apron for Mamma. Muchly as I knew living here brung me closer to freedom, I so badly wanted to see her and Delphy. I didn't dare ask, but prayed we'd return to Mount Vernon when Congress broke up. With my mind on missing Mamma and Delphy, I still caught a few words of what they talked about.

The more they talked, the more troubled Lady Washington sounded. Her voice rose up further with one sentence to 'nother, always did when she be tipped over. I perked up my ears. I'd be hearing more of it later during our quiet time and wanted to be able to comfort her. She started listenin' to me lately, and even asked me questions 'bout what I thought. It made me feel nearly as important as them toffee-nosed ladies she invited over. At times she durn near doted on me, buying me sweets and shoes and flub dubs. But flub dubs gave me no guilt about wanting to own myself someday.

"Did you see today's *Gazette*, George? Freneau is at it again, criticizing your every move." She swept the paper off the side table and thrust it before his face.

But he made no move to take it from her. "Yes, I saw it. Or was it yesterday's? I do not take the press seriously, Patsy. Let them say what they will. They need to fill the space somehow, to justify their existence. Else they'd be begging on the streets. I know what I've done every day, I needn't read about it again afterwards, skewered as it is. Although," he gave a snicker, "they're good for a laugh. They're easy vehicles of knowledge, more happily calculated than any other to preserve the liberty of free people."

He took the paper from her and flipped it to the floor.

She fetched it right back up. "That's not the worst of it. It says your birthday celebration was a forerunner of other '*monarchical vices*'." Her voice loudened on those two last words. She flung the paper to the floor and kicked it under the sofa with her little shoe. "By God you had rather be in your grave than in your present situation, you had rather be on your farm than be made emperor of the world, and yet they charge you with wanting to be a king."

Her breath expelled in a huff. "On the other foot, those vulgar, snobbish New Yorkers say you're too down-home for a president." She spat when she talked and wiped her mouth. "I'm sick to death of them slamming your every move. Sakes, it wasn't even our party. They descended upon the house like a swarm of locusts."

The general sat back and stretched his legs, his boots muddy but the polished parts still gleaming. "But the press—let them blow their bags, they've naught else to do."

Lady Washington leant over and rested her head on his shoulder. "Oh, my old man," she nestled in beside him, "what a thick skin you've grown. I wish I could take these barbs for what they're worth like you can."

"Just remember, Patsy, in one or two hundred years, no one will ever remember Philip Freneau. So don't let it go down in history how he rattled you. Because chances are, our names will live in history …" He stopped and drew a breath. "… for a while at least."

****

We came back to Mount Vernon this April, so the general could have a brief rest. My happiness at seeing Mamma and Delphy made me forget the

Washingtons' troubles during the eves we spent together. Mamma had the ague so Lady Washington gave me extra time tending her.

But when I passed their parlour on my way to chores, I heard the general grousing, " ... what kind of sickness is Betty Davis's? For every day she works she is laid up two. If she is indulged in this idleness she will grow worse and worse, for she has a disposition to be one of the most idle creatures upon earth, and is, besides, one of the most deceitful."

I halted in my tracks as if he struck a blow to my head, stunned with disbelief. How could he accuse Mamma of pretending the ague? All he needed do was walk over to that cabin and look in the door. My hurt overtook my anger and a sob escaped my throat. As I slunk away, my heart aching for poor Mamma, I heard him spew out, "If pretended ailments without apparent causes will screen her from work, I shall get no service from her, for a more lazy, deceitful and impudent huzzy is not to be found in the United States than she is."

I couldn't stand it no more. Lady Washington's voice reached my ears, but I didn't hear her words, for I ran from the hallway and the general's rampage. Oh, if only I could tell him—ask him, beg him—to go see Mamma suffering on her pallet, coughing, burning with fever, he would be so ashamed as to never utter a foul word against her again. But my place in life here forced me to hold it all inside. I ran up the stairs to my space, hurled myself atop the bed and cried my eyes out—for Mamma, for me, for all our people unable to speak for ourselves, unable to own ourselves.

But as my tears dried I forgave the general. He spoke not from hate but from ignorance.

That eve Lady Washington made me stay with her after the general opened a letter from Mr. Hamilton. Far too troubled to sit and play backgammon with her and the family in the parlour, he locked up in his study while me and her weaved—and talked.

"These are troubled times, Oney." Her hands deftly worked the loom with blue and aqua wool. "Mr. Hamilton's letter informed the general that England and France are at war."

"But we ain't—er, aren't at war with England no more." I unraveled some un-dyed wool. "And the French took our side against them. This don't affect us, does it?"

"Doesn't affect us," she said.

"Good."

"No, I was correcting your English." She took a nip of sherry from her side table. It be bad when she started tippling other than her nocturnal buttermilk. "The general told me he's writing to Mr. Jefferson with the intent of staying neutral. You know what neutral means, Oney?"

I shook my head. "Uh-unh." It was another new word.

"It means not on any side. Since war actually began tween France and Great Britain, our government must use its power to keep neutral. And right now he's writing to Mr. Jefferson asking him to draw up a document spelling out terms of neutrality. We cannot take sides."

"I don' wanna war with no one," I declared, working on my smaller loom. "What I heard about our war when I was a babe scares me."

She put down her sherry and gazed at the empty glass, looking whether to indulge in a refill. "It was horrid, simply horrid. I always accompanied the general to his camp in the dead of winter, at Cambridge, Valley Forge, wherever he led his army at the time ..."

She paused and shut her eyes tight, her brows creasing the space tween them, as if reliving a bad dream. "Starving soldiers, filthy rags hanging from their emaciated bodies, left trails of blood in the snow with their frostbitten feet. We knitted and sewed at a furious pace but could never keep up with their needs. The whole situation seemed hopeless as soldiers fled and deserted. But the general—my husband—never gave up."

Her eyes opened and focused on the glass. She reached for it, but stopped herself. "No, I've had enough drink," she near-whispered, then busied her hands on the loom.

"We wouldn'a won if it wasn't for the French, would we of?" I didn't know why I said we. The fighting wasn't for us folks's freedom.

"They helped," was all she'd admit to. "So you can see the awkwardness of the situation."

"You believe takin' no sides is the right thing?" I asked, knowing she liked speaking her feelings more and more these days. She became a strong voice of her own since the general become president. And didn't care who misliked it. That's what I admired about Lady Washington. She voiced her mind out loud but didn't care if nobody agreed, even the general. She'd say "George is always right" but knew he wasn't.

"'Tis only the lesser of three evils, Oney." Her fingers flew over the loom, faster'n mine. "Taking one side or the other would lead to complications and more fighting in the Congress. The way those dimwits can't agree makes me wonder why there hasn't been a civil war tween all of them."

"But when is war civil?" I asked, confused. "Are there wars where the armies don't shoot at each other, just slap each other ladylike?"

She wheezed a short laugh. "No, a civil war is a conflict tween groups or armies within a single country. Our war for independence was a civil war of sorts, at times, brother against brother, because not everyone wanted independence. 'Tis from the Latin, *bellum civile*. Mrs. Powel told me about that; she can read and speak Latin."

So Mrs. Powel knew about my white name bein' Latin. "But why?" I asked. "Who talks Latin round here?"

"Something to do with her church. She's Catholic and they say the services in Latin. Don't ask me why. Seems a bit backward if you ask me."

"Speakin' of church, I'd like to join the colored church on Lombard Street and go on Sundays. Hercules belongs and tells me 'bout the services, how they pray and sing and talk about what's in the Bible. Seems we all have the same Lawd, whites and coloreds, and I'd like to get to know 'im better and learn all about salvation, and heaven, and the other hot place and all that." I looked over at her concentrating on her loom. "Please can we go?"

"That's *may* we go. Of course you may. We have no objection to our people attending their churches. I believe we all have the same God but it's not our place to question some of His ways and His will. And you need not attend church to get to heaven."

"No, my lady, I never did." But *whoa*! My hands halted. I sat struck dumb. I never heard no white person say we folk could get to heaven. Almost gave me something to look fo'ward to.

I didn't tell her all the truth. It was more'n just a colored church. It was called the African Church, started by a free black, Absalom Jones, last July. He started it out of the Free African Society, which Hercules joined and went to all the time. Philadelphia had the biggest free black community in the country. Deep down I envied them, but if they be free, so be it.

As we finished for the night she said, "The general told me we're returning to Philadelphia on Monday. And as today's Friday, we've not much time to prepare. So you must help me pack tomorrow."

So soon? I sighed, my heart heavy. I didn't want to leave Mamma and Delphy again. We'd been so happy to see each other, we clung together in tears, the four of us, Austin's arms long enough to encircle us all. Now I'd have to tell them goodbye again. I dreaded those goodbyes.

But once back in Philadelphia, Lady Washington told me the neutrality proclamation—signed the day after we returned—didn't even say the word 'neutrality'. "It contains the word 'impartial'," she told me, and I learnt another word. Not words I'd use often, as I wasn't neutral or partial on nothin' but wanting liberty for us folk.

It didn't stop the press from bashing the general, even worse than before. Hercules read me the hated comments in Mr. Bache's paper, the *General Advertizer*. Real mean, being that Mr. Bache was Dr. Franklin's grandson, and Lady Washington so admired Dr. Franklin. "He says here the proclamation is a perfect nullity and a firebrand."

"Nullity?" I asked. "That something to do with bein' nuts?"

"Nah," Hercules answered. "It means zero, naught."

"Oh, yeah." I nodded. I sho' knew what that meant.

"Them Congressmen is up to their usual hijinks," Hercules said. "As usual Mr. Jefferson and Mr. Hamilton can't agree on whether to be neutral, cause Mr. Jefferson loves them French poodles. And Mr. Madison believes the general will abuse war-making powers."

I was glad I didn't have to sit in on their tiffs. They sounded to me a gaggle of bickering ol' biddies. But hearing about it was like getting a play read to me. At times all the drama sounded something Shakespeare dreamt up.

The general and Lady Washington discussed it every eve as me and Molly cleared the dishes.

"I wouldn't have believed," the general huffed, splitting apart walnuts as I swept the shells from the floor, "that while steering a steady course to preserve this country from the horrors of a war, I should be accused of being the enemy of one nation and subject to the influence of another and in such indecent terms as could scarcely be applied to a Nero."

Who's this Nero? I wondered. Prob'ly another of his congressmen.

Lady Washington had a few choice words of her own about a treaty with France from near twenty years ago. It bound the United States to aid France in their war with England. "That treaty was made with the French king, who is now dead!" her shrill voice filled the room.

"I couldn't agree with you more, Patsy," was his answer as he spilt some walnuts into her hands. "Open these, will you, my dear? You're a better nutcracker than I am."

****

Next day I opened the knocking front door to a man carryin' a black bag.

"Nobody here is sick, Doctor," I said as he doffed his hat, guessin' he had me figgered for a Washington relative.

"I am John Greenwood, miss, not a doctor. I am a dentist. President Washington called for me."

Oh, I knew what it was, then. His last tooth was botherin' him and it needed pullin'. I showed him in and asked Mr. Lear to fetch the general.

Later the general come to dinner, wrapt head to chin in bandages, and sipped chicken soup through a straw. Lady Washington put him to bed and gave him laudanum for the pain, alum to stop the bleeding, and cinnamon water to keep the wound clean. She couldn'a fussed over him more if he lay dyin'.

But afore Dentist Greenwood presented the bill and departed, Lady Washington had him clean her teeth. She had good teeth, best of any lady I ever seen, and cleaned them every day, chewin' on mint when it was just us.

Later that week, Lady Washington sat at her desk and wrote out a list of names. "I want to have another informal tea, but am not so sure the same ladies will attend." She crossed out two names and scratched out another.

"You mean Mrs. Monroe and Mrs. Adams, cause they near broke into a hissin' fight over Mr. Jefferson?" I halted my sewing and stood to uncrick my stiff neck.

"Oh, 'twas merely a difference of opinion," she rushed to correct me, "but it did liven the discussion, didn't it?" She gave me that sly grin she always displayed setting a cat among the pigeons. "If I were to invite them both again, without each other knowing, I can fully expect another spirited debate. Ha! Naught raises ladies' hackles than arguing over a man."

"Lady Washington," I finished rubbing my neck and stood 'til she bade me to sit again, "you invite them two ladies agin and bring up Mr. Jefferson's name and your views on his shortcomings, we'll see sharpenin' claws and spittin' teeth."

A wicked cackle escaped her lips. "More amusing than any Farquhar comedy. But remember your –ing's," she reminded me. "We do not drop our g's." She slid the list aside and began writing out formal invites … to Mrs. Knox, Mrs. Powel and her niece Mrs. Bingham, and of course, Mrs. Adams. Because it was informal, I aired out her violet satin gown with white petticoat.

"Bring out my queen's night cap, too." She wore this feathered headdress at official dinners, but I knew she wanted to outshine Mrs. Bingham. Married to the nation's richest man, Mrs. Bingham was the American Marie Antoinette.

One morn I accompanied Lady Washington on a visit to Mrs. Bingham's palace and gardens. It took up half a square on Spruce Street, stretching from Third to Fourth. I had to sit in the back kitchens with the other servants and didn't see inside the mansion, but from outside was enough. Rich and snooty and—best of all—she never agreed with Lady Washington. We both knew she was in for a good hissin' contest.

Whenever Mrs. Adams called, she took up most of the talking, muchly as Mrs. Knox took up most of the room. But I learnt a lot from them. They had ideas about what 'rights' they should have. I heard some loud cacklin' when these hens took tea together.

Mrs. Adams arrived first, in a plain brown dress of the same homespun Lady Washington wore when she wasn't expecting nobody important. I knew Mrs. Adams didn't know the anti-Jefferson Mrs. Powel was calling, but I reckoned she wasn't aware the filthy rich Mrs. Bingham was invited, too, or she would'a wore more flash-fawney. Lady Washington greeted her and they locked arms afore I took her hat.

"Oney, stay at the door and greet Mrs. Powel and Mrs. Bingham," she called over her shoulder. "They should be here any minute."

"Eliza is attending?" Mrs. Adams snapped. "After that last debacle?"

I didn't hear all of what Lady Washington answered, as I'd been ordered to mind the door. But I did hear, "Oh, Abby, that was hardly a debacle, merely a lively difference of opinion. When Mr. Jefferson decides to enter the real world, he will become as revered as dear Marquis Lafayette."

"I don't know if the Marquis would be too charmed to hear that," she replied. "He doesn't like having any competition."

So I waited, but not long. Mrs. Powel arrived on time, but her niece Mrs. Bingham's cream coach and four was nowhere in sight. Was she arriving fashionably late? I wondered, but daren't ask. Mrs. Powel was another of them women of intellect—educated, read books, wrote lots of letters, and played music. A genius at politicks, Lady Washington called her. But she didn't look down at none of us.

"Hello, Oney," she always greeted me.

I showed her inside and afore I went to fetch the tea and cakes, Mrs. Powel told Lady Washington, "My niece sends her regrets, she cannot call today." But no reason.

Why? I wondered. She was right rude to consider another invite over the president's wife.

"Oh, that's too bad." Lady Washington's lips scrunched in a little pout, but I know she just invited Mrs. Bingham to be polite. She only talked about herself—her matched bays, her silver-pronged forks, her silk-festooned lyre-back chairs, her Queen's ware with their crest on each piece, her Par-*ee* (as she said it) fashions ... once, I caught Lady Washington rollin' her eyes and I stifled a laugh with a cough.

As I served, they took turns round the room offering the routine small talk—the weather, Mr. Mozart died ...

Another rap on the door got me up to answer, and I opened it to a powdered, rouged and perfumed Mrs. Bingham. She bustled in past me to the parlour, her plum satin skirts rustlin' louder'n the blast of wind outside.

"Martha, why do you not observe the custom of having your servants relay the names of guests to your parlour where you're receiving?" She stood in the doorway, twirling her gloves, hand on hip.

"Ann! Why, you'd sent your regrets." Lady Washington looked more surprised than pleased to see Mrs. Bingham. Those skirts o'hers knocked the general's specs off one table and a vase of hyacinths off another. I gathered up the posies, swabbed the rug with a rag and wrang it out outside.

"I was attending a tea hosted by Betsy Hamilton, which I'd responded to sooner, but 'twas ever so dull." Mrs. Bingham shook her high-coiffed head, sprinkled with diamond sprigs. "All she ever talks about is her tots," she scowled, "and lets them run the carpets ragged through the house ... and how do you fare, Aunt Eliza? Are you over that dreadful catarrh? I hope you aren't contaminating the rest of us." With that she snapped her ivory fan open and handed it to me—"Fan me, will you, girl? 'Tis rather stuffy in here. Pity this isn't the grand scale you're used to at Mount Vernon, Martha ... you can always lodge with us at the mansion should you wish to escape these austere surroundings." She swept her eyes round with a grimace as if smelling fresh horse dung.

So there I stood fannin' her. I glanced over at Lady Washington every few blinks hoping she'd tell me to stop and rest, but she didn't. As the other ladies sipped at their tea, Lady Washington, always the gracious hostess, cut into the meat of the tete-a-tete with the matters I wanted to hear—and led into hash-slingin'. She never disappointed me. Lady Washington knew how to rustle up a row among ladies, and she always shared a good laugh with me after. This time she shied away from politicks and started the conversation about something they all knew about but had different views on—ladies.

"So, Abby," she started, turning away from the flustered Mrs. Bingham and to Mrs. Adams, "Mercy wrote me an interesting letter last week. Have you heard from her of late?"

Mrs. Mercy Warren was another smart lady friend of theirs, living in Massachusetts, near where the general and Lady Washington stayed during the war.

"Yes, indeed, she told me she saved a letter I wrote to her. Remember when I wrote to John after the Declaration of Independence, and I commented on the new code of laws?"

"The 'remember the ladies' letter?" Lady Washington leant forward and held out her cup for me to refill, purposely I reckoned, giving me leave to stop fanning Mrs. Bingham.

"Right!" Mrs. Adams raised her ample brows and smiled. "I'd told my Johnny, 'Be more favorable to them than your ancestors, and do not put such unlimited power into the hands of the husbands. All men would be tyrants if they could,' I'd told him."

A look of fond remembrance softened the lines in Mrs. Adams's face. "I was so thankful she'd kept it. John wrote me back that he laughed over it, as he never took it seriously. But you know what he said to show how far in the dark men were? He'd written back that—I'm paraphrasing now, although at the time I could've recited it—men knew that their struggle..." She counted on her fingers, "... loosed the bonds of government, children were disobedient, colleges were turbulent, and negroes grew insolent to their masters, but my letter was the first hint that another tribe, more powerful than the rest, were discontented. "And he called me saucy." Mrs. Adams tittered. "He mentioned General Washington and our other heroes, refusing to subject themselves to the repression of the petticoat."

The other ladies sat rigid, stony-faced and wordless, tea cups suspended in mid-air. But I held my mouth from droppin' open. "Oh, it was rather over-the-top at the time," Mrs. Adams went on, "but I even threatened rebellion, saying we wouldn't hold ourselves bound by any laws in which we have no voice."

"But we still don't, Abby," Mrs. Powel corrected her. "John's reaction to your letter was utter apathy. Looks like you let the matter drop."

"Not without some more effort." Mrs. Adams raised her cup towards me and I went to refill it. "I wrote to Mercy, suggesting we petition Congress to write some laws that favor women. But Mercy didn't reply. I believe she thought I was overstepping my bounds. So what if I was?" She shrugged. "I wrote one more letter to John, and to all of Congress, and said, 'Whilst you proclaim peace and goodwill to men, you insist upon retaining power over wives.'"

Now Mrs. Bingham looked ready to swoon—all the pink drained from her face, save the round blobs where she'd dabbed rouge. She snapped her fan open and didn't order me to breeze her off this time. "Abby!" she breathed. "Why, I'm surprised you didn't get a flogging for that insolence."

Mrs. Adams cast her eyes down on Mrs. Bingham as if at a fly she was fixin' to swat. "Hardly. John respects my views and always comes to me for advice. He's treated me as an equal partner in all things. He went so far as to tell my concerns to Brigadier General Palmer about voters' rights. Someday we will have the right to vote."

"The president doesn't believe women should vote," Lady Washington said. "And he is right. But alas, if every one of us did vote in this last election, I daresay my husband still would have been elected." Her voice lowered, sounding like her throat hurt to say it.

Mrs. Powel added, "I'll be the first to admit it, Martha, I'd have voted for your husband. I wish they'd taken Mr. Hamilton's advice to let elected officials serve for life."

"Bite your tongue, Eliza!" Lady Washington nearly jumped from her seat. "Neither of us wanted to be here before, but now ..." She glanced round at the posh surroundings and settled back into her plush chair. "My husband had to serve again. He believes in fate and it couldn't be any other way ... least of all my way."

"But think of the nation, Martha—" Mrs. Powel squared her shoulders. "I daresay he's the only man in America that dares to do right on all public occasions."

Lady Washington returned. "He told me I was being selfish when I didn't want him to accept again."

Mrs. Powel scoffed, waving a dismissing hand, her diamonds catching the light, shooting rays about. "Oh, you're not selfish, dear, you're his wife. I'm speaking as a citizen. And as a citizen, I can also say that I believe Mr. Jefferson and his ilk would have dissolved the union with their Frenchified ways."

As expected, Mrs. Adams puffed up, ready to spew forth some venom in defense of her gentleman friend. "I beg to differ once more on this matter, Eliza." Her stern tone didn't seem to match her small stature and kind eyes. "Mr. Jefferson loves the union as much as anyone. Some day, as president, he will prove it to you. He favors a loosely structured federal government and shuns pomp and formality," she added with a proud nod.

"He shuns pomp and he loves the French?" chimed in Mrs. Bingham. "What did he do there when invited to court, sit out at the curb?"

To my disappointment, Mrs. Adams ignored her goading. She went on, "Rather than bankers, merchants and judges ... you know, the elite ... he favors farmers ... the real working folk."

I bit my tongue. What did he—and she for that matter—think *we* were? Un-real working folk?

"But Mr. Jefferson does shun the leanings toward monarchy ..." Mrs. Adams huffed. "Naught against you and the president, Martha ... but I know he'd do away with the coach and six and the formal parties were he president."

Lady Washington slammed her cup onto the saucer with a clank. "I never wanted a coach and six *or* formal parties."

"I know, dear, but as the president's wife you need to entertain and keep some semblance of pomposity," Mrs. Powel said. "When he was first elected, your husband and Mr. Madison appealed to us ladies for an Americanized version of the European courts. What impressed me was the way you and the president entertain, very similar to those European courts. So I do credit both of you, as it is rather a paradox ..."

There was that word again, I heard ...

"... how you both organize your affairs so beautifully, after the colonies fought to banish the very monarchy you emulate."

They all bobbed their coiffed heads except Lady Washington. "Neither the president nor I want to be compared with monarchy, and if someday Mr. Jefferson does become president, though 'tis highly unlikely, Abby," she cast Mrs. Adams a narrow sideways glance, "should he dispense with the coach and parties and even if he receives senators in his carpet slippers, more power to him." She gave a staunch nod, her chins wigglin' just a bit more'n in past years.

The ladies sipped at their cooling tea, and Mrs. Adams gave a smug smile. "Huzzah. I for one am against the formality I observed in France. We're a republic, for certain, but we need not go to those extremes of protocol. "Oh, how blest I am to be in this land of freedom! When I reflect upon the advantages the American people possess, our ease in obtaining property, the personal liberty and security, I feel grateful to heaven who marked out my lot in this happy land."

And what about us! nearly burst from my lips. But as always I didn't dare utter a word."Our Benjamin Franklin didn't mind the faux pas of the French ladies from what I heard," Mrs. Powel remarked with a cocked brow, as the ladies' eyes all fixed on Mrs. Adams for another dose of juicy gossip about Mr. Franklin and his famous rond-a-vouzes with the French fair sex. Even I knew about them, from what Hercules read in the Gazette.

"Oh, that Madame Helvetius was the first French woman I met at dinner at Ben's home in Passy..." She fanned herself with her hand. "Madame entered the room with a careless, jaunty air. Upon seeing ladies who were strangers to her, she bawled out, 'Ah! Mon Dieu! Where is Frankling? Why did you not tell me there were ladies here...how I look!' Her hair was fangled, over it she had a small straw hat with a dirty gauze half-handkerchief round it, and a bit of dirtier gauze than my maids wore was sewed on behind."

"Did her and 'Frankling' have a bit of fun on the side?" prodded Mrs. Bingham, as folk never got 'nuff of the old cad's frolicks.

"I know not if even he had such little respect for his person, but their public display left not much to the imagination. Madame ran forward when he entered, caught him by the hand, then gave him a double kiss, one upon each cheek and another on his forehead. She sat twixt him and my husband, carried on the chief of the conversation at dinner, locking her hand into the doctor's and spreading her arms upon the backs of both gentlemen." Mrs. Adams gave what looked like a practiced shudder that she no doubt used on her husband. "I was highly disgusted and never wisht for an acquaintance with any ladies of this cast."

"Thank God Ben never became president." Mrs. Bingham matched her shudder. "But I wonder who our next president will be," she mused. "Certainly not my William. He has much more pressing business."

"What is more pressing than running the nation, Ann?" asked her aunt, with a haughty cock of her brow.

"William has many issues on his mind. For one, we still haven't been blest with any babes." She shook her head and expelled a breath, as if she couldn't figger out why her husband wanted childruns. "He so wants a houseful of little ones running about."

"He wants them and you do not?" her aunt asked, but Mrs. Bingham only shrugged.

"It may not be you, Ann," Lady Washington informed her. "I've only told a few close friends, but my husband and I …" She cleared her throat and fussed with the lace on her sleeves. "I advise you to purchase ginseng and insist he take it. It's known to, er … up a man's potency. And also to produce male children. I'm certain that's what he wants, at first."

"Ginseng?" Mrs. Bingham's eyes widened. "I've never heard of that before. But he has been eating enormous quantities of Boston fish and venison at dinner. He'd heard from a few prolific men that these foods would—er, invigorate him. Yet they haven't, alas." But she didn't look all too sorry for it.

"Just as any remedy, it doesn't always work," Lady Washington warned her. The others sat in stony silence. Me, my heart went out to her in sympathy. Her and the general never had any young'uns and no one ever breathed a word about it—'til now. At that moment I remembered, when I first come to the big house, he always ordered Hercules to mix ginseng into most all he ate and drank, even his slap jacks and honey cakes. But not in recent years, just when Lady Washington stopped complaining of her flux to me. Now I knew why.

Mrs. Bingham went on, "I'm not in such a hurry for babies as he is. He wants to do so much more with his businesses and keep me home in confinement. He's been engaged in running his textile factory on Market Street, and his position in building the Lancaster Pike—a worthy investment if any of you ladies convince your husbands to buy shares. The Senate is the farthest William wants to go as a public servant. But he would make a worthy president," she mused, fingering her glittery necklace.

"Sounds as if money is his sole object," Mrs. Adams said.

"I'd have thought you'd be urging him already," Lady Washington said, with a half-smile. "I'd gladly let you and William take our places. Today, if you so wish."

"You really don't want to be here, do you, Martha?" Mrs. Adams's head tilted, eyes focused on Lady Washington.

"I'm here for one reason, Abby," she admitted. "That reason is my husband. You can talk about equality and voting rights and voicing your thoughts to Congress, but given those rights, I wouldn't be happy as I would be back at Mount Vernon."

Mrs. Bingham and her Auntie Eliza departed first, leaving Mrs. Adams time to chat privately with Lady Washington.

"Ah, that was lively enough, Abby, was it not?" Lady Washington grabbed the last cake from the plate and sat back to savor it. "We need not attend the theatre for a month of fortnights."

****

At nine that night, the Washingtons' customary retiring time, her and me talked as I helped her undress. I pulled off her sweat-soaked chemise and she fanned herself.

"I'll do that." I resented Mrs. Bingham ordering me to fan her, but didn't mind fanning Lady Washington.

"No need, it will pass. Just wipe down my back, it's soaked." She held up her arms so I could wipe under them, too.

"That tea party was fun, Lady Washington." I pulled her stockings off. "I wish I could'a talked some. I'd'a asked them ladies some questions that'd make they feathers—er, their feathers fly."

"I know, Oney, you are a smart girl, but these ladies don't generally care what anyone else has to say except themselves. They don't even listen to their husbands." She stepped out of her shoes. I sprinkled corn starch in them and set them on the floor beside the others.

"Should ladies listen to they husbands—their husbands?" I combed out her hair.

"Sure, they should listen. But they don't need agree on everything. We ladies do have minds, too. But most men don't give a fig what's in them."

"Don' I know it," I muttered as she dipped into a pot of face cream and spread it over her face and neck.

"You're dismissed for the evening, Oney." She dug her fingers way down in the near-empty cream jar. "And you may have tomorrow morn to do as you wish. But if you're going out and about, make sure you're well dressed, and someone accompanies you. Then we can decide whom to invite to next week's tea." She arranged her jars in a neat row on the table top.

After bobbing a curtsey I backed out, feeling my way down the dark stairway. Then I stopped short. Did she say 'we'? Land sakes alive, she treated me like a near person, that dear lady. With another quick bop I skipped down the stairs.

CHAPTER EIGHT

This French poodle come right outta a Shakespeare play, I'd'a swore it. When Lady Washington told me about Monsieur Genet this raw cloudy morn, I begun wishing he'd come calling. He sounded a genuin' troublemaker, and that he was.

"He arrived in Charleston a fortnight ago and still hasn't come to greet the general," she huffed as I rolled her wool stockings up her legs. "Does he expect the general to go running to him?"

These days I answered all her questions, whether they be beggin' an answer or not. "Not sho, Lady Washington, but if he be French, I s'pect he may. The general ought let Mr. Jefferson go to him."

She snickered. "Not a bad idea at that. They'd cozy up to each other faster than one could ask the other to minuet."

"But why he called citizen?" Nowadays our talk became less one-sided as she let me ask her questions of a reasonable nature. "That ain't—isn't his given name, is it?" I asked.

"No, his name is Edmond, but since those French have taken to calling each other 'citizen' and 'citizeness', in French, of course, to oust the old-line 'M'sieu' and 'madame', now he's citi-*zeen*. Gouverneur Morris told the general that Monsieur Genet dresses like a fop, but is a Renaissance man of sorts—speaks several languages, plays instruments, sings ... I for one am looking forward to meeting him," she admitted with a titter.

These days I could near read her mind. She itched to get him in her comp'ny to needle him about his dress. She surprised me in not pluckin' him up for her grandgirl Miz Betsy, so far unmarriageable. But that's another story.

As days and weeks wore on, Citizen Genet proved to be naught but a nuisance to the general. He stuck his hook nose into the government's business, I learnt from the general's bellyachin' about him, and what Hercules read me from the papers.

One eve, during the dinner hour. Molly answered a rap at the door. Next thing I seen Mr. Jefferson and a man togged to the bricks, standing in the dining room doorway, uninvited.

"Why, Tom, what a surprise, and this must be Citizen Genet," the general greeted them. They pranced past him up to Lady Washington.

"Martha, always a pleasure." Mr. Jefferson kissed her raised hand and introduced the Frenchman. He shunned her hand and kissed her on both cheeks. *Cheeky*, I thought, pouring sherry and watching them fawn over her. They looked alike as brothers, tall with flaming hair like a bunch a'carrots and matching lilac suits. Watch-and-chains shone at they waists. Frothy lace peeked out from Genet's sleeves.

Genet halted at a marble bust on a table and cocked a red brow. "Displaying King Louie the Sixteenth, are you, Monsieur Washington?" He slapped the statue on both cheeks with his gloves. His gaze landed on the hanging brass medallions on the wall. "*Mon dieu*, Monsieur Washington, 'tis adding insult to injury to expose portraits of the Capets as well as King Louie."

The general opened his mouth to talk. But Lady Washington cut the general off, "We don't wish to insult or injure, but as this isn't even our house, Monsieur," and I knew she called him such, as she knew he didn't like it, "we have no control over the owner's taste or allegiance. But in deference to you … " She walked over and plucked a serviette from the table and draped it over King Louis's head, "Now he won't have to look at you either."

The general's smirk matched his snicker. He cast a sideways glance at Mr. Jefferson, who looked none too charmed his exalted Louie was now draped. "And since we're proclaiming neutrality, we'll remove the Venetian blinds from Independence Hall, send the Liberty Bell back to London and won't import any more rum. Fair enough?" The general stared them both down, tall as they were.

This got a laugh out of Genet, but not from Mr. Jefferson.

Lady Washington gestured to the two empty chairs opposite the general's. Genet swept his beady eyes over the fare of lamb, lettuce, cucumbers, artichokes and potatoes. As he approached the chair farther from her, she grabbed his elbow. "No, here! You sit here in this one, sir. At my right."

Oh, ho! I knew why she offered him that chair! In its middle was a small hole that made a loud squeak when sat in. It flustered many an unsuspecting guest upon sitting there.

Hence, Genet grabbed the offered chair, sat down, and the resulting *squeeeeeeak* made all eyes turn to him. But to Lady Washington's and mine's dismay, he cared not a whit. "Haaw, haaw … you should repair the tottering furniture here, Madame."

Then I saw what I didn't before—on his cheek a perfect round birthmark I swore he'd drew on. And them lips looked too red to be his—that had to be rouged on. "*Allors* … cognac, if you please?"

Lady Washington gave him a frosty smile with her own un-rouged lips and said, "Sorry, but we've no cognac. The closest we have is cherry brandy."

He took out a box of snuff and tapped on it. "If you must."

At that, Austin bowed out to fetch Genet's second choice.

"I just came from a rousing crowd at the City Tavern," Genet said. "I was greeted by over six thousand at Charleston. I felt like the king myself." He gave a theatrical toss of his head and his wig went slightly askew. Mr. Jefferson straightened it for him and nodded as if his self got all the fanfare.

To me, Monsieur Genet was puttin' it on like a character in one of them comedy plays, only he wasn't tryin'a be comical. I saw Lady Washington hide a chuckle. Our eyes met, but she gave me an eye-roll before she looked away.

"Yes, I read about it in the papers," the general commented, cutting his potatoes into small bits. "It would have been rather more cordial, not to mention observant of protocol, if you'd landed here first so we could have talked things over."

Genet gave a wave of his ruby-ringed hand, nails buffed to a sheen. "Ah, but Charleston was warmer, 'tis still quite cold here. Present company excepted." He gave Lady Washington a smile with those cherry lips. She smiled back after a long pull of her sherry. He got to her, I could see.

As they stuffed their faces, the general didn't waste no more time getting down to business. "I see you've done everything in your power to invalidate the neutrality proclamation, Edmond. Fanfare from fellow Francophiles notwithstanding, the majority of us in government want neutrality, which is why my proclamation went through. I don't appreciate your converting our ships into privateers to pounce on the British, recruiting Americans to access British possessions in the south. We had our own revolution here and don't wish to repeat your French one. Don't you realize this can all backfire on you?"

"But you can see it hasn't," came the answer. Genet pushed his meal round his dish with a knife as Mr. Jefferson washed down his with a generous quaff of Madeira.

"Monsieur—rather, Citizen—Genet offers everything and asks naught, President Washington," Mr. Jefferson stated. Then his eyes swept across the room, straight to me. He winked and curled his lip. I looked away, flustered. I shouldn't'a been looking right at him.

White folk took the time to ogle me, specially men. Dependin' on the man's age and *how* he looked at me, with an admiring cast into my eyes rather than a lip-licking leer, I felt either appreciated or degraded. Some foreigners leered, and I expected it more from Monsieur Genet than another Virginian. But as I cleared away some dishes, I could feel Mr. Jefferson's eyes roving me up and down. I cringed, as if bugs crawled over me. Lady Washington once told me 'don't let a man stand close 'til he's the right one'. I wondered if I'd ever find the right one. But I knew the right one wouldn't look me over like Mr. Jefferson did. Then I remembered his mulatto concubine Miss Hemings. Mayhap I looked like her.

Through all the talk with the three men, he didn't stop eyeing me. Then Lady Washington offered her opinion, and they mouths shut like flies tried gettin' in.

"Edmond, the press hasn't been very positive to us since you reached our shores either," she gave him a good what-for. "Why, just the other day, the *National Gazette* blasted the general for bootlicking England and showing base ingratitude toward France, complaining that the United States shouldn't view with indifference the struggles of our friends to support their liberties against despots."

He didn't dare open his mouth, and she went on, "If that weren't enough, a letter appeared in the paper to the general accusing him of being isolated from the masses while surrounding himself with sycophants." The paper lay at her elbow. She'd kept it there, knowing he'd show up one day, and she could throw it in his pretty face. She read right out to all of them: "Let not the buzz of the aristocratic few and their minions of speculators, Tories, and British emissaries be mistaken for the voice of the American people. The spirit of '76 is again roused."

Genet merely frowned, but Mr. Jefferson turned ruddy as his hair. Then I knew—he wrote that letter. I knew it plain as the nose on Monsieur Genet's face. My lips curled.

Lady Washington didn't give the general a chance to give Monsieur Genet a dressing down, she did it all herself. But he sat back and seemed to enjoy the volley as Monsieur Genet, now flustered that a *dame* would dare challenge him, tried to defend his self.

I perked my ears, hoping Lady Washington would chide him through the floor. He needed takin' down a few pegs and she was the one to do it. She knew how to give a good chidin'. I seen folk limp away from her, tails tween they legs.

"Madame Washing-*tone* ..." He snapped his fingers toward Austin and pointed to his empty snifter, "... there will always be lovers of France in this country. Let us not forget your history. Whom did you fight for your independence and who assisted you? So begrudge us not—neutrality to me is a slap in the face of France."

The general sat sucking his teeth and playing with the sugar nippers. But Mr. Jefferson nodded like a toy doggie.

Monsieur Genet announced, "*Allors*, I invite all of you aboard our man-of-war *L'Ambuscade* on Monday as her captain, Citizen Bompard, will host a naval dinner for a select few, so they might come to know me better. General Knox, Governor Mifflin and Tommy—our Monsieur Jefferson ..." With a nod his way, "... have already accepted. We shall drink toasts to Franco-American friendship and sing patriotic hymns. Madame, I hope you will persuade your president to accept and look forward to seeing both of you there ... as I now know you are one very persuasive lady." His drawn-on birthmark slid up as he smiled.

"We will consider it, Monsieur," Lady Washington answered sweetly. "But do not hold the toasts on our account if we're not there on time. Take none of this personally. We proclaimed neutrality because we believe it's in our best interests. Taking sides would be too dangerous. Look at it from our point of view. What would you have done in our situation? Take one side or the other? Or simply bow out, to ensure the safety of your citizens?"

"I'm inclined to help the side that helps us," he answered.

"But you truly had no right to commission Americans as privateers to attack British ships and have your pseudo-French courts here seize captured cargoes from the British," she scolded. "This is only making your war with Britain a golden opportunity for ship owners to turn their ships into military vessels."

"But Fronce is now a Republic, Madame," he corrected her. "And Britain,   as you know, is not."

"And we do not want war with them. Or with France. Ergo, we remain neutral." She placed her serviette down, signaling the end of the meal and the debate.

I wanted to clap my hands raw.

Mr. Jefferson hastened to say, "I did see to it that the word 'neutral' in the document was replaced with 'impartial', Monsieur."

"For what it is worth," added the general.

"I trust we will remain friends." Lady Washington stood, prompting the gents to rise, too.

When the guests departed, Austin and I cleared the dessert dishes. "You may leave it for later, Austin and Oney." Lady Washington pulled the serviette off King Louis's bust. "Sorry about that, Louie," she said. "But you didn't miss a thing."

As I turned to leave, I heard Lady Washington tell the general, "I do believe Citizen Genet is one of *those*."

"One of those what?" He sat at table cracking more nuts.

"Are you so unobservant, old man?" she huffed. "Something I suspected of Mr. Jefferson, too."

He chomped down on nuts. "Oh, a macaroni?" He laughed. "I did notice they both carried matching brollies."

Only effete fops toted umbrellas, that I knew. The general only used an equestrian umbrella when riding to keep the sun off his face. Walking down the street, he'd'ruther get wet. He was no macaroni.

CHAPTER NINE

On my way out to market, I passed Lady Washington and my brother in the hall. When I heard what she sayin' to him, I ducked in the doorway and forgive me, Lawd, but I needed to hear why she said it.

"Austin, I'm sending you back to Mount Vernon to visit your family and friends. You've been working hard and deserve some time off."

I stifled a gasp with my palm. Back to Mount Vernon! Working hard? Pray who *didn't* work hard round here?

We just come back from Mount Vernon nigh on two weeks ago when Congress adjourned. Lady Washington gave me time off, but a morn or eve, no trips back to Mount Vernon. I didn't begrudge my brother. I just couldn't figger why she'd send any of us back to Mount Vernon.

Knowing I'd talk to Austin about it later, I gone about my marketing. And then heard the truth from Katy Bower and Eliza Warner, paid house servants.

As I sewed in the parlour and they slid the crumb cloth from under the dining room table, I heard Katy tell Eliza, "Austin's six months must be about up."

"Hercules and his son should be next," Eliza said back.

What's Austin's six months? I wondered. A stab of fright stopped me in mid-stitch. Was they sick or dyin'? Got six months to live?

I dropped my sewing and bolted into that dining room, heart thumping in my throat. I rushed up to them, kneelin' on they knees with the crumb cloth. "Is my brother sick? Please," I added, as they were white folk. Servants, but still white folk. They halted and looked at me standing there trembling.

"Of course not, Oney, Lady Washington is sending him back to Virginia because his six months in Pennsylvania are almost up." Eliza clambered to her feet, leaning on the table.

"Up for what?" I stood, struck dumb. "What you talkin' 'bout?"

"You really don't know?" Katy sat back against the wall.

"The law in Pennsylvania," Eliza explained. "It says that if slaves are kept here longer than six months, they're legally free. That's why the

Washingtons send you and the others back to Virginia before the six months are up. So you remain as slaves. The others know about it—they cottoned on after a while. And Lady Washington finally admitted it to them." She looked at me like I was dumb. Now I felt dumb. "How could I've not known this?" I shook my head, stunned. "She ain't never tol' me 'bout no law says I can go free in six months."

Eliza shrugged. "You never asked."

But I did ask, later that eve, while brushing out her hair. The boldest I ever was. "Lady Washington, I never knew 'bout that law says we can go free in this state after six months," all came out in one rushed breath.

She glanced up, and our eyes met in the mirror. I held the look, disrespectful or not. "We don't want to break the law," she said, "so we send our people back to Virginia before the six-month limit. That's why Austin is going back tomorrow." Her eyes held mine in the mirror, as truthfully as she been telling me the time.

"Do he know 'bout the law?" I pressed on, hoping he didn't. It would'a rattled him more'n it did me.

"I don't know." She broke my gaze and flicked her hand. Course, why should she care if he knew? "We don't happen to agree with the law, but we do what we must do." She turned her head for me to brush the side.

If I'd'a sassed this way with Mrs. Bingham, I'd'a got lashed. But Lady Washington was more civilized than that. She wouldn't lash for sasssin'. "But I'm not sending you back with him," was all she said. "I need you around the house."

Oh, Lawd have mercy! I would be free tomorrow, cause my six months was up too! My spirit soared like it grew wings.

"I'm taking you across the river to New Jersey tomorrow morn," she stated.

Oh, no. I crashed back down to ground when she told me her plans for me.

****

Mrs. Dolley Todd come calling unannounced that Sunday, the only day the Washingtons didn't receive guests. They let us attend the African Church and gave us the rest of the day off after cleaning up. But now that Mrs. Todd stood at the doorstep handing me her gloves and umbrella, that meant I'd have to serve tea, whether Lady Washington wanted to receive her or not.

"Dolley!" They clasped hands in the parlour, and Lady Washington led her to the sofa. Lady Washington's eyes met mine for a second and they told me, in that brief glance, she wasn't expectin' no company. "What brings you here, my dear?"

Mrs. Todd announced, "Thee and I are now related, Martha. By the sacrament of marriage." By her sharp tone she wasn't all too pleased about it.

Lady Washington sat at the sofa's other end, adjusting her cap, not one of the frilly ones, bein' a Sunday at home. She looked ruffled bein' taken by surprise, in her muslin apron and scuffy slippers. "Whose marriage, dear?"

"Thy husband's nephew George Steptoe and my sister Lucy, she of the age of fifteen. They eloped yesterday." Mrs. Todd sighed and cast her pretty blue eyes down. I ain't never seen her so sullen. She always pranced round a room so chipper.

"Are you sure?" Lady Washington fanned herself with her hand. She'd've sopped up her sweat if it was me and her alone. "Sometimes the young act impetuously, just to gain attention. Mayhap they're bluffing."

Ringlets sprang when Dolley shook her head. "No bluffing. The Society of Friends hath wasted no time in disowning her. She needs find another church now." She bowed her head again and her curls bobbed round her shoulders.

"Yes, fifteen is a bit young," Lady Washington agreed. "But they must be in love. So many marriages are about money or political gain. That should be a consolation." Lady Washington reached over and patted her hand. "Do you want me to tell my husband? Mayhap he can—well, what do you want us to do?" She didn't look too tipped over to me ... she didn't see it a vital enough matter to come calling on a Sunday.

"Dolley," she went on, "I must confess I'm at a loss of what your distress is about. So your fifteen-year-old sister eloped. At least nobody forced them. One thing I abhor is arranged marriages."

"I hear in thy tone that you approve of this." Mrs. Todd's voice went stern and her back straightened.

Lady Washington shrugged. "They love each other. Let them be. And I'm sure the president would say the same thing." She turned to me. "Go fetch the president in his study, Oney."

Finally, somethin' to do. I didn't feel muchly like serving tea anyways, on what should'a been my time off. Annoyed, I spun on my heel and marched out the door. I fetched the general and followed him back to the parlour where he greeted Mrs. Todd.

"Good morn, sir." She stood to accept his hand clasp. "My sister at fifteen married thy nephew last night. She left us a note pinned to her pillow. What dost thou make of it?"

"How's that?" He cupped his hand to his ear. "Nephew? You have a nephew?"

"No, *your* nephew, George Steptoe!" She loudened her voice, for him to hear better or out of vexation, or both.

He grinned but wide. "Ah, my namesake. I didn't even know they were acquainted." He turned to Lady Washington. "Did you, dear?"

She nodded. "Of course. They're well matched. She could do worse, Dolley." She gave Mrs. Todd a smirk.

Mrs. Todd let out a huff. "Lucy hath made a grave mistake. She knows not what she does at fifteen. That's way too young a heart."

The general seemed to swat her away. "Let her marry, Mrs. Todd. What is the consequence? The madness ceases and all is quiet again." He began to pace as he continued, "I've always advised young ladies when the fire is beginning to kindle, and your heart growing warm, propound these questions to it. Who is the invader? Have I competent knowledge of him? Is he a man of good character? A man of sense?"

He took a breath and cleared his throat. "For be assured, a sensible woman can never be happy with a fool. What has been his walk in life? Is he a gambler, a spendthrift, a drunkard? Is his fortune sufficient to maintain me in the manner I have been accustomed to live?"

He stopped pacing and faced her. "If these can be satisfactorily answered there is but one more to be asked. Have I sufficient ground to conclude that his affections are enjoyed by me? Naught short of good sense and an easy conduct can draw the line tween prudery and coquetry. Both are despised by men of understanding."

Mrs. Todd worked her lips, but no words came out.

"And as my wife said," he added, "he's a Washington. She could certainly do miles worse than that." His tone haughty, he looked down upon her from his commanding height, even in his quilt slippers. "In fact, I'll suggest, when they return, that he look after Harewood, my late brother's estate. He died nigh on twelve years ago now, but young George never showed the least interest in his inheritance. Running it is a daunting task, but ... what else has my nephew to do with his time? And your sister will make a fine lady of the house. You should go visit there sometime. 'Tis a lovely home."

"I hope, as thee seems to know, they'll be very happy, sir," Mrs. Todd yielded, defeated, her voice weary. "I admit she canst do wrong marrying a Washington. Welcome to my family."

"Remember, Mrs. Todd, there is no adage more true than the old Scotch one, that 'many mickles make a muckle': if you attend the small things, the big thing will be taken care of. So do not fret it."

Lady Washington spoke up. "Now we must celebrate. Will you fetch us some brandy, Oney?"

Ah, well, that was easier than fetching tea.

"Oh, not for me." Mrs. Todd held up both hands. "I'll take buttermilk, and so should you, President and Lady Washington. After all, it is the Sabbath."

CHAPTER TEN

Now it wasn't just the French revolting. From what Hercules read me, and from what I heard tween the Washingtons in hushed tones, it spread to the island of Santo Domingo way down in the tropics.

"That's where Columbus sailed to, ain't it—er, is it not?" I asked Lady Washington as we sat doing needlepoint. "My Mamma told me about Columbus, and she learnt it from my Daddy who voyaged the seas."

"That's right, Columbus sailed for the king and queen of Spain, but those French now rule it," she answered. "The slave revolt in Santo Domingo drove those French from the island."

Austin came in, whistling, with some watermelon slices on a plate. Hercules always pulled the pips out first. Lady Washington took a slice and offered me one. I wouldn't dare take a slice without her offering. Watermelon was my favorite. It tasted like sweet snow.

I wanted to ask more about the slave revolt but didn't dare. I'd have to learn on my own.

"Refugees have been coming from Santo Domingo here to Philadelphia on ships by the hundreds." She talked as her needles clicked. "They're starved, and many of them are sick with some kind of fever."

Some kind of fever—that began it all—the plague that killed one in nine of Philadelphia's poor souls, over five thousand in the end. First it was simply called fever. But when people turned yellow, Dr. Rush named it 'yellow fever'.

June began with pleasant breezes and bright sunshine. But each day grew hotter'n the one afore. The air turned dry, dusty and gritty. Heat rolled into the house and up the stairs earlier each scorching morn. The sun sat high and blazed down, nary a cloud to block it and offer relief. No trees offered shade outside. Sweat poured off me. Oh, for a drop of rain on my tongue.

Flies and musketoes swarmed everywhere, landing on our arms, our legs, our faces, our food, leaving whatever filth they brang when we swatted 'em away. Sometimes I squashed 'em where they landed. When a fly landed in Lady Washington's cornmeal, I slammed my fist onto it, spattering a mess all over her.

"Oney!" She held up her cornmeal-flecked apron.

"Tha's better than swallowin' bug dirt, Lady Washington." She couldn't right argue with that.

Next day at market I seen more'n the usual number of wild pigeons for sale. We never had pigeon, and I figgered since there was so many, the price would be cheap. I bought half a dozen for two shillings and piled them in my burlap sack.

I told Lady Washington I'd got a good price on them pigeons but she recoiled in horror. "God, no!" She stepped back from me like I was poison just for touchin' 'em. "Get rid of them at once, bury them in the yard, or bring them out to the street and dump them. We will never eat pigeon. They bring unhealthy air and sickness." She waved her hands as if to clear all that unhealthy air. "Don't you know anything at all, Oney?" She tsk'd and quit the room.

"How was I s'posed to know pigeons brung sickness?" Rankled, I stomped my foot.

I brought the sack into the kitchen and asked Nathan. He laughed. "Ah, white folk don't like pigeons." He pulled them from the sack head first and laid them on the table. "Just as well, tha's all the more for us."

I walked out the kitchen with a satisfied smirk, knowing we'd have a feast tonight. And none of us got sick from feasting on bad air pigeon.

But when the general caught a fever, Lady Washington near fretted herself to death. She wrung her hands, paced circles round the house praying and begging God to make him better. "Make me sick instead, God." She lifted her head and hands to the ceiling. "The general's been through enough illness already." She sent a note to Dr. Rush. He called that eve, looking haggard his self, eyes red-rimmed, skin sallow. His grime-smeared shirt and trousers hung from his gaunt frame. He wheezed with a hacking cough.

He stretched out the general's arm and placed a silver cup under it. I turned my head as the candlelight glinted off his blade. Watching people bled made me queasy. But Lady Washington knelt at the general's side, grasping his other hand.

"Give him herb teas," the doctor ordered. "And a glass of brandy at bedtime will help him sleep, but I believe in the healing power of nature. The body takes its own measures to rid the humours of poisons and set them in balance. My job is to coax the body along in the process."

When the cup filled with the general's blood, Dr. Rush wiped the blade. She grabbed the cup from him and placed it on the nightstand. Some blood spilt over and she wiped it with her sleeve.

"Thank you, Doctor." She clasped his hands and bowed her head in worshipful wonder.

Next morn, dark circles hung neath her eyes. "He's no better."

"Lady Washington, you need get some sleep." I gave her a glass of buttermilk but she pushed it away.

"I'll look after the general," I offered.

"I couldn't swallow a thing," she muttered as she picked up a hoe cake and nibbled on it. "No, we need call for Dr. Rush again. The general is still hot with fever and cannot sit up. He won't eat either."

She stood and went into the parlour, dropped to her knees, and begged the Lawd for his recovery. I followed her in and clasped my hands as she did. Mayhap with both us praying, the Lawd would listen twice as hard. "We need him here, God. As your humble servant, please don't take him," she muttered over and over, head down.

All day she sat by his bedside, trying to spoon broth tween his lips, pressing cool cloths to his head, reading the Bible to him. In hopes to make him laugh, she brought out Shakespeare and that *Scandal* play she found so funny. When she needed a drink or the privy, I sat with him. He laid abed, unresponsive. He knew not who sat with him.

That eve Dr. Rush dragged his self up the stairs again and gave her frightening news. I stood by in case they needed me. "Something is not right in this city as of late, Lady Washington. Of course we've had the usual sicknesses over the winter—January's mumps, February's mouth infections, March's scarlet fever. However, there's something in the heat and drought that is uncommon in their influence on the human body." He turned and coughed in my face. I jumped aside.

"Well, what is it?" Lady Washington urged, grabbing his tattered sleeve. I don't reckon the man changed in three days. He smelt like it too.

"I cannot say for sure. All I know is that a French sailor at Denny's boarding house on Water Street was desperately ill with a fever for a few days." He pulled a dirty handkerchief from his pocket and coughed into it.

"Did you make him better?" she begged, and I cringed at her pathetic attempt to put all her trust in this man.

"No, he died. And so did a few others nearby."

She stumbled back and fell into her chair. "B-but that's at the waterfront. Denny's is in an alley. It's confined. You know what goes on down there in that disagreeable area. Surely no one here will succumb."

She fully refused to believe her husband was just as ill, cause we lived nowhere near the waterfront. Dr. Rush was in no hurry to feed her fears, though. "Summer fevers are common, as you know," he assured her, rubbing his red eyes.

Next morn as the general laid abed burning up, she pushed Molly and Katy out the door without stopping to write a note. "Go find Dr. Rush!" Then she took me aside, holding me by the hand. Something she never done before. By instinct I squeezed it to comfort her. "Oney, pray with me." She bade me kneel next to her beside her bed. Unsure what I prayed would cure him, as I still wasn't sure the Lawd listened to us folk, I mirrored her actions and said out loud, "Lawd, make the general better, and I really am your humble servant."

When she finished praying, I made a suggestion, more sensible than praying, I figgered. "Hercules knows of some remedies he tried when Mamma and Delphy got a fever, and they got better inside a day."

Her eyes brightened, looking more alive than in days. She stood at full height from her slumped posture. Beads of sweat glistened along her hairline. "Why, Oney, I never considered your people's remedies as being real … that would indeed be a blessing if they work on whites. 'Tis worth a try, I'm so desperate I'll try anything." Her voice a dry whisper, I poured her a glass of Madeira. So what it was daytime? She needed it.

"I know not when Dr. Rush will come back," she said tween sips. "He told me he has thirty more patients to see a day. Keep praying, Oney." She went out to the kitchen to fetch Hercules. She be desperate, going to him herself, not sending me. She came back with his mixed concoction, brandy flavored with fruit kernels, Noyau from Martinique. Did this work on white folk? I didn't know, none of them ever trying it on their selves. Durn, Hercules would deserve his freedom if it worked. But that wouldn't happen. He wouldn't get freedom if he brung the general back from the dead. Nothin' give us freedom—except our deaths.

I confess I wasn't too a'scared for the general having the dreaded yellow fever. He wasn't yellow—yet. "I don't believe he got that yalla fever, Lady Washington," I assured her. "He still white. He'll git better, I know it, even if Hercules's medicine don't do it. He'll git better himself. I know how strong the general is."

"Thank you, for I truly appreciate it. It seems everyone gives up when one of these plagues sweeps through. But I know the general is strong, too—much stronger than me. I'd be dead already after this long."

"No, you stronger'n him," I insisted, cause I was seeing it every day. Specially since this second term started. She was becoming as outspoken and forward as I ever thought she could be. What was making her so strong-opinioned and forthright? Her other forward thinking lady friends? What she read in the papers? The books she read? No, it was her position here—a most important place, as the first wife of the first president, though she griped about feeling imprisoned.

She realized she was in the most important place of any woman in the country at a crucial time and didn't want to see it lag back. She wanted to move forward with the young nation. These ladies didn't have much more voice than us folk did. They didn't make laws and constitutions and declarations. But without these ladies, men would have hardly no support or encouragement. From what Hercules read me what went on in that Congress hall, they'd rip each other to shreds. She now saw how important her role was and wanted to leave her mark on history.

Much as I resented being her property, deep down I held a place in my heart for Lady Washington—not love but fondness, and one other thing— pride. She got dragged into a role she didn't ask for or want, and out of devotion to the general and the country, she carried it out with grace.

Secretly I begrudged these rich folk their finery, their abundant meals, their fancy carriages, and what they felt was a divine right to buy and sell us along with pottery and donkeys. But the general and Lady Washington were here instead of in their own home, carrying out duties for the nation's future. For that I had to respect them. Though my name would vanish along with my bones in an unmarked grave, I wisht Lady Washington a legacy never to be forgot.

Next morn I opened the front door and reeled back. The sulphur reek of burning barrels of tar in the streets near knocked me over. As I coughed and sputtered, Mr. Jefferson huffed and puffed up the steps, clutching a purple umbrella and wiping his brow with a purple cloth.

Mr. Jefferson didn't look sick or yellow. But his shirt and breeches reeked of vinegar something awful. This time he had no Citizen Genet in his shadow.

"Good morn, Mr. Jefferson, the general is abed but able to sit up. We don't fear that yalla fever on him." I didn't say "yet."

He gave me his umbrella. "Thank providence for that. I won't disturb him but for a minute."

Without waiting for me to announce him, he galloped up the stairs and later took tea with Lady Washington, which I served. But how could they drink tea? 'Twas so brutal hot out. I reckon they preferred knocking back glasses of flip, but drinking rum wasn't polite in daytime visits. Not with these folk anyways.

"Lady Washington, I daresay the president's fevers have been from the incessant attacks in the press," he warned her. The stink of vinegar wafted across the room. Lady Washington grabbed her snuff tin and dipped some. I knew it was to mask the smell.

"He hardly takes the press seriously, Mr. Jefferson." She never called him Jeff to his face. With no shame she sopped sweat from her face with her hankie. She wasn't even wearing a cap—too hot. "I should be the one sick from the attacks. My husband laughs them off. He reads them to me during the eve and plays a little game to pick out the most scathing one. No, the fever's all over town," she chided him, frowning. "Dr. Rush has been telling me with each visit how many more patients he's been tending."

"The president might let it roll off his back with you, my lady, but when it's all of us men in the chamber, every last one of us is his underling. Let's not forget, with us men he lets fly his true feelings."

"He's my husband, he lets fly quite often around me, too, Mr. Jefferson." Her lips twisted into a wry curl.

"Does he swear and shout and fling nuts and olives about?" He scratched the shock of red hair atop his head.

"No, he reins in his spur at home because he knows I'd give him a good swift kick if he didn't. And he'd never fling nuts and olives about at Mount Vernon."

"Well, he's told us, and we know by his gestures, that he is extremely affected by the attacks made on him in those public papers." Mr. Jefferson scratched his arms. "I can sense more by what he doesn't say than by what he says. I'm ashamed of the scandal-mongers who print that bosh in the papers."

Lady Washington straightened up and gave him a lofty look, chin raised. "Ironic coming from a sponsor of the *National Gazette.*"

He shot back, "I merely helped launch it. I don't control what gets printed in it. Remember our First Amendment."

"I am not arguing with that," she mumbled. "I only wish they would find someone else to slanderize, someone who deserves it. Like your French Citiz—oh, never mind. I must refrain from stooping to that level."

"They will stop and move onto someone else," he answered. "As soon as President Washington leaves office."

"It can't be too soon for me," she said. "I feel out of place here, although I've striven to leave my mark as the woman standing in the first president's shadow." She swept her eyes round the room, halting at her books, her pen and paper, her unfinished knitting. "I keep the household ticking over and don't hesitate to offer advice whether he asks for it or not, but we don't see eye to eye on a lot of issues. The president is—the best way to describe him is that newfangled phrase 'old school'. Not in every way—wanting to be president rather than king brought us out of the Middle Ages into the future, but at heart he's a farmer, not a soldier or a statesman. He's worked at those other roles, but his farm, that's where his heart and soul are." She pointed a finger for emphasis.

"You're hardly the wallflower wife in his shadow, Lady Washington. As Mozart said about Beethoven, you are making a big noise in this world. Have no fear of being forgotten long after you've retired back to the farm. My Martha was the shy, reserved wife in the corner. But if only she were still with me …" His voice trailed off.

"I know." Her expression dissolved into softness as she lowered her lashes. She reached forward and clasped his fingers. "I only hope Miss Hemings is making you happy."

My eyes widened at the mention of Miss Hemings. I turned my back and busied myself waxing the table top. The Jefferson-Hemings open secret wasn't so secret no more. But nobody outside their circle dared mention Sally Hemings's name—to Mr. Jefferson or in the press or anywheres. But, oh, I wisht he'd bring her here. We'd have so much to talk over.

Next morn the general's valet, Jacob, sprang up with the roosters and dashed into the president's bedroom to help him dress. The president strutted out tall and hearty in his cream linen shirt and breeches. He returned to work, fever gone. Lady Washington praised Hercules's brandy remedy and Dr. Rush's bloodletting—but not a word of thanks to the Lawd—and gave Hercules a fistful of coins to buy more fancy duds.

Hercules later read to me from the papers about these poor sick folk from Haiti, and how some got shipped to France. "Let 'em spread fever there," he said. "Thank the good Lawd us folk immune to it."

"How you know us folk immune?" I jutted out my hip and placed my fist on it.

"Absalom Jones told us at the last Free African meeting. He been helping Dr. Rush tend the sick. He said, 'Us don't get yalla fever, only white folk git it. Us folk git Bronze John, come from the Caribbean. But it don't kill none.' I never seen it killing one o'us." He put the paper down and began cracking eggs into an earthenware bowl. "Nobody ever tol' you that, girl? You ever see one of us sick?"

"What of quadroons like me and mulattos like Austin?" I asked him.

"One drop of negro blood is enough," he answered. But I worried—a lot. Specially by July.

So sweltering, the air so still, clouds of steam surged from the putrefying piles of animal guts and sewage stagnant under the blazing sun. Lady Washington read from the papers about the waterfront, too. With the tides rolled in sloshing sewage and filth thrown from ships. God, what a pig stye, this whole city.

She let us go to the Ricketts Circus with Miz Nelly and Washy to see the horses from Ireland. All the money went to refugees for food and shelter. And to send more of them folk back to France, I hoped.

On July 4, with the general in Mount Vernon, us servant folk watched fireworks from the kitchen roof. Lady Washington stayed standing on the porch with the grandchildruns. It was too hot to watch from the upstairs windows.

With Miz Betsy and Miz Patty back in Virginia, Lady Washington, Miz Nelly and Washy slept on the settees and parlour floor, the upstairs bedrooms hotter'n the kitchen bake oven. Me, Molly, and the rest of us folk slept in the kitchen and scullery. The menfolk slept in the cellar. Folk with no homes wandered about, collapsing in alleys or in the street from exhaustion.

I tried sleeping on the roof, but swarms of musketoes chewed me up. Lawd, it was agony. We swatted and slapped and snatched from sunup to late night when they swarmed even more. Then came the scratching—our arms, legs, necks, chests—we stratched 'til we bled raw.

"I can't take another minute of these Liliputian lancers!" Lady Washington sprang up and closed every window on the bottom floor. The hum and buzz lessened as we walked round swatting with rolled-up newspaper, but we didn't kill 'em all. She gave us chamomile tea leaves wrapped in linen to soothe our raw scratches, but it didn't help none.

"We need extinguish all illumination. If not, we'll be eaten up alive, and the constant humming will drive us mad. The candles attract them," Lady Washington warned as she blew out all the candles in the house. Only a feeble glow of the moon cast shadows over the parlour. As our eyes adjusted, we could walk round without bumping into furniture. I felt my way to the back door and sprawled out in the garden, far from the rank odor of overflowing privies.

Lady Washington ordered twenty yards of green netting with lace border to drape over her bed. Hers was of gauze, the finest. To ease our suffering she bought us some muslin, the cheapest. It was not enough for our beds, but desperate, I wrapt my head in it. Still, a buzzing mosquito or two chewed their way through. I sewed bedclothes out of the extra. She sent me and Molly for muslin sacks to tie round our throats, and smaller sacks for our arms. Thus we lay abed, panting for breath and air, dressed in a single muslin petticoat and our sweaty shifts.

The bugs buzzed less when the fire company began wetting down the streets twice a day. "'Tisn't for bugs," Lady Washington told me as we stood in the doorway at dusk waiting for the fire engine. When it rumbled by, I stepped forth to let some droplets from their hose sprinkle my heated face. "'Tis because doctors think the fever is carried by dust because of the drought."

"What's drought?" A wave of heat returned and engulfed us as the fire engine's wheels clattered down the street.

"It means a long time with no rain. But I don't believe doctors will ever discover what truly causes this horrid disease." She dipped her hankie in a bowl of water she now kept in each room and swabbed her face and chest. "I just keep praying it won't touch us."

But she didn't pray hard enough.

Lady Washington let us do our household duties outside. Every morn dawned hotter and drier. From dawn 'til late night, not a breeze blew. I sewed cotton shifts for us and pants for the boys. The extra cloth we all used to mop up sweat. She let us splash water all over us from the pump. Even Miz Nelly and Washy joined in the fun. I wisht we were back at Mount Vernon but the general wrote it was just as hot there.

We gulped lemonade by the barrelful. In the heat we sweated out what we drank. There was no liquid to excrete in the privy.

All through the sweltering summer, flies and musketoes buzzed round us, landing all over us and our dinners. We swatted and slapped. The rolled newspapers filled up with squashed bugs from the constant swatting. Every night now we had to go back inside, shut the windows against the swarms of bugs, and blow out the candles. Every breath made me choke, the air so hot and stuffy.

On market day I walked the entire three blocks of stalls afore buying anything. I noticed prices gone way up since last week. Lady Washington had only given me a few dolls, and prices now near doubled. Why was that?

I heard two chicken merchants grousing about the stench from Ball's Wharf. As I looked over the squawking birds, checking they skin tween the feathers for disease, one merchant said, "Bad coffee all spoilt during the voyage from Santo Domingo and is just sitting on the wharf." He held his nose tween thumb and forefinger. "And it stinks something rotten."

I did recall Dr. Rush say to Lady Washington that he lived three blocks from the wharf, but "the coffee stinks to the great annoyance of the whole neighborhood."

But all I could smell was the swill, swine and chickens. Folk who chewed garlic and smoked seegars to keep fever away stank even worse. Camphor and sour vinegar assaulted me. How could rotten coffee smell any worse'n that?

The general, all recovered, went about his ruling the land from his office. But since Dr. Rush told her about that sailor and those other poor souls, Lady Washington scoured the papers, gasped in horror and fluttered her fan.

"Oh, dear God, Oney, listen to what Dr. Rush said." Then she read from the *Gazette*: "In recent days I've seen an unusual number of bilious fevers, accompanied with symptoms of uncommon malignity. The symptoms remind me of a sickness that swept through Philadelphia in the year '62 when I studied under Dr. Redman. It is my opinion that the disease we now see is the yellow fever. All is not right in our city."

Her voice trailed off as she lowered the paper. "Just as the doctor warned me, those exact words. Yellow fever. The deadly plague that I so feared is upon us." Her voice droned on in a flat monotone, "Lord have mercy on our poor souls." She stared straight ahead, her eyes unfocused, dazed.

"But that don't—doesn't mean we'll get it. The general didn't turn yalla," I tried to calm her, but began to tremble, a'scared as her. Hercules never read me this stuff from the papers, it was her reading it. He knew better'n to scare me like that.

"I'm praying we won't," she sighed, folding the paper up like a rotten pickerel lay inside. She handed it to me. "Throw this out. I don't want to read any more of this." She turned, fetched her Bible and, cradling it like a newborn babe, carried it up the stairs.

But next morn she went right on reading from that day's paper. Now a Dr. Hodge described the symptoms of this horrid plague: "I've seen it begin with chills, headache, and a painful aching in the back, arms, and legs. A high fever develops, accompanied by constipation. This stage lasts around three days, and then the fever suddenly breaks and the patient seems to recover."

"Seems to?" I stopped pouring tea and set the pot down afore my trembling hand dropped it.

She released a ragged sigh. "The next stage sees the fever shoot up again," she read on, her voice wobbly. "Skin and eyeballs turn yellow, nose and intestines bleed, and the patient vomits stale black blood. Finally, the pulse grows weak, the tongue a dry brown and the victim becomes confused and delirious."

My insides churned and my brekkus of leftover hoe cake and herring surged to my throat. Her face flushed and her hands shook. The paper crumpled where she clasped it at the edges. She flung it to the table as if it was aflame and pushed it to me with her knife. "I cannot read any more."

"How many people get like that so far? It say?" I asked her, not wanting to know, but a morbid fear overtook both of us since this all started. She said she couldn't read no more, but soon as I laid it down she always grabbed the paper and dived into the horror.

"Dr. Hodge said all the deaths happened on or near Water Street." Her eyes fixed downward, she clasped her snuff box. "His own daughter died right there."

"Then it all right, we ain't there—uh, not there," I assured her, and at the same time, myself.

"Sweet Jesus, the doctor knows the origin of the fevers—the stench in the air caused by the rotting coffee on Ball's Wharf." She flipped open her snuff box and took a pinch.

I dug in my memory. "I heard two merchants at the market talking 'bout that but I reckoned it all silly. How could rotten coffee cause fever?"

She took another pinch and wiped her nose with her hankie. "I don't know how, but we're not taking any chances. I'm going to tell the general the minute he arrives home that we must leave for Mount Vernon. Start packing, Oney." She stood and marched off.

But no, the general would have none of it. "Remember my providence, Patsy." He popped grapes into his mouth as they sat on the settee. "Besides, how would it look if I fled now? I'd be branded a coward for life." He spat out some pips into his hand and emptied them onto the newspaper.

"Would you rather be a dead hero?" she argued, but was wasting her time. She just liked to badger him.

"You take the children and go back to Mount Vernon." He waved his free hand, the other full of grapes. "I'll join you when it dies down a bit."

"I'm not leaving without you," she insisted through clenched teeth. "If you want to put your life in danger, so shall I."

That meant putting all our lives in danger. I could see her not caring 'bout us, but how 'bout her grandchildruns? It didn't bother them none. Lady Washington didn't read them the papers every day, each horror story worst than the day afore.

Rich people fled the city, Mrs. Bingham and her husband to their grand house on the New Jersey coast. Some took their servants, some didn't. All that, the first warning, the spreading, the general deathly ill, the horror stories—that was the easy part up 'til now. Then the bad news came.

Black folk began to catch fever and die. Molly told me two of Mrs. Powel's slaves died within hours of each other. "I knew Hercules's saying we immune was hogwash." Anger boiled my blood.

On market day somewhere in July, Molly and I sat stitching cotton blouses, this time for ourselves. Lady Washington and Tobias Lear's wife, Miz Polly, stepped onto the porch and rolled up their sleeves. Their chemises were unbuttoned to the tops of their bosoms. That was hardly proper, but only us girls was home. No cap adorned Lady Washington's head. She mopped the sweat off her face with a scrap of corn-yellow cotton I'd sewed her apron with.

"Girls, Polly and I are going to the shops to buy more cloth and buttons, and see if the market is open. We haven't much left to eat. If you please, you may fill the tub and soak for a while. The paper says it won't be cooling off anytime soon. It also says more folk have died, but not on the waterfront anymore. It's moved closer."

Just as I feared. All that praying for naught. Miz Polly and Lady Washington walked down the steps. We stood to let them pass.

"Oney, I made more washing soap, so you needn't do that today," Miz Polly said, swatting away a fly. "Use your extra time to stay cool."

"Thank you kindly, Miz Polly." She helped us house servants though she needn't. She just wanted something to do. Times were she worked harder'n me.

But when they returned from the shops, Miz Polly collapsed on the sofa, sweat pouring off her. I pumped water from out back and wiped her down with cool cloths. "'Tis the heat, tha's all," I assured her, too a'scared to admit what it really was.

Lady Washington had the menservants carry Miz Polly to bed, she bein' too weak to walk.

As Lady Washington opened the papers next morn, I got myself out the dining room. I just couldn't hear no more of her reading about the crying babies found in houses next to dead parents … folk who dropped dead in the street, their bodies rotting 'til the death carts came … the woman who gave birth while her husband and other child died next to her, then her and her newborn died right after. But in the eves, when the general and Lady Washington talked of it, I couldn't leave the room. Ordered to stay cleaning up or sewing, I had to hear it.

"We need not flee, Patsy," he told her once again as he swatted flies with rolled-up newspaper. "It's still confined to the wharf area. And Dr. Rush is way outnumbered by the city's other physicians in his belief that it's yellow fever. They're mocking him with ridicule and contempt."

"So what?" she shot back. "What's the difference what it's called? It's killing people at an alarming rate. And it's not confined anymore. I'd trust Dr. Rush before those other quacks. He's the best known doctor in town, so how could you ever doubt him?" She sassed at the general more'n ever these days.

"I've a country to run, Patsy." His voice raised above his usual calm level. "I've no time to flee and lose everyone's respect." He swatted another fly. "Now I've got letters to write. Go tend to Mrs. Lear. And for God's sake don't say naught about any yellow fever." He stomped from the room. She slammed her palm on the table.

"I'll tend to Miz Polly." I held a stack of dirty dishes to bring into the scullery.

"Thank you, Oney. Tell her I'll be in presently." Her voice broke small and strained now the general wasn't here. She dashed out the back door. I was a'scared to go into Miz Polly's sickroom now that I knew us folk could catch it. But I had to obey orders.

When I went in Miz Polly's dark room, a nauseating stench hit me. She leant on her side over the bed, vomiting. I heard a sickening splat as it hit the floorboards. It was that foul black bile the papers told about. As I forced myself to step inside, she spewed forth some more onto the bed sheets. I grabbed a towel from her washstand and gagged as I wiped it up.

Lady Washington come in and rushed up to Miz Polly, knelt beside her and smoothed drenched hair off her forehead."God, she's burning up." She waved toward the door. "Find Dr. Rush! Hurry!"

But afore I ran to the doctor's house, I found Hercules. "Gimme some more of your Noyau with extra brandy. Miz Polly is in a bad way."

"She dyin'?" he asked the obvious.

I couldn't answer him. I took the medicine into the sickroom and put it on the nightstand. Miz Polly lay there moaning. Lady Washington wiped her down. She surprised me—I didn't think she'd tend the dying woman that long. She showed a compassionate heart during this sickness I never seen. It must'a been from having her own childruns die.

Molly and I headed to Dr. Rush's residence on Spruce Street, walking in the middle of the street so not to pass close to infected houses. Though I hated the sharp odor that burnt my nose and chest with each breath, I clutched a bag of camphor whenever I went outside. It smelt better'n the rotten stench on the streets. Of course Dr. Rush wasn't at home, he was tending other sick folk. But soon as I said "Washington" to the servant at the door, she blathered on and on, "I'll get him to there right away, oh, God, please, not our beloved president ..."

I didn't say naught. Let her think the president was ill. It'd get the doctor there faster.

Lady Washington made me stay at the front door all night to let him in quick. I slept in the entry hall, ears perked for his approaching footsteps. But he didn't appear 'til seven the next morn. I'd got up by five, but Lady Washington didn't need dressin'. She sat by Miz Polly's bed all night, the poor girl's pulse slow and weak.

"I had to stay with her, I love her like a daughter," she whispered to me, wiping away tears when I brought her the last of our buttermilk.

Dr. Rush stumbled in looking near death, the whites of his eyes a sickly yalla, his face cloudy like rotten cheese. He shuffled like his joints pained him to move. He coughed into his hand and wiped it on his breeches, reekin' of sweat and vinegar. His body gave off the odor of urine.

Absalom Jones came with him, looking just as ragged, but not smelling so bad. "Hello, Oney," he greeted me.

"What you doin' here, Mr. Jones?" I knew Dr. Rush did much for our African church here, but didn't know he'd made Mr. Jones his assistant.

"Helpin' the doctor, since he does so much to help us."

As they looked down at Miz Polly, Dr. Rush told Lady Washington, "I've caught yellow fever, too, my lady. I knew it was a matter of time, but I cannot let it keep me abed. There are folk more worse off than I, and I'll treat them 'til I drop into a grave myself. I can only hope Absalom will stay free of it and carry on my work."

She gasped. "Can you do naught to help either of you? The poor child is throwing up black bile." Lady Washington waved in the bed's direction and pointed at the floor beside it, covered in new vomit where nobody swabbed it up yet. I couldn'a believed she had any more in her to bring up.

I was sure Miz Polly couldn't hear a thing, or didn't care. The doctor spoke as if she wasn't there. "I need bleed her again to remove more inflammatory humors, and this time I'm giving her a massive emetic and a purge." He pointed across the room. "That fireplace opening should not be stopped up with a fireboard but rather left open." Absalom went over to open it. "And keep this chamber well aired. It needs be as sweet and free from any disagreeable smell. Change the linen frequently and remove all offensive matter."

"Keep it well aired? That's nigh on impossible with all the bugs!" Lady Washington protested.

As he approached Miz Polly with another empty cup, he glanced at me. "You go shave the root of a tree so I can give her the bark with brandy. Fetch a pail of warm vinegar and dunk a blanket in it. Then wrap her in it. Drench her in a cold bath every two hours and feed her light meals." He dug into his bag. "The emetic is ten grains of calomel and as a purgative, fifteen grains of jalap. She will take three doses of this every six hours. I will continue to draw a quart of blood, taking two or three more in the next three days until four-fifths of the blood in the body are drawn away."

"What good will all these purges and emetics do?" Lady Washington demanded, but who was any of us to question a doctor?

"My new remedy," he boasted, his voice gathering volume. "It made yellow fever no more than a common cold. I have been treating patients thusly, and never before did I experience such sublime joy as I now feel in the success of my remedies. It repaid me for all the toils and studies of my life … 'tis the triumph of a principle in medicine!" The doctor came to life with his bragging. Seemed it was keeping him alive, too.

She had no more to question after that. A spark of hope shone in her eyes. "Oh, I do hope you'll be able to save her with these concoctions." Miz Polly didn't look as if she cared that Dr. Rush bled her dry.

Lady Washington turned to me. "Oney, why are you still here? You heard the doctor's orders. Go fetch a pail of vinegar."

I ran to the kitchen.

"I needs a pail of vinegar." I burst into the kitchen but none of the cooks were there. I crashed my head into a cone-shaped loaf of sugar hung from the ceiling, hard as a stone. "Yowch!" I swang it aside and searched the shelves, pushing aside whisks, rolling pins, chopping knives, brass mortars and pestles, but no vinegar. I knew it was sour wine, but they drank wine so fast round here not a drop had time to go sour.

There was always large stores of vinegar in the kitchen. But with all the sickness and fevers round here, they must'a went through every drop.

I took the biggest kitchen knife and sliced some bark off the dogwood tree out back. At least Miz Polly would have that—mayhap she'd get half better with half the remedy.

Lady Washington met me outside Miz Polly's room and softly shut the door. "Shhh, she's asleep." She placed her pointer finger to her lips.

"But we got no more vinegar!" I wrang my hands. "Please don' let her die on my account."

Lady Washington forced a thin smile. "I'll send one of the girls to the market—no, I needs get out of here. I'll go. You stay, and when she wakes, put her in a cool bath. Let a few boys help you carry the water up. And you take a soak yourself. You haven't bathed in a while, have you?"

"I rightly don' remember. But a soak would be nice."

"Make sure to scrub out the tub afterwards." She walked down the hall and I followed. We went down the shadowy stairway, clutching the banister.

Three of us and Absalom hauled the tub and pails of water into Miz Polly's bedroom. We took three trips apiece filling the tub. The boys and Absalom stayed out while Molly and I lifted her into the tub. She shuddered when her frail body sank into the water. I could'a lifted her myself. She'd got light as a bird.

But neither the bath nor the bleedin' nor Hercules's medicine worked. With Dr. Rush and Absalom tending so many other sick, a young Dr. Cathrall came over. He pressed a vinegar-soaked cloth to his face as he approached Miz Polly's bed. He bled her two cupfuls, gave her the same emetic and purge mixture, and told Lady Washington the same as Dr. Rush: "Wrap her in vinegar-soaked blankets and give her cold baths."

I could'a told her that, and I ain't no doctor. The whole house already stunk of vinegar. While he stood there, she vomited more. He bled her again. Lady Washington and Mr. Lear sat by her bed holding her hands. Late into the eve, her labored breathing ceased.

Lady Washington woke me, sobbing, "Mrs. Lear has gone to heaven, and I thank God for the blessing. It was too late for Dr. Rush's new remedy, but I cannot fault him for trying."

Surely a relief for all of us. But the silent question hung in the fetid air: who is next?

"God almighty, she was like a daughter to me," Lady Washington wailed. I stood, stunned, it happened so fast. But she wasted no time in ordering me to sew new frocks. "Oney, we need dress in mourning—and that means all of us. Including you, Molly and the others." She led me to her locked cabinet and withdrew several notes and coins. "Purchase as many yards as you need for six of us, in black and gray only."

Black and gray in this heat? I burst to protest. In the light cottons and muslins we now wore with sleeves pushed up, we stayed drenched in sweat. But I took the money and went out into the sweltering heat to the fabric shop, not knowing if it'd be open.

Clutching the money in the pocket I'd sewed in for this reason, a thought sped by me. I could'a took this money and ran. Then a shot of fear halted me there on the street. I peered round, as if folk could hear my thoughts. Head down, I hurried on. No, I needed much more time. I needed free black friends to help me. I needed courage. I had none of these today.

Miz Polly's was the only funeral the president went to. He led the procession of all his top men, Mr. Hamilton, Mr. Jefferson, Mr. Knox … them and the general bore the coffin to the gravesite in the scorching heat. But Lady Washington took me by the sleeve and turned away. "I can't bear it," she cried. I so ached to hold her. "This is as painful as when I lost my Patsy. She was so young, so full of life. Why take her, why?"

That same day the newly widowed Tobias Lear quit as the general's secretary. The general gave him his second best carriage and two bays to travel to New Hampshire. The father figure and the younger lad shed tears as they embraced for the last time. Mr. Lear shook hands goodbye with me and I wept tears of my own, so touched that he'd taken my hand. "Thank you for all you've done for Polly, Oney. I appreciate it more than you'll ever know."

"I would'a done it anyways …" I started but broke down in sobs.

"Please write to us," Lady Washington begged him as he turned to leave. "I hope the post office will be reopened before long and mail delivery will resume soon. But do write."

"Now who can take his place?" The general pulled his collar from his neck and paced the hallway, head down.

"How about my nephew Bart Dandridge?" Lady Washington suggested. "You seem to get along."

He turned round with one of his rare smiles. "Yes, he's the one. Write him, will you? I need change my shirt again. I'm peeling them off these days."

"Aren't we all?" She sat at her desk. I rushed over, but not in time. She'd already picked up the newspaper page I'd wrote the alphabet on.

"What is this?"

Durn it! In the haste of tending to Miz Polly, I'd left it there. I plucked it from tween her fingers. "It … it … it was me, Lady Washington, I'm tryin'a learn my letters from Hercules and been practicing. I didn't want you to see nothin' I wrote 'til I could write nice 'n neat like you." I glanced at my wobbly letters and cringed.

She peered at me over her specs, lips tight, but I could see she was trying to hide a smile. "Oney, if you want to learn your letters that badly, then learn them. But don't let it take time from your duties. Why do you want to learn anyway?" She picked up the pen and examined the nib, expecting to see I'd broke it. "Is it not enough I let you take speech lessons?"

"I want to learn lotsa things, Lady Washington," I rambled, so relieved she didn't hit me or threaten to sell me away for this offense. "Politicks and figgers and about the moon and stars," I took in air, "and I wanna sound smart when your ladies ask me questions 'bout certain things, like who should be president after the general."

She leant back and stared at me, eyes wide. "Who has asked you about who should be president?"

"Last time Mrs. Murray was at your tea, she asked me. You was—were out the room."

"And what did you answer her?" Her smile widened and her brows rose up her forehead. Yea, the colored pet was an amusement to her and her ladies.

"The truth. I said I wisht the general would stay president for life, but know tha's not the law, so I hope he'll be someone who'll let our country grow big as Europe, keep us outta wars, make enough jobs so there be no poor, and free us people someday." There. I said it. Did she punish me? No. But by then I knew Lady Washington good enough, I didn't expect her to punish me for wanting to be free. We could want all we wanted, that was no offense.

"Oney, you know the general abhors the institution of slavery," she lectured me. "'Tis his wish to see some plan adopted so slavery may be abolished by slow and sure degrees. He never means—unless some particular circumstance should compel him to it—to purchase another slave. He already has twice as many working negroes than he could use. And they're better clothed and fed than negroes generally are in this country."

A quart of corn meal and five ounces of bony fish a day is well fed? I itched to challenge her. *And after the hogs are butchered, they get only the guts. That's well fed?* Oh, yea, we get extra meat rations during the harvest season—but once a year. I reckon that's what she meant.

She went on, "Time alone can change it, an event no man desires more heartily than the general. Not only does he pray for it, but naught but the rooting out of slavery can keep our union alive, by holding it together in a common bond of principle."

"I'm glad he prays for it, Lady Washington. Do you pray for it?" I plowed on, well knowing my boundary, and this was it.

She glanced over at the Bible, took by surprise. "Well—of course. You see me pray every day."

I did the correct thing to do, I nodded. But I didn't see her pray every day. Just when she wanted something. She read her Bible, but that ain't praying. "So you do want to see us free?" I was never brave enough to talk about this with her afore, but we'd grown almost close as her and her grandgirls, so I knew she'd open up. And she did, eager to finally share her hopes with me.

"Oney," she went on, "liberty is the right of every man—not madmen or idiots, of course—liberty in their hands would become a scourge." She gave a slight tilt of her head and narrowed her eyes, rapt at me. "Do you understand what I am saying?"

"Yea, Lady Washington. Madmen don't deserve the liberty of right-minded folk," I agreed. "But enough of 'em roam the streets. Some of 'em even git elected to government." I purposely didn't crack a smile knowing she would.

That got a gruff guffaw and a knowing nod. "Don't I know it. Alas, one of the drawbacks of democracy. Any dolt can hold office, as we have clearly seen. But freeing slaves needs be gradual 'til the mind of the slave has been educated to perceive the obligations of the state of freedom, the gift would insure its abuse. It would take many years, even centuries, mayhap not in our lifetimes … well, mayhap in yours. You are young yet. I am an old lady, most of my years are far behind me. But you—you have your whole life ahead of you."

A whole life to be a slave? So how we s'posed to get educated, even if it takes all those many years? I opened my mouth to ask, but she went on.

"But 'tis not possible yet. There are too many other issues facing our nation that must be addressed—these wars with France and Britain, for example. Staying out of future wars. The money and banking situation. The constant fighting in Congress." She counted on her fingertips. "On and on."

Her stare at me deepened. "Oney, what I'm about to say comes from the core of my soul. I know God made everybody the same. It was man who made these laws." She couldn't meet my eyes as she said this. After a deep breath, she looked at me and asked, "But do I not treat you as one of my own?" She tapped the pen on the blotter in rhythm with her foot tapping on the floor.

I'd'a said 'almost' but didn't want to push my luck. I knew how far I could push Lady Washington, a bit farther each time. So I stopped. "Yes, you do. Can I be dismissed now?"

"That's *may* I be dismissed. Yes, you may. I have some writing of my own to do."

As I bobbed a curtsey and turned to leave, she said, "Here. Take this. You can use the other side to practice on more," and handed me the page I'd written the alphabet on. "When you eventually buy your own paper, you will see it is dear, so don't waste any. Always use both sides and the margins. See?" She held up a letter she wrote, every empty space filled, along the edges, both sides written all over. Writing paper musta been dear if someone rich as her needed write over every bit of it.

"Yes, Lady Washington. I hope I'll be just like you someday." I skipped out of there, back to my chores, knowing I could press even further next time we talked.

****

Instead of attacks on the general, the press reported how many folk still died of yellow fever—fifty a day and rising. With paper scarce, now they crammed *Gazette* onto a single sheet instead of the usual eight pages. Lady Washington made me listen to her read aloud.

"Leaving the city is impossible for the poor who have neither places to remove to or funds for their support, as they depend on their daily labour, for daily supplies," she read. She handed me the paper as she always did when she finished, to take to the kitchen. "We're fortunate we're not poor, Oney."

"Yea, Lady Washington, we very fortunate," and I well knew 'we' didn't include us, but I thanked the good Lawd and his providence. It could'a been me out there lying on the street if I didn't have rich owners.

When I could, I fled to the kitchen, but now Hercules read out loud to the other cooks. He hurled the paper onto the table in frustration. "The Washingtons is hardly poor, why won't they leave and bring us back to Virginia?"

"It would make 'em look cowards, that's why." I set the tea service on the butcher block, polishing a spot I'd missed on the sugar bowl.

"No, he stupid!" Hercules shot back. I peered over my shoulder. Thank providence the general or Lady Washington wasn't in earshot. Calling the general stupid would spur a severe punishment.

"Herc, listen wutch'you say. Just cause the general don't do his own lashin' don't mean he won't git Mr. Jefferson to do it for him. And he do lash his slaves. Calling the general stupid's as stupid as you can git, you numskull."

"Soon I be a dead numskull if we don' git outta here and jump afore long, girl." He stalked off.

I began to shake, a'scared to think of jumping during this deadly plague. All I wanted was not to turn yalla. But I knew deep down none else of us in this house would catch that horrible plague. I felt it in my soul. After Miz Polly died, the fever lingered at the doorstep but didn't dare come in. It

115

seemed a'scared itself, of the general and Lady Washington. It made me glad to be hers while this went on.

But fever spread to the better neighborhoods, whose folk could afford to flee. The death carts still rumbled over the cobbles. We heard "Bring outch'yer de-a-a-a-ad!" at least thrice a day from the shabby drivers, carts piled with stiff bodies. I shuddered hearin' the cart clatter past the house in the dead of night.

On the way to market I saw small red flags nailed to doors on Moravian Alley and Fetter Lane. I shivered, though the searing heat drenched me in sweat.

The general's new secretary, Bartholomew, used Mr. Flake as his tailor. He lived in Morovian Alley, one of the harder hit parts of town. He delivered some shirts to Bartho and broke down in tears. "I already lost six young'uns, sank into one silent, undistinguished grave."

Bartho muttered, "I'm sorry for your loss," grabbed his shirts and hurried on his way, but Lady Washington invited Mr. Flake in and treated him as if a government bigwig.

"Mr. Flake, I'm extending an invitation to you to Mount Vernon, and to stay as long as you wish. You can certainly work there," she offered as I served them lemonade. How did he escape that undistinguished grave? Did he pray more'n the others who didn't? I still wasn't clear on how prayer worked, and by the looks of things, neither was Lady Washington.

Mr. Flake chewed on raw garlic to keep the fever away. I smelt his breath from across the room. His stink blew in my face when I bent my knees to serve him the glass.

"Oh, no, Mrs. Washington, I couldn't escape to Mount Vernon, especially since you and the president are still here. Have you any plans to leave here and escape to safety?"

"No," came with a stubborn shake of her head side to side. "We have no plans to flee. It would appear most unbecoming, especially for my husband. And as long as he stays, I stay."

"But—are you not afraid?" He clasped the glass and rolled it across his forehead.

"Of course," she answered. "I live in more fear every day I read the blasted papers about the death tolls. But fate is fate. I'm not leaving without my husband. He told me to leave, but I wouldn't. I cannot think of myself in this."

When the tailor stood to leave, he promised to ponder her offer, but not 'til she and the general departed the city. On the way out, he picked up his length of tarred rope, another measure of keeping the fever at bay. For him it worked. He was still alive.

I wondered why Lady Washington wasn't a'scared of catching it from him. But she did tell me to soak his glass in vinegar. And Bartho made Molly soak the new shirts afore he wore 'em.

By August the town was a horror scene, sweltering and deserted. As death carts clattered down the streets, drivers called in mournful tones, "Bring outch'yer de-a-a-a-ad!" Churchbells tolled, "right out of the medieval plague days," Lady Washington said. Did she live through that, too? I wondered but didn't want to ask. I didn't know when 'medieval days' was.

For weeks now, going to church or market, I seen at least one black wagon on each street. Houses stood shuttered tight. Nobody roamed the streets unless they had to. I'd only see pigs, dogs and rats scurrying about, digging through the bones and putrid carcasses dumped in the alleys and gutters. When a breeze did pass, it carried the stench of open sewers, outside privies, and piles of rotting filth. Sulphur burnt in barrels on every corner. Smoke from blazing bonfires choked us. Folk sprinkled tobacco, garlic or camphor over their floors and outside to the street. Vinegar too sour for us girls, we pressed coffee-drenched cloths over our faces as we dashed by.

On Absalom Jones's instructions, Hercules mixed up some fly traps, glass tumblers filled with soap suds, a slice of bread with a hole in the center, the under side covered with molasses, and laid in the tumbler. Lady Washington made Molly wave a large peacock-feather flybrush during meal times to keep the flies off the food, but unlike Mrs. Bingham's rude commanding of me to fan her without even a thank-you, Lady Washington gave Molly money or sweets after each fanning session. When they swarmed real thick, the general covered the table with the gauze from the bed.

Absalom helped Hercules mix concoctions of fly poison—a blend of black pepper, brown sugar and cream, stirred and set about on plates. It was poison to the flies anyways.

When someone fired a musket into the air to scare away the fever, I jumped out my skin. Some of them remedies sounded downright lunatic.

Even a simple wench like me knew firing muskets wouldn't cure naught. How could bullets shoot through a fever?

"Thank providence we're in an affluent neighborhood," Lady Washington commented as she got brave and opened a window.

The house grew so stagnant, the air so stale, our mouths dried up. Since the general's first term, the city did make improvements—to the 'affluent neighborhoods' anyways. Streets now had paving, the main sewer over Dock Creek was now covered, and scavengers swept filth from the biggest streets. But no scavengers dared come out during this plague. Even in our 'affluent neighborhood' trash piled in heaps. The cooks buried kitchen scraps, but rich folk still threw out refuse, and rich chamber pot slops smelt as vile as poor ones.

"Now Mr. Hamilton and his wife are ailing," the general announced as he pushed open a front window, but nary a breeze came in. "They're leaving for Albany tomorrow."

"No, George, don't open the window!" Lady Washington dashed over to close it. "I opened it for five minutes last week, and the house went swarming with flies."

"But 'tis an inferno in here!"

"Better an inferno than hordes of wall-to-wall bugs. I'm going to send Betsy Hamilton some of that brandy water Hercules used on you." She headed out the back way.

"They'll be fine. He has a French doctor who knows about these West Indian fevers." The general fanned his self with the newspaper 'til Lady Washington gave him her hand-held palmetto fan. He waved it away. "I'm not going to use that macaroni-looking thing." He turned to the window and screwed up his mouth. "Why do we not use the netting for the windows to make curtains with? At least we won't get chewed up in here and will let some air in."

"George, how brilliant!" She wiped her brow and gazed at her husband, adoration in her eyes.

"Not really. 'Tis not like I invented it." Hence we had green musketo netting, "curtains," on all the windows to match the canopy over their bed.

Next morn an ear-shattering cannon boom shook the walls and rattled the windows. We jumped, startled. I spilt tea all over the tablecloth. A few drops spattered my hand and arm. I howled in pain and waved my arm round to lessen the scalding. All atremble, afore we finished stammering, "What was tha—" another boom rocked the house.

"Lawdy save us, the Red Coats come back to blow us all to bits!" Molly screeched and ducked under the table. I pulled her out by her braids and slid her across the waxed floorboards.

"If Lady Washington see you hidin' you'll get a good hidin'." But I shook, half believin' her shrieks could be the ugly truth. Just then Lady Washington's voice floated across the room. I was glad she seen me drag Molly out and be brave like me—sorta.

"Girls, don't be afraid, 'tisn't the Red Coats coming back. They wouldn't dare." We turned toward her, Molly's face near white as Lady Washington's with fear. I clamped onto the table to steady my trembling hands. But my knees wobbled so, I slid to the floor and wrapt my arms round my knees.

We stayed in these frozen poses nearly another thirty ticks of the clock, but not another boom blasted.

"I'm happy you put on a brave front, Oney," she heaped praise on me as I struggled to my feet. "I'll ask the general what the noises were when he comes in. Now go sit out back for a few minutes and calm down." She approached us and clutched one of our shoulders each, over our fabric. "I know how scary things are these times, but we're safe here and well protected in this sturdy house. So have no fear. The Red Coats are lily-livers and won't be back, I can assure you." Her confident tone relaxed me. I took a deep breath and whistled it out.

"You make me feel safe, Lady Washington," I lauded her on the way out as I guided Molly down the hall. "You're a fearless lady."

"Oh, I'm not so sure about that." She walked tween us 'til we reached the back door. "I had my scares, living at camp during the war, so close to enemy fire. But I always knew we'd win. Our armies were far better equipped than theirs, and we'd achieve the victory we—I mean the men—fought for. In the end, sheer will to win brought them their well-deserved overthrow of those brazen lobsterbacks."

"Y'all ladies fought for it, too, Lady Washington, not just the men." I couldn't resist pitching in, knowing what sacrifices they made, but careful not to voice the other part—what they fought for didn't include us. It wasn't like they had to fight harder for us folks's freedom. But I pushed away the sadness weighing down my heart. Letting these emotions win over me was a form of defeat.

We learnt about them booms when the general come home for dinner at three. "That was Fort Mifflin, not Red Coats." He handed me his jacket.

"They've been dragging cannon through the streets, stopping at regular intervals to fire. The College of Physicians made the state legislature tell Governor Mifflin that gunpowder be flashed through the streets." He held his glass up to my brother. "Is there any ale, Austin? I'm parched as a funeral drum."

"But what good does flashing gunpowder do?" Lady Washington sat to dinner and I laid her serviette across her lap. "Scaring citizens to death— you should have seen the spectacle here in this very house, poor Molly hiding under the table. I would've done the very same thing at her age being so naïve. But Oney here put on a brave little face."

With the nod of recognition and light clap of her hands bestowed on me, heat rushed to my face. I shut up, too overwhelmed to say naught in return. Not that I had permission to talk. But I blurted out, "I ain't so brave, Lady Washington. I could never face a war like you did."

The general took a quaff of ale that Austin poured him. "These times call for desperate measures, Patsy. Gunpowder is another alleged exterminator of the fever," he explained. "I'll have a word with Mayor Clarkson. I believe it's daft, too. Hmmf … doctors …" he scoffed, raising his glass for a refill. "At times I reckon there's more quackery now than in the Middle Ages."

He lived in the Middle Ages, too?

As the dead-carts kept a'rattlin' through the empty streets, church bells tolled nonstop 'til the general issued an order to stop them. "Is that ever a relief." Lady Washington sighed on the first morn of silence. "I'm the one who ordered the ceasing of the bells," she informed me, smugness curving her lips. "But of course the general needed to issue the command. I'm merely a citizen." But I could sense she was growing outta her citizen petticoats into something more forceful to reckon with. Not quite breeches, but close to 'em.

The Hamiltons recovered and returned to town. Mrs. Hamilton told Lady Washington their doctor gave them purges and emetics rather than bleed them.

"No bleeding? Why, that's odd indeed," Lady Washington commented. "But I did pray for you both. I prefer to believe that helped as much as the unusual treatment. But no bleeding?" she repeated, hands splayed in confoundment. "I'll have to talk that over with Dr. Rush. It could be a Greek medical advancement. They're so far ahead of the rest of us."

****

When the Hamiltons came to dinner early September, Lady Washington gave them six bottles of their best Madeira and offered the services of Mrs. Emerson, one of the paid servants. She didn't offer my services. She never let Mrs. Todd take me away to sew her frocks, neither. For that I thanked her, hoping she'd take that as a hint I didn't wanna be loaned out. Despite my bitterness at being property, I had it better'n the vast numbers of us folk. I wished not to be loaned in someone else's bondage. I would leave here for one reason—freedom.

"Not to fret, Oney, I cannot spare your talents to anyone, regardless of their needs. Mrs. Todd can make do with her own seamstress. Her habiliments are presentable enough. Besides, why would a Quaker want to dress at the height of fashion? That would be against her fundamental beliefs." Her tone soured on that last bit. Lady Washington wasn't keen on no religion but her own. She never tried to foist religion on me, tho. None of us got religion from them folk—it was entirely up to us.

But she offered all of our services to feed the poor at the Blockley Almshouse. My mouth fell open when she rolled up her sleeves and went out the door like one o'us. "Normally I'd take the coach but we'll walk the four blocks." In a sprightly pace for a woman her age, she led us to Spruce and Third Streets.

I knew why she wanted to walk. How would it look pulling up to an almshouse in their new English red-and-cream coach with painted panels of the four seasons, Venetian blinds, and silver-plated horses' harnesses? Even if she left the scarlet-waistcoated pos'tilions home. She hurried us to lessen inhaling of the odors of slaughtered animals and backyard privies. We walked nearest the houses to avoid stepping in the raw sewage and foul-smelling filth. She worked faster'n the rest of us, handing out loaves of bread, chickens, and vegetables to the beggars.

We finished our work as twilight fell, the glow of bonfires lining the street, the sewers smellier'n the thick smoke. "I'm far more useful here than at Mount Vernon right now," she told me as we turned the corner. "As during the war, my journeys to and fro camp in bitter cold were an awful hardship, but the reward was priceless. I feel similar to that now. Useful. Just as you are, Oney."

"Thank you kindly, Lady Washington." I knew her intention was sincere. But I knew what happened to the slaves who weren't useful. At least we had a choice in that. Do our labor good and we didn't get whipped or sold to the West Indies to be worked to death after two months.

The almshouse being down the street from Mrs. Powel's home, Lady Washington called on her. She sent the others back to the house, but brought me.

Mrs. Powel welcomed us both, extra cordial for her, being we'd called unannounced. She showed us into her parlour and offered Lady Washington a seat and punch. As always I headed for the kitchen behind the house, but Mrs. Powel stopped me. "You may stay here, Oney. I sent my surviving servants to New York."

She then surprised me by asking, "Would you like some punch, Oney?" She heaved a relieved breath when I said no. It wouldn't'a been proper for me to accept. It wasn't even proper for her to offer. But Mrs. Powel was ahead o'her time—yet not so ahead that she offered me a seat.

Lady Washington refused her offer, too. "No, Eliza, we just finished a long day at Blockley's. I wanted to extend an invitation to you and Samuel to visit us at Mount Vernon when we depart. I will do everything in my power to make George leave this dreadful place while the fever still rages, even if I have to resort to blackmail."

"I cannot, Martha." She shook her head. "Sam's obligations won't let him leave town either, although he's willing to let me go. But I will say, 'tis a dilemma the most painful. The conflict tween duty and inclination is a severe trial of my feelings, but it's best to adhere to the line of duty. The possibility of Sam being ill during my absence and deprived of the aid he'd derive from my attention would be a lasting affliction to me."

"I fully understand, Eliza, believe me." Lady Washington stood to leave. I handed her satchel to her.

****

Not a week later, Lady Washington near fell over reading the paper. "Oh, dear God! Look at this, George! Samuel Powel died of the fever. Oh, poor Eliza!" She lowered the paper and sunk down in her chair, eyes brimming with tears. "This fever—it won't give a soul a chance. It can take you just like that." She snapped her fingers.

"Say an extra one of your prayers in thanks that it's none of us, Patsy." The general then glanced at me, lips tight, head down in embarrassment, plain who 'us' meant. He cleared his throat and fixed his rigid gaze back on his wife. "But I now insist you return to Mount Vernon. This hit home once with Polly, so I cannot take another risk. Your staying here any longer is plain foolish."

"Not without you, old man." She stood her ground. "If I'm a fool, you're a fool right along with me."

He blew out a breath in defeat. "Very well, I'm a fool, too." He chortled. "I told you the last hundred times, I wouldn't be setting a good example by leaving. Besides, I've got to attend to those trade issues with Britain—"

"I am not leaving without you, George," she repeated, louder.

He placed his head in his cupped hands and rubbed his eyes. "All right! Have it your way. We will leave on the tenth."

I said a silent huzzah for Lady Washington who got her way more these days.

****

When we departed on the tenth, we didn't see no more carts piled with dead bodies. But the air and streets sat still and quiet, as if a heavy black cloud hung o'er the entire city.

She let me share the carriage with Miz Nelly and Washy, who prayed the entire way back, so I joined in. "Let the souls who've returned to You be in peace now, free from any more suffering and fever. Please spare the general, Lady Washington and all us folk from the sufferings of fever. We are your obedient servants, Lawd." As I spoke to God I felt a growing love for Him in my heart. Just as I finished, the gray clouds parted, bringing us a warm beam of sunshine.

"Huzzah, Oney!" Miz Nelly clapped. "Grandmama, Oney talked and God listened."

I shut my eyes and let the sun's warmth blanket me for this short moment. Mayhap He did hear me this once.

CHAPTER ELEVEN

After a jostling and exhausting five days and nights of rain, mud and muck, we arrived back at Mount Vernon on a breezy afternoon. Lady Washington leapt from her coach and skipped up to her beloved big house. She leant on the door and vanished inside. I stood scratching my head. She un-aged twenty years when she swang that coach door open. Just showed how happy being back at the farm made her. Us folk was happy to be back—that is, happier than at Philadelphia.

Afore I helped the others drag in trunks I snuck off to see Mamma. We hugged and wept our tears. I looked round the gloomy cabin and its meager furnishings. Pity pained my heart. I wept more tears—of guilt this time. There was me, livin' in the president's house in the city and in the big house here, but this shack and used leavin's was all she had.

A flash of anger tensed me up. Why did the Washingtons, with all their wealth, make their people live like this? It would'a cost less than the price of one of her gowns to build bigger slave quarters and feed 'em 'til they bellies full. I always heard the general hollin' over lack of money. Bull corn. He married the richest woman in Virginia and she ain't gambled it away on bid whist.

Oh, how bad I ached to take Mama back to Philadelphia with us, away from this! Without thinking, my hopes fell out my mouth. "Mamma, I'm'a ask Lady Washington to bring you with us when we go back to Philadelphia."

She shook her head. "No, child, I'll stay here on the farm. I'd be a'scared in the city. Tha's for young folk like y'all."

I planned to ask Lady Washington anyways. I wanted Mamma with me whether she wanted to go or not. One more servant in the house wouldn't crowd it. Mamma could share our room.

To lighten my heart and cheer Mamma, I told her and Delphy about the city. But I couldn't leave out the horrid account of the fever and Miz Polly's death. Mamma gave me an extra tight hug, sayin' "Oh, I'm so glad He spared you, my child. So many dead."

Her embrace warmed me in the chilly shack, but my feet still froze inside my thin shoes. "He spared all of us for a reason, Mamma, but I wish I know why. Lady Washington called on providence again. 'Our work here is not done yet' was her answer to it," I said. "She reads the Bible and tells me what she understands of it, and when I go to the African Church, I listen to the preacher what he says about the Lawd. What I learnt is we're all His servants, too, not just property of Lady Washington. White people the Lawd's servants, too, and save the soul who don't obey Him. Having learnt we're all servants, I'm not so resentful about being Lady Washington's property. She's property, too, and can't escape it."

Lady Washington stepped lighter these days. That skip into the house from the coach made her a new woman. She laughed out loud at the general's corny jokes and performed her chores humming Miz Nelly's pianoforte ditties. Early one morn, she flitted down the hall singing, "God save the thirteen states! Long rule the United States! God save our states!"

Next day she pranced in from the kitchen garden, her apron stained nut-brown with soil, singing, "Great Washington the hero's come, each heart exulting hears the sound, thousands to their deliverer throng, and shout him welcome around. Now in full chorus join the song, and shout aloud, great Washington!"

With a big *huzzah*! at the end. Her bell-like voice rang through the parlour down the hall. I knew the words, having heard them sing it as Miz Nelly played on the keys. I asked her, "Please sing that again, Lady Washington," and I joined along. We clapped for ourselves at the end. Our singing together bonded me to her more'n praying, for I knew her praying wasn't as heartfelt as "Great Washington".

Amidst the high-spirited mood, I asked her if Mamma could come with us to Philadelphia. "I suppose there's no harm in bringing her. But only if she wants to. I wouldn't want to force her to do something she doesn't want to do," was her answer.

I learnt a word called 'irony' but never heard it in real life 'til that moment. *No, Lady Washington*, I answered only in my mind. *Don't make your property do somethin' she don't want.*

But her permission made me so happy, I jumped up and down, squealing out loud. "Thank you muchly, Lady Washington. It means everything to have Mamma with me. Oh, bless you, bless you." I started to take her hand to kiss it but remembered who I was.

I ran to Mamma but she wouldn't budge even with her owner's permission. "I'll thank our lady myself, child, but I don't wanna leave here. The city with their bugs and plagues and sewers runnin' inna streets and heat don't appeal to me. You'll understand when you're old like me."

I trudged back to the big house, a mixture of glad and sad playing in my heart. Glad Mamma had the choice to come with us, sad that she chose not to. She'd die right there in that shack and spend eternity in the slaves' burial ground.

That eve as I helped Austin clean the porcelain plates with dry ashes, the general remarked, "It warms my heart to see you so happy to be here, Patsy. Before you know it, we'll be back here with nary a reason to go out past the gate." He voiced it every chance he got—neither of them wanted that second presidential term.

"I protested when you were summoned that second time, old man, but I don't hate it as much as I did the first term." She took his specs from atop his head, fogged them with her breath and polished them on her skirt. "Must be I've gotten used to it. It slowly grew on me, and I settled in. I'm always learning something new, whether it be about the city or the nation or the world."

Her features relaxed, and I swear she looked the age I remember her, with brown hair and smooth skin, her breasts hangin' way higher. Young, vibrant and thin Lady Washington once was.

"I knew you'd adapt, Patsy." The general nodded with that haughty look of his when "I told you so" played upon his lips. "One of the first things I learned about you after we met was how strong and resilient you are. You were widowed, yet ready to bounce back and conquer your world."

"Oh," she tittered, "I haven't hardly conquered any worlds."

"I said *your* world. You've become your own woman and stepped into the role you were meant to carry out. And I do say you make me proud to be the husband of our nation's most admired woman."

She sat up and studied him over her specs. "The nation's most admired? Now where did you hear that? I wasn't aware of a vote. If so, since women don't get the vote, it must've been all you men, and you wouldn't dare name anyone else but me!" She laughed, showing her clean straight teeth.

"No, it was in the papers. When I took the second oath of office, the articles all reprinted my speech, what I wore, what you wore … we're fashion plates now, and it proudly stated that Mrs. Martha Washington is our nation's most admired woman, from a general consensus of every citizen who followed your efforts and sacrifices during the war 'til you joined me in the president's house. Is all you read in the papers gloom and doom and the slanders slung against me?" He held out his glass for a refill. Austin dashed to the sideboard and fetched an uncorked bottle. I stood grinning ear to ear, buffing a silver candlestick.

"I must not have seen the papers that day." She studied her fingernails as she always did after gardening. "I was too busy readying the house for the feast and the mess afterwards."

As I held the candlestick up to the fire to admire its gleam, I mused over how the general's being president changed us all. Reunited with Mamma and Delphy, only for a short time, I knew city living helped me and Austin grow.

Now back at Mount Vernon my speech lessons resumed with the tutor. He made me recite words, then make my own sentences to put them in: "I ain't never seen you before" became "We've never met." "They house" became "Their house." "Dem" became "Them." "No more" became "Any more." And plenty of "-ings".

I couldn't yet read but simple words: at, is, the. But I was learning faster'n I figgered I could. "How long will it take me to read the papers like you?" I asked Hercules.

"Depends on who catches you tryin'," he answered, slicing turnips.

"Oh, Lady Washington is letting me learn. She even saw a newspaper I wrote the alphabet on and didn't bat an eye."

At that he stared me down. "She seen you write and didn't lash yo' back? I don't believe you, girl."

I gave him my biggest grin. "Tis the honest truth, boy."

He whistled in two-note wonder. "Them Washingtons is the kindest massa folk in the world. But not kind enough to free us."

He stopped his turnip-slicing and gave me a grin. "Good of the Washingtons to let us read what all we want. "Them the kindest massa folk in the world. But not kind enough to free us."

I answered my true belief, "Lady Washington may free us someday. She's becomin' real innapendent thinking like them ladies who gets educated and read a lot and write books. She's showin' her strong side. She ain't the lady of the house no more. You should hear her give the general what-for when she speaks her mind. He near shrinks inna his shirt collar. He ain't got as much quickness as her to give a comeback. I do believe she's smarter'n him." Of course I never used my fancy speech with

Hercules and the others. I couldn't rub it in their faces I was hobnobbin' with hoity-toity folk.

"She is smarter," he retorted, "too smart to free none of us." He looked me straight in the eye. "Someday you'll think of jumpin', Oney." His voice, low and husky, didn't sound like it came from him. "Ain't a slave alive who don't."

I broke into a sweat and my whole body stilled. Of course I thought of it. But I answered careful, "I ain't never thought nothin' of jumpin'. I have it good here. Why would I risk getting beat or sold to the West Indies?"

"You're young, Oney. When you're older and spent more years a slave, you'll begin to think freedom is worth the risk. Freedom, girl." He stared me down. "You might have it good here, might be well fed and comfortable, but you ain't free."

These thoughts entered my head in the dark of night when nestled under my clean covers, and more often in daytime, going about my chores. Thoughts of what it'd be like to have freedom—freedom to say, "I don't feel like workin' today" and go sit in the garden. But I thanked the Lawd for what I did have. Seeing beggars and urchins starving on the streets, I had it better than lotsa free folk. "You keep your voice quiet round here," I warned him.

He said right out, "I'm plannin' on jumpin'. Sooner rather'n later. I've had enough of bein' property. I wanna own my own body." His voice nowhere near quiet, like he didn't care who heard him.

"And go to where?" At that I started backing out of the kitchen, always a'scared to talk out loud about this.

"Not sure yet." He kicked at a chicken bone with the toe of his shoe. "Them free black folk we meet in church, they help slaves run. Absalom Jones and the Free African Society is gonna help me. I think it's 'bout time you come with me to hear how they do it."

"Shhhh!" I swatted his arm. "Not so loud, you dolt!" I peered over my shoulder, frantic that someone'd hear his loud mouth.

"I can make a livin' as a cook anyplace," he said in a lower voice. "You can, too, how good you sew." He caught my eyes and I held his stare. "I'm meetin' with Absalom and his wife Mary at they house on Powell Street when we go back to the city. We're gonna talk serious about where I can go to, and how they gon' help me. It'll do you good to join me. You might not think so now, but you will someday. So how 'bout it?" It came out so natural, as if asking me what I wanted for dessert.

I calmed a bit and nodded. "I'll go. What harm's in goin'a their house? I like to meet new folk. I ain't jumpin', though. It's easier for you, bein' a man. But when for you?" Knowing I shouldn't, I couldn't stop asking questions.

"Soon after I meet with Absalom and Mary." His eyes stuck on mine. "Surely afore the general finishes bein' president. Them folk, Absalom and Mary, and they friends, some of 'em you met at church—James Daniel, Sam Saviel, Aram Prymus, a few more—they arrange for slaves to hide places and ship passage to the north. You gotta stow away on the ship, but the captains, they don't say nothin'. They do it all the time, and nobody been caught and brung back yet."

I swallowed, this being hard to digest. "You takin' little Richmond with you?"

"If he wants. I ain't talked about it with him yet." He busied his hands chopping carrots. I could tell he was restive, cause he near chopped his fingers off.

Not so a'scared now, I stood at the kitchen doorway. "Let … let me know when you go see Absalom. If I have the eve off, I'll go. But you keep quiet 'bout it. Hear me what I say? You can trust me but don't trust nobody else." I shuddered with fear of someone hearing us—and not just some white folk.

Not wanting to talk no more about it, I turned and fled back to the big house, tripped and fell climbing up the grand stairs. As I scrambled to my feet, the black Bastille key loomed over me, dark and foreboding. It once locked prisoners away to their deaths. Now it hung on the wall, a constant reminder of bondage. I wondered why the general even wanted it in his house. I knew Lady Washington hated it. "George, take that dreadful thing down," she'd always demand, but he played deaf.

With Hercules's words tween my ears, my legs wobbled and my heart hammered. I never thought I'd hear nothin' like that spoken aloud. I knew he had free black friends, but didn't know they helped folk escape. I reckoned if a slave wanted to jump, he went alone, hid in bushes, swam rivers, starving and freezing along the way. I never knew nobody had help, and from such a big group, a church group no less. A church started by Dr. Rush, a white man—more of that irony.

Settled in my seat. I picked up a sleeve I been sewing. I looked forward to the meeting at the Free African Society house when we returned to

Philadelphia. I even began wondrin' what to wear. I had a new mint green frock I'd just finished.

Then Miz Betsy burst in. "Oney!"

I jumped out my skin.

"Oney, come here and help me do something." She turned her back and stomped out. I had no choice but to follow. We entered Miz Patty's bedroom where she lay asleep, her hair fanned over the pillow.

Miz Betsy handed me a pair of shears, pointy ends outward. "Here. Cut her hair off." She thrust the shears at my chest.

"Huh?" I stood still. "She ... she want her hair cut?" I stammered.

"No, she's got too much of it. Don't sass me, girl, I gave you an order, now do it. No sassing!" she hissed in a half-whisper as not to wake the poor victim. Again she jabbed the shears inches from my heart.

I reckoned real fast, this or that. What to do? If I cut the hair, I gets in trouble. If I don't, I gets in trouble. Then the solution hit me like a flash of light. *I am Lady Washington's girl, not hers.* With that I backed away and shook my head. "Sorry, Miz Betsy, I go check with Lady Washington first." I fled out of there to find Lady Washington but she wasn't nowhere to be found.

Miz Patty kept her shiny curls and Miz Betsy never mentioned it again. Nor did I. At least now she knew where my loyalty lied. She also knew who was in charge here, and it wasn't her.

Other than that, the entire household bustled with joy. Soft breezes blew in from the river and birds twittered. Lady Washington took me for walks and let Mamma, Delphy and other house servants join us. On her rounds of the kitchen garden and botanical garden, which she grew—her pride and joy—she delighted in showing us flowers from all over the world. "See, Mr. Jefferson took cuttings from these plants in France and grafted them to his own. He named them Jeffersonia diphylla."

"Figgers he'd name a flower after his own self." I wouldn't'a said this if I didn't know how she felt about Mr. Jefferson. But lately we traded barbs about him—if it was folk she didn't fancy, specially him, she demanded me to tell jokes.

"Tell me something queer I don't know about old Mr. Jefferson," she'd say to me, a twinkle in her eye, when the papers told too much bad news.

Then I'd need think of something queer I seen about him. "Last time him and Citizen Genet visited, they spent more time lookin' at each other than at you and the general."

She answered with a cocky grin, "They wanted to make sure each other's rouge wasn't wearing off."

In those moments I was truly her favorite pet. She had animal pets—some yappy dogs and goldfish allowed in the house, with goofy names like Bowser and Punkin. The general named his favorite war horse Nelson, but he died when I was little. His coach-horses—the blood bays he bred from the stallion Magnolia—them was stable pets, and pulled Lady Washington's coach to Philadelphia. Coachman Paris named them Ganymede, Callisto, Io and Europa—moons of planet Jupiter he learnt about at a Free African Society meeting. At them meetings they talked about more'n helping slaves escape.

Now she cupped a white bloom in her hand. "The jasmine here is about at the end of its season." I bent down to sniff the flower but she told me, "They only release their fragrance after sunset. Come back out here tonight and it will smell so sweet. These are foxgloves." She pointed to blooming purple bells. "They come up every two years. But they're poison if you breathe in the spores and pollen so don't try to smell them. You'll break out in hives and worse."

"Why do you grow poison plants, Lady Washington?" I backed away, not wanting hives.

"Because they're so pretty to look at. You don't have to touch them to enjoy them. Then again, one never knows when one will need poison," she added with that eye twinkle I saw more'n more.

That made me think. Lady Washington acted more playful lately. She always looked happier here at Mount Vernon, and the closer they got to the general's presidency ending, the more alive she became.

"This is the general's favorite, the English boxwood." She pointed to snow-white petals bordering the beds. "Over there the general planted the seeds from China, but none of us could read the labels on the packages, so we don't know what will come up."

"Mayhap when I learn to read good, I can read 'em to you," I said.

She laughed. "I mean they were in Chinese. It's hard enough to learn English first."

Pleasantly warmed from the sunshine, we strolled round her gardens, me beaming with pride now knowing most of the alphabet. I wanted to teach Mamma letters, but she didn't seem interested to learn.

Miz Betsy come striding from the big house, swinging her meaty arms, and joined us strolling across the bowling green. She huffed and puffed, her cheeks flushed and fuzzy as a peach.

"Betsy." Lady Washington shaded her eyes with her hand. "I just showed my people here my gardens. Care to take a ramble down to the river?"

"Yes, Grandmama." She wiped her brow and caught her breath. "But Patty needs Oney in the house. She tried on her new bodice and it's too big for her. But it fit me perfectly. So I'll take it. Oney, you can make her a new one for this eve." She gave me her narrowed-eyed expectant look that dared me to refuse. "She and some friends are going to stay with Thomas Peter's family in Georgetown. They leave in a few hours."

"B-but, Lady Washington," I addressed her rather than Miz Betsy, since Miz Betsy wasn't who owned me. "I couldn't sew an entire bodice by a few hours."

"Of course you can't, Oney." She turned to her granddarter. "Betsy, that's unreasonable and you know it. Patty can wear something else. And are you sure it fits you perfectly? I would venture to say it must be a wee bit tight on you if it was made for Patty."

I hid a grin behind my hand as Miz Betsy tossed her head and hmmf'd. Her hat slipt to the ground. "Get that, Oney." She waved pudgy fingers at the hat rolling on the grass.

I bent over to fetch her hat and held it out to her. She stooped to make me place it back on her head. "Not that way, girl, farther back. That's it."

Foxglove is poison, is it? The evil thought teased me.

"Betsy, why aren't you accompanying Patty and her friends to Thomas Peter's home?" Lady Washington asked her as we headed down to the river.

"Mr. Peter is courting her, and they hardly need me there," she answered a bit too resentful.

Mr. Thomas Peter, a fine gent, was courting Miz Patty, and Miz Betsy didn't like that not one bit. With naught else to do, she reared her jealous head at least once a day. She spewed snide remarks about him when she wasn't bashing on her sister, from her hats to her shoes.

"Your Mr. Peter is so homely and scrawny, what do you see in him?" she remarked to Miz Patty one morn, and "He's already half bald," shot out her mouth that same eve.

Lady Washington finally stepped in. "Betsy, you may not find Mr. Peter to your liking, but Patty is enamored of him as he is with her, and I believe it best that you keep your opinions under your hat."

"Yes, Grandmama dear," she mumbled, but I knew she'd save her 'pinions for when "Grandmama dear" wasn't in the room. Nobody could shut up Miz Betsy, even Lady Washington, the president of this house. The general didn't even try.

That eve, as I sat sewing a new bodice for Miz Patty, Miz Betsy stomped across the parlour, fists clenched, then back and fro again. She tsk'd and grunted, waiting for somebody to pay her some mind. Oh, she hated to be ignored!

Bottom lip thrust out, she crossed her ample arms over her doubly ample chest. Still nobody noticed her. She huffed, "I don't know what Thomas Peter sees in her," to her grandmother. She stood at the window, curtain pushed aside, breathing a circle of fog on the glass, watching Miz Patty and her friends climb into the Washingtons' coach for their journey to Georgetown. I'd helped Miz Patty dress in the muslin gown with heart-shaped bodice I'd made, and powdered her hair a silvery white, stringing pearls round the edges. But Lady Washington drew the line at a powdered and rouged face.

Lady Washington assured Miz Betsy, "Give it time. You will have suitors lined up at the door," but Miz Betsy was a year older than Miz Patty. Nobody knew more'n the Grandmama that Miz Betsy'd send a suitor fleeing soon as she opened her mouth.

Both girls didn't have much chance to socialize, so I 'spected Lady Washington would throw them together with the first bachelors to cross their paths. When it came to her nieces and grandgirls, she showed no patience waiting for love matches.

Miz Betsy finally stomped from the room, barking, "Pour me a bath, Oney. And it won't hurt to take one yourself. You're rather ripe." She sniffed the air. "You can bathe in the water when I'm through."

"I'm pleased to serve you, Miz Betsy, but I'll take a pass on that used water. I only bathe in clean water." As I turned to leave, she blocked the doorway, chest thrust out, fist on hip.

She raised her chin and stared me down. "You act too white at times, Oney." Her lips moved, her teeth clenched.

I answered evenly, "I'm white enough to act white at times, Miz Betsy. And my proper name, Ona, is white, case you didn't know."

Her hand dropped from her hip and she slunk aside.

"I'll fix your bath in a hurry," I assured her. "You can use one, too."

I s'pose Miz Betsy held her tongue instead of tattlin' my sassy remark to Lady Washington, cause I didn't get no reprimand. But I knew Lady Washington took Miz Betsy's tongue with a pinch of salt anyways.

As I helped Lady Washington dress next morn, she fretted over "my poor Betsy" with a dismal shake of her head as she spoke those words. Her "poor Betsy" laid on her mind more these days, since Miz Patty was courting.

"Oh, I do hope my poor Betsy"—along with the head shake—"finds a suitor soon." She released a long vocal sigh. "I need step in and seek a suitable match. Even though the general prefers me to stay out of the young ones' affairs."

As I combed her hair she lamented, "Whilst she could be absorbed in a novel or playing gay melodies on Nelly's keys, poor Betsy." Her head shake sent white powder fluttering to the rug. "She mopes about, doing naught about her luckless misfortune."

Poor Betsy's luckless misfortunes she brang about all herself, I burst to shriek, but that wasn't my place. Lady Washington knew full well, too, that luck had naught to do with poor Betsy's misfortune. 'Twas her demanding, manipulative self what sent many a prospect fleeing. But seems Lady Washington always needed some soul to feel sorry for. These days it was poor Betsy. She never pitied us folk, beyond poor, with no luck or fortune, bad or otherwise.

I was only allowed to nod agreement. She didn't want my 'pinion. Poor Betsy finding a suitor, be it by herself or with Grandmama's meddling, would get her out the house, and from Philadelphia when we returned there. So I hoped Miz Betsy snared a match—or mismatch—afore the general announced his plans to depart.

"Miz Betsy don't like me for some reason," I admitted.

"Oh, that's just her way." Lady Washington flicked her wrist, powder puff tween her fingers. "The spirited, headstrong lass takes after her father. Which is why I'm afraid she hasn't yet struck the fancy of any bachelors since she's grown into young adulthood. For her own good and for the security of her future I must intervene, and sooner rather than later," she said to no surprise of mine.

Fact is I feigned a cough to hide my grin. "Well, don' be dis'pointed with who's out and about the town, cause you won't find no one as fine as the general," I spoke my heart with no design to flatter, tying the sash of her skirt.

She gave herself a satisfied smile in the mirror, her teeth gleaming. "Of course not. I did the best of all. But I'll seek out a suitable catch—er, man—to withstand her temperament. Someone quite the opposite, else the two lovers would climb down each other's throats and neither would emerge the victor."

I gave a wordless nod, knowing she had more'n enough wisdom to have figgered that out. But where could she find a deaf mute?

She tsk'd. "Too bad George Steptoe married Mrs. Todd's sister already. He would have fallen for Betsy. He's quiet and refined and Betsy is ..." She let that hang in the air and I didn't dare finish it for her. She'd already said "headstrong" and "spirited", traits I found way too weak, not coming close.

I positioned her cap atop her head and arranged a frame of curls round her face on days she received guests. Throwing her grandgirls together with the general's relatives didn't bode well for family harmony. But it wasn't us folks's place to say.

"Twould be so unsettling for Patty to marry before Betsy, as Patty's the younger. I'll make it my business to find Betsy a suitor and have Patty hold off on her wedding plans until then," she said.

I stayed mum on this. But for a wife who stood "in my husband's shadow", she sho put on puppet shows with the strings leadin' directly to her grandgirls.

Few days later, I walked in on Lady Washington quietly weeping, hands clasped. About to turn and leave, I heard her call me. She spoke so softly I barely heard her words.

"Oh, Oney, terrible news arrived this morn from a courier, but that was preferable to reading it in the papers." She dabbed at her eyes with her handkerchief.

"What is it, Lady Washington?" The general was fine. He'd just got back from Washington City to lay the cornerstone of the Capitol building. Who was it this time? Someone she was fond of, so it couldn't be Mr. Jefferson.

"Queen Marie Antoinette was beheaded. The poor woman. I'm so sorry I never met her. She sent me a present, I'm told—which of course those dreadful British intercepted and sold. Still, it was a kind thought. Oh, when will the savages be satiated with blood?" She sighed, her eyes moist, focused on some faraway thought. "Mr. Jefferson despised her and said she brought all her troubles down on herself, but no one deserves such a fate. I wish I could have done something for her."

"What could you do?" fell out my mouth as I stood at her side. "They hate us to begin with, aside from Citizen Genet. But he made nothin' but trouble. You couldn'a saved her, Lady Washington. No one could, not even someone special as you. She been doomed for a long time."

"I wish the general had never taken that Bastille key from the Marquis." She wiped her nose.

I witnessed, that long-ago day in the big house, Thomas Paine handing the general that big ugly key from the Marquis Lafayette. I watched him hang it on the wall next to the grand staircase. I sensed it held a sinister aura about it. I always rushed past it. Lady Washington did the same many times.

"Mayhap it will fall off the wall and break," I offered.

She shook her head, pushing stray wisps of hair under her cap. "It is cast iron, indestructible. It will remain hanging here long after you and I are gone. Oh, the poor queen." She gazed upward and shut her teary eyes. "I pray it was quick and she didn't suffer the wrath of that merciless blade."

I once heard the general say the guillotine blade fell so fast, they necks didn't know what hit 'em. And as Lady Washington said every chance she got, "George is always right."

CHAPTER TWELVE

This blustery November morn Lady Washington mustered up the courage to bid another sad goodbye to Mount Vernon, and me to Mamma. Sobbing my heart out, I dropped to my knees before my mother. "For the last time, dear Mamma, please join us."

"I stay right here, my child, I live and die here. You go 'long with masta and missus. I'm too old to travel."

I stood and hugged her tight. "No, you're not!" I insisted, stamping my foot on the dirt floor. But I had an idea. Mayhap Lady Washington could convince her. After all, she gave Mamma permission.

I asked Lady Washington—rather, begged her, but not on my knees. I stumbled backward when she said yes. With a glance at the clock, she waved a hand up the stairs. "Fetch my outdoor shoes, and I'll walk over there." I tripped up the stairs, tears blurring my vision. Our merciful Lawd grew Lady Washington's heart bigger all the time.

I followed on her heels to the slave cabin, and she opened the door herself. Course she needn't knock. This door, this building and Mamma were all her property. I followed Lady Washington in. Mamma sat hunched over a bolt of material, cutting it with her tiny scissors. She straightened up and fixed her shoulders back.

Lady Washington stood in the doorway. She didn't go close to Mamma like she did me. "Betty, good day to you, I trust you have enough to keep you busy."

Mamma stood and set the material aside. "Mis'tis Washington, you didn't need come down here, I a'ready tole Oney I'm too old to travel, tha's fo' young folk like you and her." She gave Lady Washington a gaptoothed grin.

"I only ask because Oney misses you when we're away and you would like the city. Besides, you're hardly old. Why, you're no more than fifty-five, according to my roster."

"I feel old, Lady Mis'tis." Mamma shrugged and her shawl slipt off. "But I cain't leave Delphy neither, Lady Mis'tis." Mamma stooped to pick up her shawl, and I dashed past Lady Washington to drape it back round her shoulders.

Lady Washington glanced round the bare hovel as if seeing it for the first time. Then I reckoned it *was* the first time. She didn't even glance round the day she come for me. She suppressed a shiver and pulled her cloak tighter. I followed her gaze over the small space, drafts seepin' in through the cracks. She always did real good at not showing her thoughts. I hoped a strong shot of disgust hit her at seeing how her people had to live.

"Well, Betty, now that Delphy's older, she can join us, too." Lady Washington gave a resigned nod. I knew she'd never've included Delphy if I'd'a not begged her to come see Mamma. This was spur o'the moment, a true unstudied decision.

"Please, Mamma," burst outta me. I clasped her cold fingers. "We'll all be together again."

"Lemme think 'bout it some afore the next time, child." She looked past me. "But Lady Mis'tis Washington, I'm ever grateful for your kindness, to me and all of us."

I kept my face still as stone, hiding how it pained me to hear Mamma kissing her feet like that. Mamma didn't think like Hercules and I. She'd cut off her own toes afore even thinking of freedom.

"Then you may join us next time if you wish, Betty, and bring Delphy with you. It would greatly please Oney as you can see." She gestured to me. "Come now, we need leave."

I gave Mamma one last hug, convincing myself she'd join us next time.

On the short walk back to the big house, Lady Washington saw me swipe at my tears. "Don't cry, dear. If she stays behind it's because she wants to."

That's what broke my heart. Stay here or go there, Mamma would die a Custis slave. I only said back to Lady Washington, "I share yours and the general's wish, and that is for his time as president to be over."

She heaved a sigh. "Oh, if only. I counted the days 'til it started, now I'm counting the days 'til it ends."

We couldn't agree more, but for our own very different reasons.

****

With the cooling weather, the papers said the fever now killed less folk in Philadelphia. But at its most deadly, it killed one of every nine city folk who didn't flee.

This time we didn't stay at the president's house on High Street. Still fearing danger in the city, Congress met in nearby Germantown, a village where the general rented a part-furnished house. 'Til their two wagonfuls of furniture got delivered, they slept on couches, us on floors. Smaller than the president's house with only two levels, it sat across from the market square, to my temptation. I spent near all my money on sugar candy to send back to Mamma and Delphy. But I grabbed some bites myself.

Us folk was brave enough to ride to the city and bring back some market goods. Walking up Market Street, Molly and I looked round, mouths agape, eyes wide with wonder. "Mol, looka this place, they done clean it up right good!"

The streets were swept free of sewage, trash, dead birds and animals. The brown pavement and cobblestones now showed clean. I breathed in a gulp of air that didn't carry a sickening stench. Not one beggar limped along with a filthy palm out, no grubby street urchins scurried past. But folk dragged theirselves along, haggard, their trousers torn, their shirts dirty-stained, shabby, and reeking of vinegar. Their faces still kept a sick yellow hue.

More folk died, even after the first sprinkle of snowflakes powdered the ground. "The idea of danger is dissipated in a moment when we perceive thousands walking in security about their business and no ill consequences ensuing from it," Lady Washington read from the paper. "So says Thomas Adams, the Vice-President's son. But I don't believe him. He wants to be president someday, of course he has to keep hope alive. He's a politician in the making."

"Today a huge white flag hoisted over Bush Hill. It said 'No More Sick Persons Here'." Lady Washington read me it, but I read the word 'no' myself. My voice carried a lilt of pride.

"You're a smart girl and will learn to read well, Oney." She took the trouble to recognize that. "Persons might not be sick there," she countered, scanning the columns for more dread, "but the silversmith who made our goblets, Mr. Brooks, reopened his shop on October 31st and was dead on November 3rd. So it's not completely gone. But at least we're safe here." She folded the paper and cast it aside, gazing out the window, a crease tween her brows. I knew what she was thinking, and she voiced it. "I mean safer than in the city."

The president's house was safer cause Hercules told me the next day that white flag at Bush Hill got pulled down when more dead carts got there.

Even tho' we lived eight miles from Philadelphia here, we all pitched in, Lady Washington included, in scrubbing the walls and floors with vinegar, pouring lime down the privy, and had our own gunpowder barrels burning outside.

The general his self, without telling Lady Washington, got up afore the sun on Sunday morn. "I need ride into the city and see it for myself," he whispered, lest Lady Washington hear him, as I lit the hearth fire. If she knew he was fixin' to go out that door and gallop through them cursed streets, she'd'a drug him back in by his queue.

Of course she gave him what-for when he returned. "George!" She halted her scrubbing and dropped the rag when he told her he'd rode to Philadelphia. "The fever still lies in wait for unsuspecting victims. The silversmith died a week ago this very day. I don't—"

"Patsy," he cut her off, "the city is pristine. The air smells fresh, the streets are swept, and the only sign of plague is the red flag on a door here and there. I'm planning to reconvene Congress there again next month. No more waffling." His jowls jiggled as he shook his head. "The city is recovered. This nation didn't become great from being ruled by a bunch of lily livers. And that even includes Mr. Jefferson." He gave a low snicker that I matched and didn't try to hide it. Lady Washington still had no great affection for Mr. Jefferson and welcomed jokes at his expense.

"Speaking of lily livers …" Lady Washington wouldn't let him have the last word, president or not, "… Mr. Jefferson said yellow fever will discourage the growth of great cities in the nation. Oh, he is such a *bichon au citron!*"

I knew what that was, bein' Hercules baked it every time Mr. Jefferson was a dinner guest. It was a sweet French pastry, him bringing the recipe from France straight to Hercules in the kitchen.

Lady Washington raised her head in mockery of her detested French. The general didn't bother to reply. From what I seen, he had Mr. Jefferson figgered as hopeless. He didn't expect to see neither hide nor hair of him after he resigned to Monticello, Miss Hemings, and their many little ones.

I spent so much time unpacking trunks, airing out bedding, arranging furniture and cleaning, I didn't have time to sew, but Lady Washington gave me an assignment.

"I need you to make a wedding dress." She opened a book of Paris fashions and showed me the most elaborate gowns trimmed with lace and frills galore.

"I reckon this one would suit Miz Patty best, since she's slim enough for it." I pointed to a simple, elegant gown in the new high-waisted fashion. I reckoned Miz Patty and Mr. Peter would announce their engagement afore too long.

"Oh, no." She shook her head. "It's for Betsy."

"Miz Betsy?" I looked at the dress again, then at Lady Washington. That dress was more fit for a lamppost than for Miz Betsy. "Who you got to marry her?" The many young and not-so-young bachelors Lady Washington had matched up for Miz Betsy didn't last more'n two visits each, if that. Who'd she dug up I didn't know about?

"No one yet," she answered as if sewing a wedding dress with no groom was the custom. "But I must see her wedded before Patty ties the knot with Mr. Peter." She held out the book as if she herself designed all them fancy gowns. "The poor girl is so starved for attention. This will make her more confident and less prone to jealousy and, I trust, more pleasant company."

That's lotsa trustin', I thought. I hardly reckoned a wedding dress with a missing groom would make Miz Betsy any more bearable to be around, but Lady Washington gave the orders and I took'm. I began stitching soon as the patterns, satin and lace arrived from New York. She ordered the fabric and thread ahead'a time so not to waste a minute.

She wouldn't let me fit Miz Betsy during the sewing; she wanted it to be a surprise. But lately Miz Betsy put on more weight and jiggle. Her arms and hips and waist got wider, so I secretly let out stitches and added more material. If she burst it at the seams by the time she found a suitor willing to take her to wife, it be no fault of mine.

****

Hercules brought me to Absalom and Mary Jones's house next Sunday after church. Over on the walk, Hercules gave me a steady glare, saying, "I know you, Oney, you're a feisty, spirited girl who deep down wishes for freedom. Someday you will want it bad enough to take it. Believe me what I say. But you can't wait 'til the last minute, girl. You can't knock on they door and say 'I'm ready to jump now' and expect them to send you on your merry way the same day. You gonna run someday, even years from now. And you better start talkin' 'bout it now."

Those words struck my soul to the very core.

Mary Jones placed a cup'a tea in my trembling hands and I gulped it down. "Why you so a'scared, lil girl?" She smoothed my hair and guided me into their small crowded parlour.

"I ain't never talked to no one about this." My voice shook. "Sure I want freedom for me and all slaves, but I ain't never thought of takin' it myself. I keep prayin' they'll free us."

"That may not happen in our lifetime, Oney." She refilled my cup. "If freedom's that important to you, you can't wait for them to give it to you. You gotta take your destiny into your own hands."

I nodded, unable to take another sip. "In my heart I know you're right, but it ain't gonna be tomorrow."

Then her husband arrived, his bulky presence filling the doorway. I approached him, my head barely reaching his wide shoulders. He stood tall as the general, but broader with ropy muscles bulging under his bottle green jacket. I looked into his bark-brown eyes, warm and simmering under thick arched brows. His shiny hair curled neath his ears, so thick it could be a wig. Warm protection surrounded me like a comfy blanket, knowing that this man would well hide and care for me when I was ready to run.

"Mr. Jones, I am Oney Judge, Hercules's friend."

He grasped my hand tween his big paws. "So good to see you, Oney. Now, what brings you here today?" His voice boomed through the room as it did from the pulpit.

"Hercules brings me here today. Not to plan nothin'. Just to listen."

"Well, you wouldn't be here if you hadn't given it any thought at all." He placed his hand on my arm and edged me over to the window overlooking the cobbled street.

"Oh, I think about freedom every day. But I never thought of jumpin' as Hercules does. He told me, though, he knows me, better'n I know myself, that I'm the kinda person someday I'll take my freedom. Not anytime soon. It will take time and courage."

He closed his eyes and nodded, hands clasped, as if giving me his blessing. "When you're ready, you come to me or Mrs. Jones. Then we'll discuss how we secure your passage."

My mouth went drier than if I'd swallowed sand. "Thank you, sir. I can't talk of this no more right now. I need muster courage. And think about it much more. I ain't nowhere near past the thinkin' part." But as I talked of courage, my stomach churned. I shook. "I will be back, sir, you can count on that." I gave him a curtsey, same as I gave white folk, feeling more respect for Mr. Jones than I ever did for them. Then I fled. I walked the streets 'til the time to return to duty.

****

The front door slammed on this last morn of 1793 as I helped Lady Washington darn socks for her nephew. After supper and tomorrow, us folk could do as we wisht. Me, Hercules, Austin, and Molly planned to attend dancin' at the African church. I full expected to hear escape talk but didn't want my brother to hear none. Muchly as we all deserved freedom, running frightened me. But if I woke up and found Hercules gone, I wouldn't breathe a word to nobody, even the other servants.

"Patsy, do I have a new year's gift for you!" The general's voice boomed from the hall, louder'n the stomp of his boots on the floorboards. We looked up from our knitting as he marched into the parlour shaking the snow off his hat.

Lady Washington smiled at him over her specs. Seeing his coat covered in snow, she stood, led him to the hearth rug and dusted him off. "I hope you scraped your boot bottoms outside," she warned, ever the stickler for neatness.

"Of course I did, my dear. I wouldn't dare not." He slid out of his coat.

"I hope your gift isn't an invitation to go dancing tonight." She draped his coat over a chair.

"Hardly, Patsy, but the new year isn't the only cause for celebration. Our illustrious Secretary of State, M'sieu Jefferson, has resigned as of today."

She squealed, jumping up and down and clapping. "Oh, what joyous tidings! So he's put out to pasture. I do hope he finds what he seeks in his Monticello and his Sally and their offspring well into his twilight years."

"Well, 'tis hardly twilight for him." The general nodded to me as I presented him with the folded afternoon papers and his reading specs. He relaxed on the sofa and stretched his legs. I offered to pull his boots off but Lady Washington shooed me away. She wanted to fuss over him.

"Oh, is he going back to France?" A hint of hope lightened her tone.

"Much more ambitious. He wants to be our next president." The general snickered, opening the paper.

"And you call that a good news new year gift?" She sat beside him, lowered his paper so she could peer at him. "I hoped the last of this year meant the last of him."

"I'm sure it is. You don't expect him to win, do you?"

"No, I don't, and if *you* win, twill be over my dead body!" Lady Washington's shrill warning filled the room as Austin rang the bell for their brekkus. I followed the general and Lady Washington into the dining room.

I arranged their prized silver tray heavy with hot water pot, teapot and cups. Austin brought the hoe cakes I'd baked, kippers, hot water, tea leaves and a strainer. I filled the strainer and dunked it in the general's cup'a hot water, countin' to fifty, as he liked it. I didn't know all them high numbers yet, so counted to ten five times.

"Not to worry, Patsy, I told you this new year will be our year," the general assured her. "Ah, chamomile. And warm hoe cakes with kippers, my first and second new year's wishes." The general took the cup from me as I done counting.

"Of course, sir, smothered in honey jus' likes you likes 'em. I made 'em myself." I stood tall, gloating over my first attempt at the general's brekkus, as supervised by Hercules.

He took a bite with his mismatched choppers and closed his eyes. "Mmm-mmm, your talents in the kitchen will surpass those of your needle if this is your first attempt." He chomped at those hoe cakes, smacking his lips very un-presidential-like.

"Not only that, she's learning to read," Miz Patty came in and piped up as she sat at the table.

Lady Washington's eyes and mine met and locked. I began to tremble. Now I knew my final moments had come. The general would surely make Lady Washington brand me with a hot iron in the letter "I" for insolence on my cheek and sell me away. Terror rushed through me. I wet my petticoat.

But the seconds ticked away, and he uttered nary a word about it, just kept chompin' at those hoe cakes, licking his fingers and smacking his lips very un-presidential-like. Lady Washington held out her tea cup and I poured, spilling tea over the edge with my shaking hand.

She gave me a wordless glance as if to say "Tis fine with him." I could read Lady Washington's thoughts in her eyes most times. Now they crinkled as she broke into a smile that lit up her pale cheeks. "As I was saying, George . . . " Her eyes slid from me to him, as if to say my part of the discussion was over, and they had bigger matters to discuss, other than me learnin' to read. "You will serve another term over my dead body that you'll need drag back to the capital, for I refuse to permit that event to take place."

The general guffawed as he wiped his mouth with his napkin. "Not to worry, Patsy, I told Adams he'd better decide what he wants to be called, for it certainly appears he will be our next president. But he wants me to stay for a third term. And possibly a fourth." He took a breath. "Actually, 'til I croak."

"How could Adams have the brass to even suggest that to you?" She rapped her spoon against her cup with a musical clank. "I know what it is," she went on, not giving him a chance to answer. "From my talks with Abby, he knows he'll be a tyro in office, but how she feels is another matter." Her lips twisted into a smirk as she lifted her cup to sip. "At times she wears the britches in that family—his. Look under her skirt at any given time and you'll see her wearing his pair—of britches, that is."

"Does Abby want to be president, too?" The general matched her smirk, and I swore sometimes the general and Lady Washington had grown to resemble each other. They mimicked so many of each other's gestures and expressions.

"No, but as John's equal, she'll feel entitled to act as co-president, if he does win. And I daresay if he is given the honor, she'll pull his strings as if you voted in two for the price of one. You know how vocal she is in her opinions."

The general gave his wife a look with his eyes nearly crossing. "And not a morsel of that vocalization has rubbed off on you as of late?"

Her hand flew to her bosom and fumbled with her collar. "Me? I only give my opinion when asked."

"Patsy, although I don't agree with everything you say, I defend to the death your right to say it."

"Good to see at least one husband doesn't mind a wife who speaks her mind." Her voice and gaze lightened.

"Yea, I'm aware of some men who don't favor their wives being rather outspoken, but 'tis only because they know their wives are far smarter than they, and in some cases more educated, and they need save face, for their egos take a battering." He smoothed down his trouser legs.

"Why does it not bother you, then?" she taunted, picking up the last hoe cake, breaking it in half and sharing it with him.

"Because we are equally smart," came his answer, and ended that topic.

Smiling, she bit into the remaining ration of hoe cake. "And no third term for you." Her grin vanished and the thin lines reappeared round her lips. "I will personally let future-President Adams know that."

Miz Patty's head turned back and forth as if watching a lively tennis match. "A big huzzah to Grandmama!" She clapped. "And to Oney, the smartest of our people."

I forced a smile at that praise.

CHAPTER THIRTEEN

Lady Washington partly relieved me of one duty—she no longer wanted her hair dressed daily. So on non-tea party or levee or reception days, she combed it herself and tucked it under one of her low caps, saving the high ones for company, when she needed looking taller.

That gave me more time to learn my letters. Since Lady Washington didn't mind my learning, but showed no care to teach me, I depended on Hercules. He stoked the kitchen fire well past evening meals where we sounded out letters and words in the blazing warmth. When Miz Patty had free time she took me to her room and let me hold the quill pen. I fast learnt to write the letters I knew to read.

"Miz Patty, I near froze 'fraid when you told the general you'd been learnin' me to write. I afeared he'd give me a lashin' right there afore y'all! My mamma told me of the days when us folk takin' up a quill or a book was cause for a lashin' or worse."

She gave off a ringing titter. "No fear of that, Oney. Grandpapa never gives lashes. He cares not if you learn to write letters, or if Hercules reads Shakespeare. None of that's his concern. After all, you're Grandmama's sla—er, house servant. He may rule the country but she rules this roost. And Grandpapa being president, he's got much more important matters on his mind, such as ascertaining those men in Congress don't force him into serving another term. Now let's see you hold the quill…that's it, twixt thumbkin and first finger…"

I got adept at holding the pen and scratching out letters that didn't no longer look like a chicken run across the paper. "Miz Patty, I reckon this is easier'n a needle." With tongue tween teeth, deep in concentration, I managed to scratch out *Ona Maria Judge*. I held it up to the light in glowing admiration.

Afore I felt ready, she had me write to Mamma—only two lines, but in my mind I could see Mamma's eyes spilling over with tears lookin' at it— unable to read it, but knowing her child wrote it would make her heart swell with pride.

As I sewed the lace trim to Miz Betsy's wedding gown—the bride still without a groom—Thomas Peter asked the general's permission to marry Miz Patty. Of course he said yes, and Lady Washington wasted no time ironing out the financial arrangements.

Miz Patty flounced into the parlour and twirled before her grandparents in the new skirt I'd sewed her. "Grandmama and Grandpapa, Thomas and I are formally engaged as of today." Her words rushed out, breathless and run together.

Lady Washington looked up from her novel and peered over her specs. "And where is the intended groom? Shouldn't he be here for the formal announcement?"

"He's helping his mother for her levee tomorrow. Their gardener took ill and he's assisting her in arranging the floral centerpieces."

This got a chuckle from the general. "Arranging flowers? You sure you want to marry this lad, Pattycake? What's next, will he help his mummy apply her rouge? I hope to heavens he doesn't wear any himself. We don't need an Eddie Genet in the family."

"George!" Lady Washington gave her husband a playful slap on his knee with her bookmark. "He's a fine gentleman. So what he does flower arrangements? Sounds like he'll make a fastidious counterpart to Patty's ..." She glanced over at her granddarter, barely grown out of her tree-climbing and skinned-knee days. "I say they will greatly balance each other." She gave a resolute nod of her frilly-capped head.

"Sounds more like a match for your Betsy," the general muttered, then raised his newspaper over eye level, marking the end of his interest in this matter.

Lady Washington stood and hugged Miz Patty, her eyes brimming with tears. "I'm so proud of you, my dear. You'll make a model wife. And the most perfect mother. I cannot wait to hold my first great grandchild."

Miz Patty beamed at that. Lady Washington had Miz Patty's life all planned out for her; hence that was one grandgirl down and two to go. Young Miz Nelly would be easy enough to marry off, but Miz Betsy—that stayed unspoken, as Lady Washington quietly went about searching out the nation's most tolerant, easygoing ... desperate bachelors.

Neither Miz Betsy, Miz Patty nor Miz Nelly cared a whit about what went on outside their little world. They knew their grandpapa was president, but not much else about the nation. I knew more'n them cause Hercules read me the papers and now I could read a little. Then I took the papers and lined the cage of Miz Nelly's new pretty green pet, her parrot, Snipe.

Miz Nelly started learnin' Snipe to sing and talk, but he squawked words that made no sense. At times he said hallo. One eve when he chirped a dirty word, "aaaaaw, shite!" Miz Nelly blushed scarlet, but the general nearly spit out his teeth laughin'. "Oh, I thought little Snipe saw Mr. Jefferson come in. He'd have taken the words right out of my mouth."

Lady Washington tried to keep her lips from curling, but seeing the general's mirth, she cracked up herself.

"Oh, Nelly dear!" He rocked back and forth, holding his sides. "If that bird wasn't your feathered friend, I'd personally bring him to Monticello and gift Mr. Jefferson, so his ears could partake in that colorful vocabulary. Tell me, has he uttered any other like gems?"

"No, and I know not when he learned that." Miz Nelly sat froze with mortification.

"Simple, dear." Lady Washington cocked a brow at her husband. "Your grandpapa's vulgar senators. When in their cups, they forget they're gentlemen."

"No, not just when in their cups," the general corrected her. "You should hear them on the senate floor. They'd teach this feathered fellow a thing or a dozen about vulgarity."

Miz Nelly took good care of Snipe, who made a comfortable home perched in his cage lined with the detested newspapers.

Miz Betsy didn't like the bird. "We need some cats," she always snarled, a devilish gleam in her eye when Miz Nelly played with Snipe. I feared Miz Betsy's reaction—rather, outlash—to Miz Patty's engagement announcement, cause she got loud and boisterous when tipped over. And naught would tip her over like Miz Patty's engagement announcement.

Sure as Lawd made little green apples, Miz Betsy threw a string of tantrums, along with every object she clamped her hands on—a shelf of books, a candelabra, a hapless dozen eggs and every glass and dish in her reach—and smashed them to bits.

Lady Washington assured her in that soothing tone of hers, "Betsy, you will find a suitable mate, I promise. There are many fish in the sea."

Molly and I had to clean up the dregs of her rage. I growled from deep in my throat as I pushed the broom across the floor. Clawing at the floor with the broom, I watched not to cut myself as I brushed pieces into the dustpan. I bristled with resentment soppin' up runny eggs and broken shells from the floor. Lady Washington let Miz Betsy get away with so much monstrous behavior round here, with not a word of chiding. I heard of slaves tied to stakes in the ground and lashed, just for accidentally burning the edge of a waffle.

****

Fire could'a froze over that winter, and the Delaware River did. I took the extra material I hadn't used and wrapped myself up at night. Lady Washington complained of being dull here with no theatre or dancing. Not just cause of the cold, but lingering fears of yellow fever still a'scared her. Picturing mounds of dirt piled in the hastily dug graveyards, I shuddered.

The press's endless accounts of sudden deaths and warnings that the fever still raged put the fear of the reaper into folk. "They just want to sell papers." The general waved a dismissing hand as he flipped that day's *Gazette* onto the floor. "They can't bear it when the only news in the land is good. 'Tis scandal and fear that they prey on—and lies."

It didn't help the press sell papers in the president's house. Lady Washington cancelled her subscription. She made me and Molly purchase a paper when we went out, and she read only the politicks articles, but to herself. "I don't see any more nasty diatribes against you, old man," she addressed her husband.

"No." He wiped his specs on his handkerchief. "They tired of it and are building their ammo to unleash upon Adams, who they predict will be the next president. By all accounts he should be."

"Poor Abby." Lady Washington shook her head, same as for "poor Betsy" but less dramatic. "She doesn't know what she's in for. But—as she'll see—be careful what you ask for, you may get it."

Lady Washington's only lady friend in town this week was "poor Abby", Mrs. Adams, so she came to tea.

She arrived in a black coach, smaller and older than the Washingtons' but on purpose. Nobody could have a fancier coach than the president. She held some kinda gray furry animal, but pulled both hands straight outta it and handed it to me.

On close inspection I heaved a relieved sigh. It was only a muff.

"It is a muff, dear, for warming hands." Mrs. Adams stroked it like a prized pet. "Does not Lady Washington own one?"

"Yea, ma'am, Lady Washington has a few, but never of this size." I didn't dare slide my own hands inside, but held it atop my open palms. "I shall place it with your cloak, ma'am. If I may."

With an approving nod, she turned round for me to remove her cloak, patched in two places with fabric not quite matching. I could'a sewed it lookin' seamless but she clearly didn't have a skilled seamstress. I hid my smug little grin.

Now where did I see this cloak before? Course, it once belonged to Mrs. Bingham. Being so rich, I reckon she palmed her cast-offs off to the less fortunate. But the Adamses weren't poor, him being the vice-president. Mrs. Bingham could'a gave it to one of her people. What did Lady Washington think of the vice-president's wife wearing patched cast-offs? I knew she'd have a word with "poor Abby" about keeping up appearances if her husband became president.

"Abby, do come in." Lady Washington met her at the parlour door and they air-kissed each other's cheeks. Her warm welcome showed she needed female company, the kind me or her grandgirls couldn't provide. "And how do you fare?"

One thing I could count on with Mrs. Adams, you ask her how she is, she tells you. "Oh, Martha, my inflammatory rhumatism is acting up … 'tis now the sixth week since I've been out the door of my chamber or moved in a larger circle than from bed to chair."

I served the tea, but Mrs. Adams shooed it away. "No, dearie, 'tis far too cold for tea. Only a spot of English sherry can warm these cold bones." She tilted her silvery head. "On second thought, make it two spots. Fill a tumbler. You don't mind joining me in a tipple, do you, Martha?"

Lady Washington didn't mind a tipple, but she wasn't accustomed to her lady friends imbibing in daytime, since she didn't—only if some bad news sent her to the sideboard. Last time she tippled was when Mr. Jefferson quit the government, but that was for celebration.

On my way to the sideboard I passed Snipe's cage. He clung to his perch with his little claws and inched away from me when I came near. "Tweet tweet, hello, Snipe," I sang to him as I poured the ladies' tipples.

"Pretty girl," he sang back to me.

"Oh, how adorable!" Mrs. Adams took a pull of her tipple and went over to peer at the bird.

Lady Washington smiled. "He's Nelly's. Named Snipe. He already has quite a vocabulary and she's teaching him to sing *Pauvre Madelon*. But he only performs when he wants to, not when we request it." Lady Washington nodded at the chair next to her. "You may sit now, Oney."

Just lately she allowed me to sit at her teas rather than stand in the doorway awaiting orders. She ignored her ladyfriends's raised brows and one day told Mrs. Bingham, "They do get tired, dear. Even more than we do at times."

Today with only Lady Washington and Mrs. Adams present, I didn't expect a heated debate. Just ordinary gossip, but mayhap more vile, for the lack of theatre and dancing lately. I was disappointed in the end, but not too muchly. I found their visit amusing enough to be glad I was allowed to stay.

Lady Washington gave Mrs. Adams a few books and periodicals. "I'm finished with these. I thoroughly enjoyed this one, *A Simple Story* by Elizabeth Inchbald."

"But is that not somewhat ribald?" Mrs. Adams drained her glass of sherry and picked up a scone, heaping on double cream.

"To you, mayhap, with your Puritan sensibilities." Lady Washington tittered. "But we're in the capital city now. 'Tis about time you shed that New England morality and open your eyes and your mind. Even Dolley devoured it. She's the one who recommended it to me. So much for Quaker piety." She gave a lopsided grin that Mrs. Adams did not return.

But Mrs. Adams slid the book towards herself by the fingertips. "John and I don't read ..." As she talked she opened the book and her eyes bugged out. "Oh, heavens, I should not read this!" She slapped it shut.

"Oh, yes, you should," Lady Washington assured her priggish friend. "It isn't that salacious. And it was written by a woman. 'Tis only a love story, for Pete's sake."

"I heard all about it." She snuck the book open again and didn't stop reading. "Doesn't the girl have a liaison with a priest or some such equally scandalous?"

"Yes," Lady Washington answered. "The girl, Miss Milner, and the priest, Dorriforth, become undeniably attracted to each other. They give in to their passions and he gives up the priesthood for her."

"But he took vows. Cannot they refrain from indulging in such lewd behavior?" Mrs. Adams insisted, turning page after page, skimming, as if searching for those ribald bits she ranted about.

"If they did refrain, you wouldn't have a story," Lady Washington replied simply. "And it looks as if you've already indulged yourself." She looked over and gave me a knowing lip-curl. I struggled not to return it. Our place wasn't to share smiles with our owners and their guests, even if I was sitting. "Don't let the bawdy bits put you off, Abby," Lady Washington went on, but Mrs. Adams's scowl, lookin' like she walked into a root cellar full of rotten turnips, showed she was awful tipped over. "After Miss Milner dies—oh, sorry!" Lady Washington covered her mouth, "Didn't mean to give it away, but the story gets much more tame as her daughter takes over."

Mrs. Adams flipped through more pages. "John would greatly disapprove of me reading this."

"Then read it when he's not home. You need not ask his approval of your reading material. Come now, Abby, it is only a novel," Lady Washington urged.

"The author herself is a bit of a floozy, is she not?" Mrs. Adams put the book down, then lifted it again, opened it and peeked inside once more.

"She's an actress." Lady Washington shrugged.

"There's my answer." Mrs. Adams flipped to the last page and skimmed some more.

"But somehow floozies make the best actresses," Lady Washington corrected her.

Mrs. Adams hid a smile behind her empty glass, then she held it up to me. And it wasn't in a toast.

I jumped up and went to refill it—was that twice or thrice? She didn't look no warmer for having sherry instead of tea, tho. "We saw that buxom Betsy Bowen in a few plays back in New York at the John Street Theatre. She is a brilliant actress. Also a woman of ill repute I've been told, but I won't name names of her famous liaisons."

"I'll name two most famous names. Aaron Burr and Alexander Hamilton." Mrs. Adams's lips curled in a wry smirk.

Now it was Lady Washington's eyes bugging out. "How did you know?"

"Where have you been the last five years, Martha?" She raised her double chin and stared Lady Washington down. "News must trickle to Mount Vernon. But you never heard—or saw—in New York, Hamilton parading her round behind his wife's back? Goodness knows he's hardly discreet as is our charming Mr. Jefferson."

"My George considers Sandy Hamilton as a son. He'd never repeat something like that to me. But speaking of Jeff..." Now Lady Washington leant forward, the favorite subject of ladies' teas at length in the open, "Have you heard what hijinks he's been up to since he resigned his post?" Her voice rose with titillated glee.

"More than usual, with all that time on his hands, I expect," Mrs. Adams commented, still buried in that bawdy book. "He and John haven't been seeing eye to eye lately. His name is verboten around our house. What has he done now? Marry Miss Hemings?"

Lady Washington gasped. "Heavens, no, even he wouldn't..." She glanced at me and I pretended not to hear that, "No, he's been organizing his own political party and calling it the Republicans. Now how Frenchified can one get?"

Mrs. Adams scowled into the open book. "I'm so disappointed in him. Cannot George take him aside and tell him to redirect his zealous behavior? George is the president after all. All men in government defer to him."

She shook her head. "George has never been a man of extremes when it comes to these things. He is proud of his nonpartisanship. He despises the idea of political parties, as he says they pit one group of citizens against another, but he'd never interfere with politicks—he believes he's too far above it to be a politician. I agree he's above it. I hope you feel the same about John." She goaded Mrs. Adams with her sharp eyes.

The reply came but after careful pondering as Mrs. Adams also pondered her drink. "I don't feel my John is 'above' politicks or anything else, though he calls it the silly and wicked game. He's a simple farmer just like your George—well, a lot simpler—and regards politicks as a necessary evil—after all, what is the alternative? Anarchy. And our brave soldiers— and generals—didn't fight for anarchy." *So there*, said the jut of her chin.

"No, of course George doesn't want anarchy. He just hates the partisanship and power mongering. His cabinet is half and half, Fed and anti-Fed. But, in refusing to be a king, he lets it develop as it will. Our next president will have his work cut out for him." She glanced at Mrs. Adams with a knowing smile that said *chances are it'll be your John.* "So I trust he'll be up to the job of continuing the growth of our great nation."

Mrs. Adams put the bawdy book down and eyed the spines of the others. "Oh, I already have Mercy's poetry book. The poems are so pretty. A talented musician could put them to music. I relished the *Sack of Rome* story, but John couldn't get through it. Said it was too dry. John does prefer lively stories where he can imagine himself as the hero, but to his detriment he doesn't hold woman authors in high esteem. He'll never admit he's read a book by a woman author he likes."

I listened to this critique of books by ladies and couldn't wait to read better. I'd get my hands on every book ever written and read them cover to cover.

Lady Washington took a sip and put her glass down. "Mercy asked me in her last letter how I fared in my duties. But I told her I've begun to take some interest and pleasure in my duties as the presidential wife."

"I'm glad to hear of that." Mrs. Adams took a sip. "I ask myself questions about the future, especially if your husband will pass the torch to mine at the end of his term."

"It isn't a president's torch to pass, Abby. He's not king, remember?" Lady Washington fixed narrowed eyes on her.

"I mean urge him to seek the office, for lack of a better candidate." Mrs. Adams's voice lowered.

"The president wouldn't urge anyone. He might suggest it in passing. But urge? No." She shook her head. "I'm the urger among us. You and John know 'tis not an easy life." She glanced round the room at her trappings of this not-an-easy life. "I'm not complaining, I'm only telling you the truth. You'll lose your privacy and will have very little free time." She counted on her fingers. "You'll need to protect your children and their reputation. People will want to cut you down, and not because you're a woman. Your public behavior and your personal appearance will be scrutinized." She held up all five fingers. "So you must be careful about what you wear, what you say, how much you spend on china and even how you treat servants. Your every breath will be scrutinized."

Mrs. Adams looked deep in thought, her lips tight. "I will—would—fulfill my role if it was meant to be. Making history." She glanced round the well-furnished room with its rich drapery and rugs. Mayhap her farmhouse wasn't as posh.

After a few breaths, Lady Washington moved closer to her guest. "I sense you want this even more than John does, don't you?"

She pondered this a moment. "John believes it's his right to take over after George, although he's another farmer at heart. And don't ever repeat this to John, but—" She cleared her throat. "John is so sensitive. To lose the presidency would humiliate him so he'd never show his face in public again."

"Someone will have to lose, Abby." Her mouth curved downward. "But think the whole thing through. Let's face it, we're not chickadees anymore. A younger and gayer woman would be extremely pleased to be where I am—and where you may soon be. But the hard truth is this—we're defining things that will carry on long after us." Lady Washington wiped her brow with her handkerchief. "You will make a fitting Lady Adams if and when your time comes. But I'll be honest, the difficulties which presented themselves upon George's first entering upon the presidency seem to be in some measure surmounted." She let out a relieved sigh. "It took a term and a half for this to be. Of course it is owing to this kindness of our numerous friends," she gave Mrs. Adams a nod, "that my unwisht for situation is not a burden to me. Not as before."

"I admire you," Mrs. Adams heaped the praise. "I know how you enjoyed your life before all this." She waved round at the objects of hardship. "The first term did seem difficult for you. But you did a worthy job of maintaining the principles of democracy and the dignity of your positions. You're one of those warm and unassuming characters which create love and esteem."

Lady Washington laughed. "Oh, I'm unassuming, all right. You know me better than most. When I was much younger, I should, probably, have enjoyed the innocent gayeties of life as much as most my age. But I had long since placed all the prospects of my future worldly happiness in the still enjoyments of the fireside at Mount Vernon." She gazed into the blazing hearth.

"And you will again," Mrs. Adams assured her, taking another dainty sip. "Having seen all this thrust upon you, I now must prepare myself for that possible turn of events in our lives."

I wondered how Mr. Adams or any man could fill the general's shoes. I also feared for Mrs. Adams. She seemed to look forward to her husband's rise to the presidency. But she well knew what Lady Washington suffered in this role—the loneliness, stuck in the house with nowhere to go, accusations of behaving queenly, forced to step aside as her husband relished all the praise, getting credit for naught.

To me, Mrs. Adams was a bit delusional. Mayhap Mr. Adams would let her attend Congress meetings and speak her ideas. Or mayhap she'd stride in and take a seat even if uninvited. That pushy woman always seemed to get her way.

"There's no way to prepare," Lady Washington warned her. "I little thought when the war was finished, that any circumstances could have happened to call George into public life again. From that moment, growing old in tranquility…it's the dearest wish of my heart. But I have been disappointed."

"You must be somewhat content being chosen for greatness," Mrs. Adams flattered some more.

"George was chosen," she corrected. "No one voted for me, as no one will vote for you. I won't contemplate with too much regret disappointments that were inevitable, though George's feelings and my own were in unison with respect to our predilections for private life."

"John's and my predilections for private life aren't in unison," Mrs. Adams said. "If he's given the presidency, he'll carry it out to the best of his ability. He won't complain about it being thrust upon him, and I'd never discourage him from taking it."

"What if you did? Just supposing." Her brows rose. "I like to *what-if* on questions of the heart. It stretches the imagination."

Mrs. Adams hemmed a bit. "He listens to my opinions and ponders them. We usually compromise. But on rare occasions, depending on the issue, I let him have his way. It's easier that way. So, in this instance, if I really didn't want him to be president, I wouldn't stand in his way."

Lady Washington squared her shoulders. "George follows my advice—I mean on domestic issues, not on running the nation. I had more practice in marriage than he did. But he knows sometimes tis easier to give in than stand his ground."

"That's very democratic," Mrs. Adams said.

"No, it isn't," Lady Washington corrected her, and they shared an easy laugh.

I didn't share their laugh, unallowed to laugh in their company even if I found something hilarious. No, 'tis improper to make a joke out of things un-democratic. Didn't they ever stop to think how un-democratic they treated us, an entire race—even those of us near white as they?

"If that's what the people and God want for John and you, it will be," Lady Washington said. "I cannot blame George for having acted according to his ideas of duty in obeying the voice of his country. Having done all the good in his power will be some compensation for the sacrifices he made…in his journeys from Mount Vernon to this place." She glanced round the parlour again, and I saw by the lack of light in her eyes, she felt nowhere proud as when showing off her Mt. Vernon, where she was president—rather, queen. "But I, who had much rather be at home…I do not say this because I feel dissatisfied with my present station. No, God forbid. Everybody and everything conspire to make me as contented as possible in it. I'm still determined to be cheerful and happy in whatever situation I may be. I've learnt from experience that the greater part of our happiness or misery depends upon our dispositions and not upon our circumstances." She gave a decided nod and rested her head on the sofa's attached squab. "We carry the seeds of the one or the other about with us, in our minds, wherever we go."

"Sage advice." Mrs. Adams smacked her lips, the third tipple glass now empty. "I hope you won't mind my calling on you for more advice as—as time goes on and events unfold."

"Abby. I'm not saying I'll envy you when and if your time comes to walk in my shoes, but any time you need a shoulder to lean on and John isn't within reach, reach out to me."

"Thank you, dear friend." Mrs. Adams gave her a smile, lookin' like she near tears.

"Now let us forget about these matters and talk about something pleasant." Lady Washington glanced at the half empty sherry bottle. "But I assure you, Abby, sherry in daylight is hardly a habit with us. Cold notwithstanding." Lady Washington glanced at the mantel clock. "Speaking of sherry, I need to give supper orders. Senators Livermore, Bradford and Vining are expected with their wives, along with a string quartet. But I wish I could simply snuggle under a blanket with a romance novel," she sighed.

****

After that day, all winter, tea time became sherry time, and as the ladies loosened their tongues and promised to swap English trifle recipes, the neglected Snipe chirped up with "Yankee Doodle! Macaroni!" to the delight of Mrs. Adams. She sniggled behind her hand as Lady Washington laughed out loud.

"Seeing you so unscandalized by the bird's naughty palaver is the highlight of my day, Abby. If Gilbert Stuart were here, I'd ask him to paint Snipe charming the petticoats off you."

Even tho I shouldn't've, I laughed out loud. and no one chided me.

CHAPTER FOURTEEN

Next afternoon, another lively visitor arrived: Mrs. Elizabeth Peter, Miz Patty's future mother-in-law. She bustled in with hugs, jam jars, and a trail of dirt from her voluminous skirts. Along with Mrs. Peter pranced Miz Patty. Miz Betsy slogged in, lips twisted in a glower. The boisterous spinster still made suitors flee after a glimpse of her brash side. She never learnt to hide that dander under her petticoats when they came a'courtin'.

As I helped Austin serve a roasted piglet with potatoes, peas, beets and turtle soup, Mrs. Peter gave Lady Washington letters from home. She devoured them afore she blew on her soup.

"Oh, we're blest. No one has fallen ill or succumbed to the grave in over two months. Naught but glad tidings from Mount Vernon." She kissed the pile of letters and raised them up to heaven. "Elizabeth, I'm so happy Patty and Tommy have made a love match, just as George and I did. Romance is so rare among the young."

I muttered to myself as I swept crumbs from the floor, *and you ain't helping Miz Betsy any, throwing her together with every lone soul you can snag, just to get her hitched afore Miz Patty.*

She tied a pink ribbon round her cherished letters. She saved every letter in a trunk that traveled with her; she didn't trust providence enough to leave it behind.

Turning to Miz Patty, she repeated the same question on her lips every time the poor girl entered the room, "Have you set a wedding date, my dear?"

Miz Patty lowered her lashes and flashed a coy smile. "Not yet, Grandmama. I care not to rush." The same cagey answer as always.

"Well, time's a-wasting," Lady Washington urged, cupping her grandgirl's cheek in her palm. "Grooms such as yours are few and far between. Don't let this one get away."

As if Miz Patty would release him from her snare. Her coy smile became a smirk. Why hadn't she led her groom to this dinner party on a leash? Where was he? He done good having snuck out of her sight.

Miz Betsy, head down, pushed her peas round her plate. Without warning, my heart went out to her. All this fuss over Miz Patty, and Miz Betsy without a prospect nowhere near the horizon. Since I sassed back that day and refused to cut off Miz Patty's hair, Miz Betsy become ever so kind to me, so I knitted her a pretty shawl. Not as pretty as her unworn wedding dress, but she actually thanked me.

Miz Nelly, only fifteen, announced, "I am happy to be the bridesmaid at Patty's wedding, but twill be a long wait for Betsy's. I may be a great-grandmama by then." She cast a sly glance upon her mortified eldest sister.

That innocent child's remark got a deep scowl and a loud hiss out of the spinster Miz Betsy. She jumped to her feet, knocked her chair over and stalked from the room.

"Excuse me." Lady Washington dropped her serviette and hastened out to console her rebuffed grandgirl.

The other guests sat round the table, lips shut, fidgeting with serviettes and spoons.

Oh, Lawd, Miz Nelly gonna get it. I shook with fear for the poor girl. Lady Washington was indulgent, but when one of them childruns did wrong, even to each other, they suffered her wrath—no dancing, no romance books, no new hats for however long fitting the offense. Then they ran to the general for mercy, but he blustered and blushed, not wanting to invade his wife's territory. He never overstepped his bounds with Lady Washington, her childruns and her possessions—and that included us.

I never ran to the general for mercy but got in trouble so seldom, I never needed to. But Lady Washington made it plain and clear that the dower slaves she inherited from Mr. Custis were hers alone. She tongue-lashed the general many a time for giving us orders that didn't suit her. Which made life easier for us—she made sure the Custis folk did the easier chores, not the hard labor: plowin' fields, tendin' crops, harvestin' wheat, dryin' tobacco, curin' hams, picklin' apples, buildin' barns, carryin' fence rails, milkin' cows, drainin' swamps, herdin' cattle, shearin' sheep, loadin' cargoes, beatin' hominy, muckin' stables, packin' perch, sturgeon, herring, and bass, harrowin', plowin', grubbin' . . . and I didn't even mention the childruns forced to work in the trash gang.

CHAPTER FIFTEEN

With the general at Mount Vernon, the house slept in silence. I sat at the window in the sunshine and sewed ruffles as Lady Washington sat to write the general at Mt. Vernon. Every day she wrote him how much she missed him, the house so quiet without his gay prattle. And quiet it was, the only sound her pen scratchin' across paper.

She draped one of his jackets across his parlour chair and folded his specs atop his favorite book, *The Law of Nations*. His upcoming return cheered her up, for every time she entered the parlour, she strode up to the jacket and specs, predicting, "George will sit right here, and we'll resume as if we'd never parted."

Austin came in with the morn's post and she rushed over to retrieve it. Squealing like a love-filled young girl, she jumped up and down as she broke the seal of his latest letter. "Oh, how I miss my dear George. I wish he'd write to me more, his letters light up my days." Her sparkly eyes focused on the page and her lips moved as she read to herself. In an instant her smile vanished. She gasped and clutched her throat. Thinking she was choking, I rushed over, careful not to touch her, but would save her life if I could.

"What is it, Lady Washington? You sick?"

"The general had an accident ..." came out in a guttural rasp. As she caught her breath I grabbed the nearest pitcher and poured, not knowing what it was—ale, I hoped. Yet it could'a been hard cider, hard enough to choke her, bad enough to punish me. I handed her the glass. She gulped, swiping sweat from her forehead. Whew, it was only ale. She gulped again.

Calmer now that I knew it wasn't her dying, I asked, "What happened?" knowing she'd tell me, through tears and a string of uttered prayers.

"He fell off his horse." Her voice wobbled with fear. "He says he is better. I hope in God that he is so." She shook her head, her mouth a straight line, that same expression as when scolding him. "I disbelieve him." Anger crept into her tone as she mopped more sweat from her face and wiped it on her skirt.

Neither did I believe him. Knowing how she worried, he'd learnt to spare her the presidency's dramas. She read in the papers, not from him, about Congress's antics.

She scurried back to the desk, slippers scuffing. Her pen spattered ink as she scribbled to her niece, reading as she wrote, "If I could have come down with any convenience I should have set out the very hour I got the letter. I hope and trust he is better and that he will soon be able to return to here again. If he is not getting better, my dear Fanny, don't let me be deceived. Let me know his case and not say he is getting better if he is not. It would make me exceeding unhappy to be told he is getting better if he is not. I beseech you to let me know now how he is as soon as you can and often. My love to all my children ..."

She scratched out a few more words, folded, sealed, and handed it to me. "Oney, bring this to the post. It must go to Virginia immediately. I implored Fanny for the truth, knowing I won't get it from my husband." She cradled her head tween her palms, elbows propped on the desk. "God, watch over my George." She prayed when she wanted a favor from God, but I never heard her thank Him afterward.

"I know Lady Fanny will tell you the truth, Lady Washington. And if my mamma could write, I'd have her tell you, too."

She raised her head. "I do appreciate that, Oney. You are a dear companion to me when I need you." We looked at each other 'til I broke our gaze, not a second beyond how long custom said it should be. But I so longed to take one step closer and wrap my arms round her. An unexpected pang of guilt hung over me as I knew I'd be leaving here someday.

But my running to the post office provided the necessary distance from her presence and the house she let me live in. Now I could think without my emotions dueling. The more meetings I attended, the more I craved my freedom. Human beings in bondage all deserved freedom, and fleeting pangs of guilt wouldn't stop me. But the possibility of jumping still petrified me. No matter Hercules assured me I'd jump someday, risking a hundred lashes and the searing West Indies heat made my heart thump, my stomach churn and my body tremble.

****

She tore into the next letter from the general without the girly smile and giggles. "My hunch was right." She dashed the letter against her hip, crumpling it in her white-knuckled fist as she paced the room. "He wasn't as good as he'd first said. His back hurt so bad he can't even mount a horse to return to Philadelphia, and is traveling back on stages. I knew it!" She flung the letter to the floor. "He is never completely honest with me."

She strode over to me. "Oney ... " Hunched over my sewing, I pretended I wasn't listening. "Promise me you'll never marry a man who isn't completely honest with you about everything."

"How I s'posed to do that?" I stood. "The general'll be back soon, and you can take good care o'him. The best doctors are here, and he'll be good as new."

She shook her head, my consoling no help to her. "I fear it will be a troublesome complaint to him for some time." She rummaged in the desk drawer and pulled out her snuff box. "Or perhaps as long as he lives he will feel it at times." She dipped some snuff and started to sneeze, "Aaa ..." but pinched her nose shut before the "... choo!"

"And the presidency is hardly helping him." She wiped her nose. "If he is detained there any longer, I will get stage horses and go care for him myself." Her arms crossed over her bosom, head cocked. She looked so muchly like Miz Betsy in that dogged pose, I hid a grin.

But the next morn's post brought another letter from the general. "He left Mount Vernon in our own coach." She let out a groaning sigh, part relief, part anguish, shoulders slumped as she sank into her chair.

"That's good then," I assured her. "He'll be here faster'n them stages." The hope bubbling in my voice was real, for I looked forward to seeing the general. Lady Washington wasn't the only one who missed her George round here.

"Yes, and I must be patient with him." She folded the letter, pressed it tween her hands, kissed it and slid it into a slot in her desk. "As he gets older, he should be less brazen, but it seems he grows more fearless with each passing year. He's hard to keep up with." She met my eyes with a smile that I returned heartily.

"Mayhap he ain't gettin' old as you think," I offered my true belief. "The general keeps young by bein' brazen. To me he ain't aged one day since the first time I ever seen him."

"Oh, I've known him a lot longer than you." She stood and went to pour a glass of sherry. I used to jump up and insist I serve her, but she liked to pour herself. "When we first met he was a towering young soldier with thick red hair and a smooth face, always so smooth ... " She ran her fingertips over her own chin, and I knew she pretended it was him. "He must have shaved thrice a day. And so unpretentious. You know what that means?"

I shook my head. "Un means not. It means not preten—what you said." I still didn't know the big word.

"Pretentious." She smiled. "It means putting on airs. Another word to add to your growing vocabulary."

I repeated it: "Pre-ten-shus."

Her eyes shut and her smile widened. "Ah, my George hated talking about himself. I had to cajole it out of him, where he came from, who his parents were, what business they were in ... so modest." Her smile vanished. "Not like these haughty poseurs we have in government today, who haven't achieved two percent of what he has."

I knew two percent wasn't much—two of a hunnerd, I'd learnt from Miz Nelly's tutor.

"You're singin' to the choir here, Lady Washington." Now I refilled her sherry glass afore she did, knowing one nip wasn't near enough. "From what I seen of them men, they ain't naught but braggarts and full o'wind."

"Those men," she corrected.

A slave sharing opinions with her mistress was rare if not unheard of. But we'd developed this rapport bein' round each other so much, and I knew Lady Washington needed that constant companionship, someone to share thoughts and laughs. Of course I still knew my bounds.

"Well, Oney, that is the nature of men who enter politicks. 'Tis a quest for power. But in the general's case he didn't want it at all. Power means naught to him. He's a farmer first, a soldier second, and a politician third— a distant third."

"I'd say a husband first, my lady," I had to add. "He dotes on you and your grandchildruns more'n he ever doted on that farm, or the country."

"You are absolutely right." She looked at me, apology softening her eyes. "I'm ashamed of myself for having said that. I fear I'm beginning to think like those liberated lady friends of mine, whose marriages seem an afterthought."

I knew she was becoming liberated as those ladies, but to me it was naught to fear, she should'a been celebrating. Again, knowing my bounds, I offered, cautious not to overstep, "Lady Washington, these ladies are devoted to their husbands. But they want to use their own minds, too. They want to read and write and keep their books straight so no one steal from them. I do say now that I'm learnin' readin' and writin' I find more I want to learn about. Even if I am just one o'your people, put here to sew and serve."

"Remember the -ings," she warned. "No, I'm not of the mind to deny someone learning to read and write …" I saw her choosing the right words, "… when it's appropriate. You need not have vast knowledge. But I do enjoy having someone to talk to when no one else is about. 'Tis no fun trying to hold a conversation with a dummy."

"I do see that, Lady Washington. I see that whenever them men—those men—from Congress call here. And it will be much duller without Mr. Jefferson to banter about." We shared a smile.

"Oney, I'm going to teach you bid whist. I'm bored and want to play a game or two. Your duties can wait 'til we're finished. Not to mention my duties." Without waiting for an answer, as if I had a choice, she motioned me over to the card table and fetched a deck of playing cards.

I skipped over, pulled out a chair and awaited her permission to sit. Bid whist. If only Mamma could see me now. As their other three-hunnerd 'our people' toiled under the blazing sun, I sat in the house flippin' cards. Oh, yea, I'd moved on up from the slave quarters. However, as I was learning from the free black folk, 'up' was nowhere close to 'out'.

****

Two days after the general returned, walking normal but stooped over when he thought no one saw, another mess of bad news hit him in the face.

Hercules read me in the paper about the Whisky Rebellion, the first article I almost read on my own. I knew most letters and how they sounded, but I still struggled with big words. He helped me to finish the entire thing in no more'n ten minutes, 'cause I could now tell time. Some nasty stuff happened in western Pennsylvania, so it wouldn't come near us. Farmers out that way didn't want their whisky taxed no more. So they formed a mob, as did the French peasants that stormed the Bastille.

"Holy smokes, Herc, they ain't gonna storm the capital like them French did the Bastille, will they?" I trained my eyes on the headline, reading it out loud. "President Washington Calls Out Mil—Milit…"

"Militia," Hercules finished the word I couldn't pronounce.

"How can it be milisha? There ain't no 'sh' in it."

"That's the way the language is sometimes." His eyes darted across the column once more. "Letters sounds diff'rent what they look. A militia is an army. President Washington has state militias from Virginia, Maryland,

New Jersey and Pennsylvania, over fifteen thousand troops. You know how many fifteen thousand is?"

I shook my head with no idea. "Uh-unh."

"That's one thousand, fifteen times. One thousand is ten hunnerds."

"Now that's one thing I needn't learn, Herc. Counting aught to thousands."

He read on, "The president warned the western farmers to disperse and retire peaceably to their abodes by September one."

"Lady Washington talked about this with the general," I recalled. "He said it wasn't much a' nothin'.'"

"He's right. Compared to the war for their independence, it ain't much a' nothin'," Hercules said.

"You don't think they'll start a war?" Cold fingers of fear gripped my heart. "I'm a'scared for all of us. I heard stories about the real war, how people starved, got dragged off to prison, could get shot at any time. And now we got a mob of our own mad farmers to fear."

"No, Oney. Nobody'll hurt us. Go back to the house and sew a petticoat or somethin'." He put the paper down and went back to plucking chickens.

So that I did. Lady Washington sat reading with Miz Patty and Miz Betsy while Miz Nelly played her pianoforte. The melody soothed and calmed me. I took a few breaths, leant against the wall and let the strains float round my ears. All looked so peaceful and normal. I wouldn't dare speak about the chance of a war no more'n two days' ride from here.

Nelly stopped playing, looked over her sheet music at Lady Washington and asked, "Grandmamma, may I attend Mrs. Bingham's ball Saturday next?"

Lady Washington looked up over her specs and shook her head while answering. "I do believe their parties are too fast for a young lady of your age. It was rumored at their last ball the whole leg of the Bingham daughter was in view for five minutes altogether."

Miz Nelly plunked her elbows down on the keyboard, producing a clash of notes.

"Betsy, you should go to the ball." Lady Washington turned to the eldest of her 'little progeny' engrossed in that day's *Gazette*.

"I have no interest in attending balls," she retorted. "They're silly."

"You'd make Grandpapa and me very proud if you learned to dance like Nelly and Wash," she urged the girl on, but she crumpled the paper and stomped out.

But that very eve, they faced a new crisis—the general needed leave for Carlyle, several days' ride from here, to meet the troops. With a new uniform made by master tailor Mr. Graisbury, who outfitted the city's richest men, the general embraced Lady Washington and walked unsteadily, for he was still in back pain, to a plainer coach than their usual. "Going on horseback looks too war-like," he'd said as the weatherbeaten un-crested coach halted at the curb. Four non-matching horses pulled it. His postillion John Gaceer sat up front, without a scarlet coat. The general wouldn't admit he still couldn't ride horseback.

I turned round as the general and his lady whispered private sentiments to each other. But him being near deaf, her sentiments weren't so whispered. "I hug your shirt close to me at night. It's almost like hugging you," she near shouted.

When he gone, she craned her neck til the coach turned the corner, then dragged her feet back into the hall. I closed the door.

"Off goes my warrior once again," she droned, more to herself than to me as I followed her into the empty parlour. She looked round and found his specs on the couch. Picking them up, she wiped them on her sleeve and slipt them atop her head. "God knows when he will return."

"You have the girls and Washy," I tried to cheer her up. "And you have me." I wouldn'a said that a few years ago, or even last year. But our bond had strengthened, and we both knew it. She told me things she'd've told her grandgirls or lady friends if they were here. She gave me time off to go places, and let me talk to those ladies at tea, as I learnt more about politicks and events. I knew it was mainly 'cause I was a novelty—none of them other ladies had a almost-white pet like me, almost able to read, and knowing my subjects instead of sitting there dumb.

A scandal in itself among the ladies was me learning to read. At one reception, entering the parlour with the tea service, I heard that screechy voice, "My word, Martha, are you serious?" Mrs. Bingham upbraided her. "The n-e-g-r-o-e-s,"— she spelt out the word—"need not read. Why, it's downright dangerous. They're as children, incapable of looking after themselves."

I stood waiting for Lady Washington's answer but none came. She ignored Mrs. Bingham's remark and started talking about planting honeysuckle and day lilies. She told me one day, "I invite Mrs. Bingham just for show, and sometimes for laughs." Lady Washington didn't take everything serious, how most folk did.

Now she sat and picked up a book, opening to the marked page, but didn't read it. "At least I have something to look forward to. Mr. Madison and Dolley Todd are going to be wed in a fortnight." But she didn't look muchly like lookin' forward. Her eyes focused on the floor. She sat, deep in thought.

"You need me to make you a new frock, Lady Washington?"

"No, I'll wear what I have. I don't want to outshine the bride." The twinkle in her eye near lit up the dreary room.

"You will anyways, milady." And I meant it.

Her pensive look gave way to a smile. "Thank you for that, Oney, but I can't help wondering if Doll—Mrs. Todd—is acting too hastily in this marriage. He's so much older than she, and he's another Jefferson lackey, a would-be Frenchman. She will take a lot of calumny for that. I know the general is fond of Mr. Madison, but the general's closest followers consider him the enemy."

"Then they won't be invited, not to the weddin' nor none of her parties," I said. "Somehow I don' see Mrs. Todd as the kinda lady who cares what enemies think; they can kiss her foot."

"You're right about that, dear." She stood and set her book down. "She didn't seem to mind getting read out of the Congregation for marrying a non-Quaker. And I thought that would be more crucial than marrying a Jefferson lackey. Come, let's choose an ensemble for the wedding."

She led me up the stairs but I had a hunch I'd wind up sewing a new frock anyways. And I did—soon as she saw the new Paris fashion plates.

CHAPTER SIXTEEN

As I cut out the dress pattern, I noticed Lady Washington had filled out and grown plumper in a short time—time she spent frettin' over the general, and not cause of the horse fall—she just didn't want him being president no more. "Oh, Oney, the general still walks stooped over. He tries to straighten up when he sees me watching, but I know he's in constant pain. He need not hide it from me ..." Lips barely moving, she muttered, "Oh, why did I let him take that journey? I knew he was getting too old to ride horseback. He insists he's still got the stamina of a soldier ..."

Each frettin' starting with her, "George, you promised me you'd quit after two years," ended with his, "Patsy, that is the last I care to hear on the subject," which sent Lady Washington to the sideboard for a tipple. She now demanded we keep a bowl of sugar candy and Jordan almonds filled at all times. It was empty by early eve—no, not by us, we wouldn't dare touch 'em, only her. But I caught Miz Betsy snatchin' a pastry or two—or three. Lady Washington made it her morn's habit ordering Hercules to bake different varieties each time. Kept him on his toes tween cooking real meals and reading us the newspapers.

And, oh, them papers. How nasty they become. Every dress fitting of Lady Washington's for Mrs. Todd's —soon to be Mrs. Madison's— wedding, became a gripe session: "How dare Bache print these lies! Has he no shame or pride in his profession? He's blackening the entire profession of journalism with this rubbish." But I eagerly took part and even urged Lady Washington to vent her anger, easy as pie for me. I of course stood on her side of all issues, fueling her fire without creating a blazing inferno.

It wasn't just Mr. Freneau at the business end of Lady Washington's rants no more. Now Mr. Bache, Mr. Franklin's grandson, and his paper the *Aurora* sent Lady Washington into tizzies.

"Just don't read it, Patsy." The general always brushed it alongside his breakfast crumbs. "Yes, at times Freneau's and Bache's papers are outrages on common decency when treated with silence, but I cannot and will not take any forceful action against the free press." He rubbed thumb and forefinger on his nose where his specs rested. "Tis called free press for a reason. They already accuse me of monarchial leanings. What would happen if I tried to thwart their freedom of speech?" His unwavering stare told her he awaited an answer. Then he'd pronounce it wrong and march out.

"But they spew bald-faced lies." She rolled the paper and swatted at flies landing on the waffles, leaving mashed flies on flattened waffles. "Look what Lightning Rod Jr. said about you here," she branded Mr. Bache his well-known nickname as she unrolled the paper. "He has the gall to accuse you of standing against American independence during the war. He wrote an open letter to you." She adjusted her specs. "'I ask you, sir, to point out one single act which proves you a friend to the independence of America.'" She looked up and met his stare, unblinking. "How desperate is Bache to dredge up twenty-year-old events?"

"Desperate enough to stoop to that level," the general answered, tho I knew she'd asked him just to ruffle his feathers. "I wouldn't dignify that with a reply and he knows it. Bache is a tool of those wanting to destroy confidence in our government. He wants another France, just as Jeff does." The general got to calling him Jeff now he was out of office. "That will never happen and he knows it. But he still must sell papers. And by the looks of the stacks of them in this house, it is working. No wonder Bache lumbers round town in a gaudy calash and dresses like a bon vivant fop."

"Do not be flippant, George, we must read the papers." She crumpled the pages and handed them to Austin. "Here, put this half at the bottom of Snipe's cage and this half in the privy. Two fitting places for Bache's smut."

The general displayed his ill-fitting teeth in a grin. "No, we needn't read any papers, Patsy, specially poppycock of that ilk," he corrected her. "I told you, I sit there every day and listen to all the blathering in Congress. I can tell you what happens without the biased bent or the harsh opinions. You dignify Bache by reading his feculence. Even those romance novels of yours are more enlightening." The flip of his hand signaled drollery, but she went and picked up the novel that scandalized Mrs. Adams—she was now reading it for the third time—and motioned for me to follow her.

"Come, Oney, I need have that bodice fitted, and you need work on Patty's wedding dress."

Down the lemony-fragranced corridor we went, for Molly had just mopped the floor.

****

Miz Patty's wedding day loomed up fast, and the countdown didn't make the spinster sister any happier. Old Bets, as we nicknamed her in the privacy of our attic servants' quarters, dragged round the house, hrrumping and grumping. Finally Lady Washington insisted she attend a young people's dress ball for Mrs. Todd's young sister Anna.

"This is Philadelphia's main event, Betsy. You need step outside these walls or you'll never find a husband," she warned the spinster granddarter as I approached the parlour with a tray of mince pies. I halted in my tracks and ducked behind the door. I daren't walk in on this scene. They'd'a shut up if I'd'a come in, and I wanted to hear it.

"'Tis high time you step out on your own, because I've exhausted all the possibilities among the bachelors I could dredge—er, muster up. I am not fond of matchmaking, dear, but I needed try because of your refusal to even set foot out the house. And being envious of your sister—that is unwarranted. Patty met Mr. Peter at the cotillion you refused to attend. He could've been *your* groom if you'd attended and gotten to him first. You've only yourself to blame."

I held my breath waiting for Miz Betsy's reply, but she talked so low I couldn't hear the words. Unusual for her, always loud enough, to hear in Dinwiddie County. With that I walked in, the heavy tray near breaking my arms.

"Oney." Miz Betsy faced me, her back to her grandmama, forcing a smile through a quivering voice. "I plan to attend a ball Saturday next and would ask that you help me in choosing fabric for a gown, in a bright color, with lots of frills."

Help her choose? She never asked me to help her do nothin' exceptin' that time to cut off Miz Patty's hair. And that she hadn't asked—that was an order.

I set the tray down, my arms weary from the heavy weight. "I'm glad to help, Miz Betsy."

"Betsy is going somewhere in hopes of meeting a future husband." Lady Washington reached for a mince pie and took a hefty bite. Miz Betsy blushed to her roots. I made dumb and busied myself pouring tea.

"Grandmama, you needn't constantly remind these people I'm yet a spinster." But truth be told all of Philadelphia knew it. The *Aurora* seemed the only place that didn't blast it: *Lady Washington's oldest granddaughter still a spinster as the younger one weds*. What a scandal! One morn at market I heard fishwives tittering "Lady Washington's virginal granddaughter still hasn't snagged a mate ..."

I fled that market lest they see me and hammer me with questions.

****

Lawd forgive my sayin', but I rejoiced in one thing Lady Washington said muchly these days, "Oh, Oney, I am bored," over a sigh, gazing out the window into the empty street. When the grandgirls weren't home that meant either a few hours of bid whist and a break from my chores, her taking me for a stroll to the shops or planning another tea party. She held her formal Friday levees and their 'monarchial' receptions with Mrs. Adams at her side on a raised platform. In contrast, the cozy tea parties always brought forth lively chit-chat that evolved into scrappy debate, on the verge of clawin' and hissin'. But the ladies never went home mad. They agreed to disagree and air-kissed, to save their husbands embarrassment in the press.

On this blustery winter morn, swirlin' snowflakes tapped the windowpanes as if tryin'a get in. I helped Lady Washington on with her stockings as she slathered cream over her face.

Upon that despondent sigh I knew so well, her usual words followed, "Oh, Oney, I am bored. I need stir up some amusement."

I knew amusement meant one thing—a tea party with her smart-minded and smart-mouthed ladies.

I knew who I'd invite to tea next: Mrs. Judith Murray, who should'a been born two hunnerd fifty years from now. She had such revolutionary ideas about women. They flocked round her to soak up her 'pinions, and men downright quaked with respect in her presence.

"Lady Washington, please invite Mrs. Murray. I do so relish hearing her thoughts on ladies and men. Why, just 'bout everything she says makes me think for days on end as I go about my work."

She laughed, her teeth dulled in contrast to her creamed face. "I must agree Mrs. Murray has an inventive mind. But what interests you about what she says?"

"I have a mind, too, Lady Washington." Instead of feeling a'scared, I beamed with pride saying it, specially to her. "I want you to know I find other folk interesting, so you'll be proud to call me your confidante."

She nodded her understanding. "I know that, Oney. But you need not let such matters interfere with your duties."

172

"Oh, they don't. They make them easier to perform, when my mind is busy. My mind and hands can work apart from each other as well as together. So will you please invite her?"

She closed the lid of the cream jar. "That would be fine indeed." Her voice lifted with the mention of Mrs. Murray's name. "I've extended an invitation for whenever she comes this way. I'll write her again. She does enjoy calling on me. A change of scenery would do her good."

"Mayhap she's bored, lookin' for amusement, too," I ventured.

She scraped the chair back and stood, sliding into her shoes. "I'll write her now as not to forget. This will be great fun if Mrs. Murray can attend. She can talk some sense into Mrs. Adams about some books she should be reading to spice up … er, certain areas of her life."

I did notice a pattern here, specially since she left out the haughty Mrs. Bingham. All the ladies she invited were smart, forward-minded, always ready for a pow-wow, eager to haul it to the brink of mud-slinging ruckus, but of course these were ladies. The mud was always lavender snuff.

Yep, Lady Washington's spirits flew high when she brought her Judith and Abby together. I followed her down to the parlour where Miz Betsy's unfinished ball gown lay on the sewing table in my corner. I took my place and Lady Washington sat at her desk. As she got out her pen, ink and paper, she voiced her thoughts. She needn't for my sake, but enjoyed sharing with me her guest list each week—who was on and who was off. "I must invite some other ladies who will appreciate Mrs. Murray's intellectual offerings and who are near her equal…hmmm…Mrs. Powel…" She tapped her pen on her chin. "Of course Mrs. Adams and Mrs. Knox. I won't invite Mrs. Bingham. She's been too superficial lately, and I don't like the way she's looked down her nose at everyone, her own aunt included…if I invited Queen Charlotte she'd find a way to insult her."

"I know the other ladies'll prefer Mrs. Murray," I offered.

"She just moved to a new residence in Boston, so I'm not sure she'll be able to travel." She dipped her pen in the inkwell and began scratching letters. "But a visit from her would add brightness to my otherwise dull life here. Yes, Oney, and thank you for that idea. I'll be happy to allow you to converse with her when she arrives. But don't let her radical ideas about certain things frighten you."

"What radical certain things, Lady Washington?"

"Oh, about spirituality and the next life, subjects that usually aren't discussed in polite company," she spoke as she wrote, her pen scratching over paper.

"I ain't afeared o'the next life, Lady Washington. Can't be more to fear there than in this one."

As Lady Washington sealed invitations and bustled over her upcoming party, I went back to Miz Betsy's ball gown. She summoned me to her room for a fitting. I'd purposely cut out enough material for her bulging tummy and arms. As I pinned the material to her ample hips, she did something she'd never done before ... she poured her heart out to me.

"Oh, how disgraceful it is with Patty marrying first, leaving me as an old maid. I'm ashamed to even show my face anymore. I know everyone ridicules me behind my back." Since Miz Patty become betrothed, Miz Betsy kept her distance, and for now I become her replacement sister.

"I never heard no one behind your back," I assured her, tho that wasn't true, me being one of the guilty parties.

"Grandmama is right, I have no one but myself to blame for not going out when Patty did. I could have snagged a husband at any of those parties she went to." Eyes downcast, she shook her head, her voice quivering.

"Well, now you are, Miz Betsy," I assured her as I attached a sleeve.

"I have two good—what I believe are two good reasons. I cannot dance worth a whit, stumbling over my big feet." She kicked at the rug. "And I've no capacity for engaging witty banter as Patty does. My tongue sticks in my mouth when a suitor addresses me. I'm unable to give more than a yes or a no. Why would anyone care what I have to say?"

"Then get them talking about their selves," I offered. Even I knew this. "We folk never have problems finding things to talk about. The way to know someone is to ask about him. And he won't ask about you if he ain't innerested. You have lots to talk about. You're General Washington's step-granddarter, durn it. I'd'a thought men'd be tripping over they tongues wantin' to know you."

She turned to me. "Oney, you just solved a problem I've carried on my back like a heavy weight all my life. Get them talking about themselves. Oh, men fancy themselves the greatest thinkers and scholars and soldiers and businessmen. That is what I shall do at this ball. When I am introduced to a young man, I'll begin by asking about himself."

"Course, then you act like he's the most inneresting person in the world, even though he ain't. After you heard enough you move on." I finished pinning the sleeve.

I didn't talk the fancy talk with Miz Betsy. She knew how refined I was becoming.

She laughed—I'd never heard her laugh before. Ever. Her voice pealed like jingling sleigh bells. "Ah, yes, move on 'til the right one crosses my path." She stepped down from the platform as I helped her off with the pinned-together dress. She wiggled out of it and popped a stitch or two along the way.

"But the young men of my age are so unworldly, even if they've been to Europe or attended Harvard or read every book in Benjamin Franklin's library." She yanked on her dull gray petticoats. "Their interests are limited to their silly billiard games or horse racing or which ale goes best with mutton. I… " She cleared her throat. "I prefer older men," she confessed in a near-whisper. "They're so much more worldly and wise and—and gentle. Their hands don't fumble and grope and leave fingermarks on my velvets."

"I understand, Miz Betsy. When I'm ready for a husband I'm seeking an older man, too."

"You will have no trouble finding a husband, Oney," her genuine tone convinced me. She proclaimed this as if she could see the very future in my eyes. "But make sure you marry for love. I haven't told Grandmama but I am waiting to fall in love. Patty does not love Mr. Peter. She is marrying him for security and to escape the stigma of spinsterhood. But I—I know better. And so do you." She handed me the dress to finish.

With her forceful nod, we both knew I wouldn't breathe a soul of this exchange to anyone. Marry for love … it did happen at times. Lady Washington and the general, for one. But he was doubly lucky as she was so rich. Me, I had naught, so love was all I could hope for. I thought of it more and more these days, though I couldn't yet read them silly novels.

****

On a rain-spattered morn, we shivered in her cold bedroom, the fire's heat barely warming us. I helped Lady Washington dress as she sorted through the morning post. "Oh, look, a letter from Mrs. Murray. I do hope this means she'll be coming for a visit." While I arranged her cap, my fingers stiff with cold, she broke the letter's seal and read me parts of the missive.

"Your gracious invitation is an honor I shall be delighted to accept as John is traveling to Balto. and I am alone at present … but do not feel obliged to provide accommodation, as I have heard the president's house is rather crowded already … I eagerly anticipate our re-acquaintance."

She looked up and gave me a wide smile. "So you shall meet Mrs. Murray again, Oney."

"That'll be fine indeed." The thought of seeing her again warmed my hands and my heart. Mrs. Murray was so smart, no lady was her equal, not even Mrs. Powel. I appreciated her intellectual offerings and I was nobody. I couldn't wait to serve them and hear the witty banter. I knew Lady Washington would stir up a steamin' pot when them canny ladies perched on the sofas and crossed their dainty ankles.

****

Early on the morn of her lady party, I lit the fire in Lady Washington's hearth. The bed ropes creaked and she bounded out of bed. At the party I'd be allowed to sit and listen … and I always learnt lots from Mrs. Murray when she visited. Her sage ideas sounded centuries ahead of our time.

For the special day I chose my favorite flowered linen with bows on the sleeves. I'd sewed it from leftover fabric for one of Miz Nelly's frocks. Lady Washington chose her salmon-colored tabby silk with tucker, the lace ruffle I stitched round the neck. The Brussels lace at the sleeves matched the cap I'd made this season. Her unworn callimanca shoes waited at her dressing table to step into. Tabby silk came to her from Kashmere. She told me where that was. It sounded so far away I stroked the material with wonder, how something could journey from such a faraway land.

When I helped her on with the dress we both noticed it had grown tight, or her too plump. Our eyes met in the mirror. "Oney, somehow I don't think this dress shrank over the last month. Is there any way you can let the seams out in a hurry? I do so much want to wear this." She struggled out of it.

"Of course, Lady Washington." I spent the next three hours picking apart every stitch and adding a strip of fabric to the seams to make it larger. Thank goodness she had some left over, otherwise she'd be wearing a gown with unmatched fabric at the seams, lookin like it'd been letted out.

I finished minutes afore her party time, and the dress fit her as if I'd sewed it on. "Thank you, Oney." She let out a breath as she laid her hands on her tummy and sucked it in. "I must watch those sweets in future. But not today. Today is special."

As I combed powder into her hair, she chattered, "I'm so happy Mrs. Murray is coming today. I cannot wait to hear what she has to say, there's always something new."

Nor could I. Mrs. Murray always spurred deep discussion about subjects ladies never voiced in polite society—how religions differed, how scientific Unitarianism was, how females should be educated and learn to think for theirselves. She believed women didn't need men for naught more'n siring their babies. The ladies always sat rapt when she spoke—she didn't preach, she informed—with a voice that pulled listeners under some kinda spell. Her thought-spurring questions and beliefs changed many ladies' ways of thinking, including mine. But I dared not share that with a soul.

The first to arrive was Mrs. Adams at four chimes of the hall clock. When she swept off her cloak, I saw its faded and frayed edges. I so wanted to offer to mend it, but she'd take it as an insult.

"Close this door ... is anyone else here yet?" Mrs. Adams peered over my shoulder into the parlour.

"No, Mrs. Adams, but Mrs. Powel and Mrs. Murray are expected."

"Mrs. Murray is calling?" A smile brightened her eyes. "How about that! Martha ... Lady Washington, that sly fox, she didn't tell me."

As a light drizzle began to fall, I saw Mrs. Powel scurry up the street. I greeted her as she ducked through the door holding up her skirts. "G'day Mrs. Powel, welcome to President and Lady Washington's house."

"Good day, Oney, and how have you been faring?" She brushed raindrops from her overskirt, streaking the satiny material. Mrs. Powel always took the time to chat with me, more'n the other ladies. Eager to serve her well, I always poured her tea first—after Lady Washington, of course.

"Oh, just fine, ma'am. Busy with Miz Patty's and Miz Betsy's weddin'—wedding dresses—"

"Eek!" burst out. I jumped back, startled. She clapped hand to heart, grinning silly. "Betsy's wedding dress? Is she getting married too? A double wedding, how romantic." She clasped her gloved hands and shut her eyes in a dramatic fake swoon.

"Oh, no, Lady Washington is having me make Miz Betsy a weddin' dress, too, since she expects Miz Betsy to get married ... uh, someday ..."

I stood back and let Mrs. Murray enter, togged to the bricks. Her grass-green satin gown shimmered, trimmed in lace at the sleeves and cut in a low V over her décolletage. Two ivory combs gathered her dark red hair, tumbling in curls. A white gauze handkerchief circled her neck. I reckoned her waist buckle of dazzling stones wasn't of paste. Jiminy, she dressed for a ball, not an afternoon tea. She collapsed her matching green umbrella, revealing a pouf headdress of yellow satin in the form of a globe.

"G'day, Mrs. Murray. I'm much happy to see you again. I seen—saw you last in Mount Vernon when I first was allowed to work in the big house and never forgot you," I prattled on. "You wore a lilac skirt with a pink blouse and such pretty lace at the collar and sleeves. Do you know when I became more adept with my needle, I sewed one for myself just like it?"

She gave me a bright tooth-brushed smile. "That's very kind of Lady Washington to give you such liberties. In truth, when you opened the door I could've sworn you were one of her granddaughters and was ready to greet you as such. How embarrassing for me." She gave a hearty laugh that hardly sounded embarrassed. "But I'm sure you hear that all the time, don't you, being so light." She studied my features, my hair tied back and tucked beneath my cap. "But consider that a fortunate quirk of nature. I expect you enjoy privileges the darker ones will never see. Consider it the next best thing to being a true Custis."

Would that I were a true Custis ... I didn't dare voice it, even to this forward-thinking—and speaking—woman. I spoke my heart anyways, "No, ma'am, I am content enough with my lot in life and where the good Lawd put me right now." I added the 'right now' for my own reasons.

"That's a practical and realistic way to think, dear. It keeps deep disappointment at bay." She touched my cheek with her ungloved hand, which even Lady Washington never did. "But remember, no matter who we are, our lots in life can improve if we strive ourselves. And I did say ourselves." She voiced that last word with an intensity that matched her heather gray eyes holding mine. I never forgot it.

"Lady Washington didn't have a personal servant when I visited Mount Vernon last. I suppose, as the president's wife, she should have at least one. How many does she have?" She glanced round the entry hall that Eliza, Katy and me mopped and waxed 'til late last eve. Mrs. Murray ran her hand over the shiny banister and glanced at her fingertips. No, she wouldn't find a speck there.

"She got fourteen of us in the house doing the drudgery duties, but she calls me her personal servant," I said. "I spend the most time with her over all the others." I wasn't bold enough to add that she treated me as a companion. It stayed one of them secrets tween mistress and servant. "Asides my other chores of cleanin', washin' and waxin'—er, *ing*."

"What an honor for you." She stepped back and sized me up and down, full length. I was but a few fingers taller than her. "A step in the right direction."

Direction towards what? Was she hinting at something? I didn't dare ask, but led her into the parlour. The ladies chattered away, still standing.

Mrs. Murray gave Lady Washington a tight embrace. "Martha, you appear in your usual good flow of spirits."

"I am, and my little progeny are well. Do sit, ladies, do sit." Lady Washington gestured to the tight circle of touching chairs, arranged with a minimum of space tween them to create a cozy setting.

I retreated to my corner to take up my needle. I was sewing a petticoat from an old apron but wouldn't get much real work done over the next hour—this time was for list'nin'.

"Judith, how is everything in Boston? It's been far too long since we've seen each other." Mrs. Adams and Mrs. Murray kissed the air aside each other's cheeks, then sat side by side. "I am so glad you were able to make the journey. I trust it was comfortable."

"Very much so. All is calm and peaceful at home. John has been spreading his word about Unitarianism. I fill my time stepping in for him as co-minister." She settled in and spread her skirts about her. "I've been to the theatre and seen some good plays."

"Do not be so modest, Judith," Lady Washington drawled, as was her habit when gushing forth praise. "We want to hear about the plays *you've* been writing."

She took a breath as if deciding whether to divulge. "I'm working on my second play, a comedy, and may title it *The Traveler Returned.*"

"That's marvelous, Judith." Mrs. Adams tapped two fingers into her other palm in light applause. "I hope you'll use your real name this time."

"No, I'm still going to call myself An American Lady and possibly publish this and my first play under Constantia, my poetry pen name."

"But why, Judith?" Mrs. Adams persisted. "Susanna and Mercy use their own names. In fact, when Mercy wrote *The Group,* at first she wrote it anonymously, but I badgered her for so long to publish it under her own name, she relented and asked my John to verify that she'd written it."

"Oh, it's the risks, Abby ..." She sat back and folded her hands. "There's still a stigma against women associated with theatre. You know how the prim and proper consider theatre sinful and actresses whores."

Lady Washington's eyes widened. Nobody never said that word in the president's house.

"It can be very damaging to a woman's reputation, not to mention her family's, to be known as a playwright. Thusly I must protect my and John's and Julia's good names. Hard to believe," she scoffed, rolling her eyes, "that archaic mentality still exists at the brink of the nineteenth century. But I'll eventually publish them under my own name. Boston is still especially puritanical. So living there I'm at a disadvantage."

"Let us hope one day soon that way of thinking will shrivel and die," Lady Washington offered. I hid my surprise by turning my head to the wall. These days she thought more like her lady friends and spoke her mind. As a female, it gave me a shot of pride.

"My title traveler is Mr. Montague," Mrs. Murray began. "Long before the play starts, he deserted his wife who was engaging in illicit behavior with other men. When he returns to her in the guise of someone else, he's astonished to see her thriving. When he walks into her library and sees her reading a chemistry book, he realizes she's become a scholar. The premise is to show how utterly wrong males are in their presumptions about our gender."

"Bravo for you!" Mrs. Adams clapped with both palms. "You shall prove your point through your dramatic talent, which also proves members of our gender can be brilliant dramatists. Just the other night I saw the new comic play, *Slaves in Algiers*, at the New Theatre. Has that played in Boston yet, Judith?"

"*Slaves in Algiers*?" Lady Washington leant forward. "I didn't know of that, and I see all the plays that come to town."

"It just opened here, mayhap you didn't see the notices. Susanna Rowson wrote it. You know who she is. She authored that *Charlotte Temple* book everyone raved about. But I didn't quite take to it." Mrs. Adams scowled. "A bit too risqué for my tastes."

My ears perked, but I kept my hands looking busy.

"A comedy about slavery?" Mrs. Murray's voice didn't sound amused. "I must have a word with Susanna and ask the American Sappho what she finds comic about slavery."

"No, she's not making comedy about slavery," answered Mrs. Adams. "She makes it plain the comparison tween marriage and slavery."

"Some marriages, mayhap," Mrs. Murray scoffed.

But I bristled, sitting there in my corner. How dare a playwriter compare marriage to slavery, even to sell theatre tickets? If only I could write, I'd tell the naked truth about slavery, nothin' in common with no marriage!

Mrs. Adams explained, "'Tis set in Barbary, off the North African coast. American slaves plot their escape in their quest for freedom. Mrs. Rowson herself acts in it, she plays Olivia—she's an agreeable singer." She waved a dismissing hand. "Not the best, but her writing is better than her acting or her singing. She went a bit too far with the Jewish character, Ben Hassan. He borders on parody—'I wantsh to know ven you tink your ransom vil come … '" she mimicked the accent. "Way too affected. But I do say it's one of Mrs. Rawson's better works."

Truth be told, now I burnt and itched to go see it, eager to learn what these folk found comic about slavery.

When Austin brung in the tea and plum cakes, I dashed over and filled each dainty china cup, starting with Lady Washington. I then poured Mrs. Adams's sherry. I knew she wanted it full, so it spilt as I carried it over. I made sure Lady Washington didn't see that—they never let a drop or a crumb go wasted.

"So," said Lady Washington, "I'm so glad we're all re-acquainted and all is going well for everyone."

"But not so well for you, Martha," Mrs. Powel commented. "How has life been since the president's fall?" She tipped three spoons of sugar into her tea as she talked.

Lady Washington cast her eyes downward, looking sorry she'd brung it up. "Things haven't been the same. I worry about George all the time anyway, all his travels, his long hours at work, the endless demands his underlings make on his time and talents. But since the accident, he's been walking stooped over like an old man and at times merely shuffles. He hasn't stood up to his full height since." She added sugar and stirred her tea but talked too much to sip. "We have two doctors calling to give him daily massages. He feels good about ten minutes after each massage, then starts walking bent over again. So I started rubbing his back every night when the doctors aren't here. I've become quite deft at it, and am developing strong fingers." She kneaded an invisible lump of dough in the air. "Since he's spoilt with that, now he has me walk on his back every eve afore bed."

"Walk on his back?" Mrs. Adams's head pecked like Snipe the parrot. I muffled a laugh. "I wouldn't want to do that to my Johnny," she tittered. "I'd fall off!"

Mrs. Powel quipped, "Just make sure your Johnny never wants to do that to you."

Lady Washington went on, "He says I'm the perfect weight on his back, and my feet the perfect size to help loosen those muscles, so at bedtime, he lies on the floor and calls to me, 'Care to take a stroll, Patsy?' and I know that doesn't mean through the garden. So I take off my slippers and stroll to and fro along his back, til he falls asleep. Then I help him crawl into bed."

Mrs. Adams said, "John has had his accidents. He's fallen off horses and wagons, tripped over a rock and fell flat on his face . . . he was laid up for weeks so I know what you're going through." She laid a sympathetic hand on Lady Washington's arm, being she sat so close, the ladies elbow-to-elbow. "But John, oh, how he grouses. He's a terrible patient. I hope George doesn't let it whittle away at his better nature."

Lady Washington gazed up at the crown molding. "It is hardly easy. He doesn't complain when others are around. You'd think he could still leap fences, but when it's only us, he grumbles, 'How I wish I could just go back to the farm and leave the government to its own devices!"

She mimicked his gruff tone quite well, I thought. Near better'n him.

"Of course it's naught but rubbish." She tossed her head. "No one could drag him from the presidency before his term is up, 'my servitude,' as he calls it. But if I mention nary a word, he blows up at me. 'Not a chance, Patsy, I was put here by providence . . . ' he says."

"John is of the same mind. Providence put him where he is and providence will...oh..." Mrs. Adams covered her loose lips with two fingers. "I shan't say any more."

Mrs. Murray gave her a little shove. "I know what you want to say, Abby. Providence will put you in the same place Martha is in now."

Mrs. Adams shook her head. Curly wisps bounced from her cap. "I don't know providence that well. That's beyond my control."

"Come now, Abby," Mrs. Murray urged her on. "You know providence as well as I do—its powers are unlimited. Most of us Bay Staters have the same beliefs in that area. I know where your and John's ambitions lie."

"No, I'm not going to push the issue. If John wants to be president I'd never stand in his way." Mrs. Adams glanced at Lady Washington, who shot her a beady-eyed glare.

"Abby, you of all people well know I did not—could not stand in George's way when those men elected him president." Her tone sent Mrs. Adams's brows arching. "They'd have knocked me over and trampled me. I may have voiced my feelings, but I didn't expect him to heed my advice. He didn't even want the position." She looked at each lady separately. "And I wanted it even less. No one elected me, but here I am." She picked up her cup and saucer, sipped and set it back down with a clank.

Mrs. Murray said, "Our husbands are ambitious and we're blest to have them, but at the same time, they chose us as their wives for a reason. They weren't going to marry empty headed twits who want to grow lilies and host tea parties…"

They all *tee-hee*'d at that, and so did I. Quietly.

"They chose us for a good reason—I mean aside from—not to be crass, but aside from the men who married for money," Mrs. Murray went on, "and we're here for a reason. We chose each other. And we know exactly why." She brought her cup to her lips and sipped, rather, slurped—not as dainty as the others.

"Oh, yes, George and I…it couldn't have been anyone else," Lady Washington spoke with pride. "George is my God-given partner. I only wish we'd met sooner—not that I regret marrying Daniel. But I was so young when I met him." She frowned, her lines deepening. "At the time, in my young maiden's mind, I believed he was the right one, but when I met George, all the pain and grief of Daniel's death vanished into the ether. He mended me, made me feel whole again, wanted again." The other ladies tilted their heads, cradling their cups and saucers, looking enthralled at this confession. Dreamy smiles played on their lips. Now I knew why they read romance novels. They never heard naught like this in real life.

"Yea, Martha, we all think so differently when we're young things." Mrs. Powel laughed. "When I ponder my early amours, I cringe. Oh, what disasters any of those marriages would've been." She gave a theatrical shudder.

"You're very fortunate, Martha." Mrs. Murray leant over, grasped the tea pot and poured her own refill.

"I'll get that!" I sprang to my feet.

"No, dear, I've got it myself. Go back and sit." She turned to Lady Washington. "You should publish your letters to and from George for future generations to relish a true love story."

"Oh, noooo, Judith." She shook her head, tugging at the lace of her cap. "When the time comes I must burn every letter George and I ever wrote."

"But why?" she insisted. "Affaires de coeur such as yours are so rare."

"George and I share words and feelings—and pet names in our correspondence that I care not to give anyone privy to. I do share a lot with you ladies, but we're all entitled to our private moments with our spouses."

"Heavens, what's in these letters?" Mrs. Powel prodded.

Lady Washington said no more. But from what I heard of her loving exchanges with the general, I knew she had every reason to burn them letters.

Just then the parlour door groaned open and hit the wall with a thunk. Miz Betsy stomped in, munching a cookie, but seeing the crowded circle, halted.

"Oh, I didn't know you had company, Grandmama." She turned to leave, knocking a fruit bowl over as she plodded out. I scrambled to fetch up the scattered grapes.

"Stay, Betsy," Lady Washington said. "You know everyone here. Mrs. Murray came all the way from Boston to visit. Do stay." Lady Washington then called on me. "Oney, bring up another chair for Betsy. You can ask Austin to help you move it."

So with the help of Austin, we dragged Miz Betsy's favorite chair tween Mrs. Powel and Mrs. Murray. They stood for us to slide their chairs further apart to widen the circle.

"I'll have some of that tea, Oney. With a teaspoon of honey and not a drop more," Miz Betsy commanded, and I handed the pot to Austin to refill. I knew Lady Washington wanted me in the room, so I went back to my sewing in the corner.

Afore Miz Betsy even sat, they all swarmed upon her faster'n summer's muskeetoes, just as I knew they would.

"So, Betsy, how do you feel about Patty getting married first?"

"Are you courting?"

"Have you been helping Patty with her wedding plans?"

They blasted the questions like shot from a cannon. But Old Bets held her own. I smiled in secret, pleased with the stroppy what-for she gave them. "I care not if I ever get married … I don't need a man … I will marry for love if I ever do marry …" For every question fired, she shot back a terse answer.

Lady Washington, wiping flushed cheeks with her handkerchief, told Miz Betsy, "At the moment you become smitten, you'll feel different. And I do wish you to marry for love. But he won't come busting down the door and sweep you out of that chair and into his gilded coach. You'll need meet him at least halfway."

The others tittered.

Mrs. Murray, her expression solemn, drew her chair nearer Miz Betsy for a one-to-one lecture, shutting the others out for the time being. And shut they did.

"Betsy, about making sure he's the right man, even if you're an old spinster in your thirties, don't settle for a man you don't love. 'Tisn't worth any amount of riches or prestige to have a man who disgusts you, slobbering all over you in bed every night."

The other ladies nodded. Lady Washington tried to hide a knowing smirk.

Mrs. Murray went on, "The romance novels aren't realistic, but they can serve as a guide. Don't read them to escape what you hate in your life. Read them to reaffirm your own romance, to act out the scenes with your own hero, to laugh over and have the characters amuse you, the absurd situations they get into, their bickering and push-pull of tension. Don't ever read them as a substitute for what should be real. You be the heroine of your own life and let your man be your hero. Just like your Grandmama and Grandpapa."

"I should wait for a man like Grandpapa? A man I hope will be president someday?" Miz Betsy scoffed. Devouring her cookie, she reached for a plum cake as Austin entered with another teapot, hot water pot and a jar of Miz Betsy's honey. "I may die an old maid before I find someone fit to lick his boots. My husband will always put me first," she proclaimed. "I won't have that problem because I do not need a future president."

"It is more than a tad unrealistic to expect a husband to put you first. In fact it's downright delusional," Mrs. Murray lectured. "Men have their own agendas. Only rarely do they follow ours. And make sure you do have an agenda that interests you, Betsy." She pointed her finger like a pistol. "It is our duty to inform our husbands that we have interests and causes outside our marriages that might not match theirs. Our interests shouldn't put a strain on the marriage, but they should keep us busy and fulfilled. And I don't mean a dalliance on the side," she added with a saucy grin.

Lady Washington sputtered out her tea at that warning.

Miz Betsy finished her cake and licked her fingers, taking all this in.

It didn't affect me none. I heard of dalliances all the time among us folk, and nobody thought nothin' of it.

"You're young," Mrs. Murray went on. "Your generation will be much more liberated than ours. Make sure you stand up for yourself, your own person, your own body. A marriage certificate is a contract. And a contract is signed by equal partners. A thorough education will ensure your equality and fitting companionship with a spouse. We no longer have to be household drudges."

"Here here," Mrs. Adams agreed. "Women should be equally educated. After all, we are equally intelligent."

"I am well educated," Miz Betsy asserted. "But Grandmama told me that the husband makes the major decisions, and the wife runs the household—so he'll have something pleasant to come home to," Miz Betsy said with a full mouth.

"Of course you'll run your home, but that doesn't mean you're unequal. Remember, at times he won't put you first—but at times you won't put him first." Mrs. Murray sipped her tea. "It's very rarely balanced like a perfect scale. For instance right now my John is traveling and I don't particularly want to be without him, but I know the result will benefit us both."

"Then you are fortunate his absence makes your heart grow fonder," Miz Betsy said. "I see husbands and wives apart all the time. In those cases 'tis out of sight, out of mind. I want my husband with me at all times. If he travels, I travel with him."

"But it is not always possible." Mrs. Murray untied her neckerchief and flicked it off. "You cannot fret over being number two in his life, and sometimes three and four. You need bend quite a bit to make it work. If you haven't read Mary Wollstonecraft, I urge you to. I agree with her to the degree that I could have written it myself. This may sound avant-garde to the uninitiated, especially to you older ladies, but a lack of a woman's ability to support herself has a destructive effect on her mental attitudes."

"Why would I need support myself?" Miz Betsy's haughty tone filled the room, much like she did. "My step-grandfather is the president of the United States, and as a Custis, I am already rich."

"Fortunes have ways of being lost," Mrs. Murray warned. "Favor is deceitful, beauty is vain, property precarious. Women—and I also mean women fortunate as we are—who can host tea parties all day, need education to make a living. I strongly suggest training in occupations not usually practiced by women. But learn to manage business affairs for themselves and their children in the event of the husband's death."

As the others sat rapt, she went on, "Goodness me, this happened enough during the Revolution. Not every woman is as fortunate as your grandmama, to inherit a fortune as a widow. If women were educated for a wider range of occupations than, say, teaching, they'd be spared the necessity of marrying for support. Women are midwives, why not physicians? Or politicians? Or any sort of business?" She splayed her fingers. "A milliner's, a dry goods store, a tavern? At the very least, learn how to balance the books."

This made my heartbeat race. With my mastery of the needle, I could open a dressmaker shop someday.

Miz Betsy didn't look convinced. Her stuck-out tongue plainly showed her disgust at being a physician. "So where does love come into all this?" she prodded. "I want to find a man you describe, but who will fall in love with me."

"Sorry to tell you, that may never happen," Mrs. Murray answered. "Seek out respect instead. Love *can* grow out of respect. You can be happy without being in giddy love like a fictional heroine. Your Grandmama and Grandpapa were fortunate in that regard. They fell in love right away." She turned to face Lady Washington. "Didn't you, Martha?"

"It wasn't instant," she answered, a faraway look in her eyes. "It was mutual attraction, but I do confess, not love til later. After we grew to know each other—and respect each other."

"Same with us," Mrs. Adams agreed. "John and I were—I won't say it, but you ladies all know what I mean—maybe not you yet, Betsy, but John and I, say, wanted each other before we loved each other. And that wasn't til after we were married. But we're both very lucky it happened at the same time. You're better off in a loveless marriage than falling in love with a man who doesn't love you, Betsy."

"You'll find out when the time comes, love won't even keep a marriage together if you don't like each other," Mrs. Murray advised, her tone instructive.

"Abby, is all well with you and John?" Lady Washington peered at her friend with concern in her eyes.

"Yes, all is fine twixt us." She fiddled with her gold wedding band. "But John is frustrated that his vice-president position won't allow him to participate in the Congress's discussions and lawmaking. He brings that frustration home with him. But I urge him to keep busy and look forward to a bright political future. That seems to calm him, most of the time."

Mrs. Murray said, "Tis easy enough to predict, Abby, you will be sitting where Martha is now." She turned to Lady Washington. "And I daresay, Martha, you won't need tell Abby much in the way of preparing for her role. She'll take to the office naturally, for she's a strong and capable personality."

"Why, thank you, Judith, you are a diamond of the first water," Mrs. Adams said. "But Martha has shown me much for preparation. Just watching her I've retained mental notes on how to conduct myself. But I beg to differ on the title. Being called Lady Adams isn't quite my style. I'll ask to be addressed as Mrs. President."

Lady Washington stroked her chin, entertaining an inner thought. "Mrs. President would be a fitting title for you, Abby. John will value your partnership in office, not the way George regards me. But I admit tis been my own fault. Unlike you I waited way too long to assert myself. Alas, I am Lady Washington for the remaining days of George's term." The downward cast of her eyes and her defeated tone showed that it truly bothered her. "If I knew then what I know now . . . " She trailed off and waved the regrets away.

"I'd make a terrible president's wife." Mrs. Murray wound her neckerchief round her wrist. "I'd want to run the country along with him."

They all gave knowing nods as if to say, "That's Judith!"

"Now you're being unrealistic, Judith." Lady Washington's voice rose. "As the president's wife, I am very much in George's shadow, given my role as such, and I must honor that role by staying in George's shadow. You'll never see a president's wife running the country at his side."

As I served the tea, all but Miz Betsy thanked me. She just leant forward, grabbed another cake and undaintily stuffed it into her mouth.

"Oney, you may resume your sewing. When we need you, we'll let you know," Lady Washington gave me my orders, and I sat ... 'when we need you' meant I'd be invited to talk later. Goosebumps of excitement popped up on my arms. Ladies always listened entranced at my answers to their sometimes personal, sometimes silly questions, the pet learning to write and read the papers. They had views on that, for or against. So I settled in my chair, took up my needle and went back to work, ears perked. I could tell their lecturing of Miz Betsy would fast lead to the juicy goods Lady Washington really invited them for.

"Betsy, I can safely assume you've never worn that collar I gave you for posture. You need sit up straight, dear. It is essential to health and beauty to hold up the head the throw back the shoulders." Lady Washington showed her by sitting straight, chest thrust out. "You won't attract a man of any station looking the sad sack you are."

"The collar was a form of torture, for all of us," Miz Betsy snapped. "It was reminiscent of the slave collars, except those poor wretches had no ribbons to hide them." Still, she slumped over in her 'sad sack' posture.

Mrs. Powel's mouth clamped shut.

"I was confounded over how scandalized Abby was over *A Simple Story*, the novel about the priest," Lady Washington changed the subject and saved the moment.

"Oh, Martha," Mrs. Adams jumped in, "I'm no prude, but that's just not my kind of reading. I do have to agree with Tom Jefferson, reading fiction wastes time that can be employed instructively, and they poison the mind against wholesome books. Not all novels, of course. But you know the kinds of books I like."

Mrs. Powel jeered, "I suppose you and Tom Jefferson think *Charlotte Temple* is a poisonous waste of time, then."

"I read *Charlotte Temple*, who hasn't?" Mrs. Adams shot back. "Mrs. Rowson is an entertaining writer. I hope she writes more plays. Entertainment has its place, but I prefer subjects I can learn from. I read from John's vast collection of books, and our children teach me quite a bit, too. They're miles ahead of me on most subjects."

"You can learn from romances," Lady Washington argued. "I must admit I've learned one thing—George isn't the lothario everyone thought he was when I married him." They all chortled. Neither was their own husbands, I reckoned.

"We can all learn from silly novels," Mrs. Murray agreed. "It's always to our advantage to understand their theme and emulate that in our own amours. If we're lucky enough to have any."

I still wondered when they'd get to the serious talk as they prattled on about decorating, dinnerware and art.

Mrs. Murray cleared her throat loud. "Enough of this tea party palaver ... we all know Martha's real reason for inviting us ... serious discussion. I don't mean so serious that it's not enjoyable ..."

"Oh, of course not, Judith, you're a barrel of fun." Mrs. Adams gave her friend a sporting grin. "So, what do we need to talk about among us, to solve the problems of women everywhere?"

"Let's start with the women in this room," joked Mrs. Powel, giving a hearty laugh. "Then we'll spread our influence farther afield."

"Not that we need any help," Mrs. Murray remarked. "Last few times I talked to Martha, her thinking was more enlightened about certain things." She turned to face Lady Washington. "Weren't you, dear?"

"It's not just you who's been giving me ideas, Judith. It's my girls, the younger set, some of my women friends." She nodded at Mrs. Adams and her hand rose in acknowledgment. "Reading works by Mercy Warren and Susanna—ways of life are changing since the war and I need to change with them." She sighed and shook her head. "But I cannot do much 'til George is out of office. Our country gained independence, and now *we* need gain independence. We women." She gestured to all of them.

I sat sewing make-believe stitches in my corner. But rules forbade me to say a word 'til asked. I just pretended to stitch, as if my ears were shut off, no matter how it captivated me to hear this kind of talk about women—of course they omitted 'us' women. I cringed thinking how little they thought of us—and specially Lady Washington, with her own half-sister being part black and still enslaved.

Mrs. Adams gasped. "Martha! I never thought I'd hear you talk like that. You were always so dutiful and ..." She searched for a word but Lady Washington said it for her.

"Subservient?"

"No, not quite that extreme. I meant you always support George and seem content to be as you said, in his shadow."

"Seem content," Lady Washington repeated. "That is a show, Abby. Standing in his shadow is hardly satisfying. Once I finish serving in this role, I cannot go back to being the farm wife. It's hard to explain unless you've walked in my shoes. I also have three granddaughters to raise and want to make sure they—as you said, Judith—think for themselves, not as extensions of their future husbands."

"If I acquire one," chimed in Miz Betsy.

Mrs. Powel said, "Oh, your grandgirls will think for themselves, all right. I doubt it is just coincidence as we reach a new century, ideas and ways of life are changing and growing."

"Martha, I don't know if you've been reading my essays," Mrs. Murray said, "but the talk of liberty prompted me to challenge the belief about our status as women. After all, patriots wanted liberty to govern themselves. How about for women to govern ourselves? I've been writing about having equal minds and calling for a thorough education. My first published essay paved the way: *Desultory Thoughts Upon the Utility of Encouraging a Degree of Self-Complacency, Especially in Female Bosoms*," she rattled off in one breath.

Mrs. Adams grimaced. "Is that the title or the essay?"

"Do you write the essays under a pen name?" Mrs. Powel asked her.

"Yes, The Gleaner. But I do believe those in the know are aware that I wrote it—or, that a woman wrote it. No man would dare write something like it."

Mrs. Powel held up her pointer finger. "Right, I read that when it came out. It lingered in my mind for many months. I discussed it with every woman I know." Her words rushed out in an excited stream. "'Tis way ahead of its time. A few nuances told me a woman wrote it. But I didn't know it was you, Judith." She clapped. "Good work! I hope it gained the recognition it deserved."

"I read it, too," Lady Washington chimed in. "I don't remember everything in it, but that title sticks in my mind. I knew either you or Mary Wollstonecraft wrote it. But her style is more preachy."

"It was back in '84 to be exact," said Mrs. Murray with a proud air, "in the *Ladies Town and Country Magazine*, a Boston periodical."

Mrs. Powel commented, "I didn't think a man would need to use a nom-de-plume."

"A man wouldn't dare write it at all," Mrs. Adams added.

"I wish I'd kept it." Mrs. Powel gave Mrs. Murray a hinting cock of her brow.

"I'll be happy to send you one. I have several dozen. People still ask me for copies, more so in the last few years. I wonder if that's coincidence."

"What kind of coincidence?" Mrs. Powel asked.

"Well, since the release of Mary's book and the other women's books—and of course the romances, all for women—they're selling enormous quantities." Mrs. Murray's words rang out with pride. "We've been quite the consumers, carving out a huge portion of the market share. All women-driven books and periodicals. We will dominate the publishing industry someday. Women who read my essay said it stayed in their minds, as Abby said, and want to read it again. This can very well go on for the next two hundred years."

I closed my eyes, trying to imagine so far into the future. A sense of wonder drifted over me. My mind wandered as the ladies chatted. Where would women be in two hundred years? Would men let a woman be president? What about our folk? No, never a black, or even half-black president ... I'd be happy enough to know we'll be free by then.

This talk gave me a strange jolt of hope. Something inside me believed every word these ladies said and made me believe that someday us womenfolk—black and white—would be just as independent, listened to, and allowed to use our mind.

They kept up their nattering as I left the parlour and slid the tray of tea cakes from the bake oven. Hercules wasn't about, he was prob'ly at the baker buying more flour and less sugar.

When I returned, I set the cakes tray down but none of the ladies wanted to be the first to take one. Miz Betsy fixed that by grabbing the top one and taking a huge chomp. I poured Mrs. Adams's sherry and offered it to the others, but they politely refused.

"Not in daytime." Mrs. Powel shooed the bottle away.

As I turned to retreat to my corner, Mrs. Murray said, "Martha, you don't mind if I invite Oney to sit with us, do you?"

I spun back round, hoping Lady Washington didn't see my huge grin. Oh, how I wanted to sit with them and have them grill me with questions! I never read no Voltaire or Russo, or whatever his name was, but now I could talk fancy, almost—and even share what I learnt from the tutors about lots of subjects. I was their talking puppet for a while, but a smart one, aiming to make Lady Washington proud.

"Of course I don't mind." Lady Washington nodded at me to bring over another chair. "I was planning to allow her to join us anyway, after we finished discussing important matters. But Oney can discuss several topics quite intelligently now, as she's been sitting in on some of the girls' lessons."

"Oney, bring your chair over here next to me." Mrs. Murray slid her chair back to make room. The circle was still tight but Miz Betsy made sure she could still reach the tea cakes.

"So, Oney, have you been to the theatre?" Mrs. Murray asked the simplest question of all.

"I've seen lots of theatre since we moved here. I relish entering that unreal world. I remember every one like it was yesterday. Lady Washington took me to see *School for Scandal*, and us—I, Molly and Austin—went to see Shakespeare. We saw *Romeo and Juliet*, *As You Like It*, *The Merchant of Venice*, and *Richard III*, my favorite so far." I spoke slowly, with proper usage, e-nun-ci-a-ting my syllables, as the tutor taught me.

I spoke well.

I spoke white.

Mrs. Powel leant forward and rested her arms on her knees. "That's astounding. Slaves who attend plays."

"We're very liberal with them," Lady Washington stated in a bragging tone. "Oney especially is very knowledgeable about Shakespeare plays. After she sees them, we analyze them and discuss their merits and flaws." She beamed at me, pride lighting up her eyes.

"Why is *Richard* your favorite?" Mrs. Murray probed.

"Because I learnt from Miz Nelly that he wasn't really the hump-backed monster Shakespeare made him out to be. She told me the real truth, that he was a kind king and a sprightly dancer."

She asked, "What do you think about King Richard's being accused of murdering his nephews?"

"I believe he was innocent. Miz Nelly read to me from a history book that he had no reason to kill the princes. His enemies paid writers to villainize—er, vilify him—and artists painted sinister-looking portraits of him. Shakespeare made up all those lies about him, for the sake of drama. A lotta truth was tossed aside to make way for titillating the public."

"My, you're a smart girl." Her eyes wouldn't even blink, she was so taken with my speech. The smile I gave her felt so natural to me.

"Did you find it entertaining or would you rather have seen a historically accurate play?" she challenged.

"Oh, I know the answer to that. Being so fabricated made it almost farcical. I'm glad Miz Nelly tole me the real history afore I saw the play."

"That's *told*," she corrected me.

My hand covered my mouth. "Oops, that one got by."

"But you're so right, the play takes extreme license." She nodded her agreement. My heart swelled with pride, but I didn't let my head get big.

Mrs. Murray's eyes roved over me, from my face and arms down to the hem of my skirt, a bit tattered from ripping it with no time to mend it. She then shifted her quizzical look over to Lady Washington. "My goodness me, Martha, I'd never know this girl was colored—in fact, as long as we're admitting things here, I mistook Oney for one of your granddaughters when she opened the door. I almost gave her a big hug thinking she may've been Betsy or Patty—my mistake, please forgive that transgression." Her voice stayed somber, but her eyes twinkled.

Miz Betsy glared, looking none too happy me bein' mistook for a sister of hers. When nobody was looking but Miz Betsy, I grinned in glee.

"Not to worry, Judith. Many people mistake Oney for one of my own. I do treat her more like my child than my servant. She enjoys many house privileges." Lady Washington sipped her tea.

The ladies registered surprise with twitching lips touching the rims of their cups, but I couldn't bring myself to lighten my heart.

"Well, if you sew Lady Washington's habiliments, I must commend you on your talents," Mrs. Murray pressed on, her stare set on me. I suspected she'd got use to me being colored and looking white. "I've had professional dressmakers who cannot master the needle nearly as well as you."

"Thank you, ma'am." I nodded. "I do so enjoy sewing. Lady Washington shows me the latest fashion plates, and we decide together what to make. The girls, they have their own ideas of fashion. They prefer the bright reds, blues and yellows, as I do, but I expect when I grow to a woman's age, I'll prefer the light pastels—I hope to look young long as I can, though. I wish to find a husband before I'm too old, too, ma'am."

These ladies' lips now widened in true smiles.

"Oney, with your looks, intelligence and charm, you'll have many suitors," Mrs. Murray assured me. "In fact, I know several eligible young men in and around Boston who'd fall fast for you." She turned to Lady Washington, a gleam in her eye. "May I bring her back with me for a short while? Of course I'll keep her duties light."

Lady Washington's eyes nearly popped out her head. "Er, Judith … it is hardly practical for her to travel all the way to Boston just to meet men." I knew that harsh tone. She used it enough on the general. Underneath it said 'This topic is ended.'

But clearly Mrs. Murray didn't know her hostess well as I did. She ignored the warning and went on, "Just because a young lady lives in bondage is no reason to deprive her of a chance at a social life."

"Oney has a social life," Lady Washington insisted. "Among her own people."

She now had the chance to start another lively argument, on a more disputable matter than funny plays and why women should earn money.

"I've advised her many times to wait for the right suitor and marry for love rather than just wanting to be a wife. I've told her to let every suitor court her for several months to make sure he's trustworthy and loyal. But of course he must be one of her own kind."

"Then why haven't you given your own granddaughter Betsy here the same advice, instead of foisting a string of unattached men upon her?" Mrs. Murray agitated her hostess, for Lady Washington's eyes and lips narrowed. "No matter how many times you deny it, Martha, anyone who's half observant can see you're more desperate to get the poor girl married off than she is."

All eyes jumped to Lady Washington, the air so charged with tension, sparks flew tween her and Mrs. Murray.

"I am not trying to foist anyone upon her. That's an unfair assumption from someone who heard bits and pieces from five hundred miles away. I simply gave Betsy a gentle nudge to widen her circle and explore the possibilities. All the men I introduced her to are more than suitable. Alas none of them made a romantic connection with her. But that's not Betsy's fault," She added that as if an afterthought, for we all knew most of it was Miz Betsy's fault.

Miz Betsy sat, back rigid, jaw clenched, arms folded over her chest. "No, Mrs. Murray, I wouldn't let Grandmama influence me. None of those gents appealed to me in any way. Eligible they were, but one yawned all eve, another babbled about his visits to Europe, and the others rambled about their interests that in no way match my own—horse racing, gambling at cards, drinking themselves into a stupor at parties where they dance silly quadrilles ..." She gave a disdainful swipe of her hand.

"Betsy isn't much of a dancer," Lady Washington explained. "But nor am I. She takes after me in that regard. George is the dancer in the family. At the dance balls, I socialize while George prances round the floor."

"And you do not mind that?" Mrs. Murray's brows rose as her head tilted. "Your husband in such intimate physical proximity to flirty young ladies?"

"Not at all." She gave a wry half-smile. "He's oblivious to flirters. That is not George's nature. And it keeps him from luring me onto the dance floor where I have no talent or interest. I fully understand Betsy's plight. So that does narrow down the choices a bit—a man who either hates dancing as she does, or a man she won't mind sitting aside for when he wants to take the floor with other ladies. Not a pleasant choice, but I daresay your husband is far from perfect, Judith."

Mrs. Murray's eyes wandered and fixed on a distant spot. "My John is perfect for me. We have similar ideas about most things. I'm very grateful this time I found a companionable mate."

"Then I'm happy for you. And I wish the same for Betsy—and Oney, when her time comes." Lady Washington smiled at me. I smiled back, knowing my time would come.

Mrs. Murray looked at me again, clicking her tongue. "I do wish I could take you back home with me, Oney. There are so many lads who'd fall head over heals for you. White lads," she added with a nod.

My heart tumbled at these scary but tempting ideas she put in my head. I took short breaths and clasped my trembling hands. Oh, to go north with her! I opened my mouth, ready to speak my mind, knowing my boundaries, yet needing to answer her. At that moment I also learnt what self-respect meant.

I needed to speak, for my own self-respect. I took a deep breath and chose my words. "Mrs. Murray, I do wish to go back up north with you for as long as you'd have me. But my position here and in life does not allow that. So you must understand why Lady Washington won't permit it." There. I couldn't get whupped for saying what I wish to do.

"May I just borrow her, Martha?" The boldness of Mrs. Murray's question struck me like a sack of feed. "I'd be proud to introduce her as your personal servant, on loan to me. I'll compensate you handsomely."

I glanced at Lady Washington, already shaking her head. I drooped, shattered. But that strengthened my forbidden thoughts even more. If I ever got free, I'd go north, and without Mrs. Murray to borrow me.

"I can't spare her, Judith. Others have asked me, Mrs. Madison and Mrs. Maclay to name a few, but Oney is too valuable to me. Not all of them are this smart, you know," she added in a lower tone, tapping the side of her head with her finger.

"Well, she is part white," Mrs. Powel chimed in.

Now that sounded like somethin' her niece Mrs. Bingham would'a said. I s'pose there was some of that in every family. The Washingtons never said it out loud, but it was there. They believed whites smarter'n us. Even mulattoes like her half-sister, or quadroons like me. Once more I bit my tongue, holding back the words *white don't mean smarter. I seen plenty o'white dolts, you high-and-mighty ladies*!

"Oh, well, Oney, I tried to get Marth—Lady Washington—to let you visit with me," Mrs. Murray apologized to me with a forced-on frown. "But the Washingtons have an open invitation to visit us in Boston, and I do trust when they take up that invite, Lady Washington will surely bring you."

"Of course I'd bring her," Lady Washington affirmed. "But not for you to throw her together with whom you deem fitting suitors. She will find her mate when the time is right—or more likely, he will find her."

An awakening grasped me. Was now the right time? After all, I was of marriageable age. I just never got round of thinking about it, being so busy working all the time. But first things first. Getting Miz Betsy married off was the first order of business round here.

"What else do you do in your spare time?" Mrs. Murray asked me.

The other eyes fixed on me. "I relish sewing fashionable habiliment. Lady Washington lets me have extra textiles from what I sew for them, and I sew for the folk back at Mount Vernon," I rattled off my biggest interest, which lucky for me was my specialty. I added, knowing this would get them clucking. "And besides lessons, Lady Washington is letting me learn to read and write. I can write my name and simple words and can almost read all of the paper."

Mrs. Adams stopped nibbling at the cake she said she didn't want. A frown wrinkled Mrs. Powel's face.

But Mrs. Murray glowed. Her lips spread in a happy smile and she looked from me to Lady Washington and back to me. "Oney, you are such a bright girl! Why, if you lived with me, I'd hire you a tutor and let you learn as much as you wanted."

This crushed my heart. Oh, if only I'd'a been born up north with Mrs. Murray. Why did life put me where I was—lucky enough to be here and not toiling in the fields at backbreaking labor, but cursed enough to live as property unless I took action? Was there a why? I couldn't sit here and ponder that right now.

Mrs. Adams wiped crumbs from her lips and gave Lady Washington's arm a reassuring pat. "I am in full agreement of letting our people learn to read and write. They should be educated right along with women. One of my people, James, asked our permission to attend an evening school, and I gave him my blessing. When an impudent neighbor made a callous remark about it, saying all the white boys were leaving the school because James was attending, I told him point blank, 'Is this the Christian principle of doing to others as we would have others to do us? If they have no problem with blacks sitting in their churches or James playing the fiddle at their dances, then they shouldn't complain about his attending school. I have not thought it any disgrace to take him into my parlour and teach him both to read and write.' Oh, I gave that lout what-for." She looked direct at Lady Washington. "Because his face is black, should he be denied instruction?"

Judith replied by asking, "What did your neighbor lout reply to your what-for?"

"He said naught. He gave me a haughty sneer and went back to shoveling his chicken dung. But what say you, Martha? Is Oney the only one of your people learning to read and write?"

"Hercules the cook is literate. The others never asked," she replied. "But …" she hastened to add afore Mrs. Adams came down on her again, "… I have no objection, as I had none with Oney. If any of my people came to me with a wish to attend a school or classes, they'd have my blessing, just as James has yours. I would even teach them myself, as would you."

Huh? My mouth fell open. She never sat and taught me nothing.

"I'm happy to hear that, Martha, you are becoming quite the woman of our times," Judith replied with a vigorous nod. "And I hope we all meet in heaven."

"I haven't needed to teach Oney, she's been studying quite well on her own and has made astonishing progress," Lady Washington bragged. "We have long discussions about what's published in the papers. When she learns to read well she can help herself to any books she pleases. And that is more than the vast majority of owners—that is what we do here. I have other plans for Oney, too."

I displayed a knowing smile, head held high. Lady Washington told me many times I could read out loud to her when she felt like relaxin'. This was a big step up for me, another reason I hurried up to read fast and write neat.

"When Betsy does marry," she went on, "Oney will make a nice wedding gift from me to her." She looked at me, so I took it as a chance to answer.

I nodded my agreement. "I'd be happy to sew a negligee or a quilt for her wedding gift."

She held up a palm afore I finished talking. "No, I mean you'll *be* the gift. I'm going to give you to Betsy. Then you'll go live with her and her new husband, and belong to them from then on. They'll bring you back to visit, of course." She went back to eating her cake.

I stopped breathing as if shot through the head. A sudden rush of tears sprang to my eyes. *How could you do this to me?* I silently begged. *You thought of me as your own child!*

Me be a wedding gift to Miz Betsy? Oh, no. I'd leap into the sea first. I said not another word, but swore whatever wedding gifts she gave to Miz Betsy, one of them would not be I.

Mrs. Murray blinked. "Oney will *be* a wedding gift?"

Lady Washington nodded tween bites, as if she planned this for years. Now I believe she had!

Then Mrs. Murray, with more cheek than any woman I'd ever known, turned to me and asked straight out, "Do you object to this, Oney?"

Never was I allowed to say what I objected to. Never was I asked. Struck so numb with shock, I couldn't think straight. I began to shake. I glanced at Lady Washington. She looked back at me, without any sign in her eyes that defied me to reply. But I knew my place, tho Mrs. Murray was unaware she'd well overstepped hers. As Lady Washington always treated her guests with the utmost respect, the question hung in the air 'til I mustered the courage to answer her.

I swiped my tears away. "Mrs. Murray …" My voice quivered with emotion. "Lady Washington is as a second mother to me, and it will pain me greatly to be separated from her. But Miz Betsy is a fine woman and I trust she will treat me fairly."

Then my mouth quit saying lies. But my mind soared far into my future. My fears of capture and beatings vanished. The weight of a thousand worlds lifted from my shoulders. I sat straight, chin up, and in the next heartbeat, made the silent vow … *I will never belong to Miz Betsy. I will not wait for you to give me my freedom. I will take it.*

Mrs. Murray looked past me to Lady Washington. "I'm sure Oney will do fine, Martha, wherever she goes. We don't have that inclination in Boston, things are quite different. But I respect your wishes. And I'll repeat, any time you can spare Oney, I'll be more than happy to take her in. I do say your raiment and hers is exquisite, and I'd be flattered if you'd give me the honor of letting me employ her talents."

"I'll let you know, Judith." Her answer came out terser than I expected.

Mrs. Powel looked at the mantel clock and huffed out a breath as she pushed herself to her feet. "Sorry, I must leave. I have an appointment with my physician for a bunion."

I stood afore the others did. Lady Washington looked at her guests. "Ladies, I'm so happy we were able to meet today. It certainly was enlightening."

They exchanged their customary air-kisses. I fetched their cloaks and gloves as Lady Washington grasped Mrs. Murray's sleeve. "Judith, I am so glad you were able to call. Next time I'll make sure it's just the two of us. I'd like to talk further."

Her eyes brightened, with surprise or pleasure I couldn't tell. "Why yes, I'll be happy to. Mayhap in the warmer weather. Please call on me, too."

The way her entire face lit up, Lady Washington looked like that was the highlight of her day.

But me? I stared at the wall, still numb from her shocking news. *Give me to Miz Betsy?* I repeated over and over in my mind. It sounded like a cruel joke. But Lady Washington didn't play jokes. My fingers curling into fists of resolve, I vowed to the Lawd above, long as I had two legs to carry me, I refused to be a gift, presented like a silver charger. *Now*, I told the Lord and the heavens above, *I must fight their plan for my fate. I shall not live with Miz Betsy and some husband she ensnares and become their property, because I'll be gone from here and on my way to freedom.*

With Lady Washington so desperate to marry her off, I had little time to plan this. I needed hurry—fast.

****

Next morn, Miz Patty announced her wedding day. She wanted Jan'y 6, the same day as General and Lady Washington were married, also Twelfth Night. The wedding was at Hope Park in Fairfax County. Lady Washington didn't bring me, but when she returned, I could'a guessed where her new frown lines and creases come from.

She told me anyways. "Poor Betsy is still unwed." She placed her cap and gloves on the dressing table and stuck her feet out for me to remove her shoes.

We both knew "poor Betsy"'s prospects, so naught needed sayin'. But I vowed, again and again—*the day Miz Betsy announces her marriage will be the day I go back to Absalom Jones to secure my freedom.*

It happened faster'n I could ever plan for.

CHAPTER SEVENTEEN

My decision to escape gave me a reason to live. I wanted to dance, to sing, to romp through the garden. But I settled for the theatre.

"Herc, we gotta go see this play." I stood at the cutting board helping Hercules pull pits outta olives so the general wouldn't break his newest set of hippopotamus's teeth. "I got enough money. I'll pay fer yours and Austin's tickets."

"Why don' you wanna tell Lady Washington we goin' see it? She don' mind us goin'a theatre none."

"She might mind this one." I suppressed a shudder. "It's about runaway slaves. I ain't takin' no chances."

He quit pitting and looked down at me. "Chances on what, Oney? What you tryin'a tell me?"

I let out a relieving laugh. My fears now gone, I still harbored jitters. "Oh, you know me so well, Herc." I stood close, stood on tippytoe and put my lips to his ear. "Here it is," I whispered, since Mamma always said walls has ears, specially walls belongin' to *them* folk. "Lady Washington wants to hand me over to Miz Betsy when she marries. So I'm runnin'."

He flashed a wide grin. "Good for you, girl. I tol' you I know you'd do it. And not just cause o'Miz Betsy. You had it in you anyways."

"It don' matter no more." I talked in a normal tone now. "I know the risks. They can capture me and punish me. I'll never see Mamma or Delphy or Austin … ever again." My voice quivered. "I know I'll suffer— I'll be poor and hungry. But I'd rather my time and my body be my own." I swept at tears.

"I'm proud o'you, girl." Hercules took me into his arms and patted my back.

"Oh, Herc, you're a brother to me," I sobbed.

"Shhh, we can talk more later." He released me and wiped my wet cheeks with his apron. "Take this." He gave me a cup'a somethin' sweet. I gulped at it.

"P-please, Herc. Hesh yo' trap about this round here. For both our hides."

He shook his head and gave me a playful cuff on the chin. "I ain't no dummy."

My knees went wobbly and almost gave out. I peered over my shoulder in case somebody heard. I'd be doing a lotta that once I jumped. "But you know how they always list'nin'." I jerked my thumb in the house's direction.

"Yea, we talk later. You a'right now?"

I nodded and took a deep breath.

"Good. You gotta talk to some people that'll help you make some plans." He went back to his olive pitting. I breathed in deep again and calmed down, popping an olive in my mouth. It tasted rich and buttery. I popped another one—then another.

"I'll get them play tickets when I go to market Thursday." I licked my fingers. "The matinee's cheaper, so I'll get 'em for that. Then the play'll learn us how to make slavery into comedy."

"I'll be laughin' out loud once I'm free and they can't catch me." He dumped the olives into a bowl and started chopping celery, a steady rat-a-tat hitting the board.

"That's it, I'm done here." I took another olive but I put it back, my appetite lost. "We'll talk about that again. It gotta be when we ain't nowheres near the house. Mayhap onna way back from the theatre we can talk plans. But not in here." I gave him one last warning with my eyes, turned and left.

Hercules didn't go to the theatre after all. He spent his afternoon off at the house of Sam Saviel, a free colored who helped slaves escape. I now started to spend more time with them folk, and attended their church twice on Sunday. They always had a meeting after the second service. I became a regular there. I learnt who to trust, where to go and how to get there. Lady Washington never asked me about my church and I didn't tell her. She didn't care what church we went to, long as we did our work before. She knew about the African Church, but never figgered that free blacks attended.

With the help of these free coloreds, Hercules knew the day of his escape, but I couldn't runyet. They told me I needed at least a hunnerd dolls, so I began staying up half the night sewing frocks to sell. That'd take at least 'til Lady Washington handed me over to Miz Betsy, and the lady had three more hapless bachelors lined up. So it could be real soon. There had to be someone ambitious enough to marry into the Washington family. Or desperate enough to marry her.

Hercules took me to meet his free friend Sam Saviel. I walked through the door and saw all the folk from them other meetings. They greeted me like I belonged. My heart swelled, cause I did belong. These were my people.

Sam asked me what no one ever did. "How do you feel?"

"Gotta be honest about it, Sam." Tears welled up again. "I'm walkin' round a bundle of mixed emotions. I couldn't bear saying goodbye to my mamma for the last time. That's the day I dread most of all."

He nodded his understanding. "But you have a choice, Oney. And you have help. Some slaves who run, they escape into the night alone, with nothin' but the rags on they backs. You—you got us."

"I know, Sam. I love my family with all my heart, but my need for freedom gnaws away at me." I clenched my fists. "The ache starts in my head, spreads to my heart and breaks my back. I drag it everywhere."

He lay his arm round my shoulders. "Slavery took our bodies, but they can't take our souls. Now your body will be yours, too."

His speech gave me an inner strength I never knew I had. Any lingering doubts vanished. Now there was no turning back.

I went to the play with Austin. As I settled into my rickety but roomy seat in the next to last row, who'd I see promenade down the center aisle but Lady Washington and Senator Maclay's wife. I turned and hid my face, nudging Austin to do the same, so she didn't see neither of us. Being she wasn't with the general, she didn't take the private box they always did. When she went out with other ladies, she rathered sit with the real folk.

I didn't find the play all that funny, tho mayhap other colored folk would'a found amusement in seeing whites held as slaves by pirates. The songs they sung were lively, but let's say I didn't fall out my chair laughin'.

Later that eve when Lady Washington told me she saw the play, I used the talent as an actress I never know'd I had.

"It was a musical, taking place on the Barbary coast, so I couldn't closely relate, but it got me thinking about bondage …" Then her lips clamped shut tighter'n if crushed in a vise.

I stood, straight-faced and tight-lipped myself. Course I couldn't ask her what she got thinking about bondage. Mayhap she'd take that unspoken thought to her grave. But she never said another word about it again—not to me, anyways.

****

Barely a fortnight after Miz Patty's wedding, Hercules sent his son Richmond to summon me to the kitchen. I wrapt myself in Lady Washington's old cloak over my own I sewed myself. Head down against the biting wind, I ran over, slammed the door behind me and rubbed my hands afore the fire to thaw out.

He come up to me, lowered his head and whispered, "Mr. Peter, Miz Patty's husband, he sold six of her slaves."

"Lawd Jesus." A ragged breath escaped me. I stood afore the roaring fire but chills got me shivering all over again. "I don't like that Mr. Peter at all. He give me liquorish looks all the time. Another reason to jump—if I ever became Miz Betsy's property, her or her husband could sell me, too. Why ain't I never thought of that?"

"It don' matter now, cause you are jumpin.' And my prayers are with you, girl," he praised, his breath hot in my ear.

"And mine with you." I dashed back to the house, crouched in my corner of the parlour and prayed. "Lawd, watch over us when we jump—and after, wherever we get to," was all I dared ask.

Next morn as Austin and I served the Washingtons kippers and honey cakes, Miz Betsy burst into the dining room. "I have two announcements to make. I am no longer Betsy. I am now to be addressed as Eliza. Secondly, I am engaged to Mr. Thomas Law." She crossed her arms over her chest and stood, awaiting their joyful outburst.

But none came. Just a beat of silence.

The Washingtons met each other's eyes. Me, my heart crashed. I stared straight ahead. *The time has come. I must escape.*

"The name Eliza doesn't fit you, dear." Lady Washington broke the silence.

She was right—twas like stuffing her ample form into one of Miz Nelly's petite frocks. She was a Betsy, in looks, demeanor, and spirit.

The general grimaced, rubbing his teeth with his serviette. "Betsy, do you—"

"Eliza!" she broke in.

"All right, Eliza ..." He glanced at Lady Washington whose color drained to bloodless. "This is too sudden to be practical or realistic. You barely know the man. He's twenty years your senior—"

"With two sons older than you," Lady Washington finished his sentences more'n he did. This time she jumped in faster'n usual. "Not only that, he is a foreigner."

Miz Eliza rolled her eyes with a loud 'tsk' and a toss of her head. "He's English, Grandmama. We were English once. That's hardly a foreigner. And he's rich. He just bought five hundred lots in the federal district."

The general tossed his napkin down and stood at his full commanding height. No stooping, no hanging onto the chair. He towered over Miz Eliza and stared her down with eyes of ice. "Snapping up lots in a swampland does not impress me, nor should it you. He is a speculator, naught more. Will it not be asked why are speculators to pocket so much money?"

She returned his stare, eyes narrowed. "He is a businessman, Grandpapa. Why is speculation any less moral than making your fortune off the backs of slaves? Huh?" She balled a fist on her ample hip.

My heart near exploded awaiting his answer. I'd never heard Miz Eliza say nary a word in support of slaves. Mayhap she'd listened to Mrs. Murray's words of wisdom at tea that day, too.

"That is not the issue," he fended off the question as if jumping out of a bullet's path. "This entire plot sounds queer to me—the suddenness, the secrecy. You, dear girl, have more honesty than disguise, and thus I demand to know more details of this liaison. This I have a right to expect in return for my blessing so promptly bestowed, after you concealed the matter from me so long."

Miz Eliza let out a whoosh of impatient breath. "My marriage plans are hardly a queer plot. Furthermore, it hasn't been 'so long'. We haven't been conspiring for years behind your backs. It's what the romance novels call a whirlwind courtship." Her lips spread in a smirk.

"Bets—er, Eliza ..." Lady Washington spoke up, clearing her throat. That told me she had a lotta words to unleash. "We've discussed this before. This is no romance novel. Tell me—do you truly love this man? Or are you pretending you're in a romance novel? Because if you are, this marriage will be the largest disaster since the eruption of Vesuvius that buried Pompeii."

Miz Eliza stumbled back as if shoved. Her mouth opened and shut in a gobbling motion. Word fragments fell out in a string of stutters. "I-I-I-I-of course I love him!"

"Does he love you?" the grandmother prodded on, more concerned about the girl's delusions of amour rather than her financial security. After all, since she talked to Mrs. Murray, Lady Washington now knew that her grandgirls needed to learn an occupation, as not to depend on a man.

"Grandmama, I need not stand here and take this interrogation. I am not on trial. We are marrying and that is that." She turned on a heel and stomped out.

The general and lady both shook their heads as if in timed unison.

I leant against the wall like I'd been struck a physical blow—my time as Lady Washington's favorite servant now reduced to days. Her plan to hand me over to Miz Eliza hung like a cloud over me all this time, but forbidden to voice my feelings, I had to hold it all inside.

I had more than half the hunnerd dolls they said I'd need. I'd get by on it somehow.

"George," she finally spoke. He folded his self back onto the chair, grasping the table for support, his bones popping. "Mr. Law is but a stranger, and only reputed to be wealthy. We need find out more about him before we allow this to happen."

"Of course I'll find out more." The general drummed his fingers on the tabletop. "First order of business is to write to Betsy's—Eliza's stepfather. I'll instruct David to draft up a prenuptial agreement, to have Law make a settlement upon her before the marriage, of her own fortune, if no more. But not a word to the bride-elect." He wagged a finger.

"Of course not. But please, George, hurry. We must find out more about this man before he destroys her life."

But didn't she go and marry him not more'n three months after Miz Patty, on March 20. The moment I'd been waiting for finally came.

That eve as I rubbed my owner's sweaty feet, the word 'freedom' rang in my ears.

CHAPTER EIGHTEEN

As I did the mind-numbing chore of wrapping dinnerware to pack into crates for the Mount Vernon journey, an ugly truth shocked me to the depths of my soul. I halted, nearly dropping a stack of plates. Sweat soaked my hairline and under my arms.

O dear Lord, I cannot go back south. I'll never be able to escape from there.

I would never see Mount Vernon or my family ever again. Grief ripped my heart in two. Oh, I longed to hug Mamma and be her baby one last time. How I missed her.

After my chores, I walked to Absalom and Mary's house in the south section of town. As I breathed the cool evening air, I didn't gag on any stenches of sewage or filth. Then I saw workmen in dusty overalls sweeping the streets with wide brooms and splashing pails of water on the ground. These days the city aimed to ward off another outbreak of that deadly fever. God forbid that should happen again.

I trust wherever I end up will be safe from pox and plague, I spoke a silent prayer. But bein' a slave on the run for the rest of my life, I suppose pox'd be the least of my woes.

The Jonses held no meeting tonight. I simply craved their comfort—and now their guidance. With my departure date nearly upon me, I needed iron out every detail.

"The Washingtons are packing to go, Mary," burst out of me as she opened her front door.

"C'mon in." She ushered me into the small parlour and bade me sit on the horsehair sofa. "Fetch Miz Oney some tea, child," she ordered her daughter. She sat beside me and crossed her ankles. "First I'll tell you what you cannot do when you run. You cannot stay in Pennsylvania."

"Why?" I half-whispered, half-croaked. "They outlawed slavery."

She shook her head, her lips drawn into a tight line. "Remember the Fugitive Slave Act."

Those barbaric words hit me like a blow to the head. "Gosh, I forgot 'bout that. The president signed it a few feet from where I slept. It's a federal law, ain't it?"

"Yes, and it overrides state laws. Even if you escape a free state, you can get captured and drug back. Besides, staying here is far too dangerous. Too close to the president." She swept her pointer finger to and fro. "You cannot bide your time here 'til he quits the presidency," she cautioned me, her tone half-warning, half-chiding. "Even when he retires to Mount Vernon to live out his days, you'll git seen and caught. You must escape to another state. But you cannot travel on the stage. Somebody sees you, they catch you, or the president can have you seized at the landing."

All the 'you cannots', 'you'll gits' and 'you needs' overwhelmed me. A fresh wave of despair drowned my resolve. I stared at the floorboards. "Where do I go to then?" I pleaded, my voice hoarse. "And how to get there?"

Mary's daughter placed my tea on the table but my churning insides wouldn't welcome it.

"Up north. By sea." Mary held her teacup by the handle and sipped without slurping as any fine lady. Truth be told, she *was* fine. Even finer'n Lady Washington's cronies. Poised and well mannered, Mary never gossiped nor harbored hatred towards nobody—not slaveowners, not slave traders, nor nobody else who called us subhuman.

"By sea? I never been on a boat before." I lifted the cup but my hand trembled so, tea sloshed over the rim into the saucer. I set it back down.

"Your daddy crossed the ocean sea from England, so sailing a ways north won't hurt you," she assured me. "We need find out what sloops are sailing the soonest and put you on board one. Only going north, of course."

I shut my eyes, dazed. "Then what, when I get off the boat?"

"We have friends in several northern cities—New York, Providence, Boston, Gloucester, Portsmouth ..." She rattled off cities faster'n the words to *All God's Chillun Got Wings*. I silently thanked God for these folk who helped us escape. In many ways, they were braver than us escaping.

"I won't know 'til I get there?" My voice shook. The shock come and went. Now I trembled with hope. I gave the cup another try anyways. This time tea didn't slosh over.

"When we find out which vessel is sailing the soonest, then we'll tell you where you're going. You'll need to stow away, but it's only a few days' travel. Not the lap of luxury, but they won't treat you like a slave." She met my eyes and I musta looked awful a'scared. She took my cold hand and clasped it in her comforting warmth. "You're a strong girl, Oney. It sounds scary now, but when you take your first step on free soil ... you'll be reborn."

I nodded as my heart leapt. Not a leap of fear. A leap of resolve. Of courage. Of belief in myself. "Yes, I can," I vowed, not to her, but to myself.

"Over the next few days as they pack, you pack," she instructed. "Come back here to stay 'til we secure your passage, and have your brother or friends bring your belongings here. You need all your fancy dresses, hats, shoes and baubles you wore to Lady Washington's galas. That's most important." Her lips formed a wry smile. "You need to look rich and white, not a vagabond runaway slave."

She stood and helped me to my feet. "My, you're trembling. Calm down, girl." Her strong voice rang in my ears all the way back to the president's house.

"I am getting there," my own voice rang out—not dropping my 'g'.

****

Huddled in the Joneses' spare feather bed, too jittery to sleep, I heard Austin and Hercules's footsteps as they snuck my packed belongings in through the night. And yes, did I cram my every fancy dress, shoe and flub-dub into them satchels.

Next morn, as I helped cook breakfast, Absalom blew in from a driving rain. He wrung his shirt out over a kitchen pail and delivered the news that changed my life forever:

"The *Nancy* will take you to your freedom on the 25th, Oney. That's five days from now."

My heart paused. My mouth opened but nothing came out.

He went on, "The *Nancy* is a sloop that goes to and from Portsmouth round once a month. Besides his freight, Captain Bowles brings enslaved folk to freedom."

"You asked him for me?" I managed to force out my mouth.

He nodded as I poured him coffee, careful not to spill it, for I trembled more'n when I talked to Mary. "Yea, he expectin' you. I told him your name, but not you belonged to the Washingtons. That's up to you, you wanna tell him."

'Belonged', he said. In the past. But I wasn't free already—yet. "Abs, I got so little money so far, and that's 'til I can find work. I ain't got enough to pay him and for food and shelter." Defeat smacked me back down.

But his smile raised my hopes a glimmer. "He don't take no money. He ferries slaves to freedom on every voyage north—for free."

My jaw dropped. "Free? He don't want naught?" Lewd thoughts violated me. "He must want somethin' I got."

Absalom shook his head. "Nothin' but to see you free. He's against slavery, dead set against it. Why you think he takes his chances? He knows ferrying contraband from slave states is stealing and he can face the death penalty. But since the gov'ment won't free no slaves, he's doin' it." He gulped his coffee. "Besides, he don't need the money. He makes loads'a clams in his line a' business." He rubbed thumb and fingertips together. "Him and his landside partner, they sell horse gear, boots and shoes of fancy tanned leathers … and he makes free folk pay passage. But runnin' slaves, he takes for free."

I shuffled out to the parlour, my legs steadier now, and looked out at the driving downpour. Rain pelted the windowpanes in a steady thrum. I couldn't even see the street. I went over to Mary dipping her pen in an inkwell at her desk. Her calendar, with five days tween me and freedom, showed me this was no dream. "This is all happening so fast, Mary."

"It always does when a slave decides to run, doll. It goes by in a blur and you'll land in Portsmouth before you know it." She flashed a tooth-brushed smile as her pen scratched flowing letters on a sheet of paper. Born free, she learnt to read and write as a child. I admired her penmanship, with its perfect slant, wide loops and curves.

"If only I could pen letters like you someday." I peeked over at her writing. They were no letters I knew.

"You'll do whatever you set out to do. Nobody will tell you you can't, ever again." She folded the paper in thirds. "My friends Willie and Shermener Smith will expect you, shelter you and help you out any way you need."

"Shermener? I never heard that name."

"She's named after her father Sherman." She handed me the folded note. "Shermener's very active in the Ladies Charitable African Society. Do join that soon as you can. That'll be your best way to form friendships with folk who'll help you seek employment and other of your needs. Shermener's niece Dinah and her sister-in-law Rebecca started the society right off their kitchen table."

"Sounds like a ladies' version of the Free African Society right here." The thought of meeting all those ladies calmed me a bit.

She dipped her pen and nodded. "Oh, there's one there, too, and in New York."

"They sound more helpful to one another than these cronies of Lady Washington's who all they do is tipple and gossip 'bout folk who ain't there to defend theirselves." I tsk-tsk'd with umbrage.

"That's cause they *are* more helpful than Mrs. Washington's hoity-toities." She wrote some letters and numbers on a separate sheet, that I could read. "These folk may not have riches or grand mansions or satin gowns, but they got what the hoity-toities don't—a *purpose*."

"Is this note you givin' me in French, Mary?"

She laughed. "No. See, anything in writing must be in code. We take no chances. After they read it, they burn it. They live at thirty-three and a half Gates Street. You ask the captain or a deck hand to lead you there." She handed me the address note and I pressed it to my lips. This would be my first address in freedom. "Now go to the president's house and come back here on the 24th. That's Tuesday. The next morn, we'll get you to the dock in plenty of time for your sailing." She saw me trembling again and cupped my cheek. "Don't worry, Oney. No one we've helped has ever been captured."

I covered my thumping heart. "I never believed I'd see this day." I clasped the notes 'til they began to crumple. "It's because of providence. Lady Washington always speaks of providence—cause of this, cause of that—it's all providence."

She shook her head. "No, Oney. Lady Washington is dead wrong. This is cause of you. Providence might help a little. As do we and Captain Bowles and my friends in Portsmouth. But in the end, it's all up to you."

****

It was also up to me to figure when to leave the Washingtons for the last time. Not in the morn. I helped dress Lady Washington as usual. Not in the afternoon. I repaired hems as usual. Not afore dinner. I set the table as usual.

The hour finally came—while they ate dinner.

I will never forget the date—May 21, 1796. Nothing heavied my heart— not remorse, not guilt, not sadness upon fleeing my master and mistress.

Raw thirst for freedom overcame all that. I walked straight past the Washingtons and out the front door. When I shut it, I left them—and my forced bondage— behind me.

I tore through the muddy streets in pouring rain. Gasping for breath, soaked to the skin, my heart slamming in terror, I glanced behind me, again and again. No one pursued me—yet. I dreaded and expected pounding footsteps, a clap on my shoulder. *But*, I asked myself, *who would chase me through the driving rain? No, it is not possible*, I affirmed—they didn't even know I'd left the kitchen.

At the Jones house I slowed and caught my breath. When Absalom opened the door, I staggered inside, laughing, sobbing, gulping for dear life.

I spent the night pacing the attic room, hands clasped. "I beg of you, dear God, walk beside me on this journey. See me through this safe. Don't let them capture me. I only want to be your servant, no one else's."

As daybreak nudged away the darkness, I fell to my knees, weary with fatigue. "Thank you, dear God, for ending my final night of bondage."

Mary forced a hoe cake down me and hugged me goodbye. Clinging to her, I poured my heart out. "I'm still a'scared, Mary, no matter what courage I got, I'm still a'scared." I loved Mary so, but wished I'd been hugging Mamma right now.

"I know you are, dear, but you've got protection. And your freedom is worth a bit of fear."

"I'll write to you, I promise." I stood steady, prepared for my next step. "Thank you for guiding me, Mary. You're a gift from God."

"And so are you. Now go embrace your destiny … and always hold your head high. You are beautiful, intelligent, resourceful, ambitious, and remember—no one can break your spirit," were her last words to me.

I pulled on baggy trousers and shaded my face with Absalom's old tricorn. Carrying my sacks of belongings, him and two of his sons walked me, in my ratty disguise, to the dock. There the *Nancy* stood tall and majestic, waiting to bring me to freedom. I counted two, three, four sails billowing in the breeze, one towering mast in the center. Sailors loaded crates and barrels on board. Absalom's sons carried my satchels on after them.

"There he is." Absalom pointed to a tall man in a blue jacket and shaggy tar-black hair what never seen a comb. "Good morn, Captain." Absalom extended his hand and they shook. Up close the captain's eyes shone young and bright, but his face bore the ravages of the sea. Ruddy grooved cheeks sprouted a peppery beard.

"Captain John Bowles, this is Miss Oney Judge." Absalom gestured at me. "She's going to Portsmouth with you for her freedom."

"Uh … Captain, sir …" I stumbled and fumbled but he reached and grasped my hand. Never had a white man touched me in any way. Most forward and unconventional, it put me at ease. I heaved a sigh of relief, my shoulders dropping.

"Pleased to meet you, Miss Judge." Creases formed round his lips as he smiled. "Never fear, you'll be safe on board."

My mouth already hanging open at the "Miss Judge", I searched for the proper words. "Sir, I've a few dollars I can pay you. I don't deserve your providing my ferriage for free."

He held up a hand. "I despise slavery. It's my moral duty—and my privilege—to secure passage for bondspeople who seek freedom." With that he signaled to one of his sailors. "C'mere, Jack."

The stocky, medium-skinned Jack strode over, sleeves rolled to his elbows, his muscles like ropes. "This here is Jack Staines. Jack, escort Miss Oney below decks. She's coming with us."

"Hello, Miss Oney." He gave me a smile brighter'n the sun. I liked Jack's sturdy build and his near-white features, the skinny nose, the straight chestnut hair. Our eyes didn't meet but he looked me over in a curious rather than liquorish way. He didn't ask nothing. I needn't tell him either.

I hugged and thanked Absalom. All my emotion drained out of me when I'd bade farewell to Mary. Now only numbness remained.

Jack led me up the ramp. As I stepped onto the deck, he held out his hand. "Watch your step now."

I clasped his fingers and finally, our eyes met. "It still feels like I'm on land," were the first words I spoke to Jack Staines.

"Yea, but wait 'til we're at sea. Should be smooth sailing today, with the rain finally stopped, but it can get rough along the way." He led me down the length of the boat, past coiled ropes, wooden crates, boys swabbing the deck. Not a one gave me the least bit notice. We stopped at a narrow stairway leading downwards to a dark hole.

"I gotta hide down there?" Ugly tentacles of fear gripped my heart and squeezed.

"It'll be lighter when the sun rises high. You can come up at night. And it's only four or five days, depends on the currents and such. Watch your step now." He started down the stairs and I followed, clutching the rough wooden rail. A yearning for the big house's polished banister saddened me as it flashed in my heart, then vanished.

I followed him through the shadowy lower deck piled with crates and barrels to the front of the boat. The smell of leather hung in the musty air. "It's in here." He gestured to a privy-sized hideaway piled with blankets tween two crates. Next to it sat everything I owned in the world, my four satchels Absalom's sons dropped off. "It's comfortable enough in there. No one ever complained." He stood back and let me peer in.

"Who'd dare complain?" I commented and he chuckled.

"I'll bring you some vittles after we launch. What do you like?"

I turned and blinked in surprise. "I have a choice?"

"I can't let a pretty young girl like you go hungry by givin' you vittles not to your likin'." A head taller than me, he met my gaze. This time it held.

My cheeks heated up as I warmed in secret places. My goodness me, was he a flirter? I hid my delight behind my hand and faked a cough. "That's kind of you, Mr. Staines, but I'll eat anything put in front of me. I ain't— uh, never had choices before." With that I wondered if he knew I was a runaway. But I no longer worried or cared.

"Well, you got 'em now. And call me Jack. See you later." He left me and I crawled into my safe haven, clasped my hands and went back to my praying.

I learnt much about Jack Staines on my voyage to freedom. He was a mulatto, born free in New York. When he served me vittles of bread, cheese, pork and thick coffee, thrice a day and at sundown, he sat across from me and partook of his own libation in a dented tin mug. With no one to bother us, we shared stories of our lives, happy and sad, but of course mostly sad.

"I usually hear why the captain's stowaways stow away," he chatted tween sips. "But you—now I need ask you. Why is a white girl stowin' here?"

I swallowed my bite of cheese, ready to reveal my truth. "I trust you the way I trust Captain Bowles, Jack. I know neither of you would ever betray me, just as I'll never betray the captain. I'm not fully white. But I'm running. I mean—I ran. And I'm happy to say what I never thought I'd say—I took my liberty."

He nodded, his eyes trained on mine. A strong attraction brewed tween us, and not just on looks. Our souls fused. Then he said it for me. "I know I seen you somewhere. Now I know where. At the meetings. But I never approached you, figgerin' you was white."

"Ah." I nodded. "I seen—I've seen you, too, at Samuel's. Now I'm sorry I never said hello first."

"Don't have no regrets. All that matters is we're here now." He wrapped his hands round his cup.

"Are you part of the Free African Society?" I asked.

He nodded. "When I'm ashore in Philadelphia. I either board with other free folk or sometimes Dr. Rush lets me stay with him. Black folk eat up the tales of the sea, of the faraway ports ..." His smile lit up the space. "They even ask if there's sea serpents. We entertain 'em more'n the theatre. Course the folk planning to run need to know which ships ferry runaways, so I relay all the knowledge I get about that. That's how Mary and Absalom found out when Cap Bowles was launching the *Nancy* this month. I'm his usual go-b'tween. And when in Portsmouth, I belong to the African Society there," he added, his voice swelled with pride. "The president is Pomp Spring, a local baker. You'll doubtless meet him when you go for pies and bread and such sundries."

I stared, eyes wide with wonder at this man, another God-given gift instrumental in my journey to freedom. "Thank you, Jack. I'm grateful to so many people." I choked up.

"Think nothin' of it." His hand covered mine. I tingled. "We gotta help each other. No one else will."

I composed myself, not wanting him to see me in an emotional state. "So what do you tell folk about sea serpents?" I finished the last of my bread but resisted licking my fingers. Having learnt proper manners of the Washington table, I hadn't done that in public since being ordered to the big house.

He rocked back and slapped his thigh. "Oh, I tell 'em tales make they hair stand on end! Sea monsters that surface and butt the boat 'til it rocks, breathin' fire, roarin' like wild beasts ... they scared witless but always want more. They like them stories more'n they want to hear about ghosts."

"There's a lot more scarier things than sea serpents and ghosts," I stated a hard fact and we nodded, both knowing what I meant.

I lost count how many days passed, but each night Jack led me onto the deck to stroll and breathe in the salty air. As we leant over the rail together, the foamy waves lapped up against the boat and slapped its side. The *Nancy* glided over the sea, swaying to and fro. I felt being rocked in a cradle.

So excited to be on this voyage to my rebirth, I hummed and did a little jig, too restless to keep still. My crackling energy musta been catchy, cos right then Jack grasped my hand and swung me round in a joyful dance. "We must dance together to real music," he promised me as my heart skittered in its own dance.

"Is there dancin' in Portsmouth? To real music?" We clung to each other, swaying with the boat.

"Oh, yeah. And then some."

He led me in a slow waltz up and down the deck as I kept up my joyful humming to my favorite tune, *All God's Chillun Got Wings*. He knew the words and sang along with my humming. At that moment I knew Jack Staines was part of my rebirth.

One late night I saw flickering pinpoints of light in the distance. "That's New York," he told me. "We're almost halfway to Portsmouth now."

That jolted me. "I lived in New York," I chatted away, to get my mind off this audacious act I'd done.

"Yea? When?"

I emptied the bag: "My owners weren't just plain ordinary folk. I belonged to the Washingtons," I confessed, beginning with my step up to the big house to Lady Washington's heartless gifting me to Miz Eliza. "That made me run." I made sure I used the past, "belonged," as Absalom had.

"I don't blame you one bit for leavin' them. No human being has any right to own another, no matter you live in a mansion or a hut. You think the nation's president would know better'n that." He frowned, shaking his head.

"Well, he don't," I stated the sad fact. "They're all two-faced, every last one of 'em. Hercules helped plant the seeds in my head, but when Lady Washington told me she was giving me to Miz Eliza—never would I succumb to that. She's a mean cow. It ain't—isn't entirely her fault. She can't help it, she just is. A miracle she ever found a husband. But now it's my miracle, too."

He stepped closer and lay his arm round my shoulders. I snuggled into him. "Not a miracle for you, Oney. I can tell by looking at you, the intelligence in your eyes, the glow about you, you're meant to be free. Where you staying in Portsmouth?"

I unfolded the address note Mary wrote for me, tucked securely down my front. "Gates Street, name of Smiths—Willie and Shermener." I looked up and our eyes met in the moonlight. "Ain't—isn't that a poetical name?"

"Rather melodious. I know who the Smiths are. Gates Street's near the dock. I can walk you there—course if you'll let me."

My smile must've brightened the night like the noonday sun. "You mean that? Share my first walk as a free woman? Oh, Jack, how mighty fine of you!"

"If you don't mind me stoppin' by to call on you sometime, for that dancin'." He lowered his head as he shuffled his feet.

My heart tumbled upside down. "Only sometime? And only for dancin'? How 'bout all the time?" Oh, how brazen was I! I burnt so hot I musta flamed red as an apple. But I cared not—free folk did whatever they like.

****

I heard my name through the haze of sleep. "Oney, Oney!" A hand nudged my shoulder. "Oney, we're in Portsmouth." Jack's warm minty breath tickled my ear.

I sat up. No swaying, no rocking. Beneath me lay still and solid as earth. I opened my eyes to gray shadows. Weak light spilt through the hatch leading to the deck. Jack's nearness thrilled me even before his words did.

"Your journey is ended. You're free now."

I focused on him crouching before me, a ghostly haze in the pre-dawn. "Tell me this is no dream, Jack. Tell me I'm awake and this is real."

"You're awake and this is real. And you're beautiful and free. Now I'll walk you over to the Smiths." He held out his hand to help me stand.

I struggled to my feet, not knowing the day or time. I stumbled, now feeling motion as if the boat still rocked.

He caught me, his strong hands clamped round my arms. "You'll get'cha sea legs once you're on land a while."

"I'm still rockin'." I swayed left to right. He stepped closer and held me, as in a silent dance. "I don't wanna let go, Jack."

"But your new life is waiting." At the break of my first full day of freedom, Jack Staines lowered his lips to mine and captured them in a sweet, yet hungry search. My lips softened under his kiss. Our breaths mingled, and it ended too quickly as he pulled away. We took a much-needed gulp of air. "I'll send the boys down to fetch your satchels, we best get goin'."

He turned and left me swaying. I grasped onto the side, covered my just-kissed lips with my hand, jumped up and down and squealed in delight.

****

"Thank you from the bottom of my heart, sir." I clasped hands with Captain Bowles, a cheroot clamped tween his teeth. "You'll never know what this means to me. And I promise I'll never betray you."

A puff of smoke escaped his lips. "No need to thank me. I don't believe in thanks for what is right. We'll see each other again, I'm sure."

"Oh, I do hope so, sir. Any time you need cleanin', chores done, and specially sewing, you fetch me at the Smiths, hear?"

He removed the cheroot and spat out a bit of tobacco. "Sewing I always need." He raised his arm to show me a gaping hole in his shirt. "You have my word."

And though he protested, I pressed five dollars into his hand. Jack walked me to the Smiths. Two sailors followed us, bearing my loads of fancy raiment to make me look rich and white.

The clapboard dwelling stood wedged tween a tobacco shop and a stable. "This is it." I checked the number on Mary's note: 33 1/2. "This neighborhood's all colored? There's some grand houses yonder." I nodded towards a row of brick mansions even posher'n the president's Philadelphia house.

"This ain't the south." Jack rapped on the door. "Most folk don't turn coloreds away if they want to live near here. You'll see."

When the door opened I knew it was Mary's friend Shermener. Not light as me or dark as Jack, her skin a creamy almond, she glowed with health and what else? Ah, yes, I saw it in her eyes—freedom.

"Hello, Oney. We've been expecting you. Oh, hello, Jack." She nodded at him.

"Thank you so much for helping me, Mrs. Smith, I'm forever in your debt," were my first words to my gracious hostess.

"We're Shermener and Willie to you, Oney. Come on in. Boys, put those bundles down there. Now, ladies first, so Oney—" She took me aside. "What would you like first? A meal, a bed, or the necessary?"

My stomach growled, my bones ached for a bed, but I needed the other thing first. "The necessary, please."

The hardest part of my first free day was saying goodbye to Jack—for now. "The *Nancy*'ll be in port five more days, so I will see you before we launch. Now you begin your new free life."

I grasped his fingertips as we parted, waving, blowing kisses. My mind knew freedom, and now my heart knew love.

My first chore began with a pile of Shermener's sewing, as I refused to sit idle and let my hosts abide by my wishes. My first real employment came the next day from Captain Bowles, as promised, at his home next door to the recently departed naval commander John Paul Jones—but no dirty work. My duties stayed light—polishing silver, dusting, changing bedding, and of course mending his fine linen shirts and trousers. At each day's end, he placed bank notes and coins of my very own into my palm. I smoothed out the crumpled filthy notes and held them to my heart. *Never will I part with this, my first pay*, I vowed. I'd show this to my children, so they'd appreciate what I went through to earn my very own living.

Jack called on me at Shermener's when he was in port, and when I wasn't employed for the eve, for I secured several evening assignments round town. The free blacks I met through the Smiths and the Ladies Charitable African Society sent me to the white *and* black folks's homes what needed help, and seeing my quality of work, not to mention my near-white skin, they grappled over me. Many a time I overheard, "No, Oney's working here this week … no, we need Oney until week's end … I'll match what you pay and double it …"

I sauntered into dressmakers' and milliners' shops, buying up frocks and hats and stockings, attending the North Church, the theatre and taverns that allowed blacks in the snug. There I got some wild stares—*what's a white lady doin' in here*? I merely dipped my lashes and sipped at my malt whisky that I could now afford.

I dedicated my liberty to all my fellow slaves who would never escape the bonds of that atrocious institution. I enjoyed my work, my income, my romance … *ah, freedom*! "Thank you, God, for answering my prayers," I prayed on bent knees morn, noon and night. I dropped to my knees every minute I got.

But barely a month after taking my freedom, a scare jolted me as I held the papers. Now reading bigger words, I was the first each morn to fetch the Portsmouth *Oracle of the Day* and read it cover to cover. On this bright July day a public notice snagged my eye, right below Captain Bowles's latest sales announcement—*Samuel Haley warns him and all others living along the Piscataqua River that Joseph Hutchings, my 13-year-old indentured servant, absconded and he forbid all persons harbouring said boy and masters of vessels from carrying him to sea.*

"Lord, the poor boy," I whispered. "Th-that could be me," I stammered out loud, catching Shermener's ear.

"What's wrong, child? You look like you seen a ghost."

I thrust the paper at her and jabbed my finger at the notice.

She laughed, tossing it aside. "These go in here near every day. You know how many absconded servants run on these streets? Captain Bowles or any other captain don't care 'bout owners comin' after them. Believe you me, girl, if the Washingtons wanted to catch you, they would'a did already."

Oh, how I wanted to believe her. But I knew Shermener was secretly glad I'd ran and come here. The fright passed through me. I forgot all about it, and the Washingtons capturing me … 'til the very next day.

CHAPTER NINETEEN

As I carried bags of fruit and veg down Congress Street, I heard, "Oney Judge!" in a shrieky voice louder'n a cat in heat.

I knew that voice. I heard it at the Washingtons' receptions a thousand times. I picked up my pace but she caught up, clamped her claws into my arm, halted me in my tracks and peered into my face. "Oney, it really is you! What are you doing here? Are the Washingtons in town?"

I looked straight into the eyes of Elizabeth Langdon, daughter of the New Hampshire senator. "No, they are not, Miss Langdon. Now do excuse me." I stepped aside and, as the startled woman's mouth fell open, I scurried away, made a quick right onto Pearl Street and ducked into the black People's Baptist Church, where she wouldn't pursue me if I'd a million-dollar bounty on my head.

Cocooned in the holy sanctuary, I slipt into a pew and dropped to my knees on the hard kneeler. "Please don't let them find me," I begged, hands clasped over the pew in front of me. I'd completely forgotten the Langdons lived here. Would Elizabeth tell the Washingtons on me? Did I dare go to the Langdon mansion and beg her not to betray me?

Never! I trusted no one of the Washingtons' acquaintance. I went about my business, working, reading, writing, learning to draw, enjoying Jack's courting. *Elizabeth Langdon has more important things to tend to, like growing lilies*, I affirmed as I strode round town, yet my eyes darted side to side. I never voiced my disquiet to Jack, Shermener, or my new free friends. I just went about my business, but stayed alert. Truth be told, her accosting me did render me more cautious. Who knows, someday that could be President Washington strolling down Congress Street yelling out "Oney Judge!" And knowing the president, he'd sure follow me into the black church. Lady Washington wouldn't. But he would.

So I cast it aside—'til the knock on Shermener's door opened to "the assistant of Mr. Whipple, Collector of Customs."

"What can I do for you, Mr. Assistant?" I addressed him thusly, as he didn't give his name.

"Ona, Mr. Whipple wants to see you at his office tomorrow morn for an offer of employment."

Relief flooded me. I had no reason to suspect otherwise, as more folk, white and black, clamored for my services. I reckoned the Collector had a large house and wanted some light chores done, for word got round that I didn't do no scrubbin' or scourin.'

So I put on my best satin frock with a crisp white linen blouse, my wide-brimmed garden hat and my new pearl earbobs, and walked the six blocks to Mr. Whipple's office.

"Miss Judge—may I call you Ona?"

"Why certainly, sir," I replied in my most businesslike tone as he motioned to a high-backed chair opposite his desk, strewn with papers and ink blotters, a right mess. Mayhap he wanted me to start cleaning here; it sure needed it.

"Miss Judge—Ona—I've been in contact with President Washington." An oily smile spread his lips.

I froze. My heart stopped. I knew instantly. This was no offer of employment. It was a ploy to get me here. But I refused to fall into his trap. I kept my composure. And did it ever save me.

"The president first contacted Treasury Secretary Wolcott to capt—er, retrieve you. Since you, as his possession, esca—er, departed from the president's Executive Mansion here to New Hampshire, he believed that summoning me, the Portsmouth Customs Collector, was the proper protocol, since I supervise the unloading and delivering of goods within the town and I report directly to Secretary Wolcott."

"Oh, so I'm goods." I stared him down.

He looked away, yet seemed unable to keep his eyes off me, my hat, my dress. "Well, uh, legally, yes. Therefore, Treasury Secretary Wolcott has asked me to quietly send you back—not publicly. Quietly."

"Mr. Whipple, if President Washington and you read his own Fugitive Slave Act, which I've read now that I'm literate, you will both learn that he has every right to request that you apprehend me, but a slave owner must appear before a federal or state magistrate and prove ownership before removing the … ahem … *goods* to another state. This is a breach of legal process on the president's part."

He stared dumbly, tongue lolling out his mouth.

"I now realize you're not familiar with the Slave Act from your blank expression. However, the president should know better than that." I sat ramrod straight, chin up.

Of course he couldn't answer. He removed his specs and leant forward. "Why did you escape, Ona? President and Lady Washington maintain they brought you up and treated you more like their child than a servant, and you lived quite comfortably."

"That much is true, sir, but comfortable is not free. And my thirst for freedom superceded any guarantee of comfort, albeit in bondage, for the rest of my days. I simply wish life, liberty and the pursuit of happiness as proclaimed in the Declaration of Independence which Mr. Jefferson penned. Surely you can understand that. What would *you* prefer, sir? Bondage to the grave? Or life, liberty and the pursuit of happiness?" I goaded.

He couldn't answer this time, either, only steepled his fingers. He looked me directly in the eye, uncustomary for whites. "I'm greatly impressed with you overall. Your appearance, your eloquent speech, your deportment ..." He gestured up and down. "You're as poised as any fine lady to the manor born. Why, the president told me you were too simple and inoffensive to leave them on your own. He believes you became embroiled in an amorous liaison with a Frenchman who abandoned you in a state of pregnancy. I admit I had no reason to disbelieve that."

The theatrics of that yarn amused me. My mouth turned up at one corner. "A Frenchman? Abandoning me in a state of pregnancy? Do I appear in a state of pregnancy, sir? That sounds like something Lady Washington would conjure up, not him. To be precise, that's right out of her romance novels, and if I hadn't read it myself, I wouldn't venture a guess it came straight from the pages of *Charlotte Temple*."

I squared my shoulders. "No, sir, no one, Frenchman or otherwise, persuaded me to leave bondage, nor am I simple or inoffensive. The president and his wife know that full well. As you can see, sir. He's hoodwinked you, plain and simple."

Did I dare laugh? I smiled all right, but suppressed the laugh. After all, someone as proper and eloquent as myself wouldn't dare ridicule the president of the United States before one of his public servants.

"Oh, tongues will wag ..." He waved his specs through the air. "It must have been some rumormonger fabricating these romantic details to bring some titillation to their otherwise sapless existence. Heed my words, Ona

...￼" He focused on me, "... since I assured my director that I would with great pleasure execute the president's wishes, I'll secure your permanent freedom if you return to Virginia tomorrow. I took it upon myself to secure your passage on Captain Bowles's schooner *Thomas*. And in deference to your elegance and deportment, I won't have you physically restrained en route to the boat. I'll ask you to confide in my obtaining for you the freedom you so earnestly wish for."

I didn't miss a beat. Poker faced, I accepted his proposal. "Why, of course, sir. I'll make preparation with cheerfulness to go on board the vessel the very same day."

"Superb. And I propose concealing your intentions from your people lest they should discourage you from your purpose." He grinned in sly self-satisfaction.

"You are so right, sir. Now if you'll excuse me, I shall prepare for my passage. I do so want to return to my family." A genuine tear trickled down my cheek as I pictured Mamma.

But when I turned and departed, I finally let out that laugh, wishing I could guffaw right in his face. I had no intention of falling into his trap. After telling me how proper and refined and eloquent I was, he still believed me such a fool?

"He thinks he's dealing with some dummy, he's got another think coming," I said out loud, not dropping my 'g's' as I strode away, back to my freedom.

He never came for me the next day. Nor did he send any more of his henchmen to the door with bogus offers of employment or other ruses. He called on me his very self, one blustery morn as I fed Shermener's cats. No servants about, I opened the door and fought the urge to slam it in his face. *How rude of you to call on me uninvited!* nearly burst from my mouth. But when he removed his hat, grasped my hand *and kissed it* ... not in a month of Sundays could I resist hearing what he had to say for himself.

"May I come in, Miss Judge?"

Now I was Miss Judge. I stepped back and he entered, wiping his feet. In the parlour, I offered him tea to be polite but of course he refused: whites never drank from colored cups.

"Miss Judge, you must know that the president contacted me directly and I persuaded him not to pursue you. I told him it appeared to me, so obviously, that you hadn't been decoyed away or apprehended, but a thirst for complete freedom had been your only motive for absconding. I must admit to you, I offered a bargain with him, for him to free you upon his death."

I balled a fist on my hip. "Why on earth did you tell him that?"

He fidgeted with his watch fob. "I only wanted to help. But somehow the president believed the entreaty came from you. I thought it fair to read you his reply." He unfolded a sheet of paper filled with the president's wide-looped penmanship.

With two fingers I plucked the letter from his hand. "Pardon, sir, but along with eloquence and grace, I possess literacy. I shall read it myself." I read out loud, out of courtesy. Also, hearing the president's words spoken through my mouth made my cause all the more just.

"To enter into such a compromise with her, as she suggested to you, is totally inadmissible, for reasons that must strike at first view: for however well disposed I might be to a gradual abolition, or even to an entire emancipation of that description of People it would neither be politic or just to reward unfaithfulness with premature preference; and therby discontent the minds of all her fellow servants who by their steady attachments are far more deserving than herself of favor. If she does not cooperate then I have no choice but to resort to such measures as are proper to put her on board a vessel bound either to Alexandria or the Federal City, but do not use violent measures, the kind that might excite a mob or riot or even uneasy sensations in the minds of well-disposed citizens."

"Hmmf." I folded it and handed it back to him. "I shall consider returning to their servitude only if they promise to free me. Otherwise I would rather suffer death than return to slavery. I do wish to return to my native place." Mamma's face flashed before me. It tore me up inside. "But I will not take orders from the Washingtons as their property ever again."

He stammered and fiddled with the paper. "Miss Judge, I already replied to this letter, and apologized for my ill success in returning you. I stated very clearly and frankly that my personal feelings held me back … namely, my feelings for you."

He tugged at his collar. Beads of sweat glistened at his hairline. "I qualified this by saying that a servant returning voluntarily is of more value than one taken forceably like a felon to punishment. I did agree to send you to Alexandria if it be possible without exciting a riot or a mob." He jumped aside as a cat rubbed against his legs. "But I warned the president that carrying out this action would cause exactly that. After all, New Hampshire is quite anti-slavery. Hence, I will take no measures to send you back." He crossed himself. "As God is my witness."

"Thank you, sir." I opened the door to make it clear the visit was at an end. "And if you ever need any domestic help or sewing … there are many hard workers right here in town who would be most obliged to help you, for an adequate wage."

I saw him out the door and out of my life. I hoped.

****

"Oh, Lawdy Lawdy, wait 'til you hear this latest scuttlebutt buzzin' round the streets like a swarm o'skeeters!" Jack'd come back on leave and we'd barely embraced afore he started a'guffawin' and knee slappin'. Humming in curiosity, the Smiths and their help flocked to the parlour and surrounded us hand-clasped lovers on the sofa.

"Do tell!" They gathered round Jack like expecting he found the cure for pox.

"It seems Lady Washington's nephew Mr. Bartholemew Dandridge suddenly fled Philadelphia the very same day the *Nancy* pulled out o'port carrying her precious cargo, my Oney girl." His eyes met mine and he squeezed my hands. "Nobody could chalk it up to happenstance and leave it at that—oh, no, they dug for dirt, and they dug it deep. So now the latest babble is that they both run off—together."

A gasp circled the parlour, mine being the loudest. "Me and Mr. Bart Dandridge? They should know me better'n that. He cannot hope to hold a poky candle to my Jack." I gazed upon my sailor man, eager to clear the parlour of spectators so we could court in private.

"It ain't only all over the capital city, it's soarin' up and down the coast faster'n the bald eagle," Jack told the spellbound household.

"But that's good for you, Oney," Shermener encouraged me. "They'll be so busy seeking out Mr. Dandridge at his usual haunts, thinking he's entangled with you, they won't come nowhere near our town."

I nodded with a grin, amused, but deep down, flattered I'd become such big news. I'd never had any interest in Bart Dandridge, but after all, he *was* somebody.

Mayhap I'd be somebody someday, too.

CHAPTER TWENTY

Portsmouth sorely lacked people of color. When Shermener told me we were only 1% of the population—of New Hampshire that is, not Portsmouth—I wasn't a bit surprised. What a change of scenery from Virginia and even New York. Of the blacks here only a handful were slaves. My near-white skin and fine raiment opened many doors for me. I enjoyed courteous service in shops, taverns, eateries, tea rooms ... but I kept going to the black church. Instilled in me was that rule: one drop of Negro blood is enough. But heck, I was proud to be what I was.

One November eve I attended a Ladies Charitable African Society meeting where we taught folk to read. Returning home, no sooner had I shed my cloak than Shermener's daughter scampered up to me. "You got a caller, Oney, wanted it to be a surprise." Pointing at the closed parlour door in a burst of giggles, she sported a playful grin.

"Who'd be calling on me as a surprise?" Her grin and giggles assured me it wasn't no Washington lackeys. When I stepped into the parlour, I nearly fell over. Jack stood front and center, arms wide for me to step into. "Jack! You're not s'posed to be back for two weeks."

"The captain took the sloop to New York and back instead of Philadelphia. I got an extra few days. Thought I'd spend 'em with my wife-to-be." He dropped to one knee and held up a ring. A lavender-color stone peered up at me.

The entire household gathered round us now.

I still wasn't sure I heard right. "Wife-to-be? Me? Jack ..."

I dropped to my own knees and wrapt my arms round those sturdy shoulders. He slipt the ring on my finger, which one, I don't recall, but it fit snug and felt so right.

"That's sea glass, found in the sea from glass that could be from the beginning of time. Called Mermaid Tears, the story goes every time a sailor drowns at sea, the mermaids cry, and the glass is their tears washing up on shore. But that's one'a them tales like the sea serpents. I found it fitting to give you somethin' from the sea."

"Oh, Jack, I'm honored to be your wife-to-be, and even more so to be your wife!" His hug enveloped me like a warm blanket.

Everybody clapped and cheered as we shared congratulatory hugs.

Our notice appeared in the *New Hampshire Gazette* on Saturday, January 14, 1797, the proudest item I ever read out loud to my dear friends. "Mr. John Staines to Miss Ona Gudge— hey, they spelt that wrong! And who did the officiating but Reverend Samuel Haven, who'd bound Tobias Lear and poor yellow fever victim Polly Long in holy matrimony. The Reverend remembered me, gave me his best wishes, and assured me he wouldn't tell the president.

"Go ahead an' tell him," I defied my former owner's husband. I also defied the president's two-faced bootlicker Collector Whipple, who'd tried to thwart our plans by ordering the clerk to withhold our marriage certificate. We sidestepped round that molehill by going to the next town, Greenland, where town clerk Thomas Philbrook, with more honor in his little finger than Collector Whipple in his entire body, provided our proper papers. In return I promised Clerk Philbrook three hours of free sewing—if I ever got back to Greenland.

I missed Jack terribly when we were apart, but dear Captain Bowles paid him a generous wage that afforded us a tidy little home and enough to eat. But the thirst for independence that drove me to my freedom stayed with me. So with Jack away at sea, I stayed busy with my work. My extra income allowed me to pursue hobbies. I learnt to draw and paint. But I put work aside for a greatly more important endeavor—our first baby Eliza.

****

One muggy July eve I sat in our bedroom rocking the baby to sleep before the open window. The refreshing sea breeze brought the promise of a thunderstorm. Expecting Jack's return in four days, I shut my eyes, imagining the soft touch of his lips on mine.

A knock at the door jolted me from my reverie. I placed baby Eliza in her sturdy Shaker cradle, a gift from the Bartletts, a family whose home I cleaned.

Thinking it one of my friends or a customer calling to engage my services, I opened the door. But my visitor wasn't expected and the surprise wasn't a pleasant one. I gasped at the sight of the neat powdered wig, velvet coat and lace jabot. I stepped back, hoping he didn't take that as an invite in.

"Good eve, Ona," said President Washington's nephew Burwell Bassett, whom I hadn't seen last since my Mount Vernon days.

"What do you want?" was all I cared to know from him right now. Over the initial shock, I stood rigid, hand on the door, my guard up, ready to slam it shut. I knew this was not a friendly call.

"My uncle the president has asked a special favor of me. In my obedience, I must carry it out. He requested I be the instrument of recovering and forwarding the girl back to the plantation—and that girl is you." He pointed with both pointer fingers as if aiming pistols at my eyes.

Not even a bogus offer of employment this time. I opened my mouth to speak my piece, but he didn't pause for breath.

"My uncle the president further pled that I avoid any unpleasant or troublesome measures to capt—er, retrieve you and escort you back. As I am currently residing with the Langdons, you will also lodge there until my departure on Tuesday. Now—how long will it take you to gather some belongings and come with me?" He forced a smile that touched neither his eyes nor his heart, for I could tell his mission served one purpose—to gain favor, and hopefully a generous bequest—from his uncle.

Since he'd spoken in a civil tone, I didn't slam the door in his face. Nor did I invite him in. "My belongings, Mr. Basset? Does that include my infant?"

He gulped. Clearly his uncle wasn't aware that I'd given birth, and now they owned another potential piece of property they'd never see.

I squared my shoulders and lifted my head high. "Sir, I respect your need to carry out your uncle's orders. However, I've no intention of returning to the plantation and my former bondage, with you or no one else. I made that clear to the customs officer when your uncle used him and the Treasury Secretary as go-betweens. You've just become one more go-between who can relay my message. Good eve, sir." Now I flung the door shut, but he halted it midway and dared step over the threshold.

"Ona, you are in no position to refuse recapture. Mark my word, I shall return with orders to bring you and your child by force." With a disdainful glance round my home, his beady eyes narrowed. "Do not dare defy me, girl." He spat out that last disparaging threat with a turn of his heel as he stomped out.

I bolted all the doors and windows and rushed back to my child. As I wrapt my protective arms round her and held her to my breast, I promised her, though waves of terror tore at me, "I will protect you, baby. I will never let no one take us away."

Through the night, as a crashing thunderstorm raged, I sat up with baby Eliza. Eyes wide in sleepless fright, I dreaded that vicious nephew's return with an army of slave-catchers to drag me and my child from my home, never again to see my beloved husband.

I must have dozed, for a knocking on the back door jolted me into awareness. Recalling the horror of the eve before, I faced the uncertainty of my future as my heart leapt into action.

A steady rap on the window further alarmed me. I flattened my body against the wall.

"Oney, open up, it's me, Cyrus." Hearing the voice of Cyrus Bruce, the Langdons' free black butler, I heaved a relieved sigh. But goosebumps still chilled my arms. Could he be here to help me or with orders to lure me into captivity? Without the choice to ignore him and hope he went away, I went to the back door, unbolted and opened it.

He strode up to me from his perch at the window. "Senator Langdon is aware that the president's nephew called here to retrieve you. The senator urges you to leave town by midnight and hide somewhere else."

I rubbed the fuzziness of fatigue from my eyes and gaped at Cyrus. Not sure I heard right, I asked, "Senator Langdon wants to help me? But it was his own daughter who told the president she saw me on the street."

Cyrus shook his head with a half-smile. "The senator ain't like his daughter. He helps slaves go free, not get captured. The senator has a good heart. So take his warning and the baby and go."

"But go where?"

"The senator offered you go to Jack and Phillis Warner," he answered my desperate question afore I had the chance to even guess the possibilities.

"Oh, the kind man. I owe him so many thanks. As I do you."

The Warners lived in the next town, Greenland. I knew Jack and Phillis and their daughters from church and Ladies Charitable African Society meetings. When the senator freed all his slaves, he kept them on his staff as paid servants, including the Warners.

Muttering words of gratitude I needed to voice to the kind Senator later, I tossed some essentials into a satchel. Cyrus walked me to the stable up the street. I hired a horse and driver, and fled the few miles to Greenland—and to safety—for now. This time I didn't peek over my shoulder every two seconds as I did walking the streets. I felt God beside us, protecting us. I breathed easy over the bumpy rutted road to Greenland.

The Warners harbored me and the baby 'til I got word that Bassett left town. Jack fetched us when he returned from the sea. I felt safe in his arms as we embraced on the Warners' doorstep, baby Eliza between us. A sudden foreknowledge convinced me I needn't fear further capture after that terrifying ordeal.

My portent came true, for in late December, Jack returned home with disturbing news. "President Washington died of a throat ailment."

As I listened, mixed emotions churned within me. That didn't mean I was now legally free. I'd never been his property. I was hers. But knowing the lady well as I did, I knew she wouldn't send any flunkies round to threaten me with capture, brute force or otherwise.

"I must do the right thing, Jack." I went over to my desk and with my own pen and paper, wrote a note of condolence to my former owner. I expressed my sorrow at the president's passing. But not my sorrow at leaving her. I signed it "Mrs. Ona Staines."

I didn't expect to hear back from her. But I did think of her now and then, wondering how she was doing, if she was healthy and happy. I even wrote her another letter that Eastertime. I told her I was married with a baby girl, and I kept busy working and enjoying my life. I wanted to tell her I missed her, but decided against it. That night I dreamed of her, and in the dream she gave me one of her smiles that we used to share. I did miss her. So I took the letter I'd written, unsealed it and added "I miss you" at the very bottom.

Only two years later, as I nursed baby Nancy, Jack came in holding the newspaper out to me. "Read it to me, Jackie, I got my hands full."

"I thought you'd rather read it yourself, but if you say so. Lady Washington died May 22nd."

"Oh, dear." My stomach tightened. I shut my eyes and saw her kindly face before me as if she sat right across, as we always did. A summery breeze floated inside, billowing the curtains. It warmed me like the hug she never saw fit to give me. Now I believe she just did, and I smiled.

But even upon her death neither I nor my children were legally free. We all still belonged to Daniel Parke Custis's estate, meaning her nieces, nephews and grandchildren. That included Miz Eliza, who never got me as that wedding gift. My fists clenched. Determined never to be her slave, I knew how to handle any proxy they might send to retrieve me. I was aware the Custis heirs could try to bring me back south. But because I knew how to fight back, like I did those other two times, I was no longer afraid.

Moving forward through the new century, we had our own home and three little ones, Eliza, William and Nancy. But the 19th century didn't treat me kindly. I still had my freedom, but not much else.

CHAPTER TWENTY-ONE

I looked forward to the new year as 1802 neared an end. With the death of Lady Washington and nearly losing my baby Nancy, born premature, weak and frail, I gladly put it behind me to start fresh.

Jack and I celebrated extra this Christmas, knowing better times were ahead.

But in the dead of night, horrifying shrieks of "Fire!" sliced through the silence. Jack sprang from bed and ran to the window.

"God above, the sky's ablaze!" He dashed out of the room. I slid from the warm bed, wrapping my shawl round me, shivering.

The cries of "Fire!" grew louder as Jack pulled on his overcoat and boots. He grabbed a bucket and turned to me. "I'm helpin' out, you stay inside, hear?" As he fled, I stepped outside and peered up Market Street. Hellish orange flames blazed in the distance. Smoke billowed up into the frigid air. Men ran towards the fire, carrying buckets, their thumping footsteps drowning out the shrieks and wails of terror.

Explosions pierced the air, making me jump out of my skin. They sounded like those gunshots during the yellow fever. After each explosion, glass shattered. In the glaring firelight, men furiously worked their hand-operated pumper engines. But the streams of water from the hoses failed to reach high enough. They splattered below the upper floors of high buildings. A block-long bucket brigade lined Market Street. I wanted to help but couldn't leave three small children alone.

I prayed for Jack's safety.

The Great Portsmouth Fire consumed mansions along with small dwellings, numerous stores and a school. Mercifully the fire burnt itself out before it reached us.

Jack finally came home. He staggered through the door, coughing and wheezing, unable to catch his breath.

I helped him to bed and tucked blankets around him. "I ran into Judge Pickering's house to save their children, trapped on the third floor," he rasped as a fit of coughing consumed him. "I searched best I could, but the smoke blinded me, stung my eyes …"

"Jack, don't try to talk no more." I boiled water and placed a cup tween his lips but all he could do was cough.

I went to fetch Dr. Goodard, but his once-grand house lay in a pile of ashes. Nearly all of Market Street smoldered in charred ruins. Hopeless, I returned to my family.

Who could help Jack? I racked my brain for names of folk who could bring Jack a remedy. As he gasped for breath, I ran through the biting cold to Captain Bowles's house. He lived in the opposite direction, the part of town the fire hadn't ravaged.

A servant answered. I pleaded, "Please fetch the captain ... my husband ... he can hardly breathe. He got caught in the fire ..." Without a word, she tore up the staircase. I heard pounding on a door.

The captain tumbled down the stairs and gaped as if he'd never seen me afore. "What happened?"

"Jack ... the fire ..." was all I could choke out. He grabbed his coat off a rack and sprinted down the street, way ahead of me. When I reached home, he sat at Jack's bedside, clasping his hand. I sat beside him. His chest lay still. No more labored breathing, no more hacking cough. He lay at peace.

"I'm so sorry, Oney ..." the captain whispered. I collapsed. The room spun. I smelled the coat of wax on the floor. Shutting my eyes, I cradled my head in my arms. I suffered the unbearable loss of not just Jack, but part of me. Then my mind blanked.

I remember nothing more until the funeral. Half the town turned out to bid my husband farewell. "He's Portsmouth's hero," Captain Bowles declared to the stunned crowd gathered in the cold sun. I held the sea glass stone to my lips and kissed it.

"You are not gone, Jack," I sobbed, facing the freshly dug grave. "You live on in the children and I will always honor your memory. You're Portsmouth's hero, but you're my strength."

I called on that strength to get me through years of cold, darkness and poverty.

CHAPTER TWENTY-TWO

I couldn't support myself and three little ones without starving. I needed help—and fast. Even though we never starved, we still lived hand to mouth. Most I ever had were a few dollars and a handful of coin. That wouldn't last the week, and my babies already wailed for nourishment. I went hungry so that I could feed them.

Harboring more fugitive slave boarders, the Smiths' four-room house was bursting at the seams, so I couldn't go there. Since the kind-hearted Warners hid us when Senator Langdon clued me in to flee town, they took me and my babies into their cozy little home. We pooled our talents and ran an economical household, made our own soap, candles, clothing, grew a mixture of vittles. Hardly a bustling port city like Portsmouth, only ten blacks lived in Greenland, so work for us folk was scarce, but their citizens were no less generous. We gratefully accepted donations of firewood, vittles, candles and rum that made the frigid winters bearable.

Because so many folk called Jack Warner "John Jack", "Black Jack" and "Jacks," the Warners became the Jack family. Fine by me. As long as I remained Mrs. Staines.

Mayhap I thought far ahead of white folk for these times, but I saw all this almsgiving as a paradox. Why not grant us some autonomy instead of handing us alms? Allow us schooling to prepare for better jobs than working fields and domestic labor. Teach these poor folk to read. At least free them from the shame of illiteracy. Then we wouldn't need beg for handouts. But, no, not in this century, even though it was now the 19th. Mayhap we'd overcome the prejudice, poverty and indignity in the next. But first things first—outlaw that degrading institution of slavery. Who would be the brave soul to finally abolish it?

We coexisted in Phillis's two-bedroom dwelling given her by Deacon Brackett, her former owner. We grew many of the same herbs Lady Washington grew in her garden—sage, lavender, thyme—and sold them as medicines. But none of them poison purple bells of foxglove Lady Washington grew.

236

Finally able to enjoy the blooms of my very own garden, I proudly nurtured marigolds, sweet William, bachelor's buttons, and tried my hand at roses. The jams and pies from our currants and raspberries sweetened our summers.

Phillis even had the local stream named after her, Phillis Brook. It served as our very own moat, barricading our castle from invaders—that is, slave-catchers. Reaching our humble abode with its rotting wood boards entailed trampling over the weed-choked roadway and crossing the wobbly footbridge spanning the brook. To secure further obstruction, we laid logs over the road that the sturdiest carriage would not dare traverse; visitors first needed roll the logs out of their path.

If that weren't enough protection, townsfolk built us a stone wall and a gate round the property as barter for our juicy apple and blueberry pies.

And I did receive callers—mostly white folk, from the commonest laborers to Portsmouth's finest, including Senator and Mrs. Langdon—but their daughter Elizabeth stayed away. I needn't wonder why.

Seems I become a curiosity round these parts. The town'd never seen the likes of me afore—a runaway slave what once belonged to America's highest-ranking residents.

Townsfolk rich and poor, from sea captains' wives to blacksmiths' apprentices, badgered me with questions about the president and his lady. We'd chat in the garden, rocking in our chairs, sipping sweet tea with the recipe I'd brung from the south.

"What were the Washingtons really like?" "Did the president have a sense of humor?" "What did they eat for breakfast?" "Did the president tipple?" "What did they talk about among themselves?" "Did they attend theatre?" "Did they have spats with each other?" "What did they call each other in private?" "Did the president ever walk round the house without his teeth in?" On and on. Sometimes they even asked questions about me.

"Did they treat you well?" "Did you have any free time?" "Did Lady Washington ever hit you?" "Did you get enough to eat?"

I answered all that and more, relating lavish accounts of their receptions, their fetes, her ladies' teas, their dinners with Citizen Genet and Monseiur Jeffer-*sone*. Seems he wasn't all that popular round here neither, and I made sure they knew exacty how Lady Washington felt about him. I even relayed some of the jokes we'd shared, when Lady Washington goaded me to tell her something funny about Mr. Jefferson.

These folk became my following, as they returned day after day, now with neighbors and young 'uns in tow. Carts clattered and fancy carriages rolled up the road, conveying laborer folk in blue denim, chambermaids in white uniform, and the well-to-do in satin finery, their chilluns flocking to me, arms outstretched.

"Please tell the children about the Custis girls, Mrs. Staines," mammas and pappas entreated, carrying their gifts of vittles, rum, wine, and sometimes even a bag of coin or two, along with bolts of sumptuous cloths and sketches of the latest fashions for me to create their finery.

The Jacks didn't mind all the company either. They, as did my numerous callers, never tired of my adventures. But at times I did—*oh, no not another pack of troops*—dusting my hands on my apron and looking at the ball of dough that wouldn't bake itself, I sighed and opened the door to the latest swarm of unexpected callers when I needed to work round the house.

As my little ones grew big and William followed his daddy's footsteps to the sea, my girls excelled at art. They drew and painted such exquisite scenes, many upper class Portsmouth folk boasted Eliza and Nancy's works on their mansions' walls. But I never known a rich artist, and art hardly put bounty on our table. Their meagre sales forced them to toil as maids. Me, I maintained my prowess at the needle, with embroideries, dressmaking and tapestries.

Though hardship was a small price to pay for my and my children's freedom, 1816 plunged us into pauperism. As Eliza turned 18 and Nancy 14, the harsh winter thrust hunger and bone-rattling cold upon us with howling winds, snow and ice storms. Our offers of work dwindled to an occasional cleaning job or a soap- or candle-making assignment. At the brink of beggary, I lived the worst nightmare of my life—my girls become wards of the town.

Frequent ferocious snowstorms kept neighbors from bringing us firewood, so we fast run out of fuel. This sleety morn as I sat sewing, huddled in my blanket to ward off the chill, bootsteps trudged up the walk and stomped on the porch. My blanket wrapt tight round me, I opened the door to a blast of icy wind, a slap of snowflakes across my face—and the town clerk.

"Mrs. Staines, I regret to give you this news, but ..."

I don't recall no more of the ugliest words I ever heard. I thank the Lord He let me forget. *No, don't take my girls*, I begged, *take me instead*—I remember those words because I screamed them, over and over, pleading on my knees, my arms round his legs 'til he lost his footing.

Still he refused.

My girls boarded at different neighbors who hired them as needed. "I'll summon them there, thank you." Shaking me off, he backed out into the cold. I shut the door, sliding to the floor in a shivery heap. *No, don't take my girls! How can you be so cruel?*

The next day I slogged the mile to town hall through piles of snow over the frozen ground. I could've spared myself the agony of seeing my little girls sold, but they needed their mamma there for them. As I trudged, numb with cold, past snow-blanketed fields and scraggly branches, my long-ago youth haunted me, those days of defiance when I vowed *this humiliation will never befall me.*

The helplessness of that former life flooded back—slave bound to owner, with no control, not even allowed our God-given free will. But compared to the heartache of seeing my babies sold along with cookery and animals in 'free' New Hampshire's version of slavery, I could've braved my own storage in a slave pen and resale to a heartless master back then.

I finally reached the town hall and approached the mob of eager bidders nudging each other aside to get a glimpse of the goods. They bid on pots, pans, donkeys and now—a knife pierced my heart at the sight. My precious girls stood trembling on the block, sheer terror in their eyes, while the rambling auctioneer persuaded the crowd of townsfolk, many we'd invited into our home, to bid them up like chattels, "Who'll take these fine young wenches? The first item for sale is a fine animal, no defects or blemishes, in fine condition, supple, strong, can wash, plough, sew ... who will offer me ..." He rattled off numbers so fast they ran together in a blur.

Much as I grieved Jack's death, this was worse, this paradox of slavery. At least death ended the toil and drudgery, as only death set our people free.

I clasped my hands, *Oh, dear God above, please let them sell me instead*! But He ignored my pleading and instead "Sold! To Farmer Nathan Johnson ..." and a gavel bang ripped through the air.

My little girls lost their wills with that slam of gavel on wood. A wave of guilt near drowned me. How could I, their mother, having defied my owner and that savage institution, let my children lose their freedom? I failed them, I was a bad mother. Madder at myself than at the town and the winning bidder, I dug my nails into my palms to cause pain, making it linger and torture me.

You deserve to suffer, you unfit mother! I berated myself.

I smacked myself across the face and grimaced from the biting sting. *How dare you accept this. Do not turn around and go back home a free woman while those precious girls get dragged off to bondage.*

With the same courage that defied the very president of the United States, I strode up to Farmer Johnson. "Take me, sir, leave my girls alone, they're too young, spare them."

He shook his head, mouthing "It's a done deal" or some such utterance.

"Just remember they ain't field slaves!" I screamed into his face.

He backed off and nodded. "Yeah, I know they ain't. I'll let 'em go when I don't need 'em no more."

"You won't beat 'em? You won't rape 'em? You won't brand 'em?" I shrieked the words of a madwoman.

"Why, no ..." His jowls swung as he shook his head.

"You gimme yo'word?" I further defied him, grasping his collar in my fist and pulling him nose to nose 'til I smelt the whiskey on his breath. "With God as our witness?"

"Why, course I do." He backed down, and I secretly smiled at the glint of fear I seen in his eyes.

"You better mean it. Cos if you mistreat either o'them girls, you answer to *me!*" I jabbed a finger into his chest.

They ain't field slaves, I declared over and over. *They ain't field slaves, Farmer Johnson will not work them hard and will free them when he no longer needs their services, just as he promised ...*

Clerks escorted my girls off the block and we embraced. "We will survive this, my babies," I promised them. "Don't ever forget, you ain't slaves, he don't own you, he only bought your services. As long as there's breath in my body, nobody owns you."

Watching Farmer Johnson load my girls into his wagon brought back all the heart-wrenching grief of slavery tearing me from Mamma's arms every time I departed Mount Vernon.

But this savage practice would prevent my girls from starvation. With the Johnson farm only a mile away, we did see each other at church and Christmas. Mercifully, Farmer Johnson released Eliza in April, and Nancy returned to me at the next new year's. I opened the door to my most cherished new year's gift—my youngest baby girl. "I'm home to stay,

Mamma." How I'd longed to hear those words. I opened my arms for her to lay her head on her mamma's loving bosom.

The good Lord called Jack Warner that autumn. Our dear friends' generous gifts of provisions and a funeral stood tween us and pauperism once more. The town even paid a dollar a day for his care 'til he drew his last breath.

But I hardly faded into the wilderness of Greenland, New Hampshire. Oh, no, just the opposite. I'd become somewhat notable round town when word spread who I was—rather who I'd been. At this late age, no longer fearing capture, I reveled in my 'fame', attending soirees and parties in my finest calico, lawn and linen gowns as the guest of honor.

They sent fancy carriages for me, wined and dined me, and I sat at the center of many a ladies' circle, reminiscent of Lady Washington's teas when I stood in the corner in silence, my only purpose to serve the ladies their tipples or squash a bug. They lavished praise upon my person, for my "intelligent expression", and "refinement in manner". I could'a profited off this notoriety but to me that was a form of prostitution. Mrs. Langdon asked to take me on tour, but I declined. I'd done enough traveling in my time.

****

"George Washington Born One Hundred Years Ago Today" blasted the headline on Feb'y 22, 1832. Portsmouth celebrated his centennial and townsfolk invited me to their fetes and receptions. But that very day of the president's hundredth birth, fever took away my precious Eliza at age 34. I had never bore such pain or grief as I stood over that cold grave and watched my dear daughter lowered into the earth. The Jack sisters each held an arm and led me away, followed by so many of my friends who brought food and wood and rum and their comfort and sympathy. But no one could bring my baby back.

The next Feb'y dealt the final blow when my girl Nancy passed at 31. But she'd been sick so long with chills and cough and fever; she got better, she got worse—the Lord's call home came as a blessing.

My son William, still at sea, did not return.

My children were gone, but I knew my sister Delphy was thriving. Miz Eliza's husband Thomas Law freed Delphy. I never liked Mr. Law but I sat down and wrote him a note of gratitude for granting to my sister what I seized with my escape. Would Mr. Law have freed me had I not escaped? I shall never know, nor do I care to wonder.

Here's a bit of real life irony: Delphy married Lady Washington's grandson William Costin. As Delphy also learnt to read and write, we exchanged letters, though we both knew we'd never see each other again. She gave me five nieces and two nephews. So I did have family, but in faraway Virginia. But how would Lady Washington react to having Delphy as a granddaughter-in-law and part-black great grandchildren? It made me laugh.

I freely attended the anti-slavery Stratham Baptist Church. That's when my name spread all over New Hampshire.

CHAPTER TWENTY-THREE

When Rev. Chase wanted my story to appear in the *Granite Freeman*, he called on me at home. "More than a few folk told me about your former life with the Washingtons and your bravery," he poured on the flattery, but even at this age I couldn't resist lapping it up. "Your courageous escape from human bondage will galvanize all the abolitionist folk in these parts, and no doubt farther afield. You're our very own spokeswoman for freedom."

"Oh, I'm not much of a writer," I admitted, serving him a generous portion of my raspberry pie. I led him to the scarred kitchen table and put the tea kettle on. "I've written letters, but only to those close to me—my mamma, my sister … and to Lady Washington, long ago."

"I'm not asking you to write, Mrs. Staines. I want to interview you. I'll do the writing."

So I gave him a fair and unbiased story. "I harbor no ill will toward my former owners, yet I abhor slavery and pray it will be abolished in my lifetime."

By then my advancing age and resulting palsy stoked my reassurance that the Custis heirs wouldn't take the trouble to drag me back south.

So with this interview in 1846, I became even more famous. But not famous enough to end slavery. I can only hope some brave soul will emancipate every slave from bondage, at least before the end of *this* century.

Author's Note from Diana Rubino

Oney Judge did escape to Portsmouth, NH in 1796, and her interviews with reporters are cited in the bibliography. Martha Washington, although torn about the slavery issue in later years as was President Washington, could not legally free Oney. She was one of the dower slaves, who belonged to the estate of Martha's first husband Daniel Parke Custis. Virginia law dictated that when a man died intestate, as did Custis, his widow was given use of one third of his slaves until her death. However, they remained the property of his estate. This prevented Martha from freeing any of the dower slaves. They could only be divided among her grandchildren after her death.

From Mount Vernon historian Mary Thompson: "We'd have to talk to a specialist in 18th century law, but Martha Washington *might* have been able to free the dower slaves, IF (and it is a very big if) she reimbursed the Custis estate for their value *and* if she had permission of *all* the grandchildren. Since married women technically could not own property, the husbands of any married granddaughters at the time would have made the decision. Oney knew there was talk of giving her to Eliza. This was not necessarily as a wedding gift; my guess is that Eliza specifically asked for Oney, maybe in terms of after Martha's death, when the eventual division was made to the grandchildren."

Hercules escaped from Mount Vernon on February 22, 1797, George Washington's 65th birthday and about two to three weeks before the Washingtons left Philadelphia at the end of the presidency. The Washingtons did try to find Hercules for several years, but he was never seen again.

Oney's half-sister Delphy was freed by Eliza's husband Thomas Law in 1807. Delphy married William Costin, who is thought to have been Martha Washington's grandson. He is said to have been the son of Ann Dandridge, Martha's mixed race half-sister. They had five daughters and two sons.

The Washingtons found out that Oney was living in Portsmouth and tried to secure her return, but she eluded their capture.

An advertisement was posted saying: 'ABSCONDED from the household of the President of the United States, ONEY JUDGE, a light mulatto girl, much freckled, with very black eyes and bushy black hair; she is of middle stature, slender, and delicately formed, about 20 years of age. Ten dollars will be paid to any person who will bring her home, if taken in the city, or on board any vessel in the harbour—and a reasonable additional sum if apprehended at, and brought from a greater distance, and in proportion to the distance.'

In an act of unexpected lenience, Martha gave up on Oney and let her remain free. Since she'd complained, "I am more like a state prisoner" during her husband's presidency, perhaps Martha put herself in Oney's place and felt that she deserved liberty, too.

Because this is fiction, I needed to take some minor liberties with facts and dates to fit the story. People generally didn't address each other by their first names in colonial times, but in order to familiarize readers with the people in the story, I have them address each other less formally, with first names.

The Great Portsmouth Fire took place in 1813. I changed it to 1802 to suit the timeline of the story.

Any factual and historical errors are entirely mine.

About the Authors
Diana Rubino

Diana at the Fred W. Smith National Library for the Study of George Washington, Mount Vernon, Virginia

Diana Rubino specialises in historical romance, sometimes with a touch of the paranormal, her favourite areas being Medieval and Renaissance England and all American history. She recently completed a romantic thriller about Alexander Hamilton and a biographical novel about Nathaniel Hawthorne's wife Sophia. A longtime member of Romance Writers of America, the Richard III Society and the Aaron Burr Association, she has written articles for Romantic Times, appeared on The Book Swap Café, shown on Comcast channels, and is a regular guest of Dr. Art Sippo on his podcasts, Art's Reviews. She spends as much time as possible living the dream on Cape Cod with her husband Chris.

Visit Diana at:
www.dianarubino.com,
www.DianaRubinoAuthor.blogspot.com,
on her Facebook Author page at
https://www.facebook.com/DianaRubinoAuthor/
and contact her at Diana@DianaRubino.com

Piper Huguley

Piper Huguley is the author of *Migrations of the Heart*, a five-book series of inspirational historical romances set in the early 20th century featuring African-American characters. Book One in the series, *A Virtuous Ruby*, won the Golden Rose contest in Historical Romance in 2013. Book Four in the series, *A Champion's Heart*, was a Golden Heart finalist in 2013. Book One, *The Preacher's Promise*, in her 19th century historical series *Home to Milford College* was a semi-finalist in Harlequin's So You Think You Can Write contest and was published in 2014.

She blogs about the history behind her novels at www.piperhuguley.com/. She lives in Atlanta, Georgia with her husband and son.

Bibliography

Allgor, Catherine, *Parlour Politics, In Which the Ladies of Washington Help Build a City and a Government*, The University Press of Virginia, 2001

Bourne, Miriam, *First Family, George Washington and His Intimate Relations*, Norton & Co., New York, 1982

Brady Patricia, *George Washington's Beautiful Nelly, the Letters of Eleanor Parke Custis to Elizabeth Bordley Gibson, 1794-1851*, University of South Carolina Press, 1991

Britt, Judith, *Naught More Agreeable, Music in George Washington's Family*, Mount Vernon Ladies Association, 1984

Cadou, Carol, *The George Washington Collection, Fine and Decorative Arts at Mount Vernon*, Hudson Hills Press, New York, 2006 (P 126-7)

Chernow, Ron, *Washington, A Life*, The Penguin Press, New York, 2010

Custis, George Washington Parke, *Private Memoirs of Washington by his Adopted Son George Washington Parke Custis with a Memoir of the Author, by his Daughter; and Illustrative and Explanatory Notes*, Union Publishing House, New York, 1859

Decatur, Stephen, The Private Affairs of George Washington, From the Records and Accounts of Tobias Lear, Esquire, his Secretary, Houghton Mifflin, Boston, 1933

Earle, Alice Morse, *Two Centuries of Costume in America 1620-1820*, Charles E. Tuttle Company, Rutland, VT, 1971

Ferling, John, *Ascent of George Washington*, Bloomsbury Press, New York, 2009

Fields, Joseph, *Worthy partner: The Papers of Martha Washington* compiled by Joseph E. Fields; with an introduction by Ellen McCallister Clark. Greenwood Press, Westport, CT, 1994

Ford, Paul, *George Washington*, J.B. Lippincott Company, Philadelphia, 1896

Gerson, Evelyn, *A Thirst for Complete Freedom: Why Fugitive Slave Ona Judge Staines Never Returned to Her Master, President George Washington, A Thesis in the Field of Women's Studies for the Degree of Master of Liberal Arts in Extension Studies*, Harvard University, June 2000

Hess, Karen, *Martha Washington's Book of Cookery*, Columbia University Press, 1981

Hirschfeld, Fritz, *George Washington and Slavery, a Documentary Portrayal*, University of Missouri Press, 1997

Jacobs, Harriet, *Incidents in the Life of a Slave Girl, Written by Herself*, 1861

Keckley, Elizabeth, *Behind the Scenes or Thirty Years a Slave, and Four Years in the White House*, 1868

Lee, Jean, *Experiencing Mount Vernon*, University of Virginia Press, 2006

Lossing, Benson, *George Washington's Mount Vernon*, The Fairfax Press, 1870
McCully, Emily Arnold, *The Escape of Ona Judge*, Farrar Straus Giroux, New York, 2007

McKissack, Patricia, *A Picture of Freedom*, Scholastic, Inc. New York, 1997
McKissack, Patricia, *Look to the Hills*, Scholastic, Inc. New York, 2004

Moore, Virginia, *The Madisons*, McGraw-Hill Book Company, New York, 1979

Niles, Blair, *Martha's Husband*, McGraw Hill Book Company, Inc., New York, 1951

Richards, Laura Elizabeth Howe, *Abigail Adams and Her Times*, D. Appleton and Company, New York, 1917

Rinaldi, Ann, *Taking Liberty, the Story of Ona Judge*, Simon & Schuster, New York, 2004

Skemp, Sheila, Judith Sargent Murray, *A Brief Biography with Documents*, Bedford Books, Boston, 1998

Smith, Barbara, *After the Revolution, The Smithsonian History of Everyday Life in the Eighteenth Century*, Pentheon Books, New York, 1985

Smith, Thomas, *The City of New York in 1789*, Trow's Printing and Bookbinding Company, New York, 1889

Stowe, Harriet Beecher, *Uncle Tom's Cabin*, John P. Jewett, Boston, 1852

Taylor, Elizabeth Dowling, *A Slave in the White House*, Palgrave Macmillan, New York, 2012

Unger, Harlow Giles, *The Unexpected George Washington: His Private Life*, John Wiley & Sons, Inc., Hoboken, NJ, 2006

Wharton, Anne, *Martha Washington*, Charles Scribner's Sons, New York, 1897

Wharton, Anne, *Through Colonial Doorways*, J.R. Lippincott Company, Philadelphia, 1893

Wharton, Anne, *Colonial Days & Dames*, J.R. Lippincott Company, Philadelphia, 1895

White, Deborah Gray, *Ar'n't I a Woman, Female Slaves in the Plantation South*, W.W. Norton & Company, New York, 1985

Wiencek, Henry, *An Imperfect God, George Washington, his Slaves and the Creation of America*, Farrar, Straus and Giroux, New York, 2003

Wilson, Dorothy Clarke, *Lady Washington*, Doubleday & Company, 1984

Interviews with Oney:

www.ushistory.org/presidentshouse/slaves/Onainterview.htm

www.ushistory.org/presidentshouse/history/household.htm

Phila. Market: www.hmdb.org/marker.asp?marker=31304

www.weekslibrary.org/ona_maria_judge.htm

lcweb2.loc.gov/ammem/gwhtml/gwseries.html

www.paperlessarchives.com/

www.archive.org/details/plantationechoe00hendgoog

www.archive.org/stream/befodewarechoesi00gordiala****page/8/mode/2up

www.mountvernon.org/educational-resources/encyclopedia/elizabeth-parke-Custis-law

Poem about Oney:
nutfieldgenealogy.blogspot.com/2010/06/ona-judge-staines-slave-runs-away-to.html

Video about Oney:
www.youtube.com/watch?v=gnCRsK6msww

Slave Quarters in Philadelphia:
www.ushistory.org/presidentshouse/slaves/slavequartersfaq.htm

If you enjoyed *Oney: My Escape from Slavery*, please share your thoughts on Amazon by leaving a review.

For more free and discounted eBooks every week, sign up to the *Endeavour* newsletter.

Follow us on Twitter and Instagram.